lean on me

PAT SIMMONS

sourcebooks
casablanca

Published by Sourcebooks Casablanca, an imprint of Sourcebooks
P.O. Box 4410, Naperville, Illinois 60567-4410
(630) 961-3900
sourcebooks.com

Library of Congress Cataloging-in-Publication Data

Names: Simmons, Pat.
Title: Lean on me / Pat Simmons.
Description: Naperville : Sourcebooks Casablanca, [2019]
Identifiers: LCCN 2019027174 | (trade paperback)
Subjects: GSAFD: Love stories.
Classification: LCC PS3619.I56125 L43 2019 | DDC 813/.6--dc23
LC record available at https://lccn.loc.gov/2019027174

Printed and bound in the United States of America.
VP 10 9 8 7 6 5 4 3 2 1

Chapter 1

Marcus Whittington wasn't expecting to see a woman on his surveillance camera, trespassing on his domain. From time to time, he had seen maybe a stray dog. Never a lady who wore an oversize red hat that concealed her features as she strolled up to his house. According to his security video, this wasn't her first visit.

This mystery person had commandeered his porch between 6:30 a.m. and 7:15 a.m., as if she owned the deed to his property. A couple of times, the chick sat like a statue for about ten minutes—it was seven minutes this morning—before hurrying off as if a dog were chasing her. He frowned as he rewound and reviewed the evidence again.

What was going on? Marcus had lived on Overdrive Court in Pasadena Hills, Missouri, for four years. The quiet suburban neighborhood was a hidden-in-plain-sight treasure, with an unmanned, majestic, sixty-five-foot Gothic tower at the Natural Bridge Road entrance. It served as a visual barrier that guarded its residents from the questionable, blighted North St. Louis city neighborhoods in transition. Clearly, security had been breached.

He didn't have time for this. It was Monday morning, and he had to get to the office. Scratching his jaw, which demanded a razor, he decided to multitask and call the police as he shaved.

"911. What's your emergency?" a male dispatcher answered.

"I'd like to report a strange woman making uninvited visits to my property."

"Excuse me, sir?" The man paused. "Has your home been vandalized?"

"No." His morning paper deliveries were untouched. "This woman just sits on my porch."

There was silence on the other end of the phone. Finally, a

response came: "I'll connect you to the nonemergency number, sir. Please hold."

A deep voice came on the line. "Officer Roman."

Flustered, Marcus recapped and added, "Please add my cul-de-sac to your round of patrols. I'd appreciate it."

"Will do, sir," the officer said and disconnected. Now Marcus was really pressed for time. Whittington Janitorial Services, the company he had started with his older brother, Demetrius, was twelve minutes from his house, tops. Unlike his sibling, Marcus wasn't a fan of city living, so before purchasing his Cape Cod–inspired, story-and-a-half home, he had done his research about the neighborhood.

With University of Missouri–St. Louis's sprawling campus nearby, Pasadena Hills was considered one of the untouched neighborhoods of the county and touted as North County's best-kept secret. But now this woman had shown up.

Not easily intimidated, standing at six foot three and 240 pounds of muscle, Marcus could back up whatever came out of his mouth. Yet having some petite woman violate his boundaries unsettled him. "Hmph," he grunted.

"One thing for sure, lady. I'll be watching out for you," he muttered, making a mental note to check his video surveillance more often. He hoped there wouldn't be a next time, because the woman definitely didn't want a confrontation with him.

———

Tabitha Knicely sniffed the air as she strolled into her kitchen. Aunt Tweet had settled into a routine since coming to live with her two weeks ago. Her aunt rose every morning at six thirty, showered, dressed, and prepared breakfast. Today's menu was scrambled eggs, sausage patties, and bread that remained in the toaster. Yet her aunt was munching on a spoonful of Cheerios.

"You cooked a hot breakfast but settled for cereal?" Tabitha chuckled as she grabbed a plate to serve herself.

"I changed my mind."

Spying her aunt's bowl, Tabitha frowned. "You don't have any milk in there."

Alzheimer's was slowly attacking Aunt Tweet's brain cells. One moment, her aunt was absentminded, repeating tasks and craving snacks, especially sweets, as if they hadn't finished a meal not long ago. Then, in a blink of an eye, Aunt Tweet would turn into a game show junkie. She would beat the buzzer before the contestants could answer the host's questions as if she were Google.

Tabitha had been attending a medical conference in Birmingham, Alabama, when she received a call from her older sister in Baltimore.

"Aunt Tweet is in the custody of the Philly police department."

"What?" Dread came over Tabitha and she felt faint. "What happened? Is she all right?"

"They say she's fine," Kym assured her, "but someone called the police when she was stopped at a green light, lost, and couldn't figure out how to get home."

Her aunt could have caused a pileup or, worse, been killed. Tabitha exhaled. Thank God Aunt Tweet was alive, but what had happened didn't make sense. "What do you mean lost? She knows every nook and cranny of Philly, so how was she lost in her own city?"

Their youngest sister, Rachel, who was also on the line, finally chimed in. "Yeah, explain that to me too."

"Well, apparently, she left home to get groceries and wound up in Cherry Hill," Kym said.

The two sisters had gasped. "New Jersey?" Rachel asked.

"That's ten miles away," Tabitha added, knowing the area well.

"Yeah, I'm glad it wasn't farther. Anyway, they took her to the hospital for a physical and mental evaluation. Since my name is on her emergency contact, they called me. Her blood pressure and sugar levels were normal, but..." Kym became quiet before she dropped the bombshell. "They suspect her confusion could be connected with Alzheimer's."

Tabitha had left the conference early and booked a nonstop flight to Philly. Rachel coordinated her own flight from her condo in Nashville.

Kym was already on the road from her home in Baltimore. The sisters pulled together, just as they always had in a crisis. They had gone not only out of a sense of duty, but because Aunt Tweet had been too important in their lives not to; she'd meant everything to them, especially after the deaths of their parents. Once the three were gathered in Philly, they'd made a pact to share in the responsibility of their great-aunt's well-being, each taking care of her for six months at a time. As the oldest, Kym had looked after Aunt Tweet first.

Tabitha needed to refocus as she smiled lovingly at her aunt. Beginning today, Aunt Tweet would stay at an upscale adult day care while Tabitha began her first day at a new job.

After getting the milk carton out of the refrigerator, Tabitha walked back to the table and poured some into Aunt Tweet's bowl. Chalking it up to another sad oddity of dementia, she was determined to keep happy memories in the forefront of her mind as she kissed her aunt's cheek.

"Thank you, ma'am." Aunt Tweet giggled, adjusting Tabitha's red, floppy hat on her head. Since her arrival, her aunt had fallen in love with that hat and wore it practically every day, regardless of her ensemble. "I took a little walk around God's green earth."

"What?" Tabitha didn't like the idea of her aunt out of her sight. "Without me?" It was easy for anyone to succumb to the tranquility and abundance of green space in Pasadena Hills, which rivaled the nearby Norwood Hills Country Club. But in the midst of that apparent peace, they were still on the outskirts of a neighborhood not nearly so safe. It definitely wasn't safe for Aunt Tweet to wander. Tabitha shivered at the thought of worse-case scenarios.

"You were asleep."

"That's okay." She hugged her aunt. "Next time, wake me and I'll go with you." She yawned, recalling her previous night's lack of sleep. Her aunt had wanted to reminisce about her years as an airline stewardess, and Tabitha had indulged her before all of Aunt Tweet's memories would slip away. Researchers had yet to find a cure, so Tabitha hoped God would reveal a cure to eradicate or reverse this terrible disease before it was too late for her aunt.

All of a sudden, Aunt Tweet dropped her spoon, spilling milk onto the table. "I left my scarf…I left my scarf!" Panic-stricken, she trembled and scooted her chair back.

Startled, Tabitha's heart pounded, so she patted her chest to aid her breathing to return to normal. "It's all right. I'll get it from upstairs," she said, reassuring her aunt that it was okay to forget things sometimes.

While staying with Kym, Aunt Tweet had worked herself into hysterics over the vintage scarf she had gotten as an engagement gift. Her aunt boasted she'd gotten rid of the husband but held onto the expensive shawl. There hadn't been any peace in Kym's house until she'd found it behind a pillow on the sofa.

"No!" Aunt Tweet shrieked, shaking her head. "On that porch. We'd better hurry."

Confused, Tabitha tried to calm her down to figure out what was going on. "On my porch?" When her aunt shook her head, Tabitha asked, "Whose porch?"

"I don't know."

Dread seemed to pour over Tabitha like a downpour. "Okay, okay." Of all the days for a distraction, this was not a good one. This was her first day on a new job. As a pharmaceutical sales rep, Tabitha could recite medical terms, facts, definitions, and clinical studies' results in her sleep. She'd entered college as a biology major and graduated with a bachelor's in business. The pharmaceutical industry gave her the benefit of both worlds. Plus, she thrived on studying the physiological, anatomical, pharmacological, and scientific properties of medicine, so she could communicate the benefits of the company's products.

But family was family, so taking her duty as a caregiver seriously, Tabitha had resigned from her job of six years as a senior pharmaceutical sales rep to ease the stress of the demanding position. Not wanting to leave the field completely, she took a pay cut to work in a smaller territory with a competitor who demanded little to no overnight travel. The sacrifice was worth it. Plus, her aunt's trust fund designated the money for her own care.

Tabitha rubbed her forehead. "Let me put something on, then we'll go find it." Tabitha raced upstairs, hurried into her clothes, then grabbed her briefcase. Minutes later, she almost slipped while rushing down the stairs in her heels.

She reentered the kitchen, and Aunt Tweet wasn't in sight. Tabitha checked the adjacent family room, then peeped outside toward the patio. Her aunt was behind the wheel of Tabitha's rental car. Not good. She hadn't purchased a car in years. A perk for being a sales rep, after she completed her two-week training, which started today, would be a company-issued vehicle.

After locking up the house, she had to convince Aunt Tweet, who had worked herself into a frenzy, that she couldn't drive. Tabitha had to coax her own self to have patience while following her aunt's conflicting directions, thinking, *I can't be late for my first day on the job.*

"That's the place!" Aunt Tweet yelled as Tabitha jammed on her brakes in front of a stately, story-and-a-half, older brick house she had never noticed before. The massive front door was centered under an archway. Twin french doors with mock balconies were on both sides of the entrance.

"I don't see anything." She craned her neck, admiring the impressive work of building art.

Aunt Tweet snapped, "I told you that's the porch."

"Okay." *There is no reason for your sharp tone,* Tabitha thought but dared not voice. This house wasn't that close to hers at all. Despite some mental deterioration, there was nothing wrong with her aunt's physical stamina. She had obviously cut through the common ground area among the houses to get here.

After parking her car, Tabitha got out and surveyed her surroundings to make sure she wasn't being watched. "This is crazy, sneaking up to somebody's house," she muttered to herself. Since the coast was clear, she hurried toward the red scarf that was snagged on a flower in a pot and flapping in the wind. She was within her reach when the door opened. Tabitha jumped back, then steadied herself in her heels.

An imposing man filled the doorway. Under different circumstances, he would be breathtakingly handsome. That was not the case now. Judging from his snarl and piercing eyes, Tabitha felt as if she had walked into the lion's den.

Buy Aunt Tweet another scarf. Run!

Chapter 2

MARCUS SLIPPED ON HIS MARBLE FLOOR WHEN HE GLIMPSED OUT OF his window in passing and spied a blue sedan creeping to the curb in front of his house. His interest piqued when a dark-skinned beauty stepped out and almost danced her way in heels to his porch. The suit fitted her well and would capture any man's attention—his included. Even though a *No Solicitation* sign was posted at the entrance to Pasadena Hills, he would place an order for whatever she was selling.

Wait a minute… Why was she glancing around suspiciously? Was she the trespasser? Marcus had been ready and waiting for the mystery woman's return. The time was now.

He flung open his door for answers.

She froze as if she were part of that old social media craze, the mannequin challenge. His limbs couldn't move either, but his eyes did, cataloging her features. She was a showstopper, with her best assets being her gorgeous face and shapely legs. But this was not the time for distractions. He folded his arms. "May I help you?"

Her lips trembled into a smile, revealing even, white teeth. He was a sucker for good dental hygiene.

"Ah, I'm so sorry," she murmured in the sweetest voice.

Keeping his eyes steady on his target, Marcus studied her expression as she seemed to contemplate her next move. In the blink of an eye, she swiped the red scarf off the potted plant and gave him a smug expression, then smiled.

He returned it with a smirk of his own. "You do know that I knew you were going to do that. Why is it on my porch in the first place?"

She glanced over her shoulder and pointed to the car. "This belongs to my aunt."

"And this porch belongs to me." He squinted at the woman in the passenger seat. He didn't recognize her. "Why has your *aunt* been sitting on *my* porch in the mornings?"

Shock flashed on her face before she frowned. "*Mornings?* You mean she's been here before?"

What was really going on here? Was this a stalling tactic while someone broke into his house from the back? "Miss…?"

"Tabitha Knicely. I'm a neighbor," she supplied before motioning toward the car again. "That's my aunt, Aunt Tweet."

"You mean to tell me you had no knowledge that *your* aunt has been staking out my porch?"

She seemed flustered, then stuttered, "We take walks together—"

"Except for this morning and the others she was here without you knowing it," he said.

"She must have gotten tired and rested on your porch," Miss Knicely explained.

"Umm-hmm. And that's the story you're sticking with?" Her excuse was too simple though forgivable—if it had only happened once, which it hadn't. "Where do you live?"

This time, the information didn't come so freely. She was hesitant. "On Roland Drive."

Really? Roland Drive was the main entrance to the cluster of homes and touched every street in Pasadena Hills. Her deep-brown eyes and tentative smile silently pleaded with him to believe her. *Not so fast.* At thirty-four years old, Marcus had experience with good-looking ladies' charms that had twisted his common sense in the past, so he regrouped. "Where exactly?"

"By the park."

"What?" Marcus unfolded his arms and stood to his full six foot three. "Some houses are half an acre apart. That's a long way for an elderly person to wander." Beautiful or not, this woman was obviously too irresponsible to be a caregiver.

Responsibility had been drilled into Marcus as a child. When he was a little boy, three generations of Whittingtons lived under one roof. His grandparents, especially his grandmother, were kind, understanding, and stern when it came to disciplining their rambunctious grandsons. Yet Gran reminded them daily they were loved. This type of error would never have happened on his watch in his family.

Memories of his deceased grandparents touched a soft spot whenever he thought of them. Marcus would have moved them in with him without any hesitation and have twenty-four-hour monitoring, if necessary. When Gran and Pops died, he and Demetrius had bawled like infants.

Marcus would have done the same for his parents, but they had retired and relocated to North Carolina. "Older people are jewels, and I refuse to stand by and allow someone to treat them carelessly. You should know her whereabouts at all times. I suggest you keep track of your relative. Do you have any idea what could have happened to her?"

He must have hit a nerve and ticked her off. She jutted out her chin defiantly. She wore an attitude as professional as her suit. Her nostrils flared, and she cast him an angry glare.

"The jewel of my family is sitting right there." She pointed to her car. "Unless you've been a caregiver for a loved one, don't judge someone who is!" She stormed back to her car. Once there, she spun around. "You don't have to worry about any further visits from Aunt Tweet!"

"That works for me, because if she shows up on my doorstep one more time unsupervised, I'll contact the police. I'm sure they'll take her into protective custody and charge you with endangerment of a senior citizen. Don't test me, *neighbor*."

"Mr..."

"Marcus Whittington," he supplied before waving at the passenger in the car.

"Whatever. This is a test I don't plan to fail."

"For your aunt's sake, I hope not." Dismissing Tabitha, he stepped back inside and slammed the heavy wooden door for good measure, rattling the nearby windows. Her Aunt Tweet was definitely in the wrong hands.

After grabbing his computer bag, he checked his appearance, then decided to double-check his doors, just in case. Next, he activated his home security system and headed to work. During the short drive, he fumed, replaying the incident in his head. He didn't know if he was more upset about Tabitha's mistreatment of an elderly person or him losing his temper. That was so uncharacteristic of him.

In no time, he arrived at the business park that housed his company. Using the back entrance, he took the shortcut to the office he shared with Demetrius. Usually, he admired the layout of Whittington Janitorial Services' warehouse. Industrial cleaning products and supplies were stacked neatly on the shelves that lined the walls. One side had spacious lockers for employees to store their personal items. At the moment, any sense of accomplishment paled, as his irritation built with each step. Those two ladies had dared to infiltrate his home safety zone.

One of three supervisors on his cleaning staff, Chester "Chess" Gray, stopped him. He glanced at his wrist as if he were wearing a watch—he wasn't. "Something's wrong if I'm beating you to work," he joked.

Marcus wasn't in the mood for humor. He needed to vent and he didn't care who listened as he described his bizarre morning. "Who does that?" he asked, needing an answer.

"Watch it, Boss," Chess cautioned. "Old girl might be setting you up for a burglary. There was a string of robberies not far from where you live a while back."

Great. He gritted his teeth. *The day keeps getting worse.*

"She could be part of the lookout team."

Living in a crime-infested part of the city, Chess was suspicious of anybody and everybody, which made him a good supervisor—most of the time. Other times, Chess was annoying…but Marcus's employee could be onto something.

Continuing on his way, Marcus opened the door to the office. Demetrius was on his computer. "Nice of you to show up," he said sarcastically.

"Yeah, well. I had a situation this morning, but I caught them."

"Caught who?" His brother frowned. "Please tell me you didn't hurt anyone without my backup." Marcus had attended Pennsylvania State University on a wrestling and academic scholarship—both had full rides. Demetrius had boxed in college; together, they were a force to be reckoned with.

"No need. Evidently, two chicks have been staking out my place." After what Chess said, he downplayed the woman's excuse. "The older woman goes by the name of Aunt Tweet. The other was much younger." He huffed and slid his laptop out of the bag. He had to shake the bad vibes from Tabitha Knicely, so he could review the time sheets before signing off on them. *Relax and focus.*

"Interesting. A female crime ring."

Marcus frowned. "I don't really buy that, but for good measure, I instilled fear in them that they had picked the wrong house for that foolishness. And I issued a threat too."

"Well, sounds like those two won't be returning. Hopefully, they got the hint they were messing with a Whittington," Demetrius said. When Marcus didn't add any further comment, his brother cleared his throat. "Switching to work, Terrence Scott needs a random drug test. We may have to terminate him."

Not good. Their company had received awards for their exemplary efforts to give hope to the hopeless in low-income communities and to young men and women who had served time in prison for nonviolent crimes. Marcus labeled their choices as making stupid decisions. Whittington Janitorial Services' mission statement referenced assisting disenfranchised workers with a way out of poverty. He and Demetrius had both witnessed how a cleaning staff seemed invisible to people with money. It was offensive how they, most of them black, were mistreated, disrespected, and stereotyped.

Although he and Demetrius believed in second chances, after three strikes, his company had no choice but to terminate an employee. Terrence had been the exception to this rule. He was barely twenty-three, his live-in girlfriend was pregnant, and he didn't have a car. Prison had probably saved the young man's life or he would have been another statistic of a young black man killed in the streets.

Rubbing the hairs of his goatee, he spun around to admire the framed, floor-to-ceiling corkboard. It boasted success stories of former employees. The brothers had mentored, encouraged, and sometimes gave out of their own pockets to meet basic needs, like food and shelter. Marcus shook his head.

Turning to face his brother, Marcus squeezed his lips in frustration, then said, "My day seems to be going from bad to worse." When would people learn that responsibility wasn't optional? First, those women set the stage for his day to go downhill, and second, Terrence seemed to be picking up the torch. "Can you believe she got an attitude after trespassing on *my* property?" he mumbled, then grunted.

"Back to the lawbreakers, huh?" Demetrius chuckled, evidently straining his hearing, since their shared office space was at least twenty feet long and a short file cabinet served as the dividing line. It was a spacious office that could easily be separated into two, but neither felt the need to have a wall constructed for privacy. They knew each other's business anyway. "So how did she look again?"

"Like a gorgeous spitfire." He hadn't forgotten one detail. "She was a crafty diva with curves from a good workout."

"I got the gorgeous part." Demetrius leaned across his desk and smirked across the room. "I was referring to the aunt."

"Oh." Marcus shifted in his chair and reached for the chilled bottled water their administrative assistant placed on their desks every morning. To hide his blunder, he unscrewed the cap and gulped down half the bottle as if he were dying of thirst. "Ah." He smacked his lips. "Say what?"

"I asked you to describe this crafty diva with the great body." Demetrius snickered until laughter exploded out of his mouth.

Okay, so his big bro had jokes. Marcus played along. "She was a nice-looking lady who seemed completely normal from her spot in the front seat of a car. Her silver-gray hair reminded me of Gran's." Maybe the similarity was what had sparked his outrage at Tabitha's lack of responsibility.

His beloved grandparents, Gran and Pops, were the sweetest people on earth and lived into their eighties. When they became sick, Marcus and Demetrius had waited on them hand and foot. They were his idols, seemingly knowing everything about everything.

He pitied anyone who had to enter a nursing home, where some families abandoned their relatives instead of maintaining ties with visits and calls. He had witnessed firsthand the abuse and neglect when he had to deliver business orders to a few nursing facilities. Those images and odors were seared into his brain.

"But did you have to be so hard on her?" his brother asked.

"The situation forced my hand. When it comes to responsibilities, the Whittingtons take care of our own." He patted his chest with pride.

"Yeah, but usually, I'm the bad guy." Demetrius chuckled. "After your stunt today, I'd say you reign, but I understand you had to do what you had to do."

Although they were extremely close, their personalities were like night and day. Demetrius was the no-nonsense one who had mastered the "do not dare to cross me" facial expression. On rare occasions, his brother could be a pushover. Marcus was laid back and sympathetic.

Physically, there was no mistaking them as brothers.

Marcus preferred a low haircut and trimmed goatee. Outside of work, he was a meticulous dresser and maintained a regular workout routine. Demetrius's current exercise regimen was, at best, inconsistent—at this point, it amounted to whenever he felt like it.

Demetrius sported his shaved head and set off his look with a diamond stud in one ear. Marcus didn't like jewelry on a man, not even a watch—that's what his smartphone was for. He was the shade of black coffee, where Demetrius was a double dip of dark chocolate.

"Great way to start off a relationship," Demetrius teased. When they were boys, his brother had an annoying habit of baiting him. As a man in his late thirties, he still hadn't grown out of that trait.

"Relationship? Where in my conversation did you assume that?" Marcus frowned. "I'm not even sure if the chick is really a neighbor."

His brother twitched his lips. "Umm-hmm. Something tells me this story with your neighbor is just beginning." He stood and strolled toward their door, chuckling. "Chapter One: Brotha Meets Fine Sistah—I can see the fascination in your eyes. Plus, your protest is overkill."

Grabbing a piece of paper from a stack, Marcus balled it up and aimed for Demetrius's head, then fired. Hitting him, Marcus got the last laugh—or so he thought, until he realized it was an invoice he needed to mail to a client. Groaning, he closed his eyes. His day had to get better, right?

Chapter 3

TABITHA CONSIDERED HERSELF A PEOPLE PERSON. SHE HAD TO possess a friendly personality as a pharmaceutical sales rep. By nature, she believed in making friends, not enemies. However, this morning, Marcus had pushed her buttons. She didn't like him.

How was she to know her aunt had snuck out of the house—more than once—while she was sleeping? This was all new to her.

She was humiliated that he talked down to her as if she were a child and was frustrated that Aunt Tweet had done such a thing. Tabitha renamed him the Jerk. If the man had been an unattractive, out-of-shape slouch, she would have disposed of him with a few choice words—in a civilized manner, of course—but without shame.

No, the homeowner had to be disgustingly fine with a physique that made her notice. She had no choice but to take the whipping for #TeamAuntTweet. "Please, stop waving at the man," she had pleaded softly as she drove away.

"He waved first, miss," her aunt replied as if she were talking to a stranger while fumbling with the scarf Tabitha gave back to her. That was the second time Aunt Tweet had forgotten her name. Although memory recognition was symptomatic of dementia, it pricked Tabitha's heart just the same.

Gripping the steering wheel, she turned to her aunt. "Please don't leave the house without me again—please." She wanted to avoid any future run-ins with the Jerk at all costs. "By the way, do you remember how many times you've been to that man's house?"

"Hmm. Let me see." Aunt Tweet lowered her brows as if mentally calculating. "I can't remember. Three, four…a lot of times."

Tabitha gasped for air as a migraine punched her in the eye, causing her head to throb while Aunt Tweet arranged the scandalous scarf around her neck while looking straight ahead as if nothing had transpired.

Fortunately, her aunt hadn't overheard the man's rudeness. She didn't tolerate impoliteness.

Ten minutes later, they arrived in the semicircular entrance of Bermuda Place. The valet opened the passenger door and greeted Aunt Tweet. *That is how a man is supposed to treat a woman, with courtesy and respect, not Marcus's fire-breathing threats*, Tabitha mused.

The upscale adult care facility had activities, supervised shopping trips, a hair salon, gourmet meals, and movies throughout the day. There was even a napping room. It was considered the elite of upscale senior living or adult care facilities, which Aunt Tweet had outlined in her living trust.

While in Philly, the sisters had paid a visit to the law firm of Krone, Keller, and Bush. Attorney Leah Krone read the contents of Aunt Tweet's living trust: "Nine years ago, your aunt updated her will and made you all trustees on her various accounts. Miss Brownlee has savings, investments, real estate, and her 401(k). She allocated a large portion for her upkeep and health care in the event she would require a nursing facility, only after all means have been exhausted for her to live independently."

"We have decided to share in her care." Tabitha straightened her shoulders. "She will live with each one of us six months at a time."

"I see." Attorney Krone slipped on her glasses. "If that is the case, each sister will receive $5,000 a month stipend while she is in your care." She chuckled at their stunned expressions. "She insisted on the royalty of senior care."

In addition to the living trust, Aunt Tweet had named Kym Knicely, as the oldest, the primary agent for her durable power of attorney for health care. Tabitha was named the agent for financial power of attorney, and she had put her aunt's home in the Rittenhouse area of Philly on the market. It sold for half a million, and the proceeds were deposited into Aunt Tweet's trust account. Rachel was listed as their backups. All three of them were determined to follow Aunt Tweet's requests to the letter.

Bermuda Place resembled a residential condominium or apartment complex more than an adult day care that shut down at 6:00 p.m.—no exceptions, as she had been advised more than once when she completed the application.

The hours were 7:30 a.m. to 4:30 p.m., so Tabitha didn't anticipate a problem. She knew there would be occasional evening events and planned to take her aunt with her.

To Tabitha's relief, Aunt Tweet had complimented the decor and furnishings when they had toured the facility a few weeks earlier, but she still wasn't sure how her independent aunt would feel about an undercover "babysitter."

Escorting her inside, Tabitha greeted the staff and made sure her aunt was comfortable, wondering if she would remember the new environment. She didn't.

Almost immediately, one of the staff members solicited Aunt Tweet's advice on how to accessorize some outfits—personalized activities were created for each guest based on the applicants' likes, dislikes, and hobbies to help acclimate them in an unfamiliar setting.

"I have to go to work, Aunt Tweet. I'll be back—"

The woman, Carole, waved her off. "We'll be fine."

Suddenly, Tabitha's legs wouldn't move. Now, she was second-guessing her decision to leave her aunt in the care of…strangers. She was having separation anxiety. Moisture blinded her vision as she rubbed her aunt's shoulder.

"It's okay. Miss Brownlee and I will be fine." The woman spoke in a comforting tone.

Taking a deep breath, Tabitha snapped out of it. She mimicked Carole's nods and gave Aunt Tweet a lingering hug, then brushed a quick kiss on her cheek and hurried out the door.

Once she was in the car, she took a few minutes to breathe, clear her head, and think of something else besides deserting her great-aunt.

Blinking away a few stubborn tears, she dabbed her eyes, then drove off and exited on westbound I-70, which was the route to her new job in St. Charles—the first Missouri capital for five short years in the 1820s. It was one of those tidbits she'd learned in school on a field trip to the existing state capital, Jefferson City.

By the time she arrived at Ceyle-Norman, Tabitha was back on track emotionally, especially after she called Carole at Bermuda Place. Her aunt was adjusting better than Tabitha, so she left her cares at the door, including the fiasco with her neighbor—it was show time. She stepped out of the car and crossed the parking lot to the entrance, checked in with the receptionist, then took a seat.

Minutes later, a woman appeared in the lobby. "Hi, I'm Ava Elise Watkins. I'm the lead sales trainer." She extended her hand for a shake, wearing a brown, two-piece suit and an engaging smile. Tabitha pegged the woman to be in her forties.

She had never met a black woman who introduced herself with a first and middle name. "Hi, Ava."

"Feel free to call me Ava Elise," she corrected in a soft tone. "My mother prefers both names, since she couldn't make up her mind when I was born. Unfortunately, she did the same thing with my older brother." She laughed, and Tabitha did too as she trailed the trainer down the hall.

The classroom was set up theater style. Six rows of long tables with chairs on only one side could accommodate about forty students. There were only twelve of them in this class.

The first order of business was to view a short video about the business on a sixty-inch flat screen at the front of the room. Since Tabitha had already done research on the company, her mind began to drift about a minute into the vice president's greeting.

She wondered about Aunt Tweet again, and suddenly the Jerk's face flashed before her eyes. She hadn't realized she made a growling noise until a male new hire next to her looked her way. Tabitha cleared her throat, hoping to play it off.

There was plenty of paperwork to complete, including tax forms and confidentiality agreements. By midday, Marcus appeared in her head again. This time, he was smiling at her, and she noticed his eyes danced. She found herself smiling, then his smile turned to fangs as the Jerk resurfaced. She frowned.

Ava Elise must have misread her expression. "I know it's overwhelming, Tabitha, but you're a seasoned rep. You'll just have to familiarize yourself with our procedures and products. We believe you'll shine here at Ceyle-Norman as you did at Pfizer."

"Thank you," Tabitha heard herself say as her mind drifted elsewhere. *I'll have to keep a closer eye on Aunt Tweet,* she thought. One more incident, and she was confident that the man would make good on his threat to have her arrested. Tabitha would never, never knowingly put her aunt in harm's way! Of course, if she was convicted of endangering an elderly relative, she could kiss her career goodbye. She had to be more diligent about her aunt's whereabouts and keep her away from that man's property by any means necessary, even if that meant sleeping with one eye open.

That evening, after an eventful day, Tabitha relaxed with Aunt Tweet doing one of her favorite pastimes—gardening. While Tabitha was satisfied planting bulbs and bedding plants once a year, her aunt was known for planting anything and everything when the mood hit her, then admiring the fruits of her green thumb.

Her aunt had helped the Knicely sisters make countless mud pies when they were younger. Tabitha chuckled to herself at the fond memories. She wanted more good memories while Aunt Tweet was still in her right mind.

While outside, Aunt Tweet insisted on wearing the big red hat, so for fun, Tabitha donned one of her summer, floppy straw hats too. They had a couple of hours before sunset to enjoy the warm breeze and tranquil surroundings.

"I think we should plant some collard greens."

Tabitha chuckled. "Not in my front yard, but a vegetable garden by the patio sounds good," she said as the hairs on her arms raised, alerting her to impending danger. Shifting to defense mode, she glanced over her shoulder and blinked for clarity.

She pulled back the rim of her hat to get a better view of the tall figure blocking the sun. Tabitha scrambled to her feet and wiped the dirt from her hands on her jeans. "Is there a problem?" She squinted, then realized she hadn't given him her address. "And how did you know where I lived?"

Marcus slipped his hands in his pockets and rocked back on his heels.

He tilted his head toward Aunt Tweet, who hadn't given him a peep as she focused on her mound of dirt for the plant. "The hat gave it away."

Of course. Tabitha nodded. Her aunt had set in motion bad neighbor relations. "Sooo…" She paused so he would give her the reason for his visit.

"Just checking on the welfare of my neighbors. Have a good evening, ladies." He nodded his goodbye, then strolled back to his vehicle.

Did Marcus expect there to be a problem? Tabitha hoped their spacious neighborhood was big enough for both of them not to run into each other more than once a year. "That was strange," she mumbled, still not trusting the man.

Aunt Tweet said "Mmm-hmmm" and kept digging.

Chapter 4

THE NEXT MORNING, TABITHA DRAGGED HERSELF OUT OF BED AFTER a restless night. She replayed Aunt Tweet escaping from her house and then Marcus showing up unexpectedly. It was the makings for a never-ending nightmare. To make sure it wasn't a bad dream, Tabitha stretched, then crossed the hall to look in on Aunt Tweet's room. Asleep. Good. She relaxed, but her mind was still strategizing options to keep her aunt from sneaking out.

After backtracking to her bedroom, Tabitha washed her face and brushed her teeth. "God, I'm going to need Your help to get through the next six months," she whispered.

Tabitha had foolishly thought she was self-sufficient based on her financial stability, healthy lifestyle, and intellect. Aunt Tweet's diagnosis was evidence that wealth couldn't buy good health. Initially, the what-ifs had plagued all three sisters as they berated themselves for ignoring the signs of their aunt's forgetfulness during phone calls.

Even Aunt Tweet was in denial that something was wrong after she got lost in her hometown of Philly. "Oh, it was a combination of my medicine and this extreme heat that made me a little disoriented," she had said, playing it off.

Days after that harrowing experience, Dr. William Murray evaluated Aunt Tweet and confirmed the sisters' fears. "Miss Brownlee has moderate signs of dementia. At this stage, you can witness bouts of poor judgment, mood swings, personality changes, loss of interest in hobbies, difficulty communicating, long- and short-term memory loss—"

"This doesn't sound good," Kym had said, shaking her head and cutting off the doctor.

"It's not. Alzheimer's is a cruel disease," he advised. "And a person can live years with it."

"Wait, I thought you said she had dementia," Rachel asked.

"Alzheimer's is a disease and the leading cause of some of the dementia symptoms I've outlined. Other diseases can cause the same symptoms, like Huntington's, Lewy body dementia, a stroke, or a brain injury. Remember, the symptoms are caused by something. They don't just pop up," Dr. Murray stated.

But they did just pop up, Tabitha thought. None of them had seen this coming.

Dr. Murray had suggested prescribing Aricept and Exelon to slow down the progression of some of the dementia symptoms. Her sisters had immediately defaulted to Tabitha for the drugs' stats. As a pharmaceutical sales rep, she knew that every drug had its side effects.

Tabitha had collected data and created spreadsheets on the five most common medicines on the market. She had their drug names, brand names, adverse side effects, drug interaction, and whether they were FDA approved. Many of the medicines to treat dementia symptoms were still in clinical trials. Others were too new to have a track record. She had hesitantly consented to one medication, not both.

"Only time will tell if she needs more," Tabitha whispered to her reflection in the mirror. As she dismissed further thoughts of drugs, diseases, and research, somehow Marcus's face resurfaced. What was the deal with him? It wasn't her concern. She had enough on her plate with Aunt Tweet, so as long as they stayed out of each other's way, they could live in harmony in Pasadena Hills.

Leaning closer to the mirror, she noted the evidence of not getting enough sleep, which was rule number one on her beauty regimen. With a sigh, she applied more concealer under her eyes, finished the rest of her makeup, then headed downstairs to prepare breakfast.

Since her arrival, Aunt Tweet had taken over the kitchen, and Tabitha had no qualms about relinquishing the task. Her aunt had a flair for cooking—at least her memory hadn't robbed her of her culinary masterpieces, yet. But this morning, Tabitha wanted to make breakfast for her aunt, so she'd woken up early. She rattled pans in the kitchen until she yanked out a cookie sheet she preferred for biscuits. Not long after slipping them in the oven, Aunt Tweet appeared, fully dressed and wearing mismatched shoes—one teal and the other yellow. The floppy, red hat was in one hand.

"If you don't stop slamming those dishes, I'm going home." Her aunt fussed as she took a seat at the table.

But you can't, Tabitha thought sadly.

—

"Don't mistake kindness for weakness." Marcus locked eyes with the man on the other side of his desk who was five seconds away from becoming an ex-employee because of his disregard for punctuality. He needed this distraction after pulling that stunt at Tabitha's yesterday. What had possessed him to cruise through the neighborhood three times, looking for trouble and signs of the two women? Checking on the welfare of neighbors was the excuse he'd given to Tabitha, and it was as good as any. That's the story he was sticking to until he could figure out why he gave them a second thought after their run-in yesterday.

When Victor Graves blinked, so did Marcus, forcing his mind to stay focused.

Since Victor's release from prison, he had worked for Whittington Janitorial Services for almost two years; however, his good work history was in serious jeopardy. There was something about the young father of two that always swayed Marcus to give him the benefit of the doubt and treat him as a mentee or little brother. Not this time. Marcus had on his boss hat and was ready to terminate an employee. "I don't like to throw our generosity in your face—"

"But you are anyway." Crossing his arms, Victor leaned back in the chair as if he were the one in charge of his payroll.

Flaring his nostrils, Marcus scowled. "Don't play games with me. All you have to do is arrive here on time, and I don't care if you hop on a bus, take an Uber, or ride a tricycle. Our shuttle vans drop you off at the front door of the office sites for cleaning." Counting on his fingers, he listed other perks WJS offered. "Did you forget the child care—"

"It ain't free." Victor leaned forward as if putting Marcus in check. "You're taking fifty bucks out of my check a week."

Really? Did this dude realize his job was on the line? "Stop using it and see what child care costs for a one- and a three-year-old." He grunted. "You make more than minimum wage, so help me understand why those benefits aren't incentives for you to want to keep your job?"

Victor remained silent.

"I have applicants vying to take your place. Give me a reason why we shouldn't suspend you." *It had better be good*, he thought, waiting for a reply.

The buzz about the working culture at Whittington Janitorial Services had generated a waiting list of prospective employees. He and Demetrius paid their workers, many of whom were single parents, more than minimum wage and they operated day and night child care on site. Their workers were rewarded with a $100 bonus every quarter if they deposited a certain percentage of their weekly pay into savings. These perks nurtured employees' loyalty and pride in their work.

"Fire me," Victor taunted.

If Demetrius were in the room, Victor's wish would have been his brother's command. But Marcus saw potential in the twenty-five-year-old. "Where will you live? What would your babies eat? Think about others besides yourself." He tried one more time to reason with the impossible.

"Man, you don't care nothing about me. I know you're getting government subsidies for hiring us bad boys."

True, but it didn't cover the extras his company provided. "I don't do rehires, so I would think carefully about getting to work on time tonight. Last chance." Marcus stood. "Meeting over."

"Whatever." Shrugging, Victor got to his feet and walked to the door as Demetrius was entering the room.

No words were exchanged as Demetrius eyed Victor until he left the office. "You're either a fool or a better man than I am, because I'd have fired him after the second tardy, no questions asked or guilt keeping me up at night."

Rubbing the back of his neck, Marcus gritted his teeth. "Something tells me Victor is about to call my bluff, and I'll put every dime we owe him on his payroll debit card before the end of the day. What is wrong with people? First that Tabitha woman and now him." He rocked back in his chair and exhaled. "I have to be earning brownie points with God for putting up with foolishness."

Demetrius stopped sifting through a stack of envelopes and gave Marcus a curious expression. "So your neighbor came back and you called the police? You didn't tell me that." He lifted an eyebrow.

"Because she hasn't been back."

"Oh." Demetrius took a seat with a disappointed expression. "You can put the fear in the little lady, but Victor ain't scared of being on the streets hungry or going back to jail. I call him a fool." He balled his fists. "Say the word, and I'll take it from here."

"I don't need your backup, Bro. My hunch is he plans to fail."

Chapter 5

AFTER WORK, TABITHA STOPPED AT THE GROCERY STORE WITH AUNT Tweet and lingered in the produce department. She had no problem eating a salad as her meal: spinach, fruit, taco—it didn't matter.

Aunt Tweet chatted nonstop about the happenings at Bermuda Place while guiding the cart. "I told that Eleanor at the office she needs to update her wardrobe. The colors that woman puts together." She tsked and shook her head, overlooking her own fixation with Tabitha's red, floppy hat. "I requested the limo driver take us to the stores tomorrow." Her aunt hadn't stopped talking about the facility's weekly outing where the seniors could shop. Limo vans were the mode of transportation.

Tabitha smiled, relieved her aunt was adjusting well to the changes in her life. This high-spirited and animated woman was the aunt Tabitha knew and loved. Not only could Aunt Tweet coordinate fashion, but she possessed a flair for interior decorating. How could this intelligent socialite be slipping away inside before Tabitha's eyes? *Enjoy each moment*, she reminded herself.

Once Tabitha had selected all the veggies she wanted, she steered Aunt Tweet down the bakery aisle for English muffins for breakfast. Not only was her aunt a great cook, but Aunt Tweet was also a master baker of cakes and pies. She perused packages of sugary treats until she selected a sock-it-to-me cake off the shelf.

When her aunt reached for cookies and doughnuts as well, Tabitha lifted an eyebrow to draw the line. "Auntie, let's get one or the other," she suggested.

Not one for taking instructions, Aunt Tweet straightened her shoulders and jutted her chin. "I am getting one for today and the cake for tomorrow." Her tone was final.

That's two, so why was she holding three treats? Tabitha dared not argue, but she was determined to have the upper hand to keep her aunt healthy. Then, in disbelief, she watched as Aunt Tweet dumped more sweets into the cart as if to usurp her authority.

You've got to be kidding me.

"Now," Aunt Tweet said, lifting her shoulder. "I feel like making a smothered pork chop for dinner with green beans and cranberries and coleslaw." She smacked her lips as if the meal were already prepared.

Whenever her aunt cooked, Tabitha's mouth watered too. Aunt Tweet knew how to mix seasonings for unmatched flavor. Her aunt might have won the scrimmage on the sweets at the moment, but Tabitha was going to win the battle on sugar overload. "I'll get us some chops. Please, Aunt Tweet, don't leave the cart."

Tabitha suspected her aunt would use her absence to add more junk to their grocery bill. She hurried to the meat section and picked up the first package of pork chops without checking the price or expiration date. Considering Aunt Tweet's state of mind and strong will, Tabitha didn't trust her aunt to follow instructions. All Tabitha needed was to have the employees activate a Code Adam because her aunt went missing in the store.

She scrabbled back to aisle one. To her relief, Aunt Tweet hadn't moved but was occupied with her intimidating neighbor. *Uh-oh.* Bracing for a sarcastic comment about her leaving Aunt Tweet, she hesitantly joined them.

What? Marcus actually smiled at her when he looked up. "Good evening, Tabitha. When I saw your aunt and didn't see you, I was hoping you had everything under control."

So he was taking a dig at her. "Despite what you think of my caregiving skills, as you can see, my aunt is well-loved and not neglected." Tabitha made sure her aunt was clean and groomed each day before they left the home.

"Whoa." He held up his hands. "I didn't mean to offend you." His eyes sparkled.

Oh, okay. Maybe she was taking offense because they met under circumstances that were not the best. Tabitha took a deep breath and lowered her guard. "Sorry I snapped."

"Truce?" Marcus extended his hand to Tabitha's amusement. "Misssss Knicely?"

"Yes, it's 'miss,' and there is no way I can discreetly ask your status." She smiled. "So tell me."

"Single."

Accepting his hand, Tabitha wasn't prepared for the gentle strength coming from a guy who towered over her by a foot and could probably bench press two hundred pounds. At the same moment, she took note of his black, silky hair and thick eyebrows against brown, flawless skin. His facial hair was trimmed, and a hint of his cologne lingered under her nose. *Handsome.*

Tabitha lowered her lashes in embarrassment for cataloging his features. Who was she kidding? Any whimsical thoughts of a relationship with any man were on hold as long as Aunt Tweet was under her care. Besides, she had to make every minute and memory count for both of them. She was making assumptions that there was mutual attraction all because of one civil conversation.

"Well, it was nice seeing you again under better circumstances." She pivoted to continue on her mission when his deep voice stopped her.

"I see someone has a sweet tooth." Marcus smirked, tilting his head at her cart.

"That's Aunt Tweet's doing." She leaned closer. "I plan to have the cashier put most of it aside."

"Hmm, I would never have thought of that."

"When you're a caregiver, you try to think of everything and be a step ahead. Sometimes"—she shrugged—"I miss the mark." Tabitha mustered a smile. She hoped he got her hint.

———

A day later, Marcus opened his front door and was dumbfounded. "Really?"

Tabitha was guiding her aunt off his porch again, down his steps, back to her car. After seeing a softer side of her at the grocery store, he had mixed emotions, but he would not be swayed by a pretty face. He had to do the right thing.

"Sorry." She seemed flabbergasted.

He crossed his arms. "I thought this wouldn't be a recurring thing." He expected some lame excuse about how her aunt slipped between her fingers again. The thought of her being a parent scared him. When he'd noticed Aunt Tweet by herself at the store, he grew concerned, hoping her niece was nearby. He had been relieved when he'd seen her and held his tongue, since he had no right to comment about leaving her aunt alone again because it wasn't on his property. Now was a different story.

"Me too." They briefly exchanged stares.

"I didn't get it the first time your aunt found her way to my house, and now…" His nostrils flared. "If you're unable to care for her, then let someone who can take it from here."

She squinted. "I dare you to say I'm not responsible."

He stepped out of his house and looked down the stairs at her. She didn't flinch. "And I dared you not to let her out of your sight, like you did again at the grocery store. She's not disappearing. You are."

Tabitha gritted her teeth. She opened her mouth, then closed it. She walked away.

What was she going to say? he wondered. He stepped off the porch but didn't trail her to her car. "Tabitha, I'm warning you. There better not be a third time or I will call 911 and have your dear, sweet aunt taken into protective custody, or one day she's going to go missing and the results may be worse than me finding her on my porch."

That must have struck a nerve; she spun and stormed back to him. "You think I don't know that? What do you want me to do, put a padlock on her door?" Her nostrils flared and her beautiful eyes aimed darts his way. "One minute my aunt was asleep; the next, she's at your doorstep."

This woman irritated him and captivated him. He was a man with authority over seventy employees, some of whom had served time in prison, yet he had their respect. This woman didn't seem fazed by his threats or think he meant what he said, so why was he engaging her, instead of reporting her to the authorities?

"Walk in my shoes."

Her challenge made him glance down. The hem of her dress flowed around a nice pair of legs. He continued his appraisal until he stopped at her feet. The wind stirred, and a whiff of her perfume tickled his nose. A sense of how attractive she was brought his irritation down a notch. The sun cast a spotlight on Tabitha. Her dark-brown hair blended perfectly with the shade of her skin. That's what he called natural beauty. She stepped back as he scanned her attire. He briefly wondered if her hidden toes were manicured. *Stop ogling!* he chided himself.

"I don't know your shoe size, but if I could squeeze into them, I would still do a better job. You just don't get it. This is my property. I'm trying to be nice about this—"

"Try harder. While you're breathing smoke and fire, a *good* neighbor would be sympathetic and ask what they can do to help, but that's a *good* neighbor. Now, being the responsible person I am, I'll leave you to your tirade so I won't be late for work." She strutted back to her car. After helping Aunt Tweet into the passenger seat, Tabitha slid behind the wheel and drove off.

An hour later, Marcus paced the floor in his office. He was wondering if the word *fool* was stamped across his forehead, judging by Tabitha's and Victor's insulting behavior.

"So what are you going to do about this little home-invasion thing?" Demetrius snickered.

Marcus scowled. "I have no idea. Seriously, I need to call the police and at least have her put on notice about elderly endangerment."

"But something tells me you won't—no, you can't. You like her."

"Why wouldn't I? She's very polite, despite her neighborhood adventures. She reminds me of—"

"I know...Grans," Demetrius said, cutting him off. "But I'm talking about the other neighbor. The gorgeous one—your description, not mine." He held up both hands in surrender.

Huffing, Marcus didn't reply as he stormed out of his own office. Next time, he would make the call—but he wasn't looking forward to a next time.

Chapter 6

IN HINDSIGHT, THERE WAS A REASON WHY TABITHA HAD WOKEN feeling anxious. She was exhausted, mentally and physically, and had to give Ava Elise an answer about whether she would attend a work-sponsored function the following week.

She thrived at seminars, luncheons, and other work-related gatherings. It didn't matter that she often went solo, since most of the guys she had dated briefly in the past were too self-centered anyway to care about what mattered to her. That was why Tabitha had looked forward to Aunt Tweet's six-month stay. The social butterfly could accompany Tabitha to those functions. That was before her aunt's "in the blink of an eye" disappearing episodes.

"Next week, Ceyle-Norman is sponsoring a two-hour meet-and-greet with specialists to introduce our new drug to treat hyperaldosteronism," Ava Elise said. "There are no good excuses not to be there."

Tabitha's interest was already piqued. She was a magnet for information, and the topic promised to be interesting. She knew that hyperaldosteronism was caused by a benign tumor on the adrenal gland and that, before this promising drug, doctors were controlling the secondary symptoms.

At her former company, she helped organized meetings throughout the year. These gatherings were key to building rapport with professionals in the medical community and learning how new medicines impacted patients' quality of life. Tabitha sighed. If only there were a proven drug to prevent dementia symptoms instead of managing them once they manifested.

Her mind worked overtime to see how she could attend and keep an eye on Aunt Tweet. *How?* She was packing up her things after class, and Ava Elise strolled in her direction and took a seat. "It would be nice to have another sister present for a change, to increase the diversity at this function."

White males dominated the field. Despite diversity programs throughout the pharmaceutical industry, blacks and other minorities had to work harder and be better than the average worker to stand out. Tabitha understood how important the strength-in-numbers support system was. She bit her lip to keep from gnawing on it. Again, how could she make it happen? "If I didn't have my great-aunt living with me, I would be there. She's suffering from dementia and my multitasking skills as a caregiver are being challenged in my own home. She wandered away a couple of times and that was scary. I don't even want to think about her going missing at an event."

Ava Elise nodded, then patted Tabitha's hand. The gesture was comforting. "My family has been in a similar situation, so I understand your concerns. A home aide can probably watch her for a few hours." They stood. "This speaker is a big, big deal. You might be the one to pitch the drug to doctors, so I strongly suggest you rework things at home for a couple of hours. You'll want to hear what the chief surgeon and a group of endocrinologists from Barnes-Jewish Hospital's findings are on using our new drug."

"I know. It's so tempting." But an unknown home aide? Aunt Tweet was her responsibility, not a stranger's. The temptation still lingered when she picked up Aunt Tweet from the facility and continued all evening while they watched game shows.

The last thing Ava Elise said before Tabitha left was "I'm sure you'll make it happen."

Tabitha had wanted to say *It's not that simple* but held her tongue.

After a restless night, she had come to a decision that she wouldn't budge on. Sacrifices were part of her life now, so for the next six months, some things would have to be tweaked or eliminated, including evening events.

Before she used the bathroom, she tiptoed to Aunt Tweet's bedroom. Inside, it was like a whole new world compared to the rest of

Tabitha's house. The decor was Victorian influenced with vintage, dark furniture where Tabitha preferred white modern furniture in her bedroom, including wood shutters. An oversize floor rug and oil paintings gave her oasis splashes of color.

The thick curtains her aunt preferred kept the room dark day and night. Tabitha stepped closer to verify Aunt Tweet was resting peacefully and her breathing was even. Smiling, Tabitha was about to back out of the room when one of her aunt's eyes popped open. "I'm still here."

"Whew!" Tabitha almost jumped out of her skin. She patted her chest, trying to comfort her pounding heart. "You scared me."

"Didn't mean to, miss. I was just resting my eyes. I get up when the birds start chirping and fall asleep under the melody of the crickets and owls."

"I'm Tabitha, your niece." She didn't add *remember*, because her poor aunt couldn't.

Aunt Tweet only stared and nodded with a slight smile.

"It's early, so you don't have to get up yet. I'm going to take a shower, then make breakfast."

Back in her room, Tabitha spied her powder-blue business suit hanging from a brass hook in her walk-in closet, which she'd had redesigned from a nursery off the master bedroom. The sunlight continued to brighten her room by the second, giving Tabitha a mental and physical boost. It was going to be a great day!

After her shower, Tabitha dutifully checked on her aunt, who was gone from her bedroom. "You've got to be kidding me." Tabitha shook her head as she searched the entire house. She had a sinking feeling in the pit of her stomach as she imagined her aunt's whereabouts.

The good day Tabitha had hoped for turned into a nightmare. She had thought after her cordial conversation with Marcus at the grocery store—maybe even an imagined slight attraction—they had that truce he'd mentioned. Nope. This morning, he had been the same jerk she had met the first time.

Now, they were back inside the house, and Tabitha thought about indulging in a sixty-second pity party, but she didn't have the time to spare. She would schedule that later.

Sniffing back tears of frustration, she resisted asking Aunt Tweet why she was drawn to Marcus's house. Instead, Tabitha performed her tasks with her aunt, praying to God to tame her frustrations.

Unlike the first time Aunt Tweet went missing and Tabitha managed to get to work on time, she was an hour late this time and apologized for her tardiness, hoping she still had a job. Ava Elise graciously accepted and continued with the training. Tabitha wanted to cry. She wasn't one for dramatics, nor was she one to feel out of control or to be tardy. Why was her aunt pulling these stunts? Were children this mischievous, because Tabitha was starting to feel like the parent.

During the class's midmorning break, Ava Elise pulled her aside. "Walk with me."

"Okay." She braced for a tongue-lashing or verbal warning as she followed her trainer through the door to the campus's courtyard.

"What happened?" Ava Elise asked softly.

Shaking her head, Tabitha could barely open her mouth before the tears flooded her face. Ava Elise guided her to a nearby stone bench surrounded by meticulous flower beds. They reminded Tabitha that she and Aunt Tweet were supposed to work in the garden and plant flowers this coming weekend.

"Here." Ava Elisa handed her a travel-size package of tissues from her suit pocket.

Nodding her thanks, Tabitha dabbed her eyes and blew her nose.

"Take a deep breath," Ava Elise coaxed her. "Tell me what's going on."

"I'm so sorry. I've always maintained perfect attendance. I don't practice tardiness—"

"Hey, I'm not worried about you being late. I won't have you sign a verbal warning. I'm concerned about you. You looked flustered when you walked in."

"My aunt"—Tabitha swallowed the lump in her throat, conjuring up the memories—"before I showered, she was in the bed. When I finished,

Aunt Tweet was nowhere to be seen and I had the hunch she had wandered to this one neighbor's house."

Her trainer listened patiently, even though their break time had surely ended.

"My aunt and I are still adjusting to this new phase in her life. Aunt Tweet doesn't remember who I am at times. She might freak out with a nurse's aide in the house and I'm not there. I can't attend my first company function, and I can't promise to attend the next one and the one after that." Tabitha knew she was probably asking to be terminated, but with her qualifications, she could get another job. There would never be another Priscilla "Aunt Tweet" Brownlee.

After a moment of silence, Ava Elise spoke. "I know you made a sacrifice to take in your aunt, even on a temporary basis, but life goes on, and you're going to have to figure out how it goes on, juggling commitments at home and work." She stood. "Take as much as time as you need to regroup. I know you won't have any problems catching up in class." To Tabitha's surprise, Ava Elise bent and snapped the stem of a tulip, lifted it to her nose, then handed it to Tabitha. "Flowers always cheer me up."

She laughed. "I can't believe you did that." Her eyes widened in disbelief as they both looked around the garden area, hoping no one saw what she'd done.

"Me neither." Ava Elise grinned. "But I won't tell if you don't."

"You stuck me with the evidence, so I'm walking back inside with you."

⸺

On Saturday morning, Tabitha woke and stretched at the foot of Aunt Tweet's bed like a feline, then shifted on a body pillow that had been surprisingly comfortable last night. Since she couldn't bear any more of her aunt's daring escapes and Marcus's wrath, this was her solution. Although she heard Aunt Tweet's light snoring, Tabitha refused to take a shower until her aunt was awake and occupied.

After a big breakfast, Aunt Tweet helped Tabitha tidy up the kitchen. When her aunt became quiet, Tabitha glanced over her shoulder. Aunt

Tweet had found an old photo album that Tabitha had tucked away and was flipping through it. Tabitha sat and rested her head on Aunt Tweet's shoulder.

"Do you remember any of these people?" She pointed to a younger picture of her parents and Aunt Tweet.

Her aunt frowned. "That's me…" She didn't identify the others in the photograph. For the next half hour, Aunt Tweet's memory faded in and out as some photos triggered recollection of antics and travels.

Late afternoon, they enjoyed the sunshine outside gardening. There was no music or conversation, just quiet time as they worked side by side. It was entertaining and relaxing until Tabitha realized her aunt was pulling up the petunias they had just planted. "No, no." She felt as if she were scolding a kindergartener. Her frustration surfaced.

"These aren't flowers. They're weeds," Aunt Tweet argued and continued undoing their tedious work.

Getting up, Tabitha dusted off her pants, then assisted her aunt to her feet. She would have to finish later, by herself. "That's enough for one day. Let's get cleaned up and eat."

"I ain't ate in a while." *A while* was the light lunch they'd had a few hours earlier.

The rest of the day, they stayed inside and watched movies while Tabitha multitasked, reviewing her class notes. At about eight, her aunt retired to bed, so Tabitha returned to her patio and replanted the flowers that had been unearthed and finished planting the others. It was ten thirty by the time she had completed her task and watered her efforts. Turning off the lights, she climbed the stairs, checked on her elderly relative, then relaxed in the bathtub filled with bubbles. Tonight, she would sleep in her own bed.

The next morning, Tabitha felt someone nudging her from her sleep. Her sore muscles protested the interruption, so she snuggled deeper under the covers.

"I'm ready, sweetie," a voice echoed in the room.

Springing up, she blinked until a familiar face came into focus. Aunt Tweet was fully dressed with her purse dangling from her arm.

She yawned. "Ready for what?"

"Church," Aunt Tweet said as if it were obvious.

Whew. She'd thought her aunt was asking for permission to leave for Marcus's house. This was an easy one. "We don't go."

Aunt Tweet frowned. "My church is across the street from where I work."

What was she talking about? Her aunt had been retired for more than twenty years. Maybe she was referring to Bermuda Place as her job, which would make sense, since she had gone there every day that week.

If there was a church nearby, Tabitha hadn't given it a second glance. Besides, she was drained. Her body craved sleep and relaxation. Wasn't Sunday a day of rest anyway? She floated back to her pillow. "Let's do a rain check, please."

"Tabitha Faye Knicely, if you don't get out of that bed, I'll drive myself."

Tabitha sprang forward again. Aunt Tweet had said her full birth name. She was about to celebrate the baby step when she realized her aunt also knew how to drive. It was where she could end up that concerned Tabitha, so she wasn't about to call her bluff. "Give me an hour."

"Cut it in half," Aunt Tweet ordered with a suspicious grin and adjusted her pink hat.

"Why don't you sit here and watch me?" Tabitha patted a spot on her bed, then sprinted into her closet and grabbed the first dress she saw off the hanger. Before she raced into her shower, she wagged her finger lovingly. "Please don't leave this house," she begged, putting her hands together in a prayer gesture.

Although her aunt nodded and seemed content, Tabitha broke a record with her grooming. Even her sisters would be impressed.

Defiant as a toddler climbing out of a playpen for a toy, her aunt had disappeared when Tabitha hurried out of the bathroom, but the aroma of breakfast cooking meant Aunt Tweet was still in the house. Tabitha dressed, then gathered her purse and walked downstairs. Aunt Tweet was busy behind the stove, whipping up scrambled eggs, while sausage sizzled in another skillet. Toast was already stacked on a plate.

Once everything was cooked, they silently gave thanks. While enjoying breakfast, Aunt Tweet gave Tabitha an odd expression, then chuckled to herself. "You remind me of my graduation picture from George Washington High School."

Tabitha beamed at the compliment she'd heard more than she could remember growing up.

"You should've been my sister instead of Pallie."

Priscilla "Aunt Tweet" and Palmira "Pallie" were twins, though not identical. From what her father had shared, Aunt Pallie had died in her twenties from tuberculosis. Their only other sibling was Tabitha's paternal grandmother, Pearl. Aunt Tweet was the only one left out of three girls. No husband or children. The Knicely girls were the last living relatives Aunt Tweet had on Tabitha's father's side. Kinfolk on her mother's side were so distant that Tabitha wouldn't know them if she passed them on the sidewalk.

Pushing aside her plate, Aunt Tweet sat back in her chair. Though her face had held a happy expression moments earlier, it was now crestfallen. "Live so you won't have regrets."

Where did that come from? "Do you have regrets?"

Aunt Tweet stood. "I'm ready to go." Instead of taking her plate to the sink, she left it on the table—so unlike her—and walked out of the kitchen.

Was her aunt avoiding to elaborate, or had she already forgotten her statement? That was another mystery that might not be solved. Tabitha wished Aunt Tweet had forgotten about church. Tabitha could really use a couple more hours in bed.

"It's not about me," Tabitha mumbled to herself. She scooped up the last of her eggs, wiped her mouth, then reached for their plates.

During the short drive, fear struck Tabitha. What was behind the sudden rush to attend church? Did her aunt sense death was imminent and she had regrets about something she did or didn't do? *God, please give her more time, or at least don't let her die while she's in my care.* She swallowed.

Following the route to Bermuda Place, she saw the church before Aunt Tweet pointed. Tabitha admired the beautifully constructed white stone complex that housed Bethesda Temple. The entrance was inviting, as were those who greeted them in the parking lot and inside the large foyer. A representative gave them welcome badges, then a very handsome male usher led them inside a large sanctuary.

Tabitha could feel the charged energy in the atmosphere. She strained her memory and couldn't recall the last time she had been to church, whether of her own volition or at someone's invitation.

Maybe her own brain cells had started to die if she couldn't remember something so simple. From her research, Tabitha could be susceptible to early onset Alzheimer's if she'd inherited mutations in genes on chromosomes twenty-one, fourteen, and one, but late onset after the midsixties would add chromosome nineteen to the equation. In essence, her father would have been the carrier from Grandma Pearl. Could her mutations be associated with other diseases like Lewy body dementia? Hold up. She was overanalyzing things.

Dismissing all medical-related thoughts, Tabitha relaxed in her seat and noted her surroundings. She had never seen people so serious about their worship. She smiled, admiring the little girls whose braids were adorned with bows and beads. Ties accented little boys' attire.

Will I ever have a family? Tabitha wondered as she scanned the sanctuary for husband material. Every man she saw had a woman by his side. Didn't matter anyway. The timing wasn't right for dating. Her focus was on being a caregiver. Right now, she would prefer a nap over going on a date.

A melodious sound drew Tabitha out of her reverie. Facing Aunt Tweet, Tabitha could only stare as her aunt harmonized with the music. *What an angelic sound.* She vaguely remembered that her aunt had possessed such a gift. Her father once said Aunt Tweet could rival Lena Horne, but Tabitha thought it was a myth. Clearly, he had been right. *Wow.* Closing her eyes, Tabitha reveled in the singing of "How Great Thou Art."

Too soon, the singers ceased and so did Aunt Tweet. Tabitha didn't hide her disappointment as she squeezed her aunt's hand. A middle-aged man stepped to the podium and introduced himself as Pastor George

Nelson. Clean-shaven and without a minister's robe, he looked more like a businessman than a preacher.

"Will our visitors please stand so the church can welcome you?" he said in a strong voice that commanded attention.

Aunt Tweet popped up and Tabitha followed. Her aunt seemed to soak in the attention as the audience heartily applauded. Glancing around, Tabitha noted there were many visitors sprinkled throughout the sanctuary.

"Thank you for joining us. We hope you will come back again. Please, take your seats," Pastor Nelson said. He directed everyone to open their Bibles to Philippians 4:6–7. Tabitha felt embarrassed. Not only had she not brought a Bible, but she didn't even know which box in her basement contained it. Good thing the scripture was displayed on an overhead screen.

"We're stressed out today, whether it's at home, on the job, or with family obligations," he began. "Do you ever feel like giving up? Don't! The stats on depression are overwhelming. Folks don't know the antidote for stress. It's simply in these two verses: 'Do not be anxious about anything, but in every situation, by prayer and petition, with thanksgiving, present your requests to God. And the peace of God, which transcends all understanding, will guard your hearts and your minds in Christ Jesus.' This is our formula: be prayerful, petition God with your struggles, and give thanks for the good things in your life."

If only it were that simple. Tabitha's formula for reducing stress was sleep.

"If you've locked God out of your life, let Him back in. Trust the Lord to relieve you of your burdens and you'll get a good night's rest," the preacher said as if he were reading Tabitha's mind.

Before closing his Bible, he encouraged his congregants to meditate on that passage throughout the week, then paused. "Now, for those of you who came here today with a heavy heart, God's salvation is waiting for you. Stop fighting against God's perfect will for your life and surrender." He lifted his arm. "Come to the altar."

As the choir sang "Come to Jesus," Tabitha's aunt's melodious voice blended in like an instrument.

"You've been holding out on me." Tabitha smiled and patted her aunt's hand that was adorned with rings. "You could sing to me anytime."

Aunt Tweet chuckled. "I used to all the time when you and the girls were babies."

Tabitha's heart pounded with excitement. Her aunt's right mind was back. "Really? Why did you stop?"

"I can't remember." Aunt Tweet seemed frustrated.

"It's all right." She slid her arm around her aunt's shoulder and squeezed. Tabitha was experiencing a level of that same frustration too. After the benediction, they made their way to the parking lot, smiling and nodding at folks along the path.

Next, the two enjoyed a buffet at Nana's Place. When Aunt Tweet massaged her stomach in fulfillment, Tabitha knew it was time to go home. Since the Knicely sisters became caregivers, their Sunday evening ritual included Skype calls among them, so they could be briefed on Aunt Tweet's condition.

Sitting next to Tabitha at the kitchen table, Aunt Tweet peered at the monitor but said very little. Every now and then, she would add a chuckle to their chatter.

"Can you believe Aunt Tweet woke me to go to church?"

"Our Aunt Tweet?" Kym blinked in surprise.

Rachel frowned. "I don't ever recall our aunt attending church. She reserved her Sundays for brunches, luncheons, and social functions."

Tabitha nodded. "Yeah, threw me for a loop too. Then once we were there, Aunt Tweet sounded like a songbird."

"Really?" Kym grinned. "Auntie, how could you bottle up all that talent and hold it in all these years? Sing for us."

They all laughed, even their aunt, before she mumbled, "I don't think I ever learned how to sing."

Huh? Tabitha's jaw dropped. Her aunt's bout of confusion was confusing. Her sisters looked at her with doubtful expressions. Tabitha had not imagined what she heard. She wondered what other hidden talents were trapped inside, screaming to get out. Soon, their aunt said her goodbyes and headed toward the stairs for her bedroom.

"Bummer," Rachel said. "I'd give the world to have heard her. Dad said Grandma bragged about Aunt Tweet singing in clubs and at parties, then she stopped."

"Hmm." Tabitha rested her chin on a fist, wondering if something traumatic happened. "Well, add gospel to her repertoire." Should she tell them about the other developments without freaking them out? "Her angelic voice was the *good* thing that happened this week…"

"Ah, was there a bad thing?" Kym frowned. "Aunt Tweet doesn't like the adult day facility, does she? Uh-oh. Tell us about your new job. Like it?"

"First, Aunt Tweet loves Bermuda Place," Tabitha said with relief. "She thinks she's an employee instead of a client. I guess she picked the church because we pass by it every day." She paused. "As far as my job? The pharmaceutical industry is the same—different company, different drugs, and a tweaked training program. I do like my trainer, Ava Elise."

"I wish there were a drug proven to reverse these dreaded dementia symptoms." Kym gritted her teeth.

As a stall tactic, Tabitha settled into her clinical mode to delay telling them about Aunt Tweet's wandering. "The brain is considered a complex organ, so it's not a simple fix. There are about eighty drugs being tested now."

"That's a lot," Rachel said with a sad expression. "Besides the meds she's on now, we need to make sure she eats healthy and gets plenty of exercise—"

"About that exercise," Tabitha interrupted to come clean. "Our dear aunt has taken some unsupervised walks in the mornings. She's been sneaking out of the house before I wake up."

"What?" Kym and Rachel shrieked at the same time.

"I know. Unbelievable, right?" Tabitha rubbed her forehead in frustration. "Thank God she was okay, but she picked the wrong neighbor's porch to sit on. He went ballistic on me." She closed her eyes, not wanting to relive her moments of shame. When she opened them, her sisters were peering closer at the monitor.

"That's a concern," Kym stated. "What if this neighbor had abducted or assaulted her?"

"After chewing my head off about Aunt Tweet's trespassing on his property, he threatened to call the police if she showed up again."

Rachel groaned. "I don't think I can handle another police call that one of my loved ones is in custody."

"Me either. He made me feel like a five-year-old." Tabitha raised her voice.

"Sisters," Rachel cut in, "apparently, this was an isolated case. Auntie is okay, and you're aware of it. You're going to have to really watch her."

Tabitha thought twice about telling her sisters that Aunt Tweet had gone missing more than once and that the last time had caused her to be late to her new job and to have a breakdown while there. Their aunt hadn't been in her care for a month, and already Tabitha felt like a failure. Tears welled up in her eyes, then fell unchecked.

"Tab, I'm sorry," Kym said softly. "I know you have to adjust. I had winter and spring breaks when Aunt Tweet stayed with me. I took a short leave of absence in between, and when I returned to the university, she tagged along. Since she was in academia for so long, the familiar setup kept her in her element. We have to cherish our time with her before she forgets who we are."

Dabbing her eyes, Tabitha sniffed. "Sorry. That came from nowhere." *I guess that's from my unchecked stress that the minister preached about today.* "Anyway, it's already happening. She's called me 'miss' a few times." She sighed. "Kym, I'm glad you had a smooth transition as her first caregiver. Everything was going okay for me too—at first. Instead of taking a family medical leave from the other company, I changed jobs, thinking everything would run smoother. Ah!" Tabitha shook her head. "Although we're getting a stipend for her care, I'm accustomed to working."

"No need to explain to us, Sis," Rachel said. "We're in this together. My turn is after yours. I wonder if getting her a dog would keep her more settled."

No way. "I can't take on more responsibility. This is harder than I thought. I'm trying to adjust to her ever-changing versions. She looks the same, but I have to remind myself that dementia is the culprit when she says and does things out of the norm."

Kym looked thoughtful. "If you need more time to adjust with the new job and everything, I can come get Aunt Tweet and bring her back with me for, let's say for three months." Always in big-sister mode, she believed in taking charge when she didn't feel a situation was going as planned.

"Nope." Tabitha wasn't a quitter, nor did she want a rescue—yet. "I needed to vent. That's all." She exhaled. After all, she had prepared herself for the caregiver role, learning the stages and recognizing the symptoms. "Everything will work out."

"Think about activities to keep her occupied…and pets do make great companions for the elderly," Rachel said. "We're in this together."

It didn't feel like it this week. Tabitha felt alone and could have used another pair of eyes to monitor their aunt's whereabouts at all times. "I got this," she assured them before ending their Skype chat. To be on the safe side, she raced upstairs to make sure Aunt Tweet wouldn't make a liar out of her with another visit to that mean old Jerk's house. Let him call 911. She dared him.

You'll be sorry, a voice in her head admonished her, so Tabitha quickly withdrew her unspoken dare.

Chapter 7

"You were missing in action this weekend, bro," Demetrius said, ribbing Marcus when he strolled through the door Monday morning. "Everything all right?"

"Yep." He was in a good mood after a great weekend. "A college buddy popped into town, and we spent Saturday hanging out, catching up." He rested his laptop bag on the desk. "Sunday, I had brunch with the vice president of Enterprise Leasing, then we golfed for a few hours. I'd say I was in good company." He was in a great mood to begin the workweek.

"Smooth." Demetrius exchanged a fist bump with Marcus. "I heard their contract with the current cleaning crew is expiring. Best time to network."

"You know it. Hey, have you checked in with Mom and Dad? I haven't been able to reach them."

Sometimes John and Sylvia Whittington, both of whom had retired from the phone company and moved to North Carolina three years earlier, would take off for mini vacations at a moment's notice. The tables had turned. Instead of the parents trying to keep up with their two little boys, it was the other way around now as he and his brother attempted to track their aging parents' whereabouts at all times.

Demetrius shrugged. "They went sailing with a stopover on Governors Island. They said they had enjoyed it so much, they and their friends, spent the night with no hurry to return home."

Shaking his head, Marcus envied their no-cares-in-the-world lifestyle. "They are living it up."

"Yep, and they were ecstatic when I told them you were out of pocket because you were in a complicated relationship with your neighbor and possibly on a date." He snickered. "Mom seemed real interested." So amused with himself, Demetrius doubled over, laughing as he returned to his desk.

Cutting his eyes toward Demetrius, Marcus didn't appreciate being the source of his brother's amusement. "You what?" He didn't bother taming his roar. "My last and only complicated romantic relationship was with Chelsie. That was enough drama to last a lifetime."

Demetrius bobbed his head and grunted. "Glad she is old news. Only money could buy that chick's love. I'm glad you saw that and cut your losses."

"I'm still trying to figure out what possessed you to concoct a story about Tabitha and her aunt. When she's out of sight, she out of my mind." *Maybe*, Marcus said to himself. "What's your fascination with my neighbor?"

"You tell me. You come in mad about her aunt. Granted, you don't get heated easily, but I've seen you mad, and when you talk about Tabitha, you ain't mad enough to carry out your threat." He twisted his mouth into a smirk.

Hmph. Marcus didn't take the bait. His brother didn't know him that well.

Demetrius's amusement diminished to soft chuckles before more laughter flared up again. "Sorry, your love life took the attention off me not having one. Mom accuses me of being too picky. Anyway, expect her to return your call tonight." He boasted a puppy-dog expression. "You can thank me on your wedding day."

Not to that woman. He did his best to keep his irritation under wraps. "Whatever." There was a knock at their door, and Chess stuck his head inside the room, then motioned for Demetrius to step outside. If their team leader wanted to speak with his brother, it must be serious.

A few minutes later, his brother returned, telling Chess, "We'll handle it."

Demetrius cleared his throat and leaned on his desk. "As we expected, Chess said Victor was a no-show on Friday."

Marcus figured as much, but when he'd left the office on Friday, he didn't want to think about it until he came back today. Marcus reached for his phone and flipped through the employee directory for Victor's cell number. His live-in girlfriend, also an employee, Latrice, answered. He could hear one of the babies crying in the background.

After a short greeting, he asked for Victor. She was quiet for a moment. "He's not here, Mr. Whittington," she said softly.

Did Victor have Latrice lying for him? Not only did Marcus not believe her, but he also suspected Victor was probably in the same room with her.

"You're going to fire him, aren't you?" Her voice trembled.

Mm-hmm. Even she recognized her boyfriend's behavior wasn't favorable in the workplace. "I'm sorry, Latrice, but you know I can't discuss personnel matters." Her sniffles tore at his conscience. Yet, as the boss, even a pushover—according to his brother—he had to stand his ground. "It's going to be all right. God will help you."

Whoa. What made him say that? He had always been a firm believer that God helps those who help themselves. He later learned, to his shame, the phrase wasn't even biblical. It was coined in the late 1600s by an English politician, Algernon Sidney, then Ben Franklin had written it in a 1757 issue of *Poor Richard's Almanac.*

After that blunder was brought to his attention, he tried to keep God out of the conversation, since he wasn't a scripture scholar. His connection with God was limited to nightly prayers and blessing his food. Marcus rarely stepped foot in church unless a special occasion called for it—weddings and funerals. Neither was his favorite. He was getting off track. The bottom line was Victor needed to man up.

"Am I being let go too?" The panic in Latrice's voice was real.

"No," he assured her. "Your work ethic is good. I wish it had rubbed off on your boyfriend. You show up on time and work overtime when we need you."

Marcus didn't know what God's plans were for Victor, or himself for that matter. "Please ask him to call me." *I want to save him a trip to the warehouse in case he's in the mood to work.* He disconnected, then bowed his head. He had no choice but to fire the man.

"I know this is hard for you."

"Yeah." Marcus exhaled. "It's a good feeling, putting someone on the payroll... It's terrible and nothing to celebrate when we're forced to remove them." He thought about his company's success stories they had posted on a corkboard in the employee lounge to motivate everyone. Some of their former employees had gone on to college, two working toward master's degrees in social work.

"I know, Bro." Demetrius stood, walked over to his desk, and gripped Marcus's shoulder. "You gave Victor one more chance than I would have."

That didn't make Marcus feel any better. Although he and Demetrius provided their employees the best working conditions they could to avoid high turnover rates, Whittington Janitorial Services wasn't created to be a career job for employees but a step toward helping them pursue their dreams. Until Victor had other options, Whittington Janitorial Services had been his best thing going.

As expected, Victor didn't call back by four thirty, so Marcus decided to stick around to make sure there wouldn't be any fireworks in case Victor showed up. Chess and Victor never hit it off, so it wouldn't take long before an exchange of words would set them off. His supervisor had had brushes with the law too, which included two assault charges. He didn't want Victor's bad attitude to make it three.

Since Demetrius had already left for the day, Marcus locked the office, strolled into the warehouse, and settled in the employee lounge. He waved at a handful of workers who had returned from their day shifts. When his stomach growled, he realized he had skipped lunch. He ordered ten large pizzas so there would be enough for his staff, plus the little ones in the second-shift child care.

While waiting for the delivery, he stretched out in the spacious room. The acrylic wall allowed him a view into the warehouse on one side and the adjacent childcare room.

Chess strolled into the lounge. "What's up with your mystery lady?" He opened the refrigerator and reached for two bottled waters.

Tabitha wasn't his lady, so there was no mystery. After what

Demetrius inferred this morning about him dating his neighbor, Marcus had tried hard not to recall the incidents. Why did his employee have to bring her up again? Plus, he didn't like discussing his personal life, which was nonexistent, with the people who worked for him. But Chess had caught him off guard the other morning when Marcus had haphazardly mentioned the source of his irritation.

Stalling, he gulped from his bottle of water, then glanced over at the childcare area and nodded at the shift supervisor. "Nothing. I found out the old woman is suffering from dementia and wanders the neighborhood. She's not part of a crime ring. The problem is the woman's niece can't handle taking care of her."

"Sounds like this escapee needs an eight-foot fence." Chess snickered.

Marcus grunted. "Something tells me she would find a way to climb over it or dig a tunnel." He paused, then shrugged. "I had to show Victor some tough love. I guess Aunt Tweet is next."

"First-name basis," Chess teased.

"The aunt really is a sweetheart, really harmless, but she could be in danger if she meets up with the wrong type of people." His mind drifted to a few days earlier. "Friday night, the news reported an elderly woman was missing. I was in the other room and I thought the anchor said Tweet. I ran to the flat-screen and rewound the segment. The missing person's name was Theresa."

Whew. "No resemblance. While driving to work this morning, I heard on the radio that woman was found okay in Indianapolis last night. She had boarded a Greyhound, thinking it was a MetroBus. That's two days of being vulnerable." He paused. "Yeah, so the next time I see Aunt Tweet on my porch, I have no choice but to call the police—for her own protection. Then her niece can deal with the fallout."

"Wow." Chess rubbed his bald head. "That's deep. Most of the old folks in my family passed away when I was small. Well, do what you've got to do, Boss."

Exactly, Marcus thought as the lobby receptionist's voice came over the intercom and alerted Marcus that his delivery had arrived, then added, "Save me a slice of pepperoni."

Her humor was a pick-me-up as Marcus stood and walked to the front entrance to pay the driver and get the food.

When he returned, his employees had descended on the break room. One worker pulled out paper plates and napkins from the cabinets, and another set them on the table. About a dozen or so had formed a line.

"You all act like you haven't eaten in weeks," he joked, hoping they had food at home and didn't rely on the fruit and snacks he and Demetrius supplied at work.

The pizza was almost devoured when one of the two shuttle van drivers walked in and snatched a piece. Since many of the employees didn't have reliable transportation, the vans took them to the job sites. It was another perk to guarantee attendance.

As the last van drove off the lot, Marcus concluded Victor was indeed a no-show. Even though his badge had been deactivated, he could still enter the building with Latrice's and cause a scene or worse.

Not ready to go home to an empty house, Marcus returned to his office to complete more tasks. After a productive couple of hours, he called it quits and decided to cut through the warehouse to his car. Some of the children were dressed in their pajamas, their school clothes in their backpacks. It was convenient for parents who worked overnight, so they could get them to the bus stops on time the next morning.

"Hi, Mr. Marcus!" Brian, a three-year-old, shouted from the other side of the glass wall.

He laughed as his childcare worker scolded the boy for yelling. Marcus detoured toward the room. Many of the children, ranging in age from two to eleven, vied for his attention. Brian made a beeline to him, holding up a book. "Can you read me a story?"

"Seems like I have a special request," he told Gail, a retired school-teacher, who wore her gray hair in short twists. "Get the children settled and I'll read just one." He lifted up a finger to their screams of delight.

She chuckled, then instructed them to sit in a circle on a colorful floor mat while Marcus dragged one of the rockers toward them. Taking a seat, he observed their wide eyes and attentive faces. He opened Brian's book, *Darius Goes on a Field Trip*, and began reading. "Darius climbed

Mr. Funnybone's bus. He was excited to go to the zoo and see the animals. He'd never seen a giraffe before…"

Brian yawned when Marcus got to the last page, but the older children wanted more—a stall tactic to keep from going to sleep. "Sorry, the end." Marcus grinned and stood. After telling his staff good night, he headed out.

Given the chance, one day, he planned to be a good father—give baths, read bedtime stories, then tuck his son or daughter under the covers, even change diapers. He scrunched his nose as if he could smell it now.

Once inside his car, he sat there. Yeah, it was time for him to settle down. All he needed was the perfect woman for him.

Chapter 8

TUESDAY MORNING, MARCUS LEFT HOME EARLIER THAN USUAL TO spot-check behind his employees at a client located at the Westport Business Park. He was cruising on Roland Drive when a flash of green caused him to do a double take. "It couldn't be." The infamous Aunt Tweet was on the loose again. "Unbelievable."

Either she was heading to his house or to another unsuspecting neighbor's. Gritting his teeth, Marcus made a U-turn. The elderly woman was not his problem, yet he was concerned. He parked at the curb, hurried out, and walked up to her. "Remember me, Aunt Tweet?"

She squinted, scanning his face for familiarity. "Can't say I do."

He was about to explain why she would know him when her niece almost pushed him out of the way from behind. His reflexes were too quick, and his body mass was too conditioned to be intimidated, but he stepped aside anyway.

"Aunt Tweet," Tabitha said out of breath, shaking her head. "You have to stop doing this—please."

Briefly distracted by her presence, Marcus noticed the lone curler dangling from her long mane. That was the extent of his perusal as he folded his arms and frowned. "If you know she becomes confused, why don't you keep track of her? Enough is enough." He removed his phone from its case on his belt slowly punched in 91, then glanced at the distress plastered on Tabitha's pretty face. Her eyes were glossed over. *Great.*

Press the last button, he told himself, but he couldn't as his shoulders slumped. He was a sucker for sniffs, tears, and looks of defeat. But it was the helplessness he saw, as if she were throwing in the towel, that kept his finger hovering midair instead of making a landing on the last digit. Was he reading her right?

"I wasn't lost, young man. I knew exactly where I was going," Aunt Tweet snapped. The determination on the elderly woman's face made a quick believer out of him. "Home."

"You mean my house," he corrected and eyed Tabitha.

"We sold your house. You don't remember, but you're staying with me for a while," Tabitha said softly, trying unsuccessfully to appease Aunt Tweet and steer her back inside, but her aunt stiffened.

"I know where I live!" the older woman snapped and balled her fist. Apparently, her aggression surprised Tabitha too.

Oh boy, now Marcus *had* to intervene. The situation had escalated into a standoff. If he pressed the last 1, it would be for an assault in progress. Lowering his voice, he vied for Aunt Tweet's attention. "I would love for you to see the house. How about later, when I return from work?" Did he just put himself in the middle of their chaos? What was he doing, and what was Tabitha thinking about his interference?

Her response was a mixture of shock, confusion, then annoyance. That was the thanks he got?

"Thanks, but I have this under con—"

"Control?" He balked. "Trust me, lady, you don't."

Before she had a comeback, Aunt Tweet accepted his offer. "All right, but you come right home after school," she said, scolding him.

"Great," Tabitha mumbled as she wrapped her arm around Aunt Tweet's shoulders and guided her home, but not without giving Marcus a final glance. "I don't need you to encourage her," she said softly.

Jingling the car keys in his hand, Marcus stared. "I stopped to help."

"How is calling the police a truce? I don't need your kind of help," she said indignantly.

He nodded. "Okay, you want a truce. Deal with me or the authorities. Right now, I think I'm your best option."

If looks could kill, he would be a dead man. "Fine!"

To him, her irritated state was comical and cute. "Good choice." He turned to her aunt. "See you later, Aunt Tweet…and Miss Knicely."

Barely containing his amusement, Marcus jumped in his car and drove off. "Women!" He didn't make it to the streetlight before he second-guessed his decision to get involved. He was supposed to be discouraging visits, not the other way around.

He had to switch gears. Their confrontation had caused him to be stuck in rush-hour traffic, which he had hoped to avoid. It was imperative he get to Bristol-Combs today to see if his employees were as meticulous as they were trained and paid to be. Demetrius had negotiated the two-year contract for Whittington Janitorial. They both hoped the company would renew the contract before it expired.

Making an early, unexpected appearance would let his client see that he and Demetrius were hands-on businessmen they could trust. The brothers wore tan pants and the company's blue polos with their logo embroidered across the upper left pocket instead of suits and ties.

While he and other motorists inched along I-170 toward Highway 64, his interaction with Tabitha resurfaced. Even without makeup, she had the wow factor to get any man's attention. He was not exempt. Still, regardless of what was going on in her life, her aunt should be her priority.

And what was it about her that kept him from calling the authorities? What kind of invisible headlock did she have on this former wrestler? Maybe he would get answers to his questions later.

And his mother wanted answers from him too about his neighbor. When he'd reached Sylvia by phone late last night, she'd fired off questions based on the nuggets Demetrius had planted. Though he'd tried to convince her that his brother was delusional about the incidents, she had dismissed his comments to remind him of the chance meeting that brought his father and her together.

"I'll take my chances waiting for the one I'm meant to be with," Marcus had told her. "I'm not enthralled with irresponsible people." What would his mother say about this morning's incident? It wasn't attraction that made him invite his neighbors to his house out of the blue. His offer was purely in hopes of putting an end to Aunt Tweet's attraction to his house.

Changing the subject, he asked about her and his dad's sailing trip. That was an hour-long play-by-play of Governors Island's beauty and scenery.

Marcus chuckled as he recalled the conversation before arriving at his destination and verifying the client was satisfied with the services provided by Marcus's company. A few hours later, he and Demetrius arrived at the office at the same time. Both had made morning business calls in the field.

"Everything satisfactory at Bristol-Combs?" his brother asked.

"Yep." He grinned. "Bathrooms, carpets, and floors are spotless and smelling good."

After resting his laptop on the desk, Demetrius sat on the edge and folded his arms. "But we have one unhappy ex-employee."

Marcus flopped in his seat and linked his hands together. "Let me guess: Victor." That man was no longer his concern.

"According to Chess, Latrice came in and said she has to quit too, spewing Victor's mantra that if he wasn't welcome to work here, then we were disrespecting both of them." Demetrius huffed. "Does he think up this foolishness in his sleep?" He stood and walked around to his chair. "Interestingly though, Chess said she sounded like she didn't believe a word of what she was saying. Why do women let no-good men brainwash them?"

Closing his eyes, Marcus rubbed his face. "I could strangle that dude. He won't work and doesn't want the mother of his two small babies to have a job either. She's hardworking and trying to do something positive with her life. What a waste of a relationship."

Demetrius shrugged. "I know you tried, but you can't save the world, even one by one. She's going to let him bring her down, the loser. I would throw the bum out."

Growing up and even now, Demetrius was always the no-nonsense son who called it like he saw it. Marcus tried to take a wait-and-see attitude before making judgment calls, but he had to agree with his brother on this one. "I second that. Since Latrice quit, she can't collect unemployment, and Victor's unemployment checks won't be much. Without two incomes, they'll both be out on the streets." How sad. "We're clueless to what's going on at their home."

Do you know what's going on inside your neighbor's home?

Huh? The voice was so loud in his head, Marcus was surprised

Demetrius didn't hear it too. He swallowed and looked around the room. Was that God talking to him? He shivered. He dismissed whatever he thought he heard and proceeded. "We've done all we can. We've tried to reach back and pull somebody forward. They—basically, Victor—let go of our grip. I don't know what else to do."

Pray.

Spooked, Marcus blinked, took a deep breath, and exhaled. Only his mother would encourage that, and she wasn't here, but apparently, God's presence was there in his office. Okay, he was getting carried away with all this talk about Victor. He quickly changed the subject. "On another note, guess who I ran into this morning?"

"Have no idea." Demetrius opened his desk drawer and shuffled through it.

"Aunt Tweet."

He looked up. "Good old auntie, huh? You call the cops?" He tilted his head and waited. "For some strange reason, this is one time I hope you didn't make good on your threat. Please tell me you didn't."

With mixed emotions about what he did, Marcus didn't answer right away but feigned distraction as he stared at the wall calendar.

"Marcus," Demetrius said in a stern voice, reminding him too much of their father.

"Nah, I was in a good mood this morning and felt generous. I invited them over this evening, so I'm cutting out early," he said nonchalantly, as if short workdays were his norm when he usually he was the last to leave work, unless he had to meet a client. After a long pause, he couldn't hold it in any longer and released a bark of laughter at his brother's dumbfounded expression.

"You had me going there, Bro." Demetrius chuckled with him.

"I'm serious."

His brother's jaw dropped. "Excuse me? There's definitely more to this story than what you've been telling me." He squinted. "Maybe I'll invite myself to dinner."

"You can't," he said smugly and rocked back in his chair. "You're entertaining Clark Baker for happy hour."

The potential client owned an office building downtown. His business would be a major win for the brothers.

Pounding his fist on the desk, Demetrius appeared truly disappointed. "I want to meet these neighborhood menaces. Take pictures."

"Did I say they were menaces?" Marcus had a feeling that, after this evening, things would change. He didn't know if it would be between him and Aunt Tweet or him and Tabitha. Would it matter?

Chapter 9

TABITHA WAS DISTRACTED AS SHE SAT IN CLASS, RELIVING WHAT HAD happened hours earlier. Her aunt was making Tabitha look irresponsible. *Maybe I am.* She considered the possibility. Clearly, Marcus was taking advantage of her weakness to insinuate himself into her life to prove she couldn't live up to her caregivers' pact. The truce had been rescinded.

She racked her brain in self-examination instead of listening to her instructor. Ava Elise had been more than kind, not pointing out her tardiness. What was she doing wrong with Aunt Tweet that Kym had done right?

Tabitha had studied all the symptoms of dementia and what to expect—the cognitive functions, like memory loss; the behavioral, like restlessness and mood swings; the psychological manifestations, like depression; the physical signs, like unsteady walking; and a long list of others to watch out for. Tabitha knew them, could recite them in her sleep.

She had anticipated all this, but the reality was her aunt wasn't a textbook, but a real person who exhibited symptoms out of nowhere, not giving Tabitha time to process how to respond. Tabitha was starting to lose weight because of her loss of appetite, a trickle-down effect of being tired as a result of less sleep. The stress of her job wasn't helping her to retain information she should have already known.

When she had finally coaxed Aunt Tweet back in the house after Marcus drove off, her aunt had fussed while Tabitha freshened her up and dressed her. Resentment was building within Tabitha—not against her aunt, but the condition that plagued Aunt Tweet. Tabitha had to keep reminding herself that her aunt's neurological abilities weren't functioning properly.

A fellow rep asked a question, jolting Tabitha back to the present to listen to Ava Elise's response, then Tabitha drifted back to her musings. She woke thirty-five minutes earlier every morning. Her routine began with checking on Aunt Tweet, who seemed to be sleeping soundly.

At least, she thought so before jumping into the shower for seven minutes. Seven minutes! To stay on a schedule, she had everything timed down to the minute, so how had her aunt wakened, walked out the door, and paraded down the street so fast?

If Aunt Tweet was testing her as a caregiver, Tabitha was flunking. Exhausted, she yawned, feeling the effects of getting up a couple times during the night to do a head count in her house. As a result, she had become a light sleeper. One eye popped open at the slightest stir.

She sighed and shifted in her seat. *Concentrate*, she chided herself, refusing to allow her home life to interfere with her livelihood.

"Clinical trials show Portal is a proven winner to reduce spine, wrist, and hip fractures for postmenopausal women. Studies show the active ingredient is absorbed faster to help strengthen…" Ava Elise informed the class, referring to a drug Ceyle-Norman manufactured for osteoporosis.

Tabitha snapped out of her reverie.

"The best benefit of Portal is it's an injection that works with calcium and vitamin D therapy," Ava Elise added. "Well." She smiled. "I think I've overloaded your brain cells enough this morning. Take an extra thirty-minute extended lunch."

Tabitha could use some fresh air. She gathered her things as her trainer made a beeline to where she was sitting. "How about Chipotle? My treat and I'll drive."

It wasn't an invitation but a summons. Tabitha had no choice but to comply. She feared a reprimand or termination was coming. On the short car ride to the restaurant, she could feel a spike in her blood pressure while Ava Elise hummed and focused on her driving.

In the ordering line, her trainer gave no hint that anything was amiss. As promised, she paid the tab and advised Tabitha to find a table. She spied a nook that was as private as it could be for a public place where she was going to be humiliated.

After Ava Elise gave thanks in a normal tone, she sampled her burrito, then wiped her mouth.

Tabitha's appetite was on hold as she waited for Judgment Day with her job.

"So, how's your aunt?"

The gentleness in the woman's eyes caused Tabitha to relax. This time, instead of bawling, she took a deep cleansing breath and shrugged. "I don't know."

"What do you mean? Doesn't she still live with you?" Ava Elise frowned.

"Yes, she stays at my house, but she seems to always want to escape." She paused. "I know Alzheimer's is taking away the aunt I know and love, but I feel it's taking a part of me too. Once I adjust to one dementia symptom, another one pops up. This morning, my aunt balled her fist at me. I thought she was going to hit me. This disease is scary," she rambled on, then stabbed at her salad and forced herself to eat.

Ava Elise reached over and patted her hand. "Hey, I know it's hard to care for a loved one. My brother and I tag-teamed our mother's care. Her mind was sharp, but her body was weak from COPD, diabetes, and a mild stroke. We shared everything—doctor's visits, dialysis, bathing, cooking. It's a physical and emotional strain on a caregiver."

Her trainer understood her. At Tabitha's former company, she had represented a steroid drug to treat chronic obstructive pulmonary disease, COPD. She couldn't imagine struggling for every breath.

So you should have no complaints, she scolded herself. "The doctor said Aunt Tweet is in relatively good physical health," Tabitha said, relieved. "She doesn't look eighty-four, and she moves as if she's in her seventies. No thanks to Alzheimer's for her brain cells dying and memory fading." She shivered at the thought of her aunt having more complications.

Ava Elise took another bite of her burrito, then washed it down with a sip from her soda. "For three years, my brother and I watched our mother fall into depression because she felt she had become a burden on us." She blinked and turned away. Quickly regrouping, she faced Tabitha again. "In truth, she was, but no more than the burdens we had put on her when we were children. The bottom line was she was our momma, so it was our pleasure. It wasn't easy. Robert Jeffrey and I had to keep reminding ourselves that she was still alive and with us." She paused. "Hold onto the good memories. That will keep you going. When we buried her, my brother and I had no regrets."

"No regrets," Tabitha whispered. She wanted a life without apologies. Accepting the advice, Tabitha relaxed enough to enjoy her salad, realizing she was famished. "Thank you so much for sharing this. I've been a little distracted," she admitted sheepishly.

"Maybe more than a little." Ava Elise gave her a warm smile, expanding the space between her thumb and finger to demonstrate how much. "You're a seasoned sales rep. I know you'll be at the top of your game after training. Expect the unexpected with your aunt and plan accordingly, but you might consider getting help. If you get sick, who's going to take care of you?"

Tabitha had no answer. For the most part, she was healthy and seldom came down with a cold. In regard to getting help, she and her sisters had agreed to discuss other options if Aunt Tweet's condition worsened. They hoped any talk about a nursing home as an option was a long way off.

With a clear head, Tabitha returned to the classroom and didn't miss a step in the lesson. Even the thought of accepting Marcus's invitation didn't annoy her as much as it had earlier in the day.

That evening when they arrived home, her aunt hadn't forgotten about going to Marcus's house. "Hurry. You never keep a young man waiting." She sounded like a drill sergeant while sitting on Tabitha's bed.

Peeping out of the walk-in closet, Tabitha said, "I thought it was the man who isn't supposed to keep a woman waiting."

"When you're my age, that doesn't apply." She gave a dainty chuckle.

Hmph. Tabitha was thirty-two, not eighty-four. The man, especially Marcus, could wait. The longer, the better. She didn't ask or want his intervention. Only to appease Aunt Tweet was she making the effort.

Chapter 10

Questioning his judgment to get involved, Marcus arrived home early enough to shower and change. Since he had committed himself, he better put to good use his home training.

His mother had drilled into him and Demetrius's heads never to entertain a guest without offering a snack or drink—even if it was water. Although he could cook well enough to keep from starving, he stopped by Dierbergs, a local family-owned chain of grocery stores, for chicken salad, crackers, a Tippin's apple pie, and bottled water. He thought that was plenty on short notice.

It had been a while since he'd entertained a woman who wasn't his mother in his house. With his brother and other guys, it was pizza and hot wings delivery. Years ago, there had been someone special in his life. Chelsie Dennis's charm, knockout looks, and grace had stolen Marcus's heart, and he had reached out to his mother to guide him step by step for the meal via phone, versus her flying in town to cook it herself like she had wanted to do.

Marcus reflected on the evening that had been perfect. Not long after their romantic dinner, it became apparent to him that Chelsie was more interested in what she could get out of the relationship without depositing anything into it. After he moved on, Marcus met Reba Green. She looked good on his arm, but they struck out on developing a deep connection. When that ended, he took a hiatus. Now, Marcus was determined to hold off by any means necessary for as long as he could to find a lifelong love like his parents'.

Why was he even thinking about past regrets? His guests today were no big deal. He was simply doing what he did best, helping those in need, and his two neighbors needed help—big time. It was almost five thirty when he discreetly peeped out his window. Tabitha had already parked in front of his home and was assisting Aunt Tweet. Her aunt wasn't in her nightclothes this time, and Tabitha wasn't in one of her stylish business suits or high heels. In her flats, he guessed she stood about five six or seven. He smiled at her faded jeans and dark sweater. She looked youthful and carefree, which was something he only saw once when she and her aunt was gardening. Other times, the woman had *stress* tattooed on her beautiful face.

He opened the door and stepped out to escort them on the winding path to his porch. "Good evening, ladies. So glad you could make it."

"I want to see what you've done to my house, young man," Aunt Tweet said as she latched onto his elbow for support. He reached back and offered Tabitha his hand. She declined, so he assisted her aunt solo up the porch stairs.

Once they crossed his threshold, he pulled his phone off the clip. "Ladies, before I give a quick tour, do you mind if we take a selfie?"

Aunt Tweet's face glowed, and she smiled warmly at the suggestion. He imagined she was a looker when she was younger, because she was still polished and beautiful, as she'd aged gracefully.

Tabitha gave him a suspicious expression. "Why? What are you planning to do with it?"

"Fair question." It wasn't as if they trusted each other. Marcus grinned sheepishly. "Well, I kinda told my brother about this scenario. He's intrigued. He wanted to meet both of you, but a business engagement got in the way. I won't post it on social media. It's only to show my brother."

"Trust me, I'm not only embarrassed that we put you in this situation, but leery of you luring an unsuspecting elderly woman into your house. Just so we're clear, I pack Mace and will use it," Tabitha warned him, then added, "My aunt knows self-defense, and something tells me her memory will kick in and she'll give you a beat down you won't soon forget." Although she gave him an engaging smile, her stance was defiant.

Not only had she questioned his honor, but she had an attitude on top of that. It was his turn to bite back. "This seems to me like a situation you can't control. Otherwise, she wouldn't be running away from you to my house." His bark must have been too much because she flinched. The selfie would have to wait. "I'm sorry—"

"Young man," Aunt Tweet interrupted, pointing to the living room. "Kym, I'm ready for a tour of my house."

He nodded at the elderly woman. "Of course." Then he frowned and faced the woman he knew as Tabitha. "Your name isn't Tabitha?"

"It is. Kym's my older sister. Aunt Tweet stayed with her before me." She whispered, "I accept your apology. I shouldn't have said anything about my Mace. You would have found out eventually if you tried anything. I'll act civil."

Shaking his head, Marcus found himself enjoying their sparring, so he grinned. "Me too. Truce number two?"

She giggled. "I'm losing count."

"Come this way." He held out his arm, and Aunt Tweet rested her hand gently on it. He waited for Tabitha to do the same. She scrunched her nose and placed her fingers on his arm. He flexed his biceps, and she pinched him.

Marcus laughed at their antics. Even though he didn't know much about Tabitha, he admitted she was more than a beautiful woman. She was strong, independent, and, despite his initial impression of her, she did care about her aunt.

He couldn't explain his slowly growing attraction toward her; at the same time, he was concerned about Tabitha's inability to seize the upper hand as her aunt's guardian. He didn't know if his invitation would hinder or help her, but he hoped it would curtail Aunt Tweet's clandestine visits to his porch. He focused on his tour guide abilities. "As you ladies can see, the marble tile accents the bleached wood on the bannister. The railing still has some of the original pieces. Although the builders designed this house to have a grand appearance from the outside, it's only three bedrooms and three baths, and I'm updating the kitchen."

For the first time, Tabitha seemed to drop her guard and took note of her surroundings. What had drawn Marcus's attention when he had shopped for a house was the L-shaped staircase that blended well with the beige, peach, and tan of the only ceramic-tiled floor in the house. Every other room had oak hardwood floors that gleamed. His mother thought the foyer screamed elegance when she first saw it; he thought the floor would be an easy mop job.

A large glass sconce on each side of the arched opening to his living room was his mother's doing. She also took delight in strategically placing every wall hanging and piece of furniture to create what she described as the "*ooh* and *aah* effect," as two matching bold-red, cushioned benches held court under the stairs.

There was an elaborate wood carving on the King Frederic console table under a ridiculous huge painting to the even heavier round table in the middle of the foyer. Its sole purpose, according to his mother, was to display an oversize vase with silk flowers. *What a waste of space*, he thought.

Tabitha spun around slowly. "This is nice! Are those closets?" She pointed to the twin narrow doors on each side of the massive, carved-wood front door.

He nodded, amused that his house wowed her.

"Clever and a nice touch. How long have you lived here?" she asked as they both kept their eyes on Aunt Tweet, who was slowly wandering into the next room as if she were a home inspector.

"Four years," he said, stepping into his living room. A wood-carved fireplace with a mirror above the mantelpiece commanded the room, and a pair of arched french doors opened to mock porches. The sole piece of furniture was a large blue sofa with an attached chaise between the two walls. This was purely a for-show room. He essentially lived in three rooms: bedroom, kitchen, and, when he entertained, family room, also known as his "man cave."

Aunt Tweet made herself comfortable on the sofa and seemed content to stare out the window. Tabitha peeped into the adjacent kitchen but didn't step farther until he invited her.

"This is a slow work in process," he explained about some missing overhead cabinets, "but I can't update it like I want."

"That's because you purchased it after the houses in Pasadena

Hills joined the ranks of National Historic neighborhoods on the U.S. Department of Interior National Park Service National Registry of Historic Places," Tabitha informed as if she was reading from Wikipedia and without running out of breath.

"Yeah. I know. I researched the neighborhood before buying here and was impressed by the meticulous details of each home. This house..." He paused and glanced back. Her aunt hadn't moved. "I never learned so much about architecture until I became a homeowner. Pasadena Hills has Tudor, colonial, and Georgian revival designs, as well as Cape Cod, minimal traditional, and Creole French homes," he said, not to be bested by her knowledge. "I'm the proud owner of Georgian revival architecture." He grinned.

"And it is beautiful. It took about thirty years to complete the hundreds of homes and other structures in the Pasadena Hills neighborhood district. My family moved here in the 1970s."

Her tidbits of information were helping him create a character sketch of his neighbor. Tabitha had an older sister and a great-aunt and had lived in the neighborhood as a child. What about a man in her life? He froze. Why did he care? Clearing his throat, he guided his mind back to the topic of discussion. "I can't imagine any developer today taking that long to complete a project."

"You're right," she said, leaning against his marble counter. "I believe this cluster of homes was meant to be a trendsetter for suburban neighborhoods that bordered the city limits. Who would have thought to build houses for homeowners with cars when streetcars were the mode of transportation back in the day?"

A history buff. Tabitha was becoming more fascinating by the minute. He took that as his cue to serve light refreshments. "I have snacks, in case you didn't have time to eat something."

"Thanks, but we've taken up enough of your time." She spun around. Aunt Tweet was behind her in the doorway, eyeing the platters Marcus was removing from the refrigerator. "We'd better go home."

Aunt Tweet brushed past Tabitha to the counter. "Hush, girl. I'm hungry. What do you have here?"

He chuckled, then watched Tabitha's demeanor when Aunt Tweet dismissed her. She easily conceded and allowed her aunt to have her way. He felt sorry for Tabitha being reprimanded as if she was a child.

The ladies trailed him to his breakfast nook right off the kitchen. Six narrow windows were designed in a bay shape that gave him a fantastic view of the neighborhood, and Tabitha commented on that too.

After they were seated, her aunt nodded for him to say grace.

Folding his hands, Marcus closed his eyes and said a simple prayer. "Thank you, Lord, for this food and companions to enjoy it. In Jesus's name, amen."

They whispered "amen," then served themselves.

While Aunt Tweet mentioned her girls, Tabitha discreetly tried to get his attention.

Marcus frowned, trying to interpret her gestures, then slowly understood that Aunt Tweet was talking about her niece as if Tabitha were her child. Next, the woman switched subjects to name the places she had visited. He eyed Tabitha for confirmation that it wasn't a fabrication, but she gave no reaction.

"I'm a twin, you know."

He dabbed his mouth before speaking. "No, I didn't know that."

"That's right. Pearl and I were twins, and we had a big sister named Pallie."

"No, you and Pallie were twins," Tabitha corrected. "Pearl was my grandmother." She sighed. "We'd better head back. We need to get ready for tomorrow. Plus, I have a lot of homework to do." She was about to stand, but surprisingly, Marcus didn't want them to leave just yet, when he was learning so much about his guests. He scrambled to keep the conversation going. "You're still in school?"

Tabitha chuckled and shook her head. "Oh no. I'm a pharmaceutical rep. I study background information on drugs that I represent for my company." Leaning back in her chair, she asked, "And what do you do?"

His stall tactic had worked. "My brother and I founded Whittington Janitorial Services. Some of our employees have cleaned doctors' offices, as well as larger businesses. We also have a brand of industrial cleaning products we sell to our clients."

Not only was Tabitha listening, but so was Aunt Tweet. "Impressive. We need more black entrepreneurs. Congratulations." She stood. "I guess we can take that selfie now for your brother, considering you fed us." She graced him with a dazzling smile.

He blinked. "You remember that?"

"Yes," she said softly. "Do you need help cleaning up?"

"Absolutely not, but thanks for the offer." Towering over Tabitha, he stared into her brown eyes again. Wow, they were beautiful. She was a pretty woman, and under different circumstances, he would have asked her out. She spoiled the moment when she extended her hand for a shake as if they were concluding a business transaction.

"This evening wasn't all about business but getting to know each other," Marcus said as he brought her hand to his lips and kissed it.

Startled, she yanked it back, and he stepped back. They were both confused by his actions. What had gotten into him? He frowned. Did men even do that anymore?

Tabitha seemed to struggle with what to say. Finally, she replied, "That wasn't necessary."

"It's proper etiquette," Aunt Tweet said, defending him and presenting her hand. Marcus had no choice but to kiss it to show he was a gentleman. After a few selfies, he walked them to Tabitha's car and watched as she drove off while his heart did a somersault. Was it trying to tell him something?

Chapter 11

Tabitha hadn't seen that kiss coming, even if it was just on her hand. Now, days later, she still shivered as if his lips tickled her skin. Their close encounter had actually tugged at her emotions, reminding her that companionship had been absent from her life for too long.

Whew. She didn't have time for any heart-tugging. Time was running out for Aunt Tweet's memory, and Tabitha wanted to be a part of it as long as it lasted. To avoid more need of Marcus's assistance, Tabitha had taken drastic measures.

"I bought Aunt Tweet a pet," she informed her sisters during their weekly Skype chat. The scene of her aunt rocking the puppy in her arms as if it were a human baby was all the heart-tugging Tabitha wanted.

The only house rule was the dog had to sleep in the kennel at night. Her aunt had complied for four days and counting. As far as Tabitha knew, Aunt Tweet seemed content not to wander.

"See? I told you. An animal will do it every time," Rachel said in triumph, glee beaming from her face. A pet lover, the first thing her baby sister did after she moved into a condo was to adopt a spaniel named Shelby from a rescue shelter.

"Actually, I needed a replacement for Marcus Whittington. A male puppy is the only constant companion I want her to pine after." Desperation had set in after they'd returned from his house, which her aunt had sadly admitted wasn't her house. That had been a relief to Tabitha. Yet Marcus was all her aunt talked about. She alternated between calling him *mister* and *George*, never Marcus. But Tabitha knew the object of her aunt's affection.

"You mean the rude and uptight neighbor?" Kym frowned. "Okay, what aren't you telling us? Rach, you up for a road trip?"

"I would be there tomorrow, if I wasn't working on deadlines for a project. Plus, I'd rather fly." Rachel leaned out of the frame and grabbed her phone.

"That will work," Kym agreed.

No need to mention the man had kissed her, even if it was only her hand. A kiss was a kiss in her book. Who did that anymore anyway? He had watched *The Godfather* too many times. *Who cares?* she told herself and rejoined the conversation. "Any reason for the Knicely sisters to get together is good enough for me. Besides, it's the neighborhood's official summer kickoff barbecue. Remember the games they had for the children, and the food?"

"How could we forget?" Rachel sighed. "That was the only day Mom and Dad looked the other way as we pigged out on junk food." All three laughed. "But we're coming to meet the neighbor."

"Yeah, the one you first described as the Big Bad Wolf," Kym snarled.

"Well"—Tabitha squirmed in her seat—"my opinion of him might have been too hasty. It was a misunderstanding on our parts that we've resolved somewhat."

"Really?" Kym lifted an eyebrow.

"Umm-hmm. How much is 'somewhat'?" Rachel asked.

"We're civil." Tabitha shrugged.

"Good for him. He doesn't want to us to put the Knicely sisters' fear into him." Rachel giggled. Growing up, the three of them got picked on at school for using proper English and for having long, God-given braids and nice clothes. They may have seemed mild mannered, but if they couldn't talk their way out of an altercation, they fought their way out—all three of them together as one. "We'll be there in a couple of weeks. I've booked us early Saturday morning flights."

"A couple of weeks?" Kym didn't hide her disappointment. "And anyway, I happen to like to sleep late on the weekends," Kym groaned.

"It's a nonstop," Rachel said, "but if you want to sleep, I can book you with a layover from Baltimore to Louisville before landing—"

Kym waved her hand. "Never mind. I can always crash when I get to Tabitha's house." She smiled. "It still sounds funny to say 'Tabitha's house' instead of 'the house.' Now, back up about this bad wolf turning into a what? Some type of a prince charming?"

Her big sister wouldn't drop it. Tabitha wouldn't go as far and describe Marcus as a Prince Charming. "I was getting dressed for work and happened to peep out the window. Not only had Aunt Tweet escaped again, but I saw her at the corner, talking to a guy getting out of a car. I ran out of here barefoot, thinking she was about to be abducted. Girl, I was surprised and annoyed that it happened to be Marcus." Tabitha closed her eyes and shook her head before facing the monitor again. "I just knew for sure he was about to make good his threat to call the police."

Kym released words under her breath that were not worth repeating.

"His solution—or bribe—was for a tour of his home to give Aunt Tweet the satisfaction of seeing inside, since she's so attracted to his porch, and to prove it wasn't her house. I agreed, so I could get Aunt Tweet dressed and go to work. I had my reservations, but once inside his house…" Leaving nothing out, she described everything from the breathtaking design of his stairway to the refreshments he served.

"I know mental confusion and wandering are some signs of dementia, but I wish she would stay within the confines of the house," Kym said.

"Exactly. You feel my pain. I know she doesn't mean to do these things…" Tabitha choked. She had to keep reminding herself to tamp down her frustration. "Unless I move her into my bedroom or keep her in the bathroom while I shower, I'm getting desperate for any type of normalcy in my life again. This is hard, Sisters."

"Hopefully, Sweetie will do the trick," Rachel said, referring to the new pet.

"Aunt Tweet thinks he's a perfect, charming gentleman."

"The dog?" Kym frowned, alerting Tabitha that she had verbalized her thoughts.

Both sisters gave her suspicious looks.

"I think she's talking about Marcus," Rachel said in a singsong tone. "I'm really intrigued with this neighbor. If he's a 'perfect, charming gentleman' as *you* say our aunt says, then Sweetie might not be enough to keep her homebound." She snickered.

Tabitha had no comeback. Okay, Marcus had been charming, not the beast she had pegged him to be. She would give him that, but any interaction with him only reminded her of what she couldn't have in her life right now: romance.

———

Marcus was not a kiss-and-tell kind of guy. He didn't care if it wasn't the heart-pounding game-changer kiss to define a relationship. Tabitha was more than pretty and smart. He was sure being a sales rep for a pharmaceutical company wasn't easy. She was also respectful, especially when Aunt Tweet came across as condescending. Tabitha held her tongue, but he could see the hurt on her face.

The following day, when Demetrius queried him about how it had gone with his neighbors, Marcus underplayed it. "Uneventful." In truth, he wanted any excuse to see Tabitha again and see if his heart would do a backward flip or something to make it happen.

Demetrius acted disappointed there wasn't more to the story. But there was. Marcus's mind couldn't shake Tabitha's brown eyes, easy smile, and fragrance, which lingered in his house after she was gone.

He checked his home-security surveillance video every morning now, and after a couple of days, Aunt Tweet had not returned. That was a good thing. Yet he felt like a sick puppy. Since he knew where they lived, should he show up at Tabitha's place, just to be neighborly?

While waiting at a traffic light near his home, he drummed his fingers on the steering wheel. "I guess I've put out all the fires," he mumbled to himself, referring to Tabitha, Aunt Tweet, and Victor. Marcus should be happy, but he wasn't elated.

Finally, on Friday, he and Demetrius ended the workweek hanging out at a sports bar in the Ballpark Village complex across from Busch Stadium. It was just what Marcus needed to distract him from his Tabitha craving.

The place was teeming with Cardinals fans watching the game on a big screen. During a commercial break, Demetrius nudged him. "All quiet on the home front, Bro?"

"Yep." He took a sip from his cup and swallowed. "No Aunt Tweet sightings all week."

"Congrats. Your plan worked. You got rid of them." They exchanged fist bumps.

While Demetrius was celebrating an end to the neighborhood crisis, Marcus was numb. "This may sound strange, but I miss—"

"Nope, don't say it or it will sound odd," Demetrius said, cutting him off.

Suddenly, they stood from their seats. A hush spread throughout the bar as all eyes stared at the flat screen. It was as if everyone was holding their breath, following the ball until the opposing team's outfielder's glove swallowed it up. The groans in the place were deafening. It was the Cardinals' third out.

In the spirit of unity, they joined other diehard fans, then Marcus became sober. "I do miss seeing—"

"Tabitha?" Demetrius grinned.

"I was about to say Aunt Tweet," Marcus said, defending himself. "You can tell she's a classy lady. It's a shame she has Alzheimer's."

"You're pining over an old chick. I sure thought you were going to say her niece. In the photo you showed me, she's hot."

Marcus cracked a shell, then popped a peanut in his mouth. He crunched, never taking his eyes off the television. "I had a good time with them. Maybe I was too hard on Tabitha. Her aunt *is* a handful."

"Doesn't matter. When it comes to the welfare of another human being, you called it right the first time. She is irresponsible. She's worse than bad."

Taking offense at hearing his own words thrown back at him, Marcus cringed. He was on the verge of punching his brother.

"Hey, man. You're the one who had 911 on speed dial."

Did that make him a bad person? He shifted on the stool and rubbed the silky hair on his chin. "There's something about those two that I admire—Tabitha's deep respect for her great-aunt and the great-aunt's independent spirit."

"Except," his brother said slowly, "when she's coming to visit, unannounced, in the wee hours of the morning." Tilting his head, Demetrius smirked. "You know you're grinning, right?"

"Maybe I should have a cup of coffee waiting for her next time." He snickered. "And I am hoping for a next time."

Demetrius's eyes widened. "Would you make up your mind? Either you want the elderly woman to be homebound at her niece's house, or have her in harm's way, wandering around."

"Of course I want her safe. If she's going to wander, she knows the path to my house. I guess I'm a neighborhood safe house." Marcus withheld his smile. Aunt Tweet might get away, but at least Tabitha knew where to come looking to rescue her aunt.

Chapter 12

Somehow, with God's help, Tabitha had made it to work on time two days in a row. Not without challenges. Aunt Tweet wanted to stay home and play with the puppy. And Tabitha was still exhausted after work with just enough energy to prepare something for them to eat.

"When I'm gone, I sure hope folks will miss me." Aunt Tweet's comment came out of the blue, giving Tabitha whiplash as she turned away from the stove. Sorrow filled her heart as she hurried to her aunt's side. Was she trying to tell Tabitha something?

As if Aunt Tweet hadn't said anything earth-shattering, she cuddled Sweet Pepper in her arms. Her aunt alternated between calling the pooch Pepper and Sweetie, so Tabitha settled on Sweet Pepper.

Not putting up a fuss about her aunt having the beast near her table, Tabitha wrapped her arms around her aunt's shoulders. She hugged her tight while dodging Sweet Pepper's licks of love.

Her eyes misted, and she sniffed. Blinking back the moisture, she took a seat and put her hands on both sides of Aunt Tweet's face. Making sure they had eye contact, she softly said, "Miss Priscilla Brownlee, you're unforgettable. Your presence makes a lasting impression."

"So many of us are gone…" Her voice faded as she took on a dazed expression. "Seems like every year somebody else has passed by the time of our reunions. We try to keep the memory of the school for blacks alive, but when we die, who's going to remember it?"

Now her mumblings made sense to Tabitha. Her aunt was proud to be an alumna of Storer College, which opened in 1865, the same year enslaved blacks were released from bondage. "A lot of us will, Auntie." Tabitha tried to console her.

The historically black college in West Virginia had educated freedman, freedwoman, and their descendants for almost ninety years. Her aunt had graduated with honors. Five years later, the college had closed.

According to Tabitha's late grandmother Pearl, Aunt Tweet's older sister, education was an honorable and much-needed profession back then. That explained why there were so many teachers on her father's side of the family, but only one of two of the Knicely girls were drawn to be in front of a classroom.

Tabitha and her sisters were in their early teens when they had attended one of Storer College's class reunions during one of their summers staying with Aunt Tweet. Ever since Tabitha could remember, her aunt took yearly pilgrimages to Harpers Ferry, West Virginia, to attend her college reunions.

At the time, they didn't understand the significance the institution had played in their aunt's life beyond her obtaining a teaching degree. When Tabitha's parents died years apart, Aunt Tweet was there for them. Now, she couldn't think about losing her aunt.

Plus, she wanted Aunt Tweet to meet her great-great-nieces from the Knicely sisters. That could be a couple of years away, considering none of them was married and had no prospects in sight—at least she and Kym didn't. Rachel, on the other hand, had men tripping over their feet to get her attention. Tabitha's bet was on Rachel to be the first one of them to glide down the aisle to the altar as if she were on a runway.

Tabitha ceased her musing and squeezed Aunt Tweet's hand. "You're very much alive and well."

"Just miss me when I'm gone," she said with finality as the pup began to bark.

I'm missing you now and you're physically here with me. Tabitha got to her feet and reached for the dog.

"No, I'll take him. I'm getting stiff, waiting too long for supper." Aunt Tweet stood and made her way to the patio door.

"Here's his harness." Tabitha watched as her aunt descended the two steps to the brick-covered patio. Since getting Sweet Pepper as a companion, Aunt Tweet hadn't ventured past the property line on her own, to Tabitha's relief.

After washing her hands, Tabitha returned to the stove to stir the pasta for the spaghetti, and she was consumed by sadness. Her aunt's declaration twisted Tabitha's heart. She wasn't ready for her oldest relative's demise, especially not while Aunt Tweet stayed with her. Tabitha had to compartmentalize her emotions. She hadn't really known what she was up against becoming a caregiver. Her mind fast-forwarded to her next task as the pasta cooked, which was reviewing notes for a PowerPoint presentation in the morning. She peeped out the window and watched Aunt Tweet tug on Sweet Pepper's leash as he sniffed the base of one of two crepe myrtle trees. Tabitha headed for her laptop that rested on the desk in the nook tucked in the kitchen's corner. She leaned over to boot it up.

Almost immediately, she saw an error on one of her notes, fixed it, then realized her aunt hadn't come back inside. Hoping Aunt Tweet had relaxed on the lounger, Tabitha saved her work and glanced outside the door. When she didn't see Aunt Tweet, a sinking feeling overpowered her. "Please, no, not again." Slipping on her sandals, she hurried outside. Clearly, her aunt was on a walk.

Tabitha whipped her head in both directions a couple of times. *Nothing.* Her heart pounded with fear as tears trickled down her cheeks. She was about to sprint in the direction of Natural Bridge—a busy thoroughfare—then realized she should check the direction of Marcus's house first. Spinning around, she took off as if she were racing for the gold in the U.S. Olympics. Tabitha made it to his house in record time. Panting, she bent over and rested her hands on her knees. If Aunt Tweet wasn't on Marcus's porch, where could she be?

While speeding back to her house, something told her to look over her shoulder. That's when she spied her aunt and her hyperactive companion circling Roland pond. Cupping her hands around her mouth, she shouted, "Aunt Tweet, get back." She repeated her cry, waving. Her aunt didn't look her way. She was about to take off when a car rolled up beside her and honked.

"Lose somebody again?" Marcus asked. His eyes sparkled with mirth. If he was joking, she wasn't laughing. If he was being condescending, she didn't have time to be chastened.

"Not now." She pointed toward the pond and jumped in his front seat. "Can you give me a ride? Aunt Tweet moves faster than a crawling baby chasing after a toy."

Marcus raced in that direction. He parked, and they jumped out at the same time, yelling. Aunt Tweet glanced up and waved as Marcus got to the uneven slope first.

Tears of joy and fright formed in Tabitha's eyes as she reached her aunt and engulfed her in a hug. That was close. She could have fallen and tumbled into the pond. "You scared me." She couldn't check her tears.

"I didn't mean to, baby."

"Come on. I'll take you both home," Marcus offered.

Tabitha didn't refuse. In a daze, she guided Aunt Tweet and the dog into the back seat, then collapsed beside them, and held her aunt's hand. Not even a minute later, they pulled up in front of her house and heard her smoke alarm blaring inside. "Oh no!" She remembered her spaghetti.

Releasing Aunt Tweet's hand, Tabitha's adrenaline kicked in again as she bolted from the car to her childhood home.

As soon as she opened the door, smoke filled her lungs and stung her eyes.

She hurried to the stove and immediately turned off the dials. The pasta was black and brittle. How could the water have evaporated that fast? *This wouldn't have happened if Aunt...* No, Tabitha stopped herself from playing the blame game. She was mentally exhausted from constantly being on guard for her aunt's whereabouts and actions.

Her eyes were burning as she choked on the smoke. She grabbed a towel and the pot handle—even the heat-resistant handle was hot. Gagging, she covered her mouth and nose with one hand while reaching for another towel to cover her nose.

Marcus appeared, fanning the air, and snatched the pot from her hand. He carried it to the sink, dumped it, and then turned on the faucet.

"I've got it"—she coughed again—"under control. Where is—?"

He practically lifted her off the floor and ushered her toward the door. "Get some fresh air with your aunt outside. *I've* got this," he said in a stern voice, which contradicted his gentle expression.

She felt so helpless. No matter how much she loved her aunt, she couldn't do it. It was still May. She had months to go before Rachel took the reins.

As the sirens grew louder, Tabitha guessed one of her neighbors had called the fire department to protect the investment of all the homes in the historic community, or maybe Marcus had made good on his threat to summon the police, the soft kiss on her hand meaning nothing more than antiquated etiquette. No, he had been with her, so he couldn't have called any authorities.

Her good workday was going downhill fast; she was a loser when it came to being a caregiver. If Marcus had her arrested for endangerment, who would take care of Aunt Tweet? Jail might be the safest place for her once her sisters bit her head off.

When an emergency vehicle arrived in front of her house, Tabitha breathed a sigh of relief. She forced herself out of a lawn chair and met one of the firefighters who was halfway to her on the back patio.

"I left something burning on the stove that triggered my smoke alarm," she babbled, waving her hands in the air. "I was down the street at the time." She bowed her head, embarrassed that she didn't follow safety protocol she had learned in school to turn off all appliances before leaving the house.

"I opened all the windows in the kitchen to air out the house." Marcus's deep voice preceded his appearance. He looked just as powerful as the firefighters, with his bulging muscles stretching his polo shirt with his company's logo. As frantic as she was and as scrambled as her mind was, why did she see him with clarity? At the moment, she was grateful for his take-charge attitude. His presence was comforting.

"If you don't mind, ma'am, we'd rather inspect the kitchen for ourselves to assess for any possible hot spots," the firefighter said and waved for one of his crew to follow.

"Sure." Her shoulders slumped as Marcus's strong hands gently squeezed them and guided her to the patio love seat, then followed the firefighter inside.

After flopping down, she covered her face with her hands and bawled.

She wasn't a crier by nature, but lately, that seemed to be the only way to release her frustration. Next, she chided herself for being so careless not to turn off the stove. As an organized and dutiful person, she was losing her edge. "Lord, help me," she whispered to herself.

Tabitha wiped at her tears and took a deep cleansing breath and released the tension. She sat, staring at nothing, as the firefighter came outside and confirmed that the damage was limited to the smoke and suggested she purchase a new pot. His sense of humor wasn't appreciated as she went through the motions of nodding her thanks. She needed to get up and see the damage for herself, but she couldn't command her body to move, so she closed her eyes to gain strength. She sniffed and inhaled cologne mixed with smoke before the seat shifted beside her. Marcus.

"You okay?" His voice was low and soothing.

Tabitha wanted to scream no, but her lips wouldn't move. She needed to get a grip.

"I'm hungry," Aunt Tweet said. "Give me a match, and I'll cook us some supper."

Tabitha's energy returned in a flash. In unison, she and Marcus responded with a resounding, "No!" Their one accord stirred something in her heart—and kept climbing up her throat and forced her mouth open. A chuckle slipped out, and Marcus winked. The gesture made her tremble as if his lips had touched her hand again. The charged moment settled as he stood and stepped away.

—

What have I gotten myself into? Marcus wondered as he noticed Tabitha shudder. Damsels in distress pulled at his heartstrings, especially this one. He wanted to wrap her in the cocoon of his arms until she gained her strength.

Unintentionally, the two lovely ladies had reeled him in. One thing was for sure: he couldn't leave them now. Tabitha was on the verge of caving in to an emotional breakdown while Aunt Tweet, despite her declaration of hunger, hadn't moved, and the puppy rested on her chest as she reclined on the patio lounger.

Marcus didn't know there was a looming crisis underway when he turned the corner and spotted her. His heart had skipped a beat when he saw her in a casual romper that showcased her flawless bare legs and cute toes. He was on the verge of flirting, something he hadn't done in a long time.

In her business suit, Tabitha came across as intimidating. Marcus definitely liked her personality when she was off the clock. As long as Aunt Tweet's whereabouts weren't the subject of their contention, they could engage in normal banter. However, the panic on her face dashed that hope and put him on alert. Suddenly, he felt like a fool for being so harsh with her. She was struggling to be a caregiver, but who was taking care of her? He glanced back at his new charges, then tugged his cell off the clip on his belt. Tabitha might not know it, but she needed to be rescued, and firefighters had nothing on Marcus Whittington. He punched in a familiar number.

"Yeah, Boss?" Chess answered.

"I've got a situation. I need you to place an order for some entrées, hot and cold—salads, fruits, and whatever Stan can throw in at the last minute. I need the delivery at my house ASAP." Whenever his company sponsored functions, small or large, Stan Wilson, owner of Sandwiches and Stuff, always came through.

His employee chuckled. "Who are you feeding this time?"

Tabitha and her aunt weren't his charity case. This was personal. His employee didn't need to know that Marcus was putting his heart on the line. "I want the delivery faster than Jimmy John's."

"It will be there in twenty minutes, even if I have to deliver it myself. Oh, and I need to talk to you about something—"

"Not now." Marcus held up his hand. "One fire at a time." Bad choice of words. "We'll talk tomorrow when I'm in the office." Whatever was going on at the company, Demetrius could handle it. Ending the call, he walked back to the patio and joined Tabitha on the love seat.

"Hey," he said softly, coaxing her to face him. Her bright eyes were dimmed by the turn of events. She looked like she was in a trance. "I ordered some food, so you can relax."

"How am I supposed to relax?" Tabitha's bottom lip trembled. "I can't. I have research to do for work. I have Aunt Tweet."

"And you have me. I'm here." Marcus didn't know what kind of commitment he was making, but he planned to fulfill it. He wrapped his hands around her soft ones. Surprisingly, she didn't pull away. After a few seconds, her shoulders relaxed, and he exhaled. "I'll entertain her."

"But don't you have something to do?" Tabitha asked politely, but her expression was hopeful that he didn't.

He smiled and winked. "Nothing but to enjoy the company of two beautiful ladies."

Chapter 13

TABITHA EDGED HERSELF ONTO THE LOUNGER NEXT TO AUNT TWEET. Accidents happen, and she took responsibility. Linking her fingers through her aunt's, Tabitha wanted to convey a gesture of enduring love no matter what.

When Marcus returned, Tabitha whispered her thanks. With unusual clarity, she scrutinized his features. Handsome, strong…dare she say, sexy? Did she hear right? He'd ordered dinner? Add kindness to his résumé. The fight in her that she didn't need his help retreated, replaced by admiration for his thoughtfulness, so she thanked him instead.

"You're welcome." Then he did it again—he kissed her hand.

The man might as well have kissed her lips the way he made her feel lightheaded with one small touch.

When he smiled, she focused on the curve of his lips. If Tabitha were a young teenager, he would have been her crush. She cleared her head of those notions.

A chirp alerted Marcus to his phone. Pulling it out of his pants pocket, he read the text and grinned. Was that a dimple she saw? She would verify that before he left for the evening. Her sister Rachel had dimples, and it added to her beauty. On a man, his was sexy.

"Our food is here. Be back in a sec."

Tabitha watched his confident stride until he climbed into his car, then she exhaled. She rubbed her fingers through her hair and sniffed. It smelled like smoke. Although she hadn't planned to wash her hair tonight, she had to add a shampoo to her tasks. She dreaded the hair regimen that would take a couple of hours: the conditioning, blow-drying, and straightening. If she dared to want curls, shame on her, because that would add on another hour of hair care.

What she really wanted to do more than eat was climb under the covers and sleep her cares away. That wasn't going to happen. If she got five hours of rest tonight, it would be a premium, but under no circumstances was she leaving her aunt's side. "God, I need help," she pleaded, then realized it was the second time within hours she'd sent out an SOS to the Lord.

Her spirits lifted when Marcus returned with bags and a platter. Her heart fluttered, watching his determined steps and the tender look he cast her way.

"I hope you're hungry." He smiled, releasing all the handsomeness and charm she'd never taken the time to admire before.

As she studied him, she chided herself for misjudging his character instead of getting to know him. Making sure Aunt Tweet was safe and fed was evidence of his passion for the elderly.

He arranged the food on her wrought-iron table, then waited for them to join him. Once they took their seats, Marcus surprised her again as he served them before himself. There were mini packets of hand wipes. He'd thought of everything.

"Young man," Aunt Tweet said, patting the table, "please say grace over our food."

Without hesitation, he bowed his head. "Lord, thank You for this meal and for keeping my neighbors safe. In Jesus's name, amen."

"Amen," Tabitha said, joining their chorus. She sampled the first bite of chicken and savored the seasoning. "This is good. Where is it from?"

"Stan's Sandwiches and Stuff. We use them a lot for catering different events." After a few bites, he grunted.

She could see amusement on his face. "What?" Tabitha prompted, wanting in on the secret.

"This is the second time we're sharing a meal, courtesy of the lovely Aunt Tweet." Although her aunt blushed, Tabitha wouldn't consider either scenario an ideal dinner date. "Come on. Where's your sense of humor?" He took another bite and chewed, watching and waiting for her.

"I think it ran away from me," she admitted, smiling in spite of herself.

Marcus changed the subject. "What type of drugs does Ceyle-Norman manufacture?"

He had remembered her company? That was a brownie point. It wasn't a big name, so most people hadn't heard of it when Pfizer and Mallinckrodt dominated the global market. Tabitha slipped into work mode. "Spironolactone for hyperaldosteronism, Porital for osteoporosis, Ceclor for sinusitis, Dyabolin, a supplemental injection for type 2 diabetes, and Lismetol for hypertension." She paused after listing two others. "Honestly, I never had a preference on which drugs I pitched to doctors, but with Aunt Tweet's dementia, I'm more driven to know every nuance about the ingredients, research, trials, and studies of drugs."

He nodded and leaned back, stretching his legs under their small table. "When I see the commercials for a new medicine to treat an ailment, I do a double take. Some of these drugs have terrible side effects—internal bleeding, suicidal thoughts, infection, death. *Ugh*." Marcus frowned. "I can't imagine needing medicine so badly it would be worth the risk."

She sipped from a cup of freshly squeezed lemonade and enjoyed the flavor as she swallowed. "It all depends on the severity of the illness. That's where the doctor comes in to manage the patient's treatment plan. My job is to learn as much as I can about the physiology, anatomy, pharmacology, and scientific research on the drugs and convey that to the doctor. It takes a lot of homework to know how the drugs interact with other meds, because the wrong combination of ingredients can be deadly. That's why people should never play doctor when it comes to their health."

"If I were a physician, I would buy anything you sell." His eyes sparkled.

She blushed from his praise, withholding a childish giggle. Yet Tabitha was only as good as she prepped herself to be, which was what she needed to do now—but she was enjoying the respite his presence was allowing her.

"So, Aunt Tweet," Marcus said, turning to bring her into the conversation, "besides gracing the world with your beauty, what was your career?"

"I'll always be an educator..." she began.

Marcus had no idea Aunt Tweet, if given the floor, could talk for hours. Tabitha knew the story of her aunt's teaching career, then her many years as a stewardess before returning to academia at Drexel University in Philly. While he watched Aunt Tweet, she observed him, then suddenly, he turned and caught her staring. Her heart fluttered when he smiled at her. It was warm, inviting, and hypnotic.

Tilting his head toward her house, he mouthed *Go*. Taking his cue and nodding her thanks, she excused herself and slipped inside the kitchen. She almost gagged at the lingering burnt odor. How long would it take to dissipate? At least her sisters' visit was a couple of weeks away, which would give Tabitha time to add deep-cleaning to her to-do list. She sighed.

Upstairs wasn't as smelly, but she opened the windows anyway. A cool breeze would help before the official summer season arrived in less than a few weeks. She returned to the kitchen, gathered her laptop and materials, and walked outside to the patio. It wasn't that she didn't trust Marcus, but to a limit. She didn't have a background report on him for any past criminal misconduct or character references, only his word. At the moment, that had to be good enough.

"You could miss out trusting the wrong man," Aunt Tweet had drilled into her nieces' heads when it came to relationships. "Stay away from uncaring men who are full of themselves. I don't care how good-looking!"

As a result of that advice, all three of the Knicely girls were fiercely independent, polished, and free-spirited. When it came to matters of the heart, none of them had experienced a man inviting them to meet him at the altar.

Aunt Tweet had Marcus captivated with the history of her West Virginia college. While waiting for her laptop to power up, she observed him. His presence commanded attention, yet he patiently listened to her aunt. He *was* a good guy. She could feel it. What was his story when it came to romantic relationships? Why wasn't he committed to a special someone? Surely, he had admirers. Did he enjoy the variety so much that he couldn't choose just one for a happily ever after?

"It's horrible living in the South," Aunt Tweet said, breaking into Tabitha's reverie. "It was downright fearful. Those ugly Jim Crow laws made sure of it. I didn't see slavery firsthand like Grandma Beulah, but I saw the legacy. Education made us equal and wise like white folks, and they couldn't stand it. They sabotaged the school in awful ways, like they destroyed the black wealth in the Tulsa massacre in 1921, yet we survived."

"Tulsa race riots," he whispered as if to himself. "Is the school still in existence today?" he asked, seeming intrigued.

Focus on your project, Tabitha coaxed herself. Plus, she had heard the stories before and could recite them as if she'd lived in her aunt's dreadful time period.

Aunt Tweet ignored his question. "Brains were important back then, but a little beauty helped to open doors. My friends convinced me to enter the state beauty pageant: Miss West Virginia." She giggled. "Imagine a black woman winning in an all-white beauty pageant in the 1950s." She whooped and slapped her knee, startling Sweet Pepper, who was resting in her lap. "Those white folks had a handbook for that silly pageant. I snuck a peep at it and rule number seven said negroes were ineligible to enter, only the white race, and here I got in and won. Judges couldn't deny I was the prettiest girl on that stage." She chuckled again. "Black folks were surprised too. Even my mama told me she only saw colored ladies on stage as part of a music act as slaves. Yep, I beat them out."

Wait a minute. Tabitha slowed, looked over her shoulder, and frowned. She had never heard this before and didn't know if the beauty pageant was fact or fiction. Making up stories could be systematic of dementia symptoms.

"I won singing the national anthem. I brought tears to everyone in the place, even myself. It was scandalous." Aunt Tweet snickered, then scratched behind Sweet Pepper's ears. "Scandalous, I tell you, but it changed my life." She continued to ramble. "I had options, so I left teaching. That year I met Randolph Dittle."

She sighed. "Handsome, *ump, ump, ump*. He called me his songbird. I fell in love with him but couldn't stay in the South, not after that pageant. I wore that Miss Virginia crown for eight whole hours until those committee members overruled their decision and snatched it off my head. That was ugly, downright ugly." She shrugged. "Didn't matter though. That win—even short-lived—opened a door of opportunities for me. I got offers to model. Where the South didn't appreciate my dark skin, in some parts of the Northeast, it didn't seem to matter so much on any given day, and that's when my life got better."

Maybe Aunt Tweet's story could be true, Tabitha thought, but why hadn't there been any mention of this milestone in the family? This was huge. Half listening, she turned back to her computer and Googled the history of the pageant. The Miss West Virginia pageants had been held since 1922. Even though there was a list of all the winners, there were no photos. It would take time she didn't have to pull up each winner's bio and see if they were black—*colored* as blacks were called then. She found a Desiree Williams in 2013 and 2014, but no mention of a Priscilla Brownlee in the 1950s. *Fiction*.

Aunt Tweet's monologue continued. "For years, Randolph never gave up on me until I married Butch. He was the package deal—looks, money, job—but that man had baggage, which included boxing. I don't mean in the ring. After one punch, I divorced him."

Now that was a familiar story; Tabitha and her sisters had heard it throughout the years. Aunt Tweet had given back Butch Freeman's last name, plus five stitches over one eye when she walked away, childless, with a bruised heart. Butch had underestimated her aunt when he felt he had the right to tame his wife. Aunt Tweet always said marrying that mean man had caused love to pass her by.

"Coming to my senses, I tried to crawl back to Randolph, but it was too late. He fell in love with someone who loved him back." She exhaled as if she had unloaded a heavy burden, then motioned to stand. Marcus pushed back his seat to assist her. "I'm tired now. I'm going to bed."

Tabitha swallowed. Her heart ached for her aunt after hearing the last part. That's what her aunt meant when she said she had lost out on love. Getting to her feet, Tabitha gathered Sweet Pepper and kissed Aunt Tweet's cheek. "Night. I love you."

"Night to both my sweeties."

They watched as she shuffled through the kitchen, then slowly climbed the stairs. Tabitha was trying to process what she had heard. Wait until she shared this tidbit with her sisters.

"You have a fascinating aunt." Marcus's deep baritone voice reminded her of his presence, startling her.

Turning to face him, she recovered. "Ah, she is. Thank you for 'babysitting'"—she made quotation marks with her fingers—"her. Some of the things she said, I never knew."

"I would like to visit again, bring dinner, maybe a board game—"

Tabitha felt some kind of connection between them that seemed absurd. "Please don't take this the wrong way—" she started.

"Then please don't say it the wrong way," he said in a challenging manner.

Choosing her words carefully, she explained, "Thank you for the offer, but I don't have time for myself, much less for entertaining guests. I'm sorry." Tabitha pouted for good measure to soften the blow.

"Who takes care of you, Miss Knicely, while you're trying to be strong for your aunt? Who has your back?"

It was a good thing Marcus didn't wait for an answer, because she had none. "Listen, I don't need you questioning—"

"Let me have your back." He stepped closer.

"Huh?" She froze and couldn't move under his alluring stare. "Why?"

He smiled as he jiggled his keys. "Because I happen to like you, and even though I didn't miss a word your aunt shared with me, I was aware of you listening and pretending to work." He paused and looked deep into her eyes. "I'm attracted to you, and not only because you're pretty—no, you're beautiful—but there's something else about you that I want to explore."

He thinks I'm beautiful? Is this the lingo he uses to get his dates? The compliment made her heart flutter until she came to her senses, then she released a fit of laughter. The annoyed look he gave her made her laugh even more. "And you realized this when? Not long ago you wanted to bite off my head."

"Blame that on having a bad day, but today, I want to be your hero." His eyes pleaded with her to believe him. "Sue me." His lips curved into a lopsided grin, and sure enough, the dimple came into view.

Her heart swayed, but her head ruled. "I'm a caregiver, Marcus. I'm struggling to meet my aunt's needs. I think you're cute too and nice sometimes too, but I don't have time for the distraction of being attracted to any man. In case you haven't noticed, I can barely get up in the morning without her going missing." She patted her chest. "I'm being honest."

"So, you think I'm cute, huh?" He lifted a silky, thick, black brow. He bit his lip and nodded. "Challenge accepted. Good night, Miss Knicely." This time he laughed as he turned and took long strides to his car.

She went into the house smiling. He had called her pretty.

Chapter 14

THE NEXT MORNING, MARCUS STROLLED ACROSS THE WAREHOUSE floor with extra swagger. The day before had been scary, an eye-opener, endearing, then enchanting. He'd drifted to sleep dreaming of Tabitha—from the sadness to the fire in her eyes, he was hooked.

He was attracted to Tabitha—a little at first when he saw her outside his door and it was purely the outside package his eyes appreciated, but something stirred that was more emotional than physical with each encounter or clash. It clicked as he witnessed Tabitha's love and respect for her elderly aunt. To be loved by Tabitha Knicely meant to be loved hard and unconditionally, and that was what attracted him to her.

Marcus grunted at her reasoning for not wanting to get involved. A relationship was what a couple invested into it. He didn't take no for an answer when it came to something he really wanted, whether it was business, a hobby, or, now, one special woman. He had to show her that she could have it all. He was almost at his office when Chess interrupted his musings.

"Morning, Boss. Hate to spoil the good mood that you're apparently in, judging by that grin cemented to your face, but we have a situation that I wanted to tell you about last evening."

"Right." Marcus bobbed his head. "What's up?" he asked, unlocking his office door, then resting his things on a nearby chair. Folding his arms, he sat on the desk's edge and stretched out his legs. "I'm listening."

"Latrice showed up last night wanting her job back. I told her you don't do rehires."

His smile dropped at the same time his shoulders slumped. Why wouldn't Victor and Latrice go away? "I don't."

"She left Victor and—"

He perked up and stopped his employee. "Hire her back."

Chess's eyes bucked and his jaw dropped. "What? Huh?"

"She was under the influence of her ex. Maybe now, she can do something for herself and her children. I'll call her." He paused. "Any other problems?"

"Ah, no," he answered slowly, dumbfounded, then cleared his voice. "Quality control has no issues."

"Thanks, and thanks for coming through for me yesterday evening." Marcus walked behind his desk. As he turned on his computer, his thoughts drifted back to Tabitha. She was too independent for her own good. Latrice, on the other hand, was in the process of declaring her independence. He was rooting for her. Searching through the folders, he opened the document with his employees' contact numbers and called his former employee.

She answered right away. "Mr. Whittington. I know I don't deserve my job back—"

"You have it, Latrice, as long as you are committed to stand by your word and not be swayed by Victor."

"I am. I love Victor or I'd never have had his children, but I have to take care of my boys."

"Great. Stop by my office before you start your shift to fill out new paperwork," he told her and disconnected. "The things I do for my employees."

"Yeah, and Mama would be proud," Demetrius teased from his spot across the room. Marcus hadn't heard him enter.

Marcus hadn't even noticed his brother, preoccupied with thoughts of Tabitha, then focused on the task of speaking with Latrice. "We're all about helping our workers, especially our single mothers. I take pity on Latrice for getting tangled up with that loser. Anyway, I have a late lunch at the country club with Thomas Dell. He's a referral, and I hope to wow him with why our company philosophy is different."

"You coming back?" Demetrius asked.

"Nope. Anything else I need done, I can do from home."

For the rest of the morning, Marcus stayed focused on work-related tasks, gently pushing thoughts of Tabitha aside. She and Aunt Tweet were taken care of during the day. It was at night he had to watch out for her. He was reviewing company expenses when his phone reminded him it was time to go.

Marcus turned into the Fairway Grille & Lounge's parking lot off the main lobby of the country club at the same time as his prospective client. After parking, Marcus stepped out of his car and greeted the man with a handshake. Thomas Dell was a stout man with thinning hair. What strands remained were more gray hair than brown. His facial wrinkles were as deep as his tanned skin.

The good news for Marcus and his brother was Mr. Dell was sold on Whittington Janitorial Services without hearing a pitch. Word of mouth had recently landed his company new contracts. His business could double by this time next year, which meant he could hire more workers.

While they lunched, their conversation was as relaxed as the atmosphere.

"Marc," the man said, shortening his name without permission, "Randall Camp couldn't say enough great things about your company and employees. Randall is convinced your work ethic is unmatched, and that's what I'm looking for, someone to take pride in their work, whether it is sweeping the floor, proofreading a business proposal, or assembling a motor at a car plant."

Marcus accepted the compliment with a grin. Randall Camp's company was a major client. His word carried weight among other businessmen.

But the accolades weren't enough, because Mr. Dell hinted at a one-year commitment. Even though Marcus preferred two- or three-year agreements, he wasn't going to make demands. WJS had to prove their worth to Thomas Dell, and that was no problem. The mindset was based, in part, on Missouri's nickname: the Show-Me State. Residents challenged one another to show that their word was good.

"Our hard workers are the face of WJS. Some of them needed a second chance to prove their worth. My brother and I are hoping clients like you would consider them for employment if any entry-level positions become available." It was more than a spiel to win new business; for the Whittington brothers, it was a mission statement.

Mr. Dell bobbed his head. "I'll take that under consideration on a case-by-case basis."

"Fair enough." They enjoyed the rest of their lunch, chatting about sports. Before leaving, Marcus had a signed contract and a check in hand. "Yes!" he shouted in the confines of his car as he drove away. It was another open door for opportunities.

The breeze, sunshine, and blooming flowers made it easy for him not to return to work, especially when he was only ten minutes from home.

With business finished, thoughts of Tabitha drifted back to the forefront of his mind. How was her day going? What was Aunt Tweet up to? He wanted to do something to lighten her burden. Dinner—not light refreshments or something ready-made from the store, but fresh— might be a good gesture. He would stop at the grocery store for some ingredients, calling his mother for guidance on the way.

"So you're cooking for someone special again? Hmm. It's been a while," she teased. "What's her name this time?"

"Actually, it's my two neighbors." She was quiet, and he wondered if they had lost a connection. "Mom, are you still there?"

"I am, Son, but that doesn't sound very romantic." She sighed, clearly disappointed.

"You know I've always been about building friendships first."

"Yes, but that's your mantra when it comes to your business. When it comes to personal relationships, you should follow your heart. So what's on the menu?"

"I was hoping you could tell me."

"Of course!" she said excitedly. "Chicken parmesan would be perfect with asparagus…"

Marcus parked in the market's lot, put his mother on speaker, and entered the info in his phone. In the store, he picked up every item on his list. He was at the register when a floral display got his attention.

He added two bouquets to his purchase. His mother was right—it wasn't romantic with Aunt Tweet around, but without the aunt, he and Tabitha might not have met. Back in his car, Marcus detoured to her house. He left a note and the flowers on her porch where she could see them.

Hours later, in the middle of preparing his meal, it dawned on him the two ladies might already have eaten. If that proved to be the case, Demetrius was always on standby and wouldn't turn down a home-cooked meal, compliments of his younger brother.

——

Flowers? Tabitha wasn't expecting that and a dinner invitation from Marcus when she arrived home. Removing the paper wedged between her front door and screen, she read his note. He advised to bring her "homework." He included his phone number. Closing her eyes, she inhaled the roses fashioned in the bouquets. "Nice."

Her steps were lighter when she returned to the car. "We have flowers!" She handed Aunt Tweet hers, then slid behind the wheel and continued up the driveway that led to the back patio.

"Sure are pretty," Aunt Tweet said. Tabitha agreed. "Randolph used to send them to me all the time."

There was that Randolph name again. Could she coax her aunt to open up about the past the same way Marcus had done so effortlessly? "Ah, what did Randolph look like?"

She wrinkled her forehead. "I can't remember."

Tabitha groaned. She craved more details. After parking the car, she walked around and helped her aunt. Lately, she seemed to be more unsteady on her feet.

Inside the kitchen, only a hint of the smoke lingered in the air. Tabitha took two vases from her cabinet, filled them with water, and gave Aunt Tweet the honor to arrange the bouquets while she called Marcus. "The flowers are beautiful…thank you," she whispered.

"You're welcome. Are you coming to dinner?" He sounded hopeful.

"I'm beat—"

"But you have to eat," he insisted. "Come on, Tab." He chuckled.
She giggled at hearing a nickname her sisters used.

"Don't forget, I know where you live," he said, feigning a threat.

"Don't remind me of the circumstances of why you know that."
She spun around to check on Aunt Tweet, who was fumbling with the
door on Sweet Pepper's kennel. "Let me call you back. The dog needs
to go out."

"By the time you call me back, I'll be on your doorstep to pick you
up." He disconnected.

She helped Aunt Tweet with Sweet Pepper's leash. While watching
them walk the length of her patio and driveway, Tabitha had planned to
warm up the leftovers in the refrigerator. She stretched, craving a long,
hot bubble bath and climbing in bed afterward with her laptop. But
Marcus's alternate plan piqued her interest.

After about five minutes, Tabitha ushered the dog and her aunt back
in the house just as Marcus drove up and parked. He stepped out and
swaggered toward her with a fierce expression. It reminded her of his
intimidating smirk the first time they'd met, but this time, his towering
presence didn't make her tremble with fear, but shiver with excitement.

"So you weren't kidding about picking us up."

"I have a soft spot for you and Aunt Tweet. You can even bring
Sweet Pepper." She didn't move as he stepped closer. "You once said
'try walking in your shoes.' It's time to switch pairs. I take big steps, so
let me do this for you."

They stared at each other until his puppy-dog expression won her
over. "Okay. Who am I to turn down a free meal?"

He grinned. "Exactly."

"Do you mind giving us a few minutes to freshen up?"

"I'm ready," Aunt Tweet said, reminding them of her presence.

I don't think so. Remnants of lunch at the adult care facility had
stained her aunt's blouse. "Give us five minutes," Tabitha said to
Marcus. She tried to limit her aunt climbing the stairs. Usually when
they returned in the evening, Aunt Tweet stayed downstairs until
bedtime.

He nodded, slipped his hands in his pockets, and waited in the kitchen.

She hiked the stairs. In her bedroom, she ditched her suit, then slipped into a pair of jeans and an oversize T-shirt. Leaning over the bannister, she yelled downstairs, "You doing okay?"

"Umm-hmm."

Great. Tabitha rushed inside Aunt Tweet's room and rummaged through her closet for a top. Next, she grabbed shower gel and powder, then hurried downstairs to find her aunt in the pantry. She had opened a snack-size package of vanilla pudding and had it smeared all over her mouth and blouse.

Come on, give me a break, she thought. *Couldn't you have given me five minutes?* Without saying what was on her mind, she guided her to the first-floor bathroom, cleaned her up, and removed her top.

Incidents such as this were evidence of why she couldn't go to Marcus's without advance notice. Tabitha could never know what her beloved aunt would do next to cause a delay. Getting to work in the morning was challenging enough. Marcus only saw the finishing touches on her aunt. He was clueless about what it took to get her to that point.

"Thank you," Aunt Tweet said softly.

Tabitha kissed her aunt's cheek. "You're always welcome, Auntie. Always." Her aunt's unnecessary gratitude tamed Tabitha's frustration.

She opted not to take the dog. After doing a final sweep of her kitchen to make sure everything was secure, she grabbed her purse and Aunt Tweet's hand. "Sorry it took longer than expected," she mumbled, already mentally exhausted.

"You all right?" He seemed genuinely concerned.

Evidently, she wasn't hiding her distress too well. "Never ask a caregiver that unless you've got the time to listen."

"I have time," he said, escorting them to his car, then getting behind the wheel.

Tabitha didn't share. Instead, she was quiet the short ride to his house. When they strolled through his front door, the aroma of food was like a sweet fragrance. "Whatever you cooked smells good." Their stomachs rumbled at the same time.

"If it doesn't taste good, I'll owe you another dinner." His eyes twinkled with mischief, then he squeezed her shoulder. She hadn't realized how much she craved his touch.

The table was already set for three. There was no fancy china or stemware, but it was the thought that counted. "Thank you for the invitation," she said as he pulled out her chair.

"Thank you for accepting." He grinned. "After we eat, you can set up in the study, while Aunt Tweet and I play cards or watch television," he said effortlessly as if he had it all planned out.

Oh no. In her haste, she had forgotten her laptop and told him so. "I hate to eat and run, but we'll have to leave." She sighed and gritted her teeth. "I forgot I didn't drive."

"Here." He lifted the keys off a hook and handed them to her to use his vehicle. "Relax. If you trust me, you can leave her with me and go get your work. But something tells me you don't."

He was right, but Tabitha wasn't going to tell him that. "Okay, I'll go after we eat. Do you always have a backup plan?"

"No, but I think I just started with you. Come on, you both are probably hungry." Marcus gave thanks for the meal and asked the Lord to bless it.

He was charming, easy to talk to, but most importantly, he seemed to really listen, which was foreign to her, considering her past boyfriends had short attention spans. But this wasn't a romantic relationship. She could see why he was a good businessman. His attentiveness was so personable toward her, but if Aunt Tweet stirred, his eyes darted in her direction.

"Watch it. A woman can get used to this," Tabitha teased.

"Noted. I'm up for the challenge. Remember, even a caregiver needs a caregiver."

And there was no doubt in her mind that Marcus would be a top-of-the-line caregiver to anyone. They chatted about family, and she told him about her sisters' upcoming visit in a week.

"That's the same weekend as Pasadena Hills' Summer Kickoff Street Party."

"I know. When we were younger, we couldn't wait until the end of the school year for the street party."

He smiled. "I can imagine you as a little girl, getting into all sorts of trouble."

"Not with a big sister like Kym. She fulfilled her role as the oldest like a drill sergeant, and Rachel and I fell in line."

Once they finished eating, he gave Tabitha time to go home for her work and come back. "You're just like Kym: a taskmaster."

"Let me know if I'm too hard on you," he said softly. His forehead wrinkled with concern. "I'm trying to keep you on task, but I want you to relax some. Go while I clear the table."

"I didn't mean that in a scolding way. It's my dry sense of humor." She smiled.

He nodded. "I'm starting to read your body language, so I'll know when you're joking."

Aunt Tweet stood to help.

"Watch her. She'll throw silverware in the trash."

"Got it." He winked. "Now, get going, Miss Knicely."

She did as he suggested, and seconds later, Tabitha was behind the wheel of his car, adjusting his seat to fit her height and sniffing remnants of his cologne. It felt odd not to have Aunt Tweet as a passenger. Marcus was right. She didn't know him well enough to trust him with her aunt, so she hurried.

When she returned, she looked closely at her aunt for signs of anything untoward. Aunt Tweet seemed fine. Tabitha breathed a sigh of relief. Her aunt had taught her never to let her guard down when it came to men, so Tabitha was taking baby steps with Marcus.

"I'll show you to my home office."

Following Marcus, she sucked in her breath when he separated wood double doors to reveal an executive office suite. The light-colored plush carpet complemented the built-in wood bookshelves, the massive wood desk, crown molding, and even the shutters accented a window seat. This room would be perfect for her in her house. "Wow. This is like a different world from the other parts of your house."

"Yep." He slipped his hands in his pants pockets and craned his neck to check on Aunt Tweet. "At work, I share the office with my brother, which I don't mind," he was quick to add, "but when I work from home, this is my space. Demetrius has a smaller version of this layout at his loft." He pulled out the chair for her and she sat at his work space.

"Also"—he lowered his voice—"whether you think so or not, you're doing a great job with your aunt."

"Really?" Her shock escaped her mouth before she could catch it. Hearing his praise and her aunt thanking her in one day sparked a few tears to trickle down her cheek. Unexpectedly, Marcus leaned in and, without any hesitation, kissed her cheek.

"I think you needed that too." He strolled to the doorway and left it cracked, allowing Tabitha to have a view of Aunt Tweet and exhale.

Her lips formed an *oh*, but the word never came out, so she swallowed it. Marcus had kissed her hand, now her cheek... These close encounters were wreaking havoc on her emotions. *Okay, okay*, she coaxed herself back to reality and quenched any further thoughts of a kiss. Settling in, she focused on the thrilling part of her work—taking control of her income.

That morning, Ava Elise had handed out packets with information about each rep's territory, car, and drug assignments.

Her sales were based on the doctors' trust in the medicine's ability to help their patients and their writing prescriptions for it.

Pfizer developed biotech products. Some quarters, she had earned big bonuses. She had taken a $12,000 pay cut when she accepted her new position. That was the sacrifice she was willing to make because Aunt Tweet meant everything to her.

Plus, money wasn't everything or the issue. All the sisters received a $5,000 monthly stipend whenever Aunt Tweet was in their care. It was the other part of the year, when Tabitha didn't have the trust fund money or the big bonuses to count on. Unless she used her savings, she would feel the squeeze after she paid her mortgage and other perks she had grown accustomed to, like traveling, shopping, and pampering.

She did the math for the upcoming sales quarter. She could earn $20,000. Her diabetes drug accounted for 65 percent of her bonus, about $13,000, but if she could hit 150 percent, her bonus could climb up to $30,000.

Although Porital and Ceclor accounted for 20 and 10 percent of her quota respectively, she had to reach 100 percent on both, or her $20,000 bonus was in jeopardy. She didn't believe in losing money, so it was showtime.

Tabitha caught herself smiling at her friendship with Ava Elise, who had pulled her aside before she left class. Her trainer's encouragement had kept her sane. "You're on your own now, so I can't help you out in the field. If you make an appointment with a doctor, nurse, or hospital rep, you'd better keep it. I'm confident that things will work out with your aunt." She hugged Tabitha, then added, "I'll be waiting to hear good reports."

"You will." *I hope*, she kept saying to herself. She had made a plan. Now, she had to work it.

After saying goodbye to Ava Elise, Tabitha drove away from the office, not doubting her ability but the circumstances that were beyond her control. *God, help me.*

She had already contacted the rental company to meet her at Ceyle-Norman to pick up the car because she would have keys to a company car—a new blue Ford Taurus.

Next, she checked her emails to see which doctors had confirmed meetings to hear her drug pitches. Her schedule was packed; she had to make ten office calls. She had no choice if she was going to make her bonuses. Hopefully, after she gave the physicians her spiel, they would agree to take her samples and monitor the effectiveness on their patients.

"So what do you like to do besides teach and model?" she heard Marcus ask Aunt Tweet, pulling her back to the work in front of her.

Model? Her great-aunt never modeled—or did she? The stories he was able to pull out of Aunt Tweet were entertaining, but were they true?

"Oh, I used to travel. I've been to a lot of places…" Her aunt's voice was perky.

That was true. Souvenirs from those exotic locations were tucked away for safekeeping in Tabitha's bedroom. Her sisters had also received keepsakes from places like Vietnam, Italy, the Philippines, and Indonesia. Yes, her aunt had been a world traveler.

"During the Korean War, I learned to speak Chinese."

What? Chinese? Who? Her aunt? *Yeah right...* Then Aunt Tweet said something that sounded like an authentic dialect.

Marcus chuckled. "What did you say?"

"Good morning." She giggled. "My mind isn't as sharp as it used to be."

How much do I know about the woman who lives in my house? Tabitha wondered.

"I'm at the age now where I'm tired of traveling. I'd rather go to church. My sister and I went a lot as kids. I hated it. I had to sit still or get a whipping if I didn't. Mama used to say the difference between a Christian and sinner..." She paused.

He prompted her to continue. Tabitha's curiosity was piqued too.

"Oh. A Christian repents. A sinner never will tell God or anybody else they're sorry. I'm going to tell Jesus I'm sorry a lot before I die."

Lord, please don't let her die in my house, Tabitha prayed.

Aunt Tweet was the quintessential entertainer. Her life experiences and intellect captivated Marcus as they watched *Jeopardy!*

He was also in tune to Tabitha. The saltiness of her tear was still on his lips. He had thrown caution to the wind at signs of her distress. At least she didn't slap him. There was something pulling them together. Aunt Tweet was just the surface; deep down, there was more of an emotional bond.

Without skipping a beat of Aunt Tweet's chatter, he had gotten up and checked on Tabitha, who was working feverishly. She seemed like she belonged in his study, in his house, and in his life. Okay, he was just going to say it—but not out loud: dating had to be a possibility between them. He couldn't let her walk away.

She gnawed on her shapely lips when she was concentrating. Free of makeup and she was still gorgeous. The ponytail added to her relaxed, youthful look. When she yawned, he couldn't help it and stifled one too. By his third trip to check on her, she was beginning to rub her eyes. It was time to call it a night—for her sake.

He knocked to announce his presence. Looking up, she smiled, but the tiredness in her eyes verified she needed her rest.

"Come in. Oh." She smiled. "It's your office." Tabitha chuckled.

"Which you can use anytime." Sitting in one of the chairs in front of his desk, he studied her. Marcus had never asked a woman to leave, so this was a first, especially when he selfishly wanted her to stay so they could talk. "Your aunt is nodding, and I think you need to get some rest too. Aren't you glad I drove?" He grinned.

"Yes, it's a long way to my house," she joked, then stretched gracefully. "It's early for me, but I do need to get Aunt Tweet to bed." She started packing up her things. "Marcus." She paused. "Thank you for letting us invade your space and time."

"You're more than welcome. See? I know how to take care of the caregiver." They shared a soft laugh, then headed to his family room, where Aunt Tweet was nowhere in sight. He began to panic.

"Where is she?" Tabitha raced to the front door to look out—nothing.

"She was just sitting in there. You look down here. I'll check upstairs." He hadn't chatted with Tabitha *that* long, had he?

"I doubt she would've climbed the stairs. They're getting hard on her knees." Tabitha wandered into his kitchen.

He hurried upstairs anyway. Aunt Tweet wasn't in the weight room or in the master bedroom. Opening the third bedroom door, he blinked. She was lying on the floor in a fetal position, asleep. Marcus grunted in disbelief. He scooped her up in his arms and slowly walked downstairs.

"I found her," he said as loudly as he could without waking her.

"Upstairs? Is she okay?" Not waiting for an answer, Tabitha rushed to him with relief and helplessness flashing across her face. He was sure if he had extra arms, she would have collapsed in them after examining her aunt for herself.

"Tabitha, I owe you an apology." He felt bad for all the times he had misjudged her. "I didn't know she could move that fast."

"Me either at first. Welcome to the life of a caregiver."

"Grab my keys. I'll carry her to the car." While she did as he asked, Marcus couldn't help but wonder if Aunt Tweet was really suffering from confusion and memory loss or playing a game of hide-and-seek and winning.

Chapter 15

A FEW DAYS LATER, MARCUS HAD RETURNED FROM A LATE LUNCH with a client when there was a knock on his door. "Come in."

Victor's ex-girlfriend, Latrice, stuck her head inside his office. He waved her inside and immediately noticed her demeanor as he nodded for her to have a seat. What was going on? If she quit this time, he wouldn't rehire her.

"Mr. Whittington," she said hesitantly, then swallowed. "I need a favor."

He lifted a brow, linked his hands together, then leaned across the desk and waited.

Fumbling with her fingers, she wouldn't look at him. Her lips trembled as she uttered, "Victor…is in jail."

Again? he thought. When tears filled her eyes, he shifted in his seat. *Oh boy.* He wasn't immune to tears.

Sniffing, she bowed her head. When she glanced up, her cheeks were wet. *Oh man.* He grabbed a fistful of tissues and handed them to her.

"Thank you." She dabbed her eyes. She swallowed and took a deep breath. "Please, Mr. Whittington. We don't have any money. Can you put up bail money for him to get out?"

"What?" Marcus roared as he shot up from his chair. Was she crazy? Seeing her flinch made him regain his composure and take his seat. This time, he took a deep breath. "Latrice, I like you as a person and enjoy seeing your boys." He paused. "There are no polite words to describe my sentiments toward Victor."

On numerous occasions, he had gone out of his way to help his ex-employee with groceries, copay for one of his boy's doctor visits, and most recently last month, a loan to buy Latrice a gift for Mother's Day. Marcus considered his gestures an investment in people. "When I've tried to help him, he threw it back in my face. Not only do I not choose to help him this time, I doubt he'd want my charity." He grunted, disgusted with himself for trying to pay it forward. There were so many choice words he could repeat at the moment. "Did he put you up to this?"

"No," she said softly. "I don't know if you're a praying man…"

"I am." Who in their right mind didn't pray? If not at bedtime or over a plate of food, most definitely in a jam. Victor better get busy.

"Do you listen?" She cast him a hopeful expression.

Latrice had him there, but no way was he going to fess up. When he didn't answer, she proceeded. "I cried and prayed and asked God for mercy. I didn't sleep all night, listening for Jesus to tell me what to do. I don't know what to do, so I'm here, hoping you can help me."

She had lost her mind. If God wasn't helping her, who was Marcus to interfere? "I thought you and Victor split."

"We did, but I still love him—from afar. I have two little boys who need their mother and father, whether we're in the same household or not."

"I can't come to Victor's rescue this time. He's on his own. Sorry," he said with finality in his voice.

She seemed slow to accept his answer. When it sunk in, she graciously thanked him, then quietly left his office. If she had put up a fight, he wouldn't have felt nearly as bad. Rubbing his head, Marcus exhaled. He pushed Victor's status to the back of his mind. The man was officially a repeat offender, but that had been his choice. On the other hand, Latrice's plea nagged him throughout the day. The next day too.

Friday couldn't come fast enough. That afternoon, while Marcus was making plans to hang out with Demetrius later downtown, his cell rang. Tabitha. "Hey." He grinned and turned away from his brother.

"I need a favor," she said in a frantic voice.

His senses went on alert. "You've got it. What is it?"

"I'm behind on making my physician visits. I have to see this doctor today before he leaves for vacation, which means I'm not going to be able to get Aunt Tweet before six." She paused. "I wouldn't ask, but I have no one else."

His heart twisted, waiting for her to tell him what she needed. "Don't worry about that."

"I'm not trying to take advantage of your kindness."

"Talk to me. I don't have anything special planned." He heard Demetrius clear his throat. Marcus ignored him. Tabitha gave him the name of the adult care facility and the latest time Aunt Tweet had to be picked up by. "I'm sorta a caregiver, remember? Thanks for calling me."

"Thank you for saying yes." He didn't miss the relief in her voice. "I'll call Bermuda Place and let them know you're coming."

When the call ended, he turned around. Demetrius had his arms folded and a scowl on his face. "Nothing planned, huh? What am I, invisible?" He huffed. "Don't tell me, the neighbor again." He swore, then spat, "You're a sucker when it comes to women."

"Watch it. Besides, one look at her and you would be a sucker too." Yet his attraction went beyond looks. It was a magnetism that made him want to know more about her. "She has a good heart too. Now," he said, lifting his keys off his desk, "if you'll excuse me, I can't keep a lady waiting."

When Marcus arrived at the place Tabitha sent him, he advised the receptionist who he was and who he was there to pick up. Once he showed his license, another woman escorted Aunt Tweet to the lobby.

"Look who's here to get you," the staff member said.

"That's my son." Aunt Tweet smiled and lifted her cheek for a kiss.

He delivered, thanked the staff, and walked her to his car. Once behind the wheel, he teased her. "So, I'm your son, huh?" He chuckled.

She nodded and matched his chuckle.

Was she playing games with him? During her game shows, Aunt Tweet was an intellectual powerhouse. Other times, her memory was fuzzy.

He drove away, thinking about his parents. Their mental health was good. What about himself and the woman who would be his soul mate? Marcus planned to wake up with her every morning and kiss her every night. He cringed at the thought of not being able to recognize the important people in his life, especially his wife.

———

Tabitha told herself she was desperate for help as she waited impatiently in the lobby of Dr. Aaron Bernard's office. He was a highly sought-after expert on type 2 diabetes treatment. She was hyped about her company's drug, because it truly would benefit patients who dreaded the daily insulin injections.

If Dr. Bernard had been her last appointment, she might have made it from South County to North County to get her aunt. There was no way now. She had two more stops to doctors who had requested samples of Ceclor for sinusitis.

When the door opened, Tabitha stood, ready to sing the praises of Dyabolin. She stopped in her tracks, recognizing her former coworker and sales rep Evan Carter as he stepped out. When he saw her, he grinned and headed toward Tabitha.

Keena Johnson, the head nurse (or gatekeeper), motioned with her finger to wait. She remembered Tabitha as a rep for Pfizer. In addition to the samples Tabitha brought to the office, she toted bagels for the staff. "Right after his next patient," Keena said.

"Okay." Tabitha exhaled.

"What are you doing here?" Evan asked and gave her a hug before she could blink. When it came to male acquaintances, she wasn't a hugger, so that caught her off guard. It seemed, recently, Marcus had been the exception to the rule.

"Same as you. I'm with Ceyle-Norman now."

"Ouch." He gave her a look of pity. "I heard you quit, which was a shocker. I know that was a pay cut. Why?"

Not that he deserved an answer, but Tabitha didn't want him to think she had gotten fired because she didn't meet her sales quota. "My sisters and I are taking turns caring for our aunt. Traveling wasn't an option anymore."

"They have some great nursing homes."

"I'm sure, but I'd rather not leave my aunt in the hands of strangers."
She swallowed. Marcus wasn't a stranger—not anymore, right? Yes, she
could trust him with her most precious relative, right? She was second-
guessing her decision to call Marcus.

Evan bobbed his head. "So, what are you peddling?"

She hated that term, as if pharmaceutical reps were drug dealers.
"Dyabolin—"

The door opened, and the nurse waved her forward. "You've got
seven minutes."

"Great. Take care, Evan." Tabitha picked up her case and disappeared behind the door.

Keena directed her to the first office. Dr. Bernard stood from behind
his desk and extended his hand, then offered her a seat. She didn't waste
any time. "Thank you for seeing me." She began her spiel. "Dyabolin
may be revolutionary for your diabetic patients who fear needles."

Folding his hands, he leaned back in his chair. She recognized the
look. He was challenging her to convince him.

"Dyabolin isn't insulin, but it helps the body release its natural insulin continuously to maintain blood sugar for seven days." Tabitha was
proud that the results from the clinical trial had proven successful.

"What are the active ingredients and the time frame for stabilization
in the bloodstream?" he asked.

"Depending on a patient's metabolism, it could take six to eight
weeks before the medicine is effective, so they would have to be monitored closely."

"So, to introduce this medication, my patients would have to be
monitored every week for two months, instead of bimonthly visits," he
summarized.

"Yes." She nodded. That was the truth.

"Will the benefits outweigh the side effects?"

"In the best candidates, yes. Possible concerns could be tumors, some
cancerous. Besides serious allergic reactions, the drug could cause kidney
failure or pancreatitis." Doctors were well aware all drugs had side effects,
some more severe than others. That's how medicine worked.

Her mother once said doctors practice medicine, but God was the healer. Tabitha believed that; however, until God healed, the medicines were the best option. "Dr. Bernard, may I suggest you identify patients whose quality of life would benefit from this new drug. With your extensive research on the complications of this disease, especially in certain ethnic populations, I hope you're willing to consider prescribing it."

He pushed his circular glasses up on his nose. "You've done preliminary research for me. I appreciate that."

"I don't believe in wasting a physician's time. I'll leave samples and check back with you. Please call me with any questions."

He accepted her packets, then stood. Thanking him, she left for her last two appointments in Midtown. On the way, she called Marcus. "Hey." She greeted him hesitantly.

"Hey, yourself." He sounded upbeat.

"Have you had a chance to get my aunt?" Her heart pounded, hoping nothing came up on his end too.

"Of course. As a matter of fact, we're enjoying a light dinner at Ol' Henry's."

Some of her tension subsided. "Thank you sooo much, but I'm jealous," she teased. "But seriously, you didn't have to feed her. I'll reimburse you."

"Our dinner—just us—is waiting to be cashed in. I'll ignore your offer to pay me back. When we finish, my lady friend and I will do a little sightseeing, then head home. Without you, I don't want to take her too far from familiar surroundings, so you'll find us at the pond."

Exhaling, she whispered, "Thank you." The man was thoughtful. "Can you put her on the phone?"

There was some scuffling, then Aunt Tweet said hello.

"Are you are okay?"

"Of course. We're eating supper. He's handsome, you know."

No comment. Once this crisis had passed, she could bask in Marcus's handsomeness, kisses, cologne, hugs… That would come later. "See you soon, Auntie. Love you."

———

Sunday morning, Tabitha couldn't open her eyes. They were too heavy with sleep. Her body begged for another hour—three hours to be generous, but Aunt Tweet's memory never faded on this day of the week. She didn't know what time it was, nor did she care as she rolled over. She could try playing possum.

"Miss, it's time to go," a voice echoed in the distance, forcing Tabitha to open her eyes.

As her aunt came into focus, fully dressed, Tabitha sat up to get her bearings and scrutinize the person before her. Aunt Tweet's appearance needed tweaking, including recombing her hair, replacing her pantyhose, which had a run, and removing the wool sweater. It was almost summer. Plus, Aunt Tweet should take her red purse to match the red hat she insisted on wearing.

"Okay. Let me shower." She sniffed. Even though Tabitha had assisted on bathing Aunt Tweet last night, she still needed freshening up.

Aunt Tweet said she would start breakfast while Tabitha showered. She had to believe her and trust that she wouldn't go anywhere. When Tabitha walked into the kitchen ten minutes later, she determined it was time for Aunt Tweet to retire from the cooking. Her aunt was scrambling eggs with an uncut onion in the skillet.

"I'll take it from here," Tabitha said. She threw the onion away, finished the eggs, and made toast. While her aunt ate, Tabitha took Sweet Pepper outside for a potty break and to stretch his legs. Back in the kitchen, she made sure the puppy was fed, then gave her aunt a final inspection.

"Let's go."

They arrived at Bethesda Temple in time to hear the praise singers lead the congregation in worship. It wasn't long before Aunt Tweet hummed a melody before singing the lyrics Tabitha followed on the screen. Her aunt's eyes were closed, and she seemed to know every word.

There was something familiar about the song. Wracking her brain, Tabitha realized she had heard her aunt humming it in her sleep.

Pastor Nelson stepped to the podium to welcome visitors and give announcements, then he flipped through his Bible. Tabitha yawned as she opened her Bible app. One extra hour would have made a difference. *Marcus is right. Who is going to take care of me?*

"What is your reality today?" The pastor paused and folded his arms. "Are your circumstances putting you into situations that you'd never thought you would be in?"

My reality is being a caregiver, Tabitha thought. It was the source of her stress. As the pastor continued with his sermon, her mind drifted. In truth, her life had ben stressful before the caregiver's pact with her sisters. As a sales rep, her income was based on performance, which was the driving force to excel for her quarterly bonuses.

The minister continued. "God knows. He cares, and He is waiting for you to come to Him. The Lord has your back. Give Him all your cares, worries, and frustration. Proverbs 12:25 says, 'Anxiety makes the heart heavy, but a good word makes it glad.'" He lifted his Bible. "I got good news for you. Your inspiration is right here. Read it daily, meditate on it always, and never stop praying. God is listening."

It seemed like in a blink of an eye, Pastor Nelson had concluded his sermon, imparting more tidbits of wisdom from Proverbs. Then he beckoned those who needed prayer to come to the altar, and many people heeded the call. What was heavy on their hearts? What were their realities? Tabitha watched as the ministers laid hands on heads and fervently prayed. Soon, the pastor asked for an offering, then gave the benediction.

Standing with the others, Aunt Tweet gave her a smile that warmed Tabitha's heart and eased some of her stress. Her aunt's *happiness* was her reality. Feeling inspired, she looped her arm through her aunt's and strolled behind others to the parking lot. Maybe she could find time to start reading her Bible. *But when?* her mind challenged her.

"I haven't eaten since yesterday." Her aunt chuckled, and Tabitha shook her head, growing accustomed to her aunt's constant declaration of hunger.

A half hour later, they were enjoying a scrumptious brunch. While sampling a serving of blueberry pie, Tabitha tried to pry childhood memories from Aunt Tweet but didn't succeed as Marcus had. When they returned home, Sweet Pepper greeted them at the door. *Uh-oh.* In her haste to leave, she hadn't put him back in the kennel. There was a trail of an accident from the kitchen to the hallway. Tabitha nudged her aunt away before she stepped in it.

Although the sermon had inspired Tabitha, her feeling of lightness was snatched away. She settled Aunt Tweet in the family room, then cleaned up the puppy's mishaps. She sighed, wishing for a twenty-four-hour respite where the Lord took all her cares away. Her reality was waiting for Rachel to take over.

Talk about stress—Tabitha lived it during the week with her sales calls. When she returned home, she was exhausted. She couldn't wait for her sisters to arrive the next weekend.

Chapter 16

THE FOLLOWING SATURDAY MORNING AT LAMBERT AIRPORT, Tabitha screamed her excitement at seeing her sisters exit the Southwest terminal. Even her aunt's eyes lit up. After a group hug, they chatted on their way to the baggage carousel.

"You two look well." Kym smiled.

"Thanks." Tabitha accepted the compliment despite her casual attire. She wore suits throughout the week, but off the clock, she believed in slumming it in jeans. On the other hand, Aunt Tweet had to be dolled up before leaving the house. "Then I guess my makeup is working." She half teased. "I'm so glad you're here." She hugged them again.

"It is, Sis." Rachel squinted. "Add more contour and your features will pop," she stated in her dramatic, sultry voice. Their personalities were as diverse as their looks. Rachel had a flair for fashion and was meticulous when it came to her personal appearance. She knew how to capture any man's eye and keep his attention with little effort. Blame it on baby-sister syndrome—screaming for attention.

Tabitha was not an attention seeker unless it was a room of medical professionals. Surprisingly, men often took her as the youngest. She didn't mind being mistaken for a teenager with her hair in a ponytail and wearing jeans. If someone didn't appreciate her natural beauty, then he could move on.

As the oldest, Kym was on another level as a role model. She was a nurturer, protector, and counselor on matters of the heart when it came to first love as teenagers. She was their idol.

Her big sister stepped forward to lift her luggage off the carousel.

"There's mine." Rachel pointed and moved closer. As she reached for the handle, a gentleman intercepted.

"Need help, pretty lady?" He didn't wait for her to answer—and he was cute.

Tabitha and Kym exchanged knowing glances, then giggled. Even Aunt Tweet was fully aware of the vibes. Tabitha may favor their aunt's features, but Rachel had inherited her charm.

Once they left the airport, Tabitha took them to Ol' Henry's for a soul-food brunch. They discussed highs and lows in their lives as they devoured chicken and waffles. It felt like old times. Their aunt didn't add much to the conversation, but her eyes twinkled every now and then.

"We heard you've been singing." Kym leaned forward and waited.

Aunt Tweet shrugged and patted the table. "I can't sing."

"I heard you in church." Tabitha nudged Aunt Tweet.

"I don't remember."

Clearing her throat, Kym changed the subject. "What are we doing for the next three days?"

"I thought we'd chill." Tabitha was looking forward to some much-needed rest. Between work and Aunt Tweet, the thought of sleeping late made her smile.

"What? We can't play tourist? No cruising through Forest Park or Creve Coeur Park?" Rachel knitted her arched brows together. "I checked out the local events online last night, and there's a play at the Muny."

The Municipal Opera Theatre of St. Louis, also known as the Muny, reigns as the largest and oldest outdoor musical theater in the nation. The amphitheater could accommodate eleven thousand seats, and fifteen hundred were always reserved free on a first come, first served basis.

"It would be nice to check it out," Rachel said.

Tabitha shook her head. "That's too much effort. Save your excitement for Pasadena Hills Neighborhood District's summer kickoff."

"As many times as we've been back home, it's never during the kickoff." Kym laughed. "I'm glad the district is still hosting that summer kickoff. It'll be interesting to see who still lives in the neighborhood."

"And meet new neighbors." Tabitha smiled, thinking about Marcus.

Once they were finished eating, she drove the short distance home. She turned on Roland Avenue to find the beloved landmark fountain circled by food vendors. Game booths and lawn chairs dotted the street corners. Some neighbors were dressed in costumes and handed out balloons.

Tabitha inched along until she made it to her driveway. Her bedding plants around the patio were bursting with color—the evidence of her and Aunt Tweet's labors of love.

"Looking good, Sis," Kym complimented. "The lawn is green and lush the way Daddy used to keep it."

"It's called lawn service," Tabitha admitted and snickered.

Rachel agreed. "The flowers around the garage bring back memories of us playing upstairs," she said with a nostalgic sigh, referring to the spacious attic above the two-car garage. As little girls, they had spent hours entertained with their doll collection, a collection started by their aunt. Whenever Aunt Tweet traveled, she would bring back different dolls for all three of them.

They had a makeshift classroom to teach their dolls lessons. Tabitha's whimsical thoughts faded as she helped Aunt Tweet out of the car and inside the house.

Rachel kicked off her heels and slipped into comfortable, stylish sandals to stroll through the festival. It didn't take long for the sisters to note their aunt's stubbornness at the simple suggestion of changing her attire to something more casual.

"I wouldn't sweat it. We won't be out there long anyway," Kym said.

"Hmph." Aunt Tweet powdered her nose. "A lady should always look as if she's about to step on a runway."

Hands down, Rachel was the winner on that one. Even in her casual outfits, she was polished. Her nails, hair, and makeup were always on display. Called "the accessories queen," their youngest sister knew how to sassy up any outfit.

Kym was the color trendsetter. She would wear the same shade for months and dare anyone to question her color binges. Despite the temperature expected to be in the low eighties, she was still in her all-black phase. Her big sister was going to burn up.

At the moment, Tabitha was satisfied with what she had on. What brought her joy was her sisters were there to help. Of course, Marcus had made it known that he was there to rescue her anytime. His words and his kindness made her heart flutter, but the bottom line was Aunt Tweet wasn't his responsibility. This was the Knicely sisters' caregivers' pact.

Yet the other day, Marcus took responsibility for Aunt Tweet's care when he picked up her from the adult facility. Tabitha had arrived home to see them sitting on the park bench by the pond. He had fed and entertained her aunt and even had a carryout for Tabitha from Ol' Henry's, which was why she'd taken her sisters there, to try something else on the menu. *Enough thoughts about Marcus.* Her sisters were in town and Tabitha wanted to enjoy every moment with them.

Caving in to Aunt Tweet's demands, the sisters let her stay dolled up as they left the house and took a leisurely walk toward the activities around the fountain. Kym recognized some familiar faces from their childhood, like Mrs. Pope, who was now an elderly widow. They also introduced themselves to new families who had moved into the neighborhood.

"You might get a chance to meet Marcus," Tabitha said casually. "Despite our rough start, he was willing to help me out in a pinch." She told them he had picked up their aunt. "That's what neighbors do."

"How well do you really know him, besides his address?" Always the cautious one, Kym was definitely alarmed. "Does he have a criminal past?" she asked in a hushed voice, so Aunt Tweet wouldn't hear as she strolled ahead of them with Sweet Pepper on a leash.

"I'm with Kym on this one. Why would he be willing to drop everything he's doing to help you when he threatened to have you arrested? I don't trust him..." In the middle of her rant, Rachel paused, then stuttered, "Whoa. If these are guys are neighbors, you've got another roommate, Sis."

Looking in the direction that had Rachel in such a daze, Tabitha sucked in her breath. Two men commanded the sidewalk with their presence. Of course, Marcus was the more handsome one.

"Good eye," Kim said with an *hmph*. "A man's confidence shows up in his walk, and those brothas have the swag."

Did her big sister just say that? Kym was usually nonchalant about men, but clearly Marcus and the other guy had piqued her attention. It was a good sign he had made a good impression. A hint of a smile tugged on his lips when they made eye contact, and he held her stare until he invaded their space.

"Ladies," he greeted.

His eyes sparkled as he leaned closer and kissed Aunt Tweet's cheek. Tabitha blushed as if it were she who was graced with his adoration. Sweet Pepper yelped for attention, so Marcus squatted and scratched behind the puppy's ears.

Tabitha caught herself waiting in line for whatever affection he was doling out. She didn't want to have any romantic fantasies concerning him, but he was the mold those heroes in romance books were made of. He winked. "You look pretty."

"Thanks." Her blush spread.

"And you are?" Kym arched her eyebrow the way their mother often did when they were in trouble.

He smiled and extended his hand. "Marcus, one of Tabitha's neighbors. I hope she mentioned me." He glanced at her, and mischief danced in his eyes.

"Oh, she has." Kym nodded, accepting his hand.

His grin widened, which confirmed a faint dimple.

Tabitha made the introductions. "This is my older sister, Kym, and our youngest sister, Rachel."

"Nice to meet you, ladies. This old guy here is my brother, Demetrius." With a low grunt, Demetrius gave a curt greeting. Clearly, he wasn't the friendly sibling.

"Need an escort?" Marcus asked them.

"Sure do," Aunt Tweet said. "You snooze, you lose, girls." Latching onto his elbow, she allowed him to lead the way.

———

Marcus had been distracted all morning—until he saw Tabitha. She seemed to have the ability to bring a sense of calmness to his life, although she probably thought it was the other way around.

When she smiled, he grinned like a preteen boy with a crush. What was amusing was watching his brother's infatuation with her younger sister. Rachel was a beauty. Marcus had to give her that. She acted older and a tad bolder than Tabitha, who was low-key, soft-spoken until pushed, and had no problem fading in the background, but she couldn't hide from him. Marcus would always sense her presence, even if his eyes were closed.

Those qualities were attractive. She was a woman who could speak her mind to show her strength, yet she was feminine and vulnerable enough to make him want to be her hero. In hindsight, how could she have irritated him?

But Marcus was irritated. Another woman was becoming a thorn in his side, which explained his earlier bad mood. It was as if his employee wasn't taking no for an answer, judging from Latrice's morning phone call.

"Good morning, Mr. Whittington, I'm sorry to bother you at home, but you always said if there was an emergency, your employees were free to call you." She released a sigh. *"I was hoping you've changed your mind about helping Victor. Maybe you've had a chance to sleep on it."*

"I slept very well, thank you, because I gave Victor's situation no further thought."

Every time he thought about Latrice's ridiculous request, it irked him. What was next, Latrice and her boys picketing in front of his house for Victor's release?

Marcus didn't realize he was frowning until Tabitha came to his side. "You okay?" The genuine concern in her eyes and the brief touch on his arm rescued him from the mental nagging.

"Yeah," he sighed, trying to put Latrice and Victor's situation out of his mind. He was in the company of a woman he *wanted* to think about.

"It's getting hot, so we're all getting a drink from the food stands, and I'll treat." Tabitha's smile brought them back to the present.

That gesture made his knees weak. She could make an army of soldiers surrender when her lips curled. "Not on my watch."

She nudged him and whispered, "You're not on Aunt Tweet duty. It's the weekend. You're off."

"When are you off?" He stared into her eyes and tried to read her emotions. She had no answer, so he continued, "If you need me, I'm here." He didn't realize that they were the center of attention until Demetrius cleared his throat.

"The ladies ate, but I'm hungry, man," Demetrius said.

"Sorry." He and Tabitha led the way with Aunt Tweet sandwiched in between them. Tabitha's sisters and his brother followed behind.

Although the ladies were stuffed, they did agree to lemonade. Aunt Tweet, on the other hand, pointed to a corn dog at the food truck. "Sure am hungry."

Marcus frowned and looked to Tabitha.

"Trust me, she was well fed, but I guess one won't hurt." No wonder her aunt's clothes were getting snug. After the ladies placed their lemonade orders, Tabitha fumbled in her pocket for money.

He was faster and handed over cash for their drinks, the corn dog, and his greedy brother's plate of food.

They sat at a vacated table. While the various conversations were lively, Marcus went through the motions that he was following their every word, but Latrice's request invaded his thoughts again. Why was the woman hard to shake?

When a small band began to play, some residents began to dance in the street, which had been closed off except for residential traffic. Tabitha's sisters convinced Aunt Tweet to dance with them. Placing Sweet Pepper in Tabitha's lap, their aunt gave them a show with her moves until she became winded. They guided her back to her seat. Immediately, she gathered the puppy.

"I bet she was something back in the day," he whispered.

Turning to him, Tabitha chuckled. "Don't let her hear you say that, because she'll tell you it's still her day."

"Aunt Tweet," Kym said, "you've still got it."

"Umm-hmm." Their aunt chuckled. "I guess I do. I was in a dance troupe, and we toured the world…"

The sisters exchanged curious expressions, as if it were the first time they'd heard this. Even Marcus was beginning to question whether Aunt Tweet embellished every tale she told him.

Somehow, the conversation bounced from dancing around the world to singing at church.

"She's up at eight thirty, and we're out the door by ten for church. That seems to be the trend," Tabitha told them.

"Any plans to barbecue on Memorial Day?" Marcus changed the subject. He had no plans to add church to his Sunday schedule.

"I haven't decided; since my sisters leave late that night, we might get some takeout and bring it back to my house."

"Nonsense." He reached out and squeezed her hand. "Come to my company's barbecue."

"She'll be there, and we'll tag along," Rachel said, clearly eavesdropping when he thought she and his brother were in a conversation.

Whether Rachel enjoyed St. Louis–style baby back ribs or had just picked up on Marcus's vibes, he was glad she was on his side.

Everyone waited on Demetrius to clean his chicken bones and wipe his mouth, then they discarded their trash. As the festival crowd swelled, Tabitha suddenly froze in her steps. "Aunt Tweet, where's Sweet Pepper?"

Her aunt shrugged. "He went for a walk."

"Walk?" Tabitha panicked. The four-pound Yorkie could be anywhere. "You can't let go of the leash."

"Calm down," Kym said. "Let's split up and look for him."

Before she could work herself into a frenzy, Marcus placed his hand on her shoulders and softly squeezed.

Weariness filled Tabitha's eyes. "The dog has put an end to Aunt Tweet's wandering, and now he escapes."

"Hey, we'll find him." Marcus hoped so, because he didn't like the sound of hopelessness in her voice.

Soon, neighbors joined in the search. Finally, Rachel sent a group text.

Demetrius and I have found Sweet Pepper playing with some children. After Tabitha read the message, they started toward the location Rachel had given.

Tension seemed to peel off of Tabitha when they saw the dog. "Thanks for playing with him," she told the children, taking the leash, "but we need to give him back to my..." She looked around. "Where's Aunt Tweet? I thought she was with you," she said, frowning.

"I thought she was with *you*," Kym said defensively.

"While you two argue, I'm going to look for her." Rachel huffed and marched off.

Splitting up again, they moved in different directions. Marcus and Tabitha weaved through the crowd and spotted her at a booth, devouring a double scoop of ice cream. The evidence was splattered on her face.

"She sure has a sweet tooth." He joked, but Tabitha didn't laugh.

Minutes later, her sisters joined them, fussing as they wiped at the spills on Aunt Tweet's dress. Not knowing who and what Rachel, Tabitha, and Kym were really complaining about, he and Demetrius stayed on the sidelines and said nothing.

Evidently satisfied with the outcome, Tabitha announced they were heading back home. Any other time, he wouldn't have hesitated to escort them. Not today. The sisters' body language shouted *don't butt in*. With his hands jiggling the keys in his pocket, Marcus rocked on his heels and watched their retreat. None of them looked happy as Tabitha toted the puppy in her arms and Rachel and Kym held on to their aunt's hands like little children.

"Whew," Demetrius mumbled under his breath, then slapped Marcus in the chest with the back of his hand for fun. "I'll give you credit that Tabitha is fine—all the sisters are—but that's a lot of drama right there." He pointed in their direction.

"I'm not scared of a little drama...when it comes to her."

Demetrius rubbed his head. "That's a busload of drama, and if I were you, I would get off at the next stop."

Shaking his head, he squinted until the group faded in the distance. "I bought a round-trip ticket. I'm not getting off until she gets off." He returned his brother's backhanded slap, his to Demetrius's stomach, but of course, done in jest. Now they were even.

Whew. Marcus had hoped with Tabitha's sisters in town, there would be harmony. Unfortunately, Aunt Tweet's antics this weekend might touch off a storm. From the brief finger-pointing he had just witnessed, Marcus might need to carry an umbrella.

Chapter 17

"THAT WAS AN INTERESTING OUTING," KYM STATED LATER THAT night after Aunt Tweet had retired to her room.

It was a comical task, as everyone had a hand in their aunt's nightly grooming. Kym helped bathe her. Rachel tidied up the bedroom and discovered snacks their aunt had hoarded behind closed doors. Tabitha used the time to wash clothes, especially towels for Aunt Tweet to fold, since she had become increasingly restless when she didn't have anything to do.

Finally, the sisters collapsed on the furniture in the family room, too tired to drag themselves upstairs to bed. "Now you see how things are with Aunt Tweet?" Tabitha asked.

Kym patted her chest. "That was the second scariest moment of my life. The first was when she got lost behind the wheel in New Jersey. Today, she could have easily slipped away in that crowd. Is this what you're dealing with on a regular basis?" The concern on her big sister's face was evident.

"Yes." Tabitha nodded. "Looking at her, she appears to be in her right mind. If I didn't know the severity of the dementia symptoms, I would say she's playing a cat-and-mouse game. I see the frustration when she can't recognize or remember things." She shrugged. "I wonder if she has moments where she knows what's going on around her, but helpless to react in the way she wants, because she's trapped in a body she has lost control of."

The room was quiet, except for the ice maker. They all were focusing on Aunt Tweet's health. "If it wasn't for the adult day care and Marcus, I might have been unemployed by now. The stress is overwhelming." Tabitha closed her eyes and exhaled.

"Speaking of Marcus, how much of a distraction is he?" Kym asked.

Tabitha folded her legs under her bottom, giving herself time to decide how to take her sister's inquiry. It sounded more like an accusation. "What are you saying?"

"Aunt Tweet is our focus. She needs closer supervision." Her older sister paused. "Don't get me wrong. Marcus seems nice and all, and beyond good-looking, but ask yourself if you have time to get deep in a relationship."

Hmph. Tabitha didn't have to ask herself. She knew the answer the moment Marcus hinted he was interested in her. She thought her crisis would scare him away, but he bounced back stronger. Now, she drew on his strength to keep her sanity.

When it came to relationships, Kym was skeptical, picky, and untrusting of hot looks and sweet words. A teenage crush had done her in many years ago, and it seemed to change her idea of happily ever after, even decades later.

"Do you think she is wandering as a way to get your attention? Maybe she feels threatened by Marcus," Kym said, voicing her concern.

Tabitha laughed at the absurdity. "Did you forget that Marcus is in my life because of Aunt Tweet?" She pointed toward the stairway. The sisters rarely bumped heads about anything growing up because she and Rachel would follow the leader. That's what made their relationship harmonious. But since they'd reached adulthood, they'd had no problem discussing opposing viewpoints.

This was supposed to be a stress-free weekend. "I know she was in good hands with you as her caregiver, Kym. Since I've picked up the torch, I live and breathe Aunt Tweet from the time I wake until my head hits the pillow. I look for and crave those moments where I can inhale more of her pearls of wisdom." Her eyes watered, but she refused to release the tears. Her caregiving journey was making her emotional. This wasn't about whining but stating a point. "After my rocky start with Marcus, he has shown himself to be caring, kind, and there when I call. He's not a part of this discussion because he genuinely cares about us."

"A man who is at your beck and call." Rachel gave a slow grin. "I love it. I think it's sweet he wants to be a part of our lives." Lifting her hand, she leaned over for a high five.

Amused at her baby sister, who supplied the comedy relief the moment it was needed, Tabitha tapped her hand against Rachel's.

"Okay." Kym conceded with a shrug. "So what's on the agenda tomorrow?"

"Church," Tabitha told her. "Aunt Tweet likes the one across the street from Bermuda Place. I think the music pulls out a happy place within her, which has sparked her to sing or hum."

"Umm-hmm." Kym scooted up from her resting position on the sofa. "I don't recall her mentioning growing up in church or wanting to attend one while she lived with me in Baltimore, but who are we to deny her whatever she wants?"

"Exactly," Tabitha agreed. "Every day she surprises me. She's convinced Marcus that she was once a model, performed in a dance troupe, and won an all-white beauty pageant."

Kym laughed and threw her hands up in disbelief. "This Aunt Tweet you're describing is foreign to me."

You're not the only one. She kept her thoughts to herself. "Dementia has so many symptoms, and I don't know if Aunt Tweet is making things up to entertain herself or sharing a piece of her that she's kept hidden." With that said, Tabitha stood, stretched, and announced she was going to sleep. Her sisters would sleep in the bedroom Tabitha and Rachel had shared growing up.

After saying her prayers, Tabitha snuggled under the covers. She hugged her pillow, then reached for her phone on the nightstand. She preferred not to text or email folks after eleven at night in case they were sleeping, and the alerts might disturb them. This time, she couldn't resist reaching out to Marcus.

Thank you for today.

Surprisingly, he responded right back. Anything for you!

I believe you.

Resting her phone back on the nightstand, she smiled and drifted off to sleep, wondering what a real date with Marcus Whittington would be like if she wasn't a caregiver. Of course, dating wasn't part of her reality, but she could dream about it every night.

———

Marcus smiled as he read Tabitha's text. He would give anything to talk to her right now. Instead, he was still stuck with his brother at a sports bar. Before glancing up, he could feel Demetrius staring at him. "What?"

"Oh nothing," Demetrius answered. He displayed a teasing grin before he lifted his glass in salute. "She has you wrapped around her finger, Bro."

"They both do." He wasn't shy about admitting his deep attraction to Tabitha and his affection for Aunt Tweet. For hours, he had gone through the motions of enjoying himself hanging out with his brother. In honesty, he desperately wanted to check in with Tabitha to make sure she was all right. Her sisters' presence hindered that. However, the trade-off was she had a temporary respite from caring for Aunt Tweet solo when he wasn't around.

"Yup." Demetrius took another sip and scanned the bar, then, in a casual manner, stated, "I can see why you've been distracted all evening." He pointed his fingers at his eyes, then turned his two fingers at Marcus's eyes. "She's pretty, but her sister Rachel...wow. But too young for me. At thirty-eight, I don't date women in their twenties. I'm not babysitting someone who is ten years younger than me."

He tilted his head. "And you know that how?"

"I asked."

"I see, so...if you asked, you're interested." When his brother remained silent, Marcus pressed. "Well, aren't you?"

He was more than interested in Tabitha. He really cared for her. What was the definition for true love?

Latrice making her plea for Victor flashed before his eyes. They couldn't be his answer as a model couple. Wasn't out of sight supposed to be out of mind? How was their relationship a model example?

"Hey." Demetrius nudged him. "I said I'm more curious than interested in Rachel, but I guess your mind was on another Knicely sister."

"Nope." Marcus rubbed his face in annoyance. "Actually, Latrice got in my head, and she jumps out when I least expect it and somehow keeps nagging me."

Finishing his drink, Demetrius smacked his lips while shifting his weight on an unsteady stool. "Man, let that go. Victor is history. He messed up, so he's out."

"Yep. I agree, hundred percent." Marcus bobbed his head.

"Give her a warning that if she approaches you again with that nonsense, she could lose her job too."

I have. Marcus tapped his finger on the bar counter. "You're so rough around the edges."

"No, I'm a businessman who follows the rules. You may have the heart, but I have the brains to run a tight ship. Did you forget I earned my MBA first and graduated magna cum laude?"

Marcus shrugged. "You got me there." He had received his MBA last year at the state university near his home. "Well, let's call it a night." He summoned the bartender for their bill.

Demetrius gave him a dumbfounded look. "Really?" He checked the time. "This early? Tomorrow's Sunday, so what's the deal with an early bedtime?"

"It's called 'getting some rest.'"

Chapter 18

Sunday morning, Latrice didn't wake Marcus with a phone call, but her voice and her request were revolving in his head, so much so that he couldn't get back to sleep. When it came to helping people, Marcus's pockets were deep. His employees, Tabitha, and Aunt Tweet were witnesses to that. Victor, on the other hand... He had to draw the line. It seemed like the more he pushed back on that request, the more Latrice got into his head.

Staring up at the ceiling, Marcus groaned. He told Demetrius he was going to get some rest, but it didn't appear his mind was going to let him do that. He thought about Tabitha and remembered she was attending church with her family. Not that church was on his agenda, but wherever Tabitha was, he wanted to be near her. Why did the old Michael Jackson hit "Got to Be There" come to mind? *Because you got it bad.* He grinned. Yeah. He did.

Marcus wasn't opposed to church, but it had never been a priority. After getting out of bed, he shaved and showered. He chose his brown suit and a light-colored tie—attire rarely worn to the office.

Tabitha had mentioned Aunt Tweet dragging her to church. Maybe Aunt Tweet had a hand in getting him there this morning too. He called Tabitha to let her know his intention but got her voicemail.

Not knowing the time service started, he drove to Tabitha's, seeing her car was parked in the driveway. A playful thought came to him as he was about to ring the doorbell. She would see the humor of him perched on her porch. This scenario was how it all started for them—Aunt Tweet staking her claim on his property.

He perused their neighborhood: solid and unique-styled houses and groomed landscapes. "Old money" was one way to describe the neighborhood back in the day. Somehow, this suburban upscale neighborhood near the city limits had survived the white flight. The residents were mixed in ethnicity and income. One thing everyone had in common was their commitment to preserving the historic value of their homes.

Not wanting to wait, Marcus opted to ring the doorbell. Seconds later, he rang it again. When the door finally opened, his jaw dropped, his heart pounded, and the scent of Tabitha's perfume made its way to tickle his nose.

Tilting her head, she graced him with a smile. "Wow, Mr. Whittington. You clean up real good, but what are you doing here, commandeering my porch?"

She got his joke. "Hey, it's fair game." It felt nice that they could tease each other about earlier incidents that caused a wedge between them. He measured his steps until he towered over her. When her long lashes fluttered, he could feel his nostrils flare. "You're the one who's wowing me." He scanned her from head to toe. The dress she wore looked femininely soft and flirty and curved around her hips.

Mesmerized, he leaned forward. "You're gorgeous." His heart rate still hadn't recovered. He inhaled and exhaled without taking his eyes off her. "I had an urge to be at church today. I hope you don't mind me tagging along with you."

Aunt Tweet appeared at Tabitha's side decked out in white—a large hat, suit, thick stockings, shoes, and purse. Even the Bible she held was white. She reminded him of a nurse, except for the hat and Bible. "We're going to be late." She was clearly ready to go.

"Give us a few minutes." Tabitha paused. "Can you believe she overslept, and I had to wake her up?" She chuckled and Marcus was a goner. "So, you're on guard duty until my sisters come down." She tilted her head at her aunt.

"Got it." He stepped farther into the foyer and placed a kiss on Aunt Tweet's cheek. He turned back to Tabitha and lowered his voice. "I don't care how long I have to wait to kiss your lips, it will be worth it, Miss Knicely." Stepping back, he stared into her eyes and enjoyed watching her blush. Yep, he was wearing down her defenses.

"Didn't expect to see you this morning," Kym said with a mischievous smirk. "Are you my aunt's driver on Sundays?"

"Actually, this is my first time going to church with them, but I do have enough room in my car, so I can be the designated driver." He sniffed the air. "It will cost you a strip of bacon, if any is left." He missed the hearty breakfasts his mom used to prepare. He couldn't remember the last time he'd cooked bacon and eggs. When the craving hit, he usually visited a restaurant for breakfast with his brother or clients.

"Not a problem. There is plenty." Tabitha made a beeline to the kitchen. He admired the way she glided across the floor in heels.

"Is Demetrius coming with us this morning?" Rachel asked. She looked nice too.

"Nope." Knowing his brother, he was probably sleeping in, as Marcus usually did on Sunday mornings.

A flash of disappointment crossed Rachel's face, then she wiped it away with a smile and a shrug. "His loss. We're going to hear Aunt Tweet sing."

Aunt Tweet began to fuss, ready to go. Marcus was certain that if Tabitha's aunt got behind the wheel, she would be halfway to the church. Other drivers beware.

Tabitha handed him two strips of bacon in a napkin, then appeared to do a head count before ushering them out the door and locking it. He held off the urge to wrap his arm around her waist and pull her closer.

He took a bite—"Crispy"—and finished by the time all the ladies were in the car. He drove off, taking a shortcut through side streets to get to Bethesda Temple Church in no time.

Once they had parked, he escorted his passengers inside. The Knicely sisters were eye-catching individually, but together, they were showstoppers. An usher led them to a pew. Minutes later, an elderly woman was reading her fourth or fifth announcement when he overheard Kym mumble, "Music please, so we can hear Aunt Tweet sing."

What was the fascination with Aunt Tweet's singing? he wondered. Soon enough, musicians took up their instruments. Three women and two men stood behind microphones and rallied the crowd.

"Praise the Lord! Praise the Lord, everybody!"

Aunt Tweet didn't move, then the group started singing "How Great Thou Art," and the melodious words spilled from the older woman's mouth like a young songbird.

When another tune began, Aunt Tweet picked up that beat to "I Know I've Been Changed." Marcus wondered if she had stored all the melodies in a hidden compartment. By this time, they all were standing and clapping.

Soon, the minister approached the podium and introduced himself as Pastor Nelson. "If you are a first-time visitor, please stand so we may acknowledge and welcome you."

Marcus got to his feet, along with Kym and Rachel.

"Amen. It's no accident you're here today. God has been expecting you, so please make yourself comfortable and listen for the message the Lord has tailored for each of you," the pastor advised before leading the congregation in a prayer.

After a chorus of "amen," Pastor Nelson cleared his throat and scanned the sanctuary. "Not long ago, I preached on stress. Another way to reduce it for Christians is to forgive without keeping score—no exceptions. In Matthew 18:22, the Bible tells us to forgive seventy times seven. You're using too much wasted energy to track 490 offenses. You'll feel better when you do, get a good night's sleep…"

"Hey, you okay? You look so intense," Tabitha said in a low voice.

Marcus sat straighter. "I'm paying attention." He patted her hand. Her softness begged him not to let go. He couldn't, and she let him hold on.

Aunt Tweet shushed them.

The pastor continued, "When it comes to forgiving others, we have to remember their walk, hardships, and mistakes in life may be different from our own. They may do things you never would, but Jesus says to forgive them."

Forgive. Victor came to mind, and Marcus immediately dismissed his former employee from his memory bank. He had been good to the man and had overlooked many of his indiscretions.

"We have to extend mercy in order for us to receive God's mercy when we mess up," Pastor Nelson pressed. "Forgiving is not the same as forgetting, so don't get it twisted. Don't have any regrets beginning now. Forgive and allow the Lord to show you how to relate to the offender…"

Becoming uncomfortable, Marcus tuned out the remainder of the sermon and didn't relax until the preacher closed his Bible.

"Has God spoken to your heart today? Will you listen? You no longer have to be a sinner. Your salvation journey can start today right here at the altar."

While Marcus refused to move his legs, Aunt Tweet popped up.

"Where is she going?" Kym asked with a bewildered look.

Tabitha didn't seem fazed. "She probably wants prayer. That's what usually happens at the end of the sermon. I'll go with her to make sure she doesn't wander off."

"God spoke to me, miss. I heard Him, and I'm not going to live another day with regrets."

Aunt Tweet seemed determined to get in the prayer line. Marcus stood, so she could exit as his mind wandered. So Sunday's message was about forgiveness. Latrice and Victor's dilemma resurfaced. Would he regret not helping Victor later, or would he be a fool to help the loser now?

—

Tabitha was disappointed Marcus declined her invitation to join them for dinner after church. Once everyone else feasted on dinner purchased from Lee's Famous Chicken, Kym was back to peppering their aunt about her church experience. "Now…Tell me again what happened?"

Squinting, Aunt Tweet seemed to strain her brain to remember. "I'm too old to go to the grave with regrets of things I said to folks, the way I acted or other things. I needed forgiveness. That young man prayed for me, and something inside of me exploded." She sighed and smiled.

"Really?" Tabitha asked. Not only could Aunt Tweet sing, but she used her lungs to release an inner voice that was strong, youthful, and let out piercing cries to God.

"This is not the same woman who lived with me." Kym looked bewildered.

"Sometimes, she's not the same woman I've known all my life either," Tabitha admitted. "But the doctor advised us to expect the unexpected. Every morning when I wake, I don't know how much of the old Aunt Tweet I'll see or how much of me she'll remember."

Rachel frowned. "What kind of state will she be in when she comes to live with me to celebrate my birthday at the end of October? They've found cures for everything under the sun. When will dementia sufferers get a break?"

Tabitha shrugged. "I read so much on dementia's symptoms and Alzheimer's to prep me to be an efficient caregiver that I thought my brain would burst." Shaking her head, she pulled her legs to her chest, then rested her chin on her knees. "The textbook barely scratches the surface. The brain tissue of Alzheimer's patients can't be studied until"— she swallowed—"they pass away. There are some things we can do now, like participate in preventive studies."

"I am so not feeling that one." Kym shook her head. "You know I'm not the one for those research and clinical trials. I don't care how much they pay me." She folded her arms.

"It's not about the money. You want a cure? It's about prevention. While scientists may test drugs and therapies in clinical trials, prevention trials are geared toward keeping diseases from developing. If they determine we're high risk, researchers will study whether a certain medicine, vitamin, or lifestyle change might prevent us from getting it." Tabitha didn't realize she had switched to her sales rep mode until her sisters started grinning at her. "What?"

"You sound so…clinical," Kym said with pride.

Rachel hmphed. "I still think we need to have her doctor change her meds to something stronger."

"The more potent the drug, the greater the chance for worsening side effects. She's already on Razadyne for mild to moderate dementia symptoms like confusion. I've done my homework the best I can, even scrutinized other drugs. A couple have a one-to-three-week adjustment period, and during that time, Aunt Tweet could suffer with diarrhea, nausea, vomiting, urinary obstruction, ulcers, and the symptoms go on."

Adjusting to medicine was never fun. "Do we want to subject her to those side effects? She's healthy, except for high blood pressure and osteoporosis. She's in the hands of God," Tabitha said, trying to convince her siblings.

"You said Aunt Tweet has been wanting to go to church, and today God gave her something that she came for. The ministers called it her Nicodemus experience." Kym twisted her lips. Her strong voice became soft and shaky. "She's eighty-four. Maybe she's dying and wants to make peace with God?"

Rachel sniffed. "I can't imagine our lives without her in it."

Tabitha rubbed her arms as if a cold blast hit her. "I don't want to think or talk about death." Tabitha blinked away the onset of tears.

"Right." Kym concurred.

Tabitha changed the subject. "Since Marcus invited us to a Memorial Day barbecue at his company, want to go?" She looked to her sisters. If they wanted to opt out, they would do something else, but surprisingly, they agreed—Rachel more enthusiastically.

Chapter 19

SINCE MARCUS COULDN'T STAY ASLEEP THE NEXT MORNING, HE opted to work out his frustration in his home gym. After the treadmill, Marcus began to lift weights when his doorbell rang. Returning his dumbbells to the holder, he reached for a towel to wipe his face, then glanced out the window. There wasn't a car in front of his house.

The bell rang again as he hurried down the stairs. Marcus doubted it was Aunt Tweet. Number one, she had never rung his doorbell. Number two, the puppy and his own frequent visits to Tabitha's had seemed to cease her urge for wandering.

He opened the door and came face-to-face with the woman who had invaded his life in a good way because of Aunt Tweet.

"Ah, hi." Tabitha scanned his attire and smiled. "Sorry for the early visit. I was walking to clear my head and was hoping you were up and... decent."

He panicked immediately. "Is everything all right?" She nodded, but that wasn't good enough. "Is Aunt—" He slowed down. "Are you okay?"

"Yes."

"And Aunt Tweet?"

"Yes."

He exhaled and grinned. "Give me a sec to shower. Do you want to come inside?"

"No. I'll wait out here." She glanced down at the puppy at her feet. "I have Sweet Pepper."

Her sisters must be babysitting. That meant it was just the two of them. "Be right back."

He showered quickly but opted to shave later. After slipping on a shirt and shorts, Marcus returned to the porch and sat next to her. "Now, where were we?"

She angled her head. He admired her as she studied his face. The moment would be perfect to share their first kiss. He was about to act on his desire when she frowned.

As if she had come to a decision, she smiled, but not wide enough to show her white teeth. "I bet you would look handsome with a beard."

"Huh? So now I'm ugly?" he teased and lifted an eyebrow.

Giggling, she nudged his shoulder. "Not even on a bad day. I'm not giving you any more compliments today." Tabitha's eyes twinkled, then in another surprising move, she rested her head on his shoulder.

Her closeness was making him weak in his knees—and he was sitting.

She exhaled. "I needed to vent."

He chuckled. "You haven't said much." He chuckled and enjoyed inhaling the scent of her hair.

Tabitha pulled away, to his disappointment, and faced him. "Being a caregiver is harder than I thought."

"I see that now, and I'm on the outside looking in. Sorry I misjudged you."

"It's okay." Tabitha shrugged, then anchored her elbows on her knees. Again, she became quiet.

"Do you realize this is the first time we've ever been alone…without Aunt Tweet?"

"Yeah." The sadness in her eyes made his heart ache. "I know you care for me and Aunt Tweet, or you wouldn't be in our lives"—she squeezed her lips as if to trap her words inside—"but somehow, you caught me off guard and captured my heart." She patted her chest as if she were about to recite the Pledge of Allegiance. "But it wouldn't be fair to you or Aunt Tweet to try to juggle a relationship. I have nothing to give. I'm not in control of my own life. My evenings and weekends are booked."

Now she was venting. Only, he wasn't buying what she was trying to sell. Marcus had witnessed her frustrations, but hearing them tore at his heart. He sensed she needed to be cuddled and loved, so he took the liberty of guiding her head back to his shoulder, then put his arm around her.

"Tab, I'm not convinced you believe the words coming out of your mouth. I'm hearing you say you don't have room for us in your life…" He rubbed his jaw against her head. "But the vibes I'm getting are you want to try. I vote to try."

He waited for her to voice her thoughts. He yearned to hear Tabitha say she wanted to try, but she said nothing as she pulled away, stood, and dusted off the back of her pants.

No! Their one-on-one time was too short. "Then I guess we'll be having 'working-to-build-a-relationship' lunches during the day," he suggested.

"Despite my protest, I like the sound of that." She laughed, and her killer smile reached her eyes. He got to his feet as she began to stroll away with Sweet Pepper.

"Miss Knicely," he called after her. When she whirled around, he asked, "Are you and the ladies coming later for the barbecue?"

"Absolutely, Mr. Whittington," she said, then continued on her way.

Folding his arms, he leaned against the porch and watched her and the pooch disappear through the park. Her presence, her smile, and her sass filled his heart with contentment, and he wanted more of it. If Aunt Tweet was part of the package, he would take the deal—plus the dog.

———

Tabitha felt refreshed after the leisurely walk to Marcus's house. But their brief private moment only left her heart and mind playing tug-of-war. Tabitha wanted him to be in her life, and it had nothing to do with him helping her with Aunt Tweet, but it was because of Aunt Tweet that Tabitha couldn't put her all into a relationship. Marcus had seen firsthand that her aunt was a handful.

She opened the door as Rachel glided down the stairs with the pure artistry of a *Project Runway* model, dressed in a romper with an airy, see-through skirt attached at the waist. Her baby sister had a walk that turned heads—men with lusty eyes and ladies with envy.

"I'm hungry and ready to go," Rachel said.

Kym walked out of the kitchen and exchanged smirks with Tabitha. "Are we talking about barbecue or Marcus's brother?"

Hmph. "Both. Let Demetrius decide if he's ready for me," Rachel boasted.

"Aren't you and Kym leaving tonight?"

Rachel grinned and lifted an eyebrow. "Even better to leave a lasting memory."

Sometimes she wished she had Rachel's confidence when it came to men. Her sister knew how to play the game. Tabitha didn't want to put the energy into being a player or the center of attention.

Before they stepped into the car, Kym pulled Tabitha to the side. "This morning I watched Aunt Tweet read her Bible."

"Okay." She gave her sister a clueless stare, waiting to hear the problem. "And?"

"It was upside down," Kym said in disbelief with a frown, "and she looked as if she was studying it. Do you think, maybe, she can't remember how to read now?"

Tabitha understood her sister's concern. "Don't know. It's possible. A couple of times while watching game shows, she's asked me what they said. At first, I thought she was becoming hard of hearing, then I figured out she wasn't understanding certain phrases anymore. It's heart-wrenching!" She shook her head. "I guess as her brain cells die, she'll become more confused."

"Her deterioration is hard to watch." Kym's eyes teared. "Maybe I'll look into the preventive trials—for all the other Aunt Tweets out there."

"I know." Wrapping their arms around each other's shoulders, they walked in sync as they had as little girls. Aunt Tweet and Rachel were already in the car. After putting Marcus's company's address into her GPS, she drove off. "Wow, he does live close."

Twelve minutes later, Tabitha turned into a crowded parking lot in front of Whittington Janitorial Services.

Tabitha felt a sense of pride for the Whittingtons' accomplishments as single, successful black entrepreneurs, employing seventy workers. The big white stone building bore their name in bold maroon lettering. Getting out, the ladies followed the smell of barbecue and trail of voices. Not surprisingly, the door was locked. Tabitha rang a doorbell. Minutes later, a young woman appeared and cracked the door open while balancing a plate in one hand. "Hi. May I help you?"

"They're my guests, Casey," Marcus said, walking up behind the woman.

"Oh, sorry, Mr. Whittington." She stepped back, then disappeared down the hall.

"Good afternoon, ladies." He kissed Aunt Tweet's cheek, then Tabitha's. She felt the softness of his lips and closed her eyes to enjoy it. She could imagine them cuddling to watch a movie, or talking in front of a roaring fire, or doing absolutely nothing. The more she protested a relationship between them, the more she craved it.

"This place is huge—and clean," Tabitha complimented as they trailed him inside.

He grunted. "We're a cleaning company. It had better be. If my place of business isn't sparkling, then I can't sell my services to prospective clients."

"Good point." Tabitha nodded. The landscape changed when the group rounded a corner. The party was in the open space of a loading dock where tables were laden with desserts, drinks, and barbecue. Outside in the sun, children played in a bounce house, and the adults lounged in chairs and ate at the picnic tables. The smell of barbecue tickled her nose.

"Want a tour?" Marcus asked.

"Food first," Rachel mumbled. Aunt Tweet seconded that.

"Give Tabitha the tour," Kym said as she and the others headed to the tables to survey their food choices. "We skipped breakfast for this, so it's about to go down."

Tabitha laughed as Marcus linked his fingers through hers and tugged her outside. A group of small children ran up to him for hugs or vied for his attention. Employees waved, nodded, or saluted him with cans of soda or bottled water.

"You're well loved." She used her free hand to shield her eyes from the sun as she verified his handsomeness that she'd cataloged up close a few hours earlier on his porch. Tabitha didn't know what possessed her to pay him a visit. Maybe it was nothing more than a desire to be near him. His presence was like a balm. She smiled to herself.

"You're probably hungry too. Have a seat, and I'll fix your plate. Are you a hot dog, hamburger, ribs, or chicken type of woman?" He wiggled his brow mischievously.

"I'll let you figure me out, so choose very carefully, Mr. Whittington," Tabitha flirted back. She was losing the battle to push him away. Her heart pounded wildly whenever she was near him.

———

With paper plates and utensils in hand, Marcus strolled in the direction of the grill. "What's ready, Chess?"

"Chicken and burgers." He wielded his barbecue tongs as if he were a master chef.

"I'll take both on each plate."

"Is that your lady friend?" his employee asked casually, peeping over his shoulder.

"Friends—definitely." The "his lady" part was a work in progress. Marcus smiled at the thought of him and Tabitha officially being a couple, not her caregiver. He rejoined her minutes later with a full plate.

"You don't expect me to eat all of this, do you?" She blinked, then chuckled before accepting his offering.

"Whatever's left, take back to the house." They bowed their heads and gave thanks for their meals. "How's Aunt Tweet doing after her church experience?" He was the first to speak.

"She seems to be in perfect peace. What about you?" Her brows knitted together with concern.

"What do you mean?"

"Your expressions were all over the place yesterday—distracted and confused. This morning—"

So she *could* read him. "I saw you and everything was all right in my world." Feeling slightly embarrassed, Marcus looked the other way before meeting her brown eyes again. "Was I that transparent?"

She chewed then swallowed her baked beans before nodding. "Honestly, I thought you were going to beat Aunt Tweet to the altar for prayer, but you acted as if you were scared to make a move."

"I was trying my best not to—" Marcus stopped midsentence. Latrice was strolling carefree through the warehouse, headed outside to the patio. While she anchored Vance on one hip, she kept Little Victor close by her side. The boy's eyes grew wide with excitement when he saw the other children, then Marcus. Breaking free, he made a beeline to Marcus's table.

Lifting the child on his lap, Marcus asked how he was doing and listened as Little Victor spoke and pointed to the swings. Latrice appeared moments later. "Hi, Mr. Whittington." Was there an unspoken tension between them, or was it just him feeling uncomfortable? Whatever the vibe, now was not the time to revisit any discussion of her ex. He hugged her son one last time and set him down, then made introductions.

"Nice to meet you," Tabitha said, unaware his employee and the woman's boyfriend—ex-boyfriend, father of her sons, or whatever was her current situation with Victor—were thorns in his side.

When Latrice and her sons strolled away, Tabitha tilted her head and studied him. "What's bothering you?"

"You just met her."

"Oh." Her eyes widened, then a blank expression flashed on her face.

"Before you even think it—no, those aren't my children. I don't have affairs with employees. My problem with her is rescuing a damsel in distress."

"O-okay...like me."

"No, no." He shook his head. "My interest in you is personal."

"But it didn't start out that way," she quietly mumbled. "I know I was a hot mess in distress."

Marcus wiped his mouth and set down his utensil before resting his hand on top of hers. "My attraction to you began day one."

"So did your annoyance," she teased with a chuckle.

"You got me." He grinned. "We got started on the wrong foot. I may not be walking in your shoes, but I'm right there beside you, not because you asked for help, but because I want to be."

The adoration on her face made Marcus take a deep breath and exhale slowly. Tabitha had a way of jumbling his thoughts, but he wanted to get her take on the situation with Latrice. He shifted in his seat to shake the deep trance her brown eyes held him in.

"Listen." He leaned closer and lowered his voice. "I'm not trying to brag, but I think my brother and I do a great job of giving back to the community. We hire ex-felons—except sex offenders—and pay them more than minimum wage. We provide transportation to job sites and offer on-site day care for our employees." He paused and scrunched his nose. "Sounds like I'm boasting, huh?"

Shaking her head, Tabitha gave him a warm smile. "Sounds like you're a great guy, but I have it on good authority that you can be a little rough around the edges."

"Fake news." They laughed together. She was a good stress reliever. "Anyway, Latrice's boyfriend is one I took under my wing. I gave him one chance after another, but the brother was unappreciative. I had to let him go."

Tabitha bobbed her head. "I get it. So the mother of his children is mad at you about it?"

"Actually, she's not mad at all. Last week, the dude got arrested *again* and is in jail. Latrice wants me to pay his bond." He grunted. "Look at me. Do I look like a fool?"

"No. You look like a smart businessman with a kind heart. I take it you turned her down."

He wanted to ask her *Wouldn't you?* But he might not like her answer, considering Tabitha was more compassionate than he was. The way she doted on Aunt Tweet, Marcus doubted she would turn anyone down who needed help.

"Yep. My decision was final." He tapped his finger on the table as if he were typing periods at the end of a sentence. "But Latrice seems to think otherwise. The Sunday sermon on forgiveness brought Victor's situation to the forefront of my mind. I was mentally gripping that pew, silently shouting 'No way!'"

"But now? Did something change?" She scooped up a bite of potato salad and chewed, waiting for his answer. For once, neither one of them was looking over their shoulders to monitor Aunt Tweet's whereabouts. Her sisters were on duty, allowing them to focus on each other's concerns.

Marcus shrugged and twisted his jaw before making his confession. "If forgiving him means helping Victor one last time, I'd rather look the other way. But the message was like a screwdriver drilling deeper into my psyche. It messed me up! God wants me to forgive seventy times seven… or seven times seventy? Whatever the formula, same answer." He continued his rant. "I thought Sunday sermons are supposed to be inspiring, not necessarily Bible-based. I couldn't wait for the sermon to end and to get out of there. That didn't help because even then, it seemed like the preacher's voice followed me from room to room. My parents didn't raise any fools." He swiped his bottled water and took a swig.

"Maybe you're overthinking this," Tabitha softly said. "We're both caregivers in a sense. My charge is a loved one. The object of your frustration—"

"Is no blood relation to me," Marcus said, "so I think I should be off the hook, right?"

Tilting her head, Tabitha seemed to study him. "Do you have to have a reason to do good?"

He gave her question some thought. She was right. "No," Marcus admitted.

"Just like you're doing good for me and Aunt Tweet." She rested her hand over his again. "If Victor is in jail, surely he could use some goodness right now. Too many of our black men are incarcerated for no criminal offense. Rescue him." She shrugged. "That's just my two cents, but I'm not in your shoes." She snickered and Marcus got the joke.

"I knew there was a reason why I liked you. Beauty, brains, and a soft heart—the best combination."

Wrapping his hand over hers, he brought it to his lips and brushed a kiss on it. He watched as she shivered, while he concealed his own reaction. He couldn't wait to kiss her.

"Stop flirting with me," Tabitha teasingly scolded. "We're having a serious conversation, and I know how it feels to be frustrated. I live in that state every day. I signed up to be my aunt's caregiver thinking I knew what I was in for. I didn't."

She sighed. "But here I am. Aunt Tweet's needs supersede the Knicely sisters' lives as long Aunt Tweet is alive, which I hope is a long time," she added quickly. "Sometimes I go to bed so exhausted… I've become a light sleeper, listening for any movement from her room. Now, I notice her hygiene isn't the best, so I'm helping her with bathing. I tell myself it's a pleasure to take care of her as she was always there for us." She paused and glanced over her shoulder. "Sometimes I don't have any pleasure in doing certain tasks."

Suddenly, the weight on her shoulders seemed to reappear and Marcus took the blame. "Aunt Tweet gives me a reason to spend time with you. Otherwise, we might never have crossed paths."

"Marcus, I will never regret how we met—never." She smiled, stood, and gathered their discarded plates and cups. "We'd better head back. My sisters have already given me a half-hour respite."

"What about the tour?"

"I'll come back—promise." She smiled.

When they strolled into the warehouse, they were surprised to see children gathered around Aunt Tweet.

"They've tricked her into reading them a story." He chuckled. "They love story time."

Tabitha gnawed on her lips. "Her Alzheimer's is preventing her from recognizing certain words."

"But she's pulling it off." Taking her hand, they slowly approached the group. Even though Aunt Tweet had an opened storybook on her lap, the tale she was weaving wasn't coming from it.

"The little boys and girls had a contest to see who could whistle the loudest and longest," Aunt Tweet said.

"Who won?" Gregory Harvey waved his hand in the air. He was the five-year-old son of a new employee.

"I did." Aunt Tweet's eyes sparkled as her audience laughed. "They would whistle after they'd done their schoolwork, or I would keep them after school."

Tabitha nodded and tried to whistle like her aunt. "Every day, I'm learning more about my aunt's younger years," she said to Marcus. "Thank you for the food and company. I need to get back home so my sisters can pack for their flight."

Now? Marcus didn't want to see her go. He wrapped her in his arms and gave her a hug. He stepped back, realizing his actions had shocked her.

"What was that for?" Her smile melted his heart.

"*I* needed that." He winked, then escorted them to their car.

Chapter 20

THE NEXT MORNING, TABITHA'S LIMBS REFUSED TO MOVE. SHE WAS tired after the long weekend with her sisters.

Rolling out of bed, she dragged her body across the hall. After hearing a light snore, Tabitha returned to her room and rushed through a shower. Next, she gave Aunt Tweet the sponge bath that was overdue from the previous night. She dressed Aunt Tweet, then admired her handiwork. Her aunt looked polished—minus the big, floppy red hat. Remembering Sweet Pepper, she hurried back downstairs to let him out.

How did working mothers do this day in and out? she wondered while preparing a quick breakfast. Single moms especially deserved an award. She had one elderly great-aunt, yet Tabitha woke up feeling exhausted, as though she mothered a house full of children and tried to remember to do mundane tasks. Half an hour later, the dog was in his kennel, her aunt was color coordinated, and Tabitha opened the door.

Marcus's presence startled her, then gave her a jolt of energy. He was leaning against his car with his ankles crossed, holding a flower. Her morning had just gotten better. He pushed off the hood and took long strides toward her.

"Morning." She stared at his five o'clock shadow, which had thickened overnight. She yearned to feel its texture but denied herself the temptation. "What are you doing here?"

"I wanted to see you before we both went in opposite directions today." He handed her the rose, kissed her cheek first, then her aunt's. Without another word, he strolled back to his car with a stride that made her lift an eyebrow.

That gesture kept a smile on Tabitha's face as she drove Aunt Tweet to Bermuda Place, then headed to Ceyle-Norman to sign out more physician samples. Breezing through the lobby, she waved at Ava Elise. The woman always inspired her to smile. Tabitha missed seeing her every day to soak in her encouraging tidbits about life.

"Hey. How was your weekend?" Ava Elise's smile was warm. "Did you get some much-needed rest?"

Tabitha released a mock laugh. "Anything but that. Saturday was the neighborhood's summer kickoff. We attended church on Sunday, and then enjoyed a barbecue at my neighbor's company on Monday. I wish it were Friday already instead of Tuesday."

Ava Elise chuckled. "How did your aunt interact with your sisters?"

"Good. They got a chance to see firsthand some of the things I'd mentioned about her behavior. She even wandered off at the summer kickoff."

"Oh no." Her friend covered her mouth in shock, then removed her hand. "Well, don't scratch off a nursing facility from your list yet. With them gone, there goes your extra helping hand."

Although Tabitha liked Ava Elise, the mention of a nursing home for Aunt Tweet was almost offensive. "I'm determined to hang in there. I don't know how much longer my aunt might live anyway."

"What do you mean?" Ava Elise gasped. "Is her health declining that rapidly? What's really going on?"

Shaking her head, Tabitha wished she knew. "At church on Sunday, my aunt mentioned no regrets and then joined others at the altar for prayer and to be baptized. I've never seen anything like it." She sighed, because she didn't have answers. "Then I got to thinking—maybe she was asking me if I had any regrets."

Her former trainer frowned.

"I can't help but wonder if she was asking me if I had regrets, either about taking care of her, or about my life." She paused. "I do have some regrets. I had hoped taking a job that required less travel and handpicking an upscale adult day care would make the transition easier, plus give us more quality time together, but each day makes that more doubtful."

Tabitha stared at nothing, thoughtful. "There is nothing easy about being a caregiver. I leave one job to go home to another one until Aunt

Tweet goes to sleep. I never thought being a caregiver for someone you love could be so challenging and exhausting."

Ava Elise reached for some tissues, but Tabitha stopped her. "Nope, I refuse to have a breakdown today." She mustered a smile. "I better go so I can get on the road."

"Now, that's the right attitude of a top sales rep." Ava Elise gave her a thumbs-up. "You know it's about to get crazy in the field with reps striving to make those bonuses. If a nursing facility is out of the question, you might want to join an Alzheimer's Association support group."

Aunt Tweet's doctor in Philly had recommended that too. At the time, the Knicely sisters had balked at the suggestion. They had each other and the situation seemed to be under control. That was then. This was now.

"Have a nurse's aide come in the evenings for a couple hours, so you can get some rest," Ava Elise suggested.

"I would have to think long and hard about having strangers in my house." Tabitha turned to check out samples.

"Don't rule out that option. God can provide you peace and rest through help from others. I'll be praying that you receive both," Ava Elise said softly. She turned and continued down the hall to the conference room, where another training class was waiting to get started.

Throughout the day, Marcus revisited Tabitha's mind whenever she was sitting in traffic or waiting in a doctor's office. Her heart warmed. She thought she didn't have room in her hectic schedule to date. Somehow, he had effortlessly changed that. If she could rearrange her schedule to see him, she would.

⁓

Demetrius was in the office when Marcus arrived. The good mood he possessed earlier after seeing Tabitha had taken flight. No question, his brother would give him grief about the biggest mistake he was about to make in his life, be called the biggest fool ever.

Yet Tabitha's gentle nudge toward doing good for the sake of just doing it seemed to settle the turmoil in his heart. His parents had taught their sons to be kind and be of good character, regardless of how people treated them.

Reluctantly, he accepted his fate to pay Victor's bond. As long as he convinced himself it was for Latrice and the boys, he felt better about it.

"What's up?" Demetrius was too upbeat this morning. What energy drink did he have?

"You don't want to know," Marcus mumbled without making eye contact.

"What's wrong with you?" His brother leaned across his desk. "I thought the way you were hovering over Tabitha yesterday, you'd be grinning from ear to ear. And what's with that hairy stuff on your face?"

"It's called growing a beard," Marcus said.

"Why?"

"Because she likes it." He didn't have to look at Demetrius to know his brother was amused. Exhaling, he prepared himself to break the news. "Ah, listen, I made a decision about something, and I know you're not going to agree with it, but hear me out."

"As long as it's not taking money away from our business or affecting our business, then it's your business." Demetrius folded his arms and leaned back in his chair.

"I'm glad you said that because it does involve *my* money. I decided to put up the money for Victor's bond." Marcus counted to three and braced for his brother's thunder.

Demetrius snarled before he roared, "What? If my name were on your bank account, I would freeze the assets."

"I know." Marcus scratched his jaw.

"I can't believe my younger brother, business partner, and a college graduate with an MBA is being played as a fool." He banged his fist on his desk. Demetrius was beyond mad.

Ouch. That hurt, even if the punch wasn't to his jaw. His brother was right, but Marcus had to believe something good would come out of it. Besides, as long as Victor showed up for court, he would get his money back, so in a sense, he wouldn't be out the money. If Victor skipped town, then Marcus would hunt him down himself. He sighed, then called Latrice with his decision.

"God bless you, Mr. Whittington." She sniffed.

From Marcus's viewpoint, it looked like Victor was getting all the blessings. "Right. Give me the particulars, and he'll be out before the end of the day."

Even though Marcus agreed to do it, his mind tried to overrule the generosity he had planned. He waited until the last minute to get a cashier's check from his bank, then hoped a construction slowdown would prevent him from making it to St. Louis County Courthouse—anything to extend his former employee's confinement another day. Unfortunately, everything seemed to be in Victor's favor. There were no delays getting to Clayton to pay the bond, a parking space was available in front of the building with the meter paid for an hour and forty-five minutes, and Marcus didn't run into anyone familiar who could engage him in conversation and eat up time until the office was closed. So he begrudgingly conducted his business, and minutes later, he watched as an officer removed Victor's cuffs and escorted him out of confinement. When he met Marcus's eyes, a cocky grin spread across his face.

"Well, well, well, if it isn't Mr. Big Shot, coming to my rescue. I'm sure I didn't put a dent into your savings."

Marcus refused to take the bait from this loser. "Trust me, I'm doing this as a favor for Latrice and your sons." He folded his arms.

"Me and her ain't together no more."

He cringed at the use of improper English, but this was not a mentoring moment. "Good for her. A shame for your boys." He snorted. "And for the record, your bond money came from my children's college fund."

"Right. You ain't got no kids."

"Not yet, but one day I will." He thought about Tabitha. Could she be the one? She was the perfect candidate. "As a matter of fact, my lady friend was on board with helping you." Shaking his head, he continued his march to the door, then felt an overwhelming power that could only have been God stopping him from taking another step.

Gripping his keys, he spun around. "I'm sure you don't have bus money, cab fare, or an Uber driver on standby. Would you like a ride somewhere?"

"I don't have nowhere to go." Victor's rough exterior slipped, and his vulnerability peeked through.

"Come on. I'll drop you off at a shelter, and you can figure out your life from there," he offered.

"Nah. I got this."

"Suit yourself." Marcus shrugged and walked away.

Chapter 21

Tuesday evening, Tabitha craved a nap—fifteen minutes tops—to get rid of the tension headache that had lingered all afternoon. Maybe she could do it with one eye open, watching Aunt Tweet.

Her aunt's appetite was increasing while her interest in cooking was wavering, even cooking the occasional hot breakfast on the weekends. Tabitha prepared a quick meal of chicken, pasta, and stir-fry vegetables. She wondered if Marcus would stop by. When the doorbell rang half an hour later, her heart fluttered as she tried to stifle a yawn before opening the door.

He stepped into her foyer and gave her a hug. *Umm.* The hugs were better than the sweet kiss on the cheek. Reluctantly, she broke their embrace to close the door. He followed her to the kitchen, where Aunt Tweet hadn't moved from her spot at the table, but she was chewing on something.

Tabitha squinted. "What are you munching on?" Her aunt chuckled but didn't answer, so she asked again.

"I found a piece of candy."

"Where?" Not a sweets eater, Tabitha didn't have candy jars in her house and especially not on the table.

Her aunt frowned as if she was straining her brain. "At the school where I teach."

Taking a peep into her aunt's purse, which rested on her lap, Tabitha was shocked to find an arsenal of peppermints and butterscotch candies. Clearly, the staffers at the adult care needed to supervise Aunt Tweet near the candy jar. "Dinner's almost ready, so please don't eat another piece."

Her aunt nodded, and Marcus brushed a kiss on her aunt's cheek. "Need any help?" he asked.

You have no idea. He must have read her mind because he scooted her over at the sink and washed his hands. He searched the cabinets for plates and glasses, then set the table.

"I should have brought some barbecue. We had plenty left over," he said.

"Next time, do that, Mr. Whittington," Tabitha said, recalling the sauce that melted on her tongue. Yep. She definitely wouldn't have minded a second serving.

"Noted."

Soon, they were gathered around the table. Marcus gave thanks for their meal and asked the Lord to bless it, then they all said amen. "This is tasty," he told her. "I have no complaints."

"So...did you bail out Victor?" She shoved a forkful of vegetables in her mouth and waited for his answer. He eyed her aunt and seemed hesitant to answer. "It's okay. She's doesn't know who we're talking about."

His shoulders slumped. "Yes, and I'd hoped, wished, and thought I'd get a glimpse of gratitude from him. Nope." He shook his head. "The only way I can keep from regretting my good deed is to convince myself I did it for the sake of his children. I dipped into my children's college fund to post bond for the ungrateful loser." He caught himself and looked up. "Sorry. Bad day."

He had started a children's fund? Immediately, she chided herself for her own pity party earlier. Her day had been busy, so busy she'd skipped lunch, and when her energy level plummeted, the fatigue from her weekend's activities hit hard. Her fatigue was physical, and she could bounce back after a good night's sleep.

On the other hand, Marcus was mentally conflicted. What could she say to ease his turmoil? She doubted he would find rest when he closed his eyes tonight. The vulnerable side of Marcus was just as endearing as his warm personality. Both were attractive.

"You did the right thing." She reassured him as a yawn escaped before she could trap it. "Sorry, it's not the company." She smiled and hoped her eyes twinkled to back it up.

He wiped his mouth, then clasped her hand. "Thanks for the pep talk. Why don't you take a nap on the sofa? I'll load the dishwasher."

What kind of host would she be if she did that? But common sense told her to take his help for her body's sake, so she pushed aside proper etiquette and accepted Marcus's offer. "Just a power nap for a few minutes." After that, she would check her emails to confirm her appointments for the next day and review the doctors' bios before meeting with them. The last task of the night would be tending to Aunt Tweet's needs before going to bed.

She turned on her aunt's favorite game show. With Aunt Tweet at one end of the sofa, Tabitha cuddled up at the other. Instantly, her mind faded to black.

When she woke, the house was quiet, and all the lights were off, except for the lamps in the den. Sitting up, she got her bearings and checked the time. Her nap had been two hours! She jumped to her feet and was about to race upstairs and check on Aunt Tweet when a note taped to her refrigerator stopped her.

You really are a sleeping beauty. Judging from your cute light snore, you needed your rest.

"Hmph. I do not snore," she mumbled.

I tagged along with Aunt Tweet as she walked Sweet Pepper. She said she was going to bed. She looked tired too, so I don't think she'll be sleepwalking tonight. A few times, I caught you smiling. I'm heading home, so I can have some sweet dreams too. Oh, and thanks for letting me know it's okay that Victor doesn't appreciate what I did for him. I guess we can say God knows and I'll get a star or something.

Marcus

Marcus pointed his remote to the flat screen in his man cave and clicked off Sports Midwest. Tabitha was good for him—they were good for each other. Whether she vented or not, he had to interpret her silence, read her body language, and be on guard for any mood swings. When he griped about Victor, she listened. He had every reason to complain. His mother taught him and his brother to say *please* and *thank you* growing up. He was still waiting to hear those words from Victor.

Getting to his feet, he took a deep breath. Obsessing over the situation with Victor was only going to cause him grief, so he shut down all thoughts of his ex-employee.

He decided to take a stroll through his neighborhood—again. The night air was warm, but every now and then, a cool breeze swayed the trees. It wasn't officially summer, but the evenings were longer.

Instead of allowing Victor's situation to taunt him, Marcus walked and let his mind recall pleasant thoughts of being at Tabitha's house. He automatically smiled.

One minute, Aunt Tweet was content watching *Wheel of Fortune*, the next minute she was antsy, wanting to take the puppy for a walk.

Not letting her out of his sight, knowing what happened when anyone did, he'd put a leash on Sweet Pepper and off they went, not waking Tabitha.

"I can't remember Mama's name," Aunt Tweet had said with no prompting on his part.

His heart dropped at her admission. He couldn't imagine not recognizing his parents or forgetting their names. Looping his arm through hers, he rested her hand on his arm and patted it. "It's okay. Tabitha can tell you."

She paused. "Who?"

"Your niece," he explained. How much had she forgotten? Physically, no one would know she suffered with dementia symptoms. Ask her a few questions or listen to her ramblings, and the evidence that something wasn't quite right was as glaring as a flashlight.

"When God speaks to you, you'd better listen." She paused when the puppy took a potty break, and she looked up at him. "Don't worry about doing good for folks. Let them live with the regrets. Not you."

Marcus froze. So she had followed their conversation at the dinner table. The dog tugged her along, so he took a few strides to catch up. "Aunt Tweet, you're remembering more than you're letting on," he joked.

She chuckled. "I forget a lot," she said sadly, "but I'll never forget my name or true love. That will last a lifetime."

"Are you trying to tell me something?"

"I just did. You have to pay attention, young man. Whew." She was becoming winded. "I'm tired now. I guess I'm getting too old to teach every day."

As Marcus steered her back toward Tabitha's house, he got an idea. She'd seemed to be in her element when she'd interacted with the little ones at his on-site child care. Maybe she would enjoy telling them a story a couple times a week. That could be a temporary distraction so Tabitha could relax in the employee lounge or do some homework. The big benefit was he could be near Tabitha. Would she go for it?

When he returned to Tabitha's, she was still knocked out. She looked so peaceful. He hated to disturb her. Aunt Tweet said good night and disappeared upstairs while Marcus put Sweet Pepper back in the kennel for the night.

Grabbing a nearby throw off a chair, he gently covered Tabitha. Leaning down, he was careful as he brushed his lips on her cheek. That's when he heard her faint snore. He smiled.

Once Marcus stole his kiss, he scribbled a note for her and left. He couldn't help but reflect on what Aunt Tweet had said about having no regrets. Currently, his only one had been coming to the rescue of a man who acted like he didn't want to be saved.

One thing was for sure, he didn't have any regrets about how he'd met Tabitha. Whether she admitted it or not, they were building a relationship—one that would be ripe by the time her aunt moved in with Rachel. Then look out, Miss Tabitha Knicely. Nothing would stand in the way of real dates.

Chapter 22

THAT WAS SWEET OF YOU LAST NIGHT. BUT I WISH YOU'D WOKEN ME UP, Tabitha texted Marcus the next morning as she waited in the lobby to speak with Dr. Roland. She blushed as she added I DO NOT snore.

In reality, she was glad he hadn't woken her. She hadn't felt that well rested since she'd started with Ceyle-Norman. She had awakened before the alarm and checked on Aunt Tweet. Although her aunt was resting, Tabitha got her up to bathe and dress her, then cooked a hot breakfast. By the time they walked out the door, Tabitha felt as if she had consumed a couple of energy drinks.

She read Marcus's reply. Happy Wednesday, sleepyhead. I have the evidence. I recorded it, and it's probably gone viral by now on social media.

Tabitha blinked and panicked. What? Please tell me you're kidding.

I am. Just said it to make you smile.

You made my heart drop first. When Dr. Roland approached, she shoved her phone back into her briefcase and switched to business mode. "Good morning. I'm following up to see if you feel our drug would be a good fit for your patients."

He signaled her to follow him back to his office, where he said, "I do have some concerns about one active ingredient interacting with a couple of medications." He frowned and seemed to be contemplating his next words. "At least ten of my patients could benefit from the drugs. Leave me samples and I'll monitor them. If they can tolerate the medicine, then I'll prescribe it for them."

She exhaled. "Thank you." Ten wasn't a small number. She could exceed her quota and bump up her bonus if the doctor saw positive results and refilled their prescriptions in this quarter.

Back in the car, she checked her voice messages for missed calls from doctors' offices—none—then her texts. Marcus had sent one after she'd put her phone away.

Seriously, I slept better knowing you got some rest.

Every caregiver should have someone like Marcus Whittington to make them smile amid the frustration, the exhaustion, and the brink of losing all sanity.

Sorry. Had to go earlier—business.

Can you talk now? he texted back almost immediately.

Yes.

Her phone rang instantly. "I would really like to treat you to lunch."

She gnawed on her lipstick while deliberating whether she could make it happen with stops in St. Charles, St. Peters, and O'Fallon, cities far west of where they lived. Yet Tabitha couldn't resist seeing him, if only for five minutes. "My aunt told me long ago never to turn down a free meal when a gentleman offers."

"So is that a yes?" He sounded hopeful.

"It's a wish, but I'm stuck out west for the rest of the day."

"Then I'll come to you before I meet with one of my clients. Name the place and time."

The man was so easy to like—and love. If only the timing were better.

⟶

Grinning, Marcus stood from his desk. "I'm out for the rest of the day," he advised Demetrius.

His brother stopped tapping on the keyboard and gave him a side-eye. "Admit it. You're in love."

"Nothing to deny there. I am," he said softly, "but Tabitha's not ready to hear it."

Demetrius was quiet. Something was on his mind. "No denying the attraction between you two, but…"

"But what?"

"Before you flip, consider whether her feelings aren't based on… Well, are you sure she's not using you as a babysitter?" Demetrius looked concerned.

"I guess you'll find out when it's Rachel's turn." Marcus smirked. "Don't think I didn't notice you watching her sister and putting in a lot of effort to show that you weren't. And I've also noticed you step out of the office when a certain ringtone chimes."

Marcus patted the keys in his pocket and checked for his wallet. "Have a good day." He whistled until he reached the door, then his amusement exploded into laughter. "I do believe I've upped you, Bro," he mumbled to himself, closing the door as he spied Chess walking down the hall. "Any problems at the work sites?"

"Nope. You know I run a tight ship." Chess gave a mock salute, then continued toward the supply room.

"Not too tight that you don't respect other employees."

"Yes, sir."

Although he had pending business matters downtown, his craving to see Tabitha was worse than any hunger pangs he had ever experienced. Their agreed meeting spot was Chick-fil-A on Mid Rivers Mall Drive.

Whittington Janitorial Services was centrally located off I-170, so he could get to the three major interstates in no time. Twenty-five minutes later, he reached his destination when he turned into the restaurant's parking lot. He looked for her car, then remembered she drove a company-issued blue Taurus. He parked.

Once he entered, Marcus noticed her right away. Her light-gray suit was classy and professional. The heels were high, showcasing a pair of shapely legs. Apparently, she had a group of admirers and was unaware of their interest. She hadn't noticed him either as she texted away on her phone. Suddenly, as if sensing his approach, she glanced up and smiled. "Hey. Give me a sec." She finished her text, then slipped her phone into her bag. "Ready."

Staring into her eyes, Marcus knew his brother had called it right. He was ready to reveal his feelings, but would she believe him after less than two months? He decided to tuck away his declaration until he could no longer hold it and when he felt she would return the sentiment.

Still, he had to let the men in the corner know she was taken, so he placed his arm around her waist. He grinned when she leaned in to him as a playful gesture, but he didn't let go. "Have you ordered?"

"And deprive you of springing for lunch? I wouldn't dare," she joked, batting her lashes.

"And I don't want to be deprived of treating you like the lady you are." He winked, and they approached the counter together to place their orders.

After paying the bill, the cashier gave them a numbered tent, so the server could find them. Thanking the young man, Marcus accepted it and guided her to a vacant table.

"How's your day going?" they asked each other at the same time, then chuckled.

"I'm always better when I see you," he answered, which caused her to smile, and that made him grin.

"I'm having a typical day, meeting with doctors or bribing gate-keepers to get to them to give my three-minute spiel, leave samples, or encourage those who have them to write prescriptions for targeted patients." She paused when their meals were delivered in record time. Taking her hand, he gave thanks for their food and asked the Lord to remove all impurities, then they dug in.

"Sorry I fell asleep on you last night, but I've been exhausted lately. I don't know if it's a combination of summer heating up early, the demands of the new job and being a first-time caregiver, or a vitamin deficiency."

"I would guess all of the above. You have a lot on your plate, and I'm not talking about food." Marcus maintained a straight face, wanting her to see there was no pun intended.

Tabitha nodded. "Yeah, I know. A woman at the company suggested I join a support group." She sighed. "Maybe it's time. Aunt Tweet's doctor in Philly said the same thing. Honestly, my sisters and I were in denial it would get to this point."

Marcus squeezed his lips together to keep from commenting, but the words spilled from his mouth anyway. "I thought I was your support group." He dipped his fry in ketchup to mask his bruised ego. He wanted to be the person she could depend on.

She rested her hand on top of his. "You are." She captured his eyes and held them. "When you're around, I have to keep reminding myself my aunt is my concern, not yours." Tabitha shook her head and her long mane bounced side to side. "Every time I make demands on your time, I'm taking you away from doing something important."

Her eyes pleaded for understanding before her lashes fluttered and she looked away. "You make me want to be selfish, and I'm trying my best not to," she said so softly an untrained ear might have missed it.

Not him. He was in tune with her and caught the sadness. This was proof his brother was wrong about Tabitha using him. She had too much class and compassion for that. "Hey," he said a couple of times to regain her attention. "I'm good. Trust me."

"I'd be disappointed if I couldn't be there for you." Marcus chuckled. "Speaking of your aunt, it seems strange not having her nearby." He bit into his grilled chicken sandwich and chewed, watching Tabitha dip her chicken strip into the sauce. "While you've been busy feeling guilty about being selfish, I've been selfishly thinking about options to give you more downtime—for naps, minus the snoring," he said, ducking as she balled up a napkin and threw it at him. "Seriously. What do you think about having Aunt Tweet read a couple times a week at the warehouse to the children? She seemed to enjoy herself."

"You mean telling them stories? I've seen her get frustrated trying to read her Bible." Her mouth turned down with sadness. "That sounds like more work for me. Once I get home in the evening, I don't want to leave, but if she likes it, I think it's important to do stuff that makes her happy while she can remember."

"Yes!" He balled a fist in victory. "If I notice it's too much for you or her, then we'll think of something else." In his peripheral vision, he noted admiring stares coming from a table not far from them. He grunted.

She tilted her head and seemed to study him. "You amaze me, Mr. Whittington..." She seemed to want to say more but switched gears, keeping her thoughts to herself. "Aunt Tweet said God was talking to her on Sunday."

Marcus squeezed his lips in thought. "Maybe the Lord's been talking to me to forgive Victor of his attitude and help him."

"I'm jealous." She dabbed her last waffle fry in ketchup. "I mean, God seems to be speaking to everyone but me."

"Trust me, if He's trying to get your attention, Jesus won't let you rest. I've done my deed, so you won't see me back in church for a long time."

She looked disappointed. "If I ask you to go with me, you won't come?"

"Woman, don't call my bluff. When it comes to you, I'll backtrack in a minute." Marcus wiped his hands and mouth, then pushed his trash aside. "To tell the truth, I've near felt God urging me to do something like I did with Victor."

After wiping her hands, Tabitha checked the time, then relaxed. "I've got about fifteen minutes, then I have to get on the road."

"You know, despite the time crunch, this is nice—us having lunch. I guess we can call this a pre-real date."

Tabitha slapped his hand. "You won't give up, will you?"

"I can't, don't want to, and won't." Again, he kept a straight face, so she would know he was serious.

"Somehow, you're making a believer out of me. Although I still don't think this is an ideal way to start a relationship—me as a caregiver. When Aunt Tweet isn't at Bermuda Place, she's with me."

"I already knew that when I signed on as *your* caregiver, but I've seen your kindness, love, and support of your loved one. I'm attracted to all those qualities and more."

"You make me wonder what it would be like in a real relationship with you." She exhaled. "But I'm not convinced it would work."

"If there is even a hint of a challenge in what you just stated, I plan to convince you otherwise." Marcus smirked. "You can't stop caring about Aunt Tweet, but neither can I cut off my feelings for you. Trust me, your aunt can't get in the way of this." He escorted her outside, then opened her car door. "I'll bring dinner tonight, so don't worry about cooking."

"Did you hear a word of what I said?" She looked up from her seat.

"Your heart was louder, and I have selective hearing." He grinned, then leaned down.

Tabitha lifted her cheek for the expected kiss. Instead, he cupped her soft chin in his hand and brought her lips to his. The kiss was too brief. "You have been warned, Miss Knicely—I'm not going anywhere."

―

One kiss. One short, sweet kiss, and Tabitha's heart hadn't stopped dancing. Her lips still tingled from Marcus's touch as she drove to the next doctor's office. She had a hard time recovering from the dreamy state and getting back in work mode. "What am I going to do?"

She waited to see if God would answer her. Nothing. *Bummer.* Tabitha honestly didn't know what she should do. Her heart, lips, and eyes screamed *Don't you dare let that man walk away!* at the same time her mind said *You can't handle him and Aunt Tweet at the same time. Stay focused.*

Since they weren't in sync, she needed advice. Who could she confide in? Not her sisters, especially since Kym thought Marcus was a distraction.

Her aunt had always been her confidante, even when her parents were alive, giving her straight talk from a woman who had seen the world. Tabitha's heart dipped. The thought that Aunt Tweet was fading—or had already faded—away made her eyes water. She sniffed. Weren't her days of instant boo-hooing over? Isn't that what she thought earlier when she chatted with Ava Elise?

Tabitha connected with her more as a friend than her former trainer.

When Ava Elise could have had her terminated from the training program, she'd reached out with a sympathetic ear instead and served as a silent cheerleader to see her succeed.

Hopefully, they could chat in the morning. Right now, her mission was to see her remaining four doctors, pick up Aunt Tweet from Bermuda Place, and go home.

That evening, true to his word, Marcus arrived at her door with carryout from Boston Market in his arms, but tiredness lingered on his face. "Hey."

Her guilt trip was back. She swallowed her sorrow. "You look beat," she said, accepting his kiss on the cheek but wanting more.

"And you look pretty. Sorry I'm late. I needed to go over some things with my crew first."

"You don't owe me an explanation." She allowed him entry, then closed her door.

"I feel I do." The smile he gave her was so endearing she felt faint. She ignored that feeling until she could get Ava Elise's take on her dilemma.

Within minutes, all three were gathered at the table, thanks was given for their meal, and they ate, barely pausing for conversation. Afterward, Aunt Tweet retreated to the family room for her game shows while Marcus helped Tabitha tidy up her kitchen. When he made a move toward the family room, she gathered up the courage to say something she didn't feel. "Thanks for dinner, but you need to go home."

"Huh?" He gave her a confused look. "I was just about to play cards with Aunt Tweet, and you want to put me out?"

"Yes, for your own good," she said softly with a smile. "Go home and get some rest...please."

He hesitated, but the pleading in her voice must have convinced him that she was looking out for him. "Okay. I am tired. What about you?"

"I think we're going to head to bed soon. I'll get up early in the morning and do some reading."

"Okay, babe." He hugged her.

A kiss and an endearment on the same day—she'd scored big.

The next morning, Tabitha walked into the Ceyle-Norman break room on a mission. As expected, Ava Elise was camped out in the corner, sipping on coffee and working a crossword puzzle. Since she carpooled with her husband, the woman usually arrived at the office at least an hour early.

Ava Elise glanced up. "More drug samples two days in a row? You know that could send a red flag for illegal drug activity or that you're exceeding your quota big time." She folded her hands. "I'm hoping it's the latter, because I like you." Her eyes twinkled.

"No samples today." Taking the seat across from her, Tabitha grinned as Ava Elise didn't hide her relief. "I need advice in confidence, since you know what's going on in my personal life."

"Of course." The lines etched across Ava Elise's forehead were evidence of her concern.

"I'm stressed," Tabitha confessed.

Closing her book, she gave Tabitha her full attention. "O-okay—the job or your aunt?"

"Both, to be honest. I love my job. I had everything mapped out to care for my aunt...but being a caregiver is more intense than any textbook could detail. A few times..."

She paused because she was ashamed to admit this, which is why she hadn't told her sisters. "My mind is sending mixed messages. I feel my life would be better if Aunt Tweet were in a nursing home—I also thought about quitting my job to become a full-time caregiver. Since I'm not eligible for Family Medical Leave, and I'm a one-person household, my savings would be drained, even with the stipend from my aunt's trust fund for her care."

"If you're not getting any help—"

"I am," Tabitha said slowly. "This is where I could use some unbiased advice. My neighbor has been stepping in to ease my burden."

"Excellent! That's great news." Ava Elise grinned. "My neighbors are one of the reasons I haven't moved. We've babysat each other's children..."

Tabitha lifted her hand to stop Ava Elise's roll. "You don't understand. My neighbor is fine, strong, and compassionate...and he thinks we should date."

"Even better." Her friend beamed. Her eyes sparkled as she folded her arms and leaned across the table. Clearly, she was waiting for more details.

Her excitement was making Tabitha exhausted. "I have no room on my schedule for free time."

"What about having a nurse's aide to sit with your aunt for a few hours to make room for this hunk?" Before Tabitha could shoot down that idea, her confidante continued, "Any man who is willing to help with the care of a loved one who isn't related to him—whether it's an elderly relative or child—is a jewel. There are men who walk away from their responsibility and don't look back. Think hard about this before turning him away."

Tabitha sighed and tapped her fingers on the table. She hadn't thought about that. "There's something about Marcus that makes me dream about candlelight dinners, movies, and picnics. But doing that"— she paused and frowned—"would make me feel like I'm casting Aunt Tweet aside. She's a guest in my home because I love and idolize her, and she's family." She shook her head. "I don't know… It seems so wrong to me."

Ava Elise moved her lips from side to side. She was conjuring up a solution. "Didn't you tell me she's in your care for six months?"

"Yes. It's a six-month rotation with my sisters. That's what we agreed upon. It's been almost two months, and the wear and tear on my mind and body make it seem like years. I can accept putting my wants and desires on hold, but I feel like I'm aging at a faster rate, if that makes sense."

"My advice to you is number one, take the neighbor and all he's willing to give you. Two, get a nurse's aide so you can go out for a few hours and breathe. I would definitely suggest you pencil in a monthly spa visit to ease some of that tension." Ava Elise stood. "I wish I had more time to walk you through this, but I need to prepare for my class."

"Thanks for listening and not judging me. In the past, my sisters and Aunt Tweet have been my confidantes. Under the circumstances, I didn't want to bring this up with Kym and Rachel."

"Every caregiver's situation is different, depending on the needs of the loved ones. My situation was different from yours, so I can't judge you." She shrugged. "I'll be praying you won't have any regrets about how you cared for your aunt when she's no longer on this earth."

Tabitha froze as a chill ran down her spine. Didn't the minister mention something like that in the sermon? Was God finally talking to her? The Bible reading she'd claimed she was going to do had been hit or miss. *Thank You, Lord, for not holding it against me.* Maybe God would speak to her at church. She couldn't wait to find out.

Chapter 23

SUNDAY MORNING, TABITHA FORCED HER EYES OPEN DESPITE HER desire for more sleep. She stretched and braced for Aunt Tweet to barge into the bedroom any minute. Then she realized it was too quiet in the house. Tabitha slipped out of bed and crossed the hall. Peeping into Aunt Tweet's bedroom, she noticed her aunt was still sleeping. Tabitha scrunched her nose; the room didn't smell fresh. After church, she would change the sheets, although she had just done the task four days earlier.

Backing out, Tabitha walked downstairs to feed Sweet Pepper and let him outside. Next, she started a breakfast of eggs, rice, and turkey links.

With twenty minutes to spare, she showered, finished her makeup, and dressed. Almost giddy with excitement, she sat in the chair, looking out of the window, waiting to surprise Aunt Tweet. Glancing at her watch, she frowned. Why hadn't her aunt made an appearance? Going back into the bedroom, she nudged Aunt Tweet. "It's Sunday. We're going to be late for church."

Aunt Tweet moaned. "I'm tired this morning. Don't feel like going." She rolled over.

Five days a week, Aunt Tweet was on a laborious schedule that Tabitha had created, so perhaps it was a good idea to let her eighty-five-year-old aunt sleep in. Tabitha had made some serious effort this morning to go to church, eager to see if God truly had a custom-made message just for her. Maybe the Lord would put it on hold until next time.

"It's okay. Rest as long as you need to." Disappointed, she covered her aunt, kissed her cheek, then strolled out of her room, slipping out of her heels in a few steps. She spied her toes and exhaled. She was way overdue for a soothing manicure and pedicure. Maybe later, if her aunt felt up to it, they could treat themselves with an outing.

She was undressing when she heard Aunt Tweet's feet dragging on the floor. The door opened and her aunt came out, rubbing her eyes. "Why didn't you wake me? It's Sunday, ain't it? We're going to be late if you don't get up."

Huh? Aunt Tweet's absentmindedness could be exhausting at times, but not today. Tabitha laughed with joy. "I'm ready. Let's find you something to wear."

While she helped Aunt Tweet bathe, her aunt mumbled, "You never know whose hand is going to give you that last piece of bread. I appreciate what you're doing for me."

Tabitha held her breath as her heart seemed to float. "I know you do." Again, she felt ashamed for her thoughts of *woe is me* when her aunt was possibly dying and trying to prepare her. "I appreciate everything you've done for me over the years, so it's my pleasure to do things for you now." She smiled wide, so her aunt could see she meant what she said. *Lord, please don't let her die in my care. Please.*

Even with their late arrival at church, they were able to find a parking spot not far from the door. Moments after settling in their seats, Marcus surprisingly appeared. Overjoyed but perplexed, Tabitha scooted over to make room. "I thought you weren't ever coming back."

"Well," he said, linking his fingers through hers and bringing her hand to his lips, "I could tell you were disappointed when I said that, so here I am."

The things this man was willing to do for her—both spoken and unspoken requests—was humbling. Pleased, she squeezed his hand. As expected, Aunt Tweet blended her voice along with the singers. When she didn't know the words, she hummed.

Closing her eyes, Tabitha took a deep breath, prayed, then opened them to scan the sanctuary. The music was so stirring that many people were on their feet rejoicing. Even Marcus stood. He reached for Tabitha's hand and tugged her to her feet. In unison, they clapped to the group's rendition of Hezekiah Walker's "Total Praise."

As the music faded, Pastor Nelson walked to the podium with his Bible tucked under his arm. He followed protocol with announcements, then welcoming visitors.

Tabitha was hyped to hear the sermon. She wanted God to speak to her through the message.

"Now, for the good stuff. Some of you may have been carrying a heavy load this week—or maybe for a while. Trust me. Believe that God is working behind the scenes on our behalf. I have only two scriptures for you today: 1 Peter 5:7. Know that the Lord cares for you, so give Him your burdens. The other one is in the Old Testament: Psalm 149:4, God delights in doing great things for His children. He doesn't get weary… like we do." Pastor Nelson preached until Tabitha could feel God's presence consume her being, then she heard the Lord speaking to her spirit, and somehow, she knew things in her life were about to change.

⸻

Sunday at church, Marcus could only accredit the Holy Ghost with propelling him to the altar for prayer after he repented of sins, then consent to the water baptism in Jesus's name. What followed was an anointing so heavy that a heavenly language flowed from his mouth.

Days after his Nicodemus experience with the Lord, Marcus glanced around his work space and shared office with thanksgiving and acknowledged that the Lord had blessed his business. He was on a spiritual high when he left his office for an appointment. As he headed toward the main parking lot, Marcus spied an unexpected visitor standing at the entrance desk, speaking to the receptionist.

"Mr. Whittington, I told Victor he was banned from the premises, but he refuses to leave without seeing you," Sandra said.

Really? He stared Victor Graves down. *There goes my good mood.*

Marcus took a cleansing breath. "What can I do for you?" he asked curtly.

"A few minutes. Just hear me out." Victor held up his hands in surrender, and Marcus noted that Victor's cockiness was gone and his tone was nonthreatening.

Yet the man didn't have a good track record, and Marcus didn't trust him. "Sandra, alert security." Marcus had to consider the safety of his employees. There had been too many mass shootings at workplaces from disgruntled former employees.

This receptionist gasped and picked up the phone.

"I guess I deserve that." Victor nodded and bit his lip.

Marcus kept his eyes locked on the Victor, trying to anticipate the man's next move, and watched as Victor reached into his pocket, possibly for a weapon. Marcus wasn't a wrestling champ for nothing—his adrenaline kicked in, and he charged his ex-employee.

Younger and faster, Victor moved out of harm's way. "Hey, man. I just wanted to give you this."

"Hands in the air, Victor!" Edward, the security guard, yelled. An envelope fell from Victor's pocket. "Step back from the package," Edward ordered. "Should I call for backup with a K-9 bomb-sniffing dog, sir?"

Talk about overkill from the retired cop turned security guard. "That won't be necessary." Marcus bent to pick up the envelope.

"Step back, sir. It could be laced with an illegal substance," Edward warned.

"Is it?" He eyed Victor, folding his arms and leaving the envelope on the ground.

"No. It's a money order." Victor's hands were still up.

"Stand down, Edward," Marcus said, then motioned for Victor to pick up the envelope. "Let's have a seat over there." He pointed to a corner nook that was private yet still in the open.

"I'll stay close by, sir." Edward gave him a salute and waited near Sandra's desk. His eyes were trained on Victor like a German shepherd waiting for his next meal.

"What's going on?" Marcus waited for Victor to sit, then sat across from him. Checking the time, he waited impatiently.

"I came to say thank you for bailing me out." Victor leaned forward and rested his elbows on his knees, then looked away before meeting his eyes again. "I don't know why you did it. I mean, you took away from your future children's college fund for me, Latrice, and my sons." He choked and handed over the envelope.

"My bond money will be returned unless you skip your court date." Marcus squinted. "You plan on skipping town?"

"I'm not going anywhere." He stared.

"Good answer." Marcus nodded and hesitantly accepted the envelope and peeked inside. It was a money order for $5,000. He blinked. "Whoa. Where did you get this type of money?" He hoped it wasn't drug money or from other illegal activity.

"I got a settlement the other day, and it kept bugging me why would you help me when I know I wasn't showing you any respect."

Yeah. It bugged me for a long time too, Marcus thought. "You weren't." He gave him a deadpan stare. "What settlement? Did you scam someone or file a bogus claim?"

The accusations put Victor on the defensive. "Why couldn't it be because *I* was the victim for a change?"

"Hold that thought." Marcus pulled out his cell and texted Demetrius. Bro, still at work. Something came up. Can you go by Redscape and meet with James Locke? He wants samples of our products. Please tell me you have some with you.

Everything okay? Demetrius texted back seconds later.

Yep. I'll explain later.

On it. Have samples in car. Like a Boy Scout. Always ready.

Leaning back, Marcus folded his arms. "Go ahead. Start from the beginning and break it down to me how *you're* a victim."

"I'm a black man who happened to be stopped by a Jennings police officer. 'Bout time the government called them out for their racist practices. Thousands of us poor, black residents who were jailed because we didn't have the money to pay court fees for traffic tickets got a lot of money from a lawsuit."

Marcus whistled. He had followed the news after the Ferguson shooting and applauded the Justice Department for serving notice to almost one hundred municipalities surrounding Ferguson whose revenue was generated through fines and fees that targeted poor people in black communities.

It came out in the news that when offenders couldn't pay, they had to serve jail time or have their driver's licenses suspended, which violated their constitutional protections. Marcus didn't know the $4.7 million settlement had been reached. "That's a lot of money. I hope you invest it wisely."

"Yep. I started a college fund for Little Victor and Vance."

Shocked, Marcus's jaw dropped. His mouth started moving. Seconds later, words spilled out. "You what? Does Latrice know about this?"

Sadness cast a shadow on Victor's face. "We're not together anymore, and she refuses to talk to me unless it has to do with the boys, even though this is about our sons." His shoulders slumped as he dropped his head.

Any other day, Marcus would have been Latrice's cheerleader. Today, somehow, he was convicted to switch sides. He felt sorry for his former employee.

Victor looked up again. "I'm going back to school in the fall and plan to work hard. Maybe I can open up my own business one day and help folks the way you and Demetrius do."

Marcus couldn't believe what he was hearing. The language seemed foreign coming from Victor. But this was exactly what his company strived to do—make a difference in people's lives.

Victor stood and extended his hand. "I wanted to say thank you."

Grinning, Marcus accepted the shake, then wrapped the younger man in a bear hug. "I'm proud of you, man. If you need to talk, call me. Just don't ask for your job back, because that's still a no. I'll invite you to the church where I began my salvation walk."

"I might check that out."

Watching Victor walk out the door a different man made Marcus exhale. "Lord, You made that change."

Chapter 24

LIFE WAS GOOD. TABITHA NEVER THOUGHT SHE COULD SAY THAT AS a caregiver, but it was true. In a short period of time, her growing relationship with the Lord had stabilized the chaos in her life. When she became frustrated, she prayed. On a bad day, she prayed. On the good days, she still prayed.

Surprisingly, her life was blissful when she thought about Marcus. He always seemed to consider her needs before his. She hadn't been sure if his plan for Aunt Tweet reading to the children would give her some breathing room, but it had.

So now, twice weekly, she had a new routine: pick up her aunt from Bermuda Place and drive to Whittington Janitorial Services, where Marcus had dinner waiting for them. Aunt Tweet would bask in the children's attention as she settled into the rocker the staff had provided for her comfort. Her presence meant story time, and the children didn't seem to mind whether she turned pages in a book or not.

Tabitha didn't expect this kind of pampering, not as a caregiver and not when she could barely contain her anguish until she was behind closed doors. "So, how's my girlfriend today?" Marcus teased. Once they were alone in the employee lounge, his eyes twinkled with mischief as he slid next to her at the table.

There had been no official declaration of their status, but he had taken liberty of claiming her. She didn't put up much protest, not because she didn't have the energy, but because he had put so much energy into nurturing their relationship that she craved spending any time with him.

"Girlfriend, huh?" Tabitha liked to hear him call her that. She shrugged as she opened her laptop to review some follow-up notes on doctors in her territory. "Who said I was your girlfriend?" she teased back in a sassy tone without looking his way.

"I can't fall in love if you're not my girlfriend," he said it in a playful manner.

Love? Tabitha stopped breathing as she slowly turned to face him. The intensity of his stare verified he wasn't kidding. Her heart fluttered. He loved her?

"I love you, Tabitha, and it grows more each day," he said almost in a whisper. "I want us to be an official couple."

At the worst possible time, a little boy rushed into the room and patted her arm, interrupting a pivotal moment between them that Tabitha would never forget. "Miss Tabby," the child called out, "Aunt Tweet won't let me play with my car." He turned and pointed.

Tabitha's jaw dropped as she looked up and witnessed her aunt slip the child's toy in her purse.

She and Marcus stood at the same time. "I'll handle it," she advised, taking the child's hand and going into the area where her aunt held court. Lowering her voice, she asked, "Do you have…" She paused and looked at the child.

"Kenny." His bottom lip trembled.

"Do you have Kenny's toy?"

Indignant, Aunt Tweet straightened her shoulders and defiantly stated, "Nuh-uh."

Stealing? Lying? What's next? "I saw you put Kenny's toy car in your purse. Let's give it back, okay?" She reached for the shoulder bag, but her aunt snatched it back until it became a tug-of-war. The more Tabitha pulled, the more her aunt strengthened her grip. To make matters worse, the children were watching them.

Marcus tried to intervene. "Ah, ladies, please."

The commotion had gotten the attention of the childcare supervisor. Even the night security guard was on her heels.

"Ma'am, please put the purse back on the table and step back," the guard whose badge showed that his name was Edward ordered with his thumbs tucked into his belt.

All this to recover a toy? Then again, Aunt Tweet wasn't relinquishing that purse.

"Edward, that won't be necessary," Marcus told him while helping Aunt Tweet to her feet. "Let's go for a walk." He guided her out of the play area, down a long corridor, all while she still clutched the purse. He turned back and mouthed to Tabitha, *Now what?*

Kenny patted her leg again. "Miss Tabby, I want my toy." He began to rub his eyes. The child was close to tears.

"It's okay, sweetie. I'll get it back." *Hopefully.* Although she was aware of the combative side of Alzheimer's, Tabitha never thought her aunt would be so stubborn and hostile, and in front of children. Her own eyes blurred with moisture as she hurried after Marcus and her aunt.

Besides her parents, Aunt Tweet had been the most loving, caring person she knew. She had to keep reminding herself of the person that was inside, no matter what she saw on the outside.

She wrapped her aunt in a hug, then kissed her cheek. "How are you feeling?"

"Tired, I guess."

Tabitha nodded. "Let's go home, but first I need to borrow something out of your purse."

Aunt Tweet frowned, but a few moments later, she handed it over. Accepting the purse, Tabitha turned her back and removed the toy. She exhaled as she handed the shoulder bag to her aunt. Discreetly, she gave Kenny's car to Marcus. "Will you tell him we're sorry and grab my things?"

"Sure, babe." As he began to walk away, he paused. "Oh, and don't think I'm not waiting to hear you say you love me back." He brushed a kiss against her cheek. She welcomed the feel of the velvety hairs of his ever-growing beard.

"I need a hug to go with that," Tabitha said. Marcus accommodated her request with a strong hug that was soothing before she reluctantly stepped out of his arms, so he could return Kenny's car.

The embarrassing turn of events had her emotions jumbled. A pity party descended on her while waiting for him to bring her purse and laptop. Hearing Marcus say he loved her would always be clouded with Aunt Tweet's antics.

Marcus reappeared. He wrapped his arm around her shoulders, then walked them to her car.

Once she was inside her car, Marcus leaned down until their eyes met through the driver's-side window. "Call me if you want to talk," he whispered.

She nodded sadly and drove away.

———

Marcus had a gut feeling she wouldn't call him. His bright idea to keep Aunt Tweet occupied had backfired at the worst possible way and time. The vibes between them were right, so he'd been in a playful mood. He desired to flirt with Tabitha and coax her to flirt back. Saying he loved her had felt right. His ears itched to hear her surrender to her love for him.

And she probably was on the verge. He would give anything to know what she was thinking. He had witnessed so many emotions cross her face—mainly the embarrassment from Aunt Tweet's stubbornness. Marcus was resolved to give her space to process her aunt's behavior and acknowledge what he had revealed tonight. After patting her hood, he stepped back.

Stuffing his hands in his pants pockets, he swallowed his disappointment. This wasn't how he envisioned the night going when he'd professed his love. Of course, it wasn't the most ideal situation, but he had to work with what time they had without Aunt Tweet in range.

He stayed rooted in place as her blue Taurus disappeared from the parking lot and exited on I-170, heading home.

"What's going on in that beautiful head of yours?" he said as if Tabitha could hear him, then he spun around and headed back into the building to do damage control.

———

The next morning, Marcus checked his phone for texts and voicemails—not one word from her. Sitting on the edge of his bed, he dropped his head in his hands. He wanted to call her, hear her voice, but she hadn't reached out to him.

"Lord, please don't let what happened last night be a setback for our relationship." It wasn't his imagination that her face had lit up when he'd told her he loved her.

He had nothing but adoration for Aunt Tweet, but at that precise moment, he was frustrated at her timing. Marcus wanted to send Aunt Tweet to her room as punishment. Now, he understood firsthand what Tabitha endured constantly when he wasn't around. His poor baby.

Feeling helpless, Marcus slid to the floor to pray after giving thanks for everything in his life.

He didn't know how long he stayed on his knees, but when he said, "Amen," he hoped for a word from the Lord. God was silent, so he picked up his Bible. Maybe God would speak to him through His Word, so he flipped through the pages until he stopped in Romans 12. He scanned the chapter, looking for a message. He paused at verse fifteen: "Rejoice with them that do rejoice, and weep with them that weep." He mediated on the meaning, then closed his Bible. He was hurting because Tabitha was hurting, and when she was happy, Marcus was happy. Without realizing this verse existed, he was already committed to enacting it. "I'll have to keep praying until we can get into a happy place again together."

Praying for her was easy. Waiting for the fruit of his petitions was torture. Marcus went through the motions of getting ready for work, but once he dressed, he couldn't stand not talking to Tabitha. He called and got her voicemail, so he texted her.

I know there are a lot of things you might want to forget about last night. I hope my love for you isn't one of them. He hit Send and waited for her reply. After a few minutes and nothing, he left for work.

Demetrius was finishing up a call when Marcus strolled through the door. They exchanged waves before he settled behind his desk and checked his phone for missed calls or a text from Tabitha. Again, nothing.

Regroup and focus. Pushing his personal life aside, Marcus used all his mental energy to concentrate on his business.

"Hey, man, did you hear about the fight in the day care last night?"

his brother asked after ending his conversation on the phone. Before Marcus could turn to face his brother, Demetrius was howling with amusement. He gasped for air as he laughed uncontrollably.

"Not funny, man." Marcus rubbed his lips in annoyance.

"B-but it is." Demetrius tee-heed. "An old woman and a young boy fighting over a toy. It doesn't get any better than that."

"Unfortunately, it does. It happened to be at the exact moment I told Tabitha I loved her. The tug-of-war interrupted us, big-time."

Demetrius put clamp on his amusement. "Ooh." He frowned and snapped to serious mode. "So you told her you loved her. Aww, man. That is *not* good. How's she doing this morning?"

"She hasn't returned my text." Marcus scratched his beard and exhaled.

Demetrius was quiet with a pensive expression. "Maybe that was a sign it isn't meant—"

Holding up his hand, Marcus cut his brother off. He didn't want to hear that. "It's a sign that my love for Tabitha is worth fighting for. Nothing and nobody is going to get in the way of that," he said with finality.

Chapter 25

THE NEXT MORNING, TABITHA STARED AT HER REFLECTION IN HER bathroom mirror. There wasn't enough primer, concealer, or foundation to mask the puffiness under her eyes. She had cried herself to sleep last night after the fiasco at Marcus's company. She thought Marcus might recall his love after witnessing the proof that a romantic relationship with her had too many uncertainties because of Aunt Tweet's condition. He called and texted, but honestly, she was still too embarrassed to talk to him.

She would have called in sick if she wasn't still in her trial period. Somehow, she made it through the motions of getting dressed, eating, and getting out the door with Aunt Tweet dressed to perfection. After dropping her off at Bermuda Place, Tabitha remembered she didn't have enough Porital samples, for osteoporosis, for today's appointments. She detoured to the office first with the intention of checking out samples, then getting back on the road ASAP.

"Sorry," she mumbled after almost knocking Ava Elise out of the way.

"Whoa, you must be in a rush." Her friend chuckled. "Hey, I like those sunglasses."

"Thanks." She didn't remove them. The cool cucumber cream she'd applied to reduce the puffiness should produce results by the time she met with the first doctor.

Resting her hand on Tabitha's arm, her friend wouldn't let her continue. "Are you all right? Is everything okay with your aunt?"

The dam broke before Tabitha could answer. Tears poured from her eyes without prompting. Ava Elise nudged Tabitha out the door to the courtyard. Once outside, her friend gave her a hug. "I thought you might need that."

That's exactly what she wanted and got last night from Marcus. Tabitha nodded and rummaged through her purse for tissues to blow her nose. "I did."

Removing Tabitha's sunglasses, Ava Elise inspected her face. "Whoa. Please tell me you have allergies. There are over-the-counter and prescription meds for that."

"Not anymore. I grew out of them." She hiccupped. "Sorry. I'm having an emotional day."

"I see that." They sat on a stone bench. "Did Aunt Tweet wander off again?"

"No." Tabitha's shoulders slumped.

Her friend exhaled. "Whew. So what's wrong?"

"Marcus told me he's in love with me." She blinked and a tear fell.

Ava Elise chuckled. "Honey, that's a good thing. I've heard of crying tears of joy, but…"

"The moment"—Tabitha closed her eyes—"was almost perfect." She mustered an uneasy smile. "The way he said it was so sweet." Then she explained how the night went downhill after that and how she'd left the warehouse in shame. "I'd never guessed my aunt would be so defiant— and in front of children. How embarrassing." She sighed. "Marcus has texted and called me, but I don't know how to pick up the pieces after last night. I'm afraid he's going to say I'm not worth it."

"He knows about her condition. I'm sure he doesn't blame you or her. What any woman wants is the love of a good man—you have it, but you didn't tell Marcus you loved him back?" Ava Elise paused. "I know you do. A good man is hard to find and he deserves to hear it from you." She stood, and Tabitha followed. "Separate your personal life from your livelihood and call that man. I'm sure he's worried about you."

Once back inside the building, they went separate ways.

Idle in construction traffic on I-70, she took her friend's advice and called Marcus. He answered right away.

"Baby, are you okay?"

"Yes," she whispered. "I'm sorry it's taken me overnight to say it, but I love you too."

"You're telling me now, and that's all that matters to me."

Tabitha's heart fluttered, but she had to address last night's scene. "I'm also sorry about Aunt Tweet's behavior." It still didn't seem real. Tabitha wished it had been a bad dream. She sighed.

"I get it. She can't help herself," he reassured her.

"I know that, and I can't help her from being the person she is now. It's heartbreaking. I'm suffering, too, silently, along with my aunt. I'm tired mentally, emotionally, physically... Sometimes, like last night, I want to run and hide under a rock. If I vent my frustration to my sisters, they may think I don't want Aunt Tweet, and that's not the case. I love her!"

"Hey, hey, I know you do and you're a great caregiver—you are. And I'm here for you to vent. I love you, and as far as hiding under a rock, I heard a Scripture about that but don't know where it is."

Me either. She really couldn't think straight. "Was little Kenny all right?"

"Yep. As soon as he got his toy back, everything was forgotten." He chuckled.

She sniffed. "Good, but I don't think it's a good idea for me to bring her back there."

Marcus tried, but he couldn't convince her to rethink her decision. By the time Tabitha made it to her first appointment and parked, they whispered their love again, and this time, she allowed it to melt her heart.

———

For the next couple of days, it was tempting not to count down the months and weeks until Rachel took over the reins of Aunt Tweet's care. As the Fourth of July holiday approached, Tabitha was grateful that Marcus didn't pressure her to join him for the company barbecue. She had no choice but to put a self-imposed ban on visiting his job. Her aunt might not remember the skirmish, but she was sure the children would.

At least she could look forward to her sisters coming to town and celebrating the holiday together.

"I decided to wait and come next weekend. That way we can celebrate

Aunt Tweet's eighty-fifth birthday," Kym said during the sisters' weekly Skype call.

"Personally, I really wanted to come for the Fourth, but I'd rather wait until all of us are together," Rachel added.

They had no idea how badly Tabitha needed their company. Masking her frustration, Tabitha smiled, then chatted a few more minutes before signing off.

No matter where the Knicely sisters were, they had always met at their parents' home—hers now—for Thanksgiving and Christmas, and as many holidays as possible. The summer holidays were the best when the sisters took trips together, despite living in different cities. Growing up, Tabitha's heart ached for her friends who didn't have siblings to enjoy things with.

Without Marcus or her sisters for a distraction, it was business as usual when she woke on July 4. After checking on Aunt Tweet, who was still in her bedroom, Tabitha returned to her room to say her morning prayers. She showered quickly and checked on her aunt again. Everything was calm. Next, she grabbed her Bible and prayed for direction, opening to a random scripture: Philippians 4:6–7. "Be careful for nothing; but in everything by prayer and supplication with thanksgiving let your requests be made known unto God. And the peace of God, which passes all understanding, shall keep your hearts and minds through Christ Jesus."

"God, I need Your peace," she whispered as she reread the verses and took a moment to meditate on them. When Aunt Tweet stirred, Tabitha helped her freshen up and dress. Once they were downstairs, Sweet Pepper yelped for attention, so they prepared for a leisurely stroll. As Tabitha inhaled the aroma of barbecue in the air, she mused. So what if it was only the two of them for the holiday? It was going to be a good day anyway.

Not long after that back at the house, Tabitha was drying her hands when her bell rang. She opened the door and a courier greeted her, holding two bouquets. She smiled.

Aunt Tweet's eyes lit up when Tabitha returned to the kitchen with the bold, bright-colored flowers. "That from Papa?"

Her aunt had called Marcus "mister" a time or two, but "Papa"? Her dementia symptoms seemed to be worsening. Tabitha nodded, then arranged the bouquet in water.

"I see you're really into the holiday spirit. The red, white, and blue arrangements are beautiful," Tabitha said when she called to thank him.

"And so are you. See you later on, babe."

"I look forward to it." After ending the call, Tabitha seasoned her chicken and hamburgers for the grill. Like old times, she and Aunt Tweet worked side by side, preparing potatoes for the potato salad. It didn't go unnoticed that her aunt had left a lot of the skin on some of the potatoes.

When they stepped outside, the humidity had kicked in, so Tabitha retrieved Popsicles from the freezer. Listening to the squeals and laughter from the neighborhood children and the occasional firecrackers that someone couldn't wait to set off, Tabitha knew it wouldn't be long until the heat was unbearable.

By the time the meat was cooked, her aunt had finished a third Popsicle. Suddenly, Aunt Tweet began to hum one of the church songs they'd heard.

Without realizing it, Tabitha herself joined in singing, "I love you, Jesus…" When her aunt sang the last note, she closed her eyes and drifted off to sleep, and Tabitha watched peace descend on her aunt.

Going inside for a platter, Tabitha returned and removed the meat, then urged her aunt inside to lie on the sofa. For the first time in a long time, her work didn't consume her day and she enjoyed her own down-time. She sat in the recliner, then grabbed her phone when a text chimed.

Love you. Miss you. Crazy about you. Can't wait to see you. Open your door.

"What?" She slowly got to her feet and followed Marcus's instructions, expecting more flowers, but outside her door was the best gift. Tabitha fell into Marcus's arms. He brushed a kiss on her head, squeezed her tight, and literally lifted her off her feet as he crossed the threshold. She giggled at his playfulness as he closed the door.

"Not that I'm complaining, because I'm not, but I didn't expect you until later this evening. I don't want to take you away from the time you spend with your employees. I know it's a tradition you and your brother started." She didn't want to be selfish and demanding.

"Couldn't stay away from my girlfriend." He gave her a slow grin. There was something about the way he said *girlfriend*, as if the word was created for her.

Linking their hands together, they walked to the kitchen, and he sniffed. "Hmm. Your barbecue smells better than ours. What's on the menu?" He craned his neck to peek into her family room. "Where's Aunt Tweet?"

"Napping," she said, pointing to the sofa instead of her aunt's favorite chair. She shook her head when she spied her aunt open one eye and then close it just as fast. Deciding to play along, Tabitha walked closer and gently nudged her awake. "Look who's here."

"There's my friend." Marcus made a big production of giving her a kiss on her cheek and complimenting her earrings.

Tabitha admired his loving nature. Even Sweet Pepper wagged his tail for attention and Marcus didn't disappoint.

"I guess we all want a piece of you," she whispered to herself.

As if the wind had carried Tabitha's words to his ears, he stopped and glanced over his shoulder, meeting her eyes. He came back to her. "You, Miss Knicely, have all of me." After washing his hands, he asked if she needed help.

"It's early, but the food is ready, if you want to eat."

"Woman, it's a holiday. There is no set time to eat, and I'm starved." He patted his stomach.

"I'm ready to eat supper," Aunt Tweet said, seconding the sentiment.

"What about eating outside on the patio?" Marcus nodded toward the door.

"I think it may be too warm. Let's stay in until the sun goes down and it cools off some," Tabitha advised.

"Good choice, *my* girlfriend." He grinned wide.

It was such a juvenile term, but Tabitha loved hearing him say it.

Marcus set the kitchen table and gave thanks for their food. As they ate, Aunt Tweet conjured up tales, causing Tabitha to wonder if they were true or not.

Once they finished, Tabitha snuggled next to Marcus as they watched game shows with Aunt Tweet. A couple of times, her aunt became frustrated with the host's questions. Tabitha tried to rephrase the question so Aunt Tweet could understand, to no avail. When her aunt lost interest, they turned off the television and enjoyed gospel tunes Marcus had downloaded on his phone. The music inspired Aunt Tweet to hum along until she dozed off with Sweet Pepper on her lap.

Too soon, the dog stirred and whined to go outdoors. The short trot around the block seemed exhausting for her aunt and Sweet Pepper; they collapsed in the patio lounger when they returned to watch fireworks from neighbors far and near. Tabitha and Marcus claimed the double-seated rocker. Facing her, he tugged at a strand of her hair and twirled it around his finger. "So, baby, did I tell you I missed you?"

"Yes." She giggled. "And I missed you too, like crazy." Everything seemed all right in her world when he was around. Their lips were about to touch when a big boom exploded nearby. She jumped, laughing.

Startled, Aunt Tweet stood, disoriented. "What was that?"

Sweet Pepper barked.

Tabitha pointed to the sky. "See the beautiful colors?"

Her aunt jumped at every boom until she finally made a dash for the door. Sweet Pepper got in the way, and Aunt Tweet began to tumble to the ground. Marcus was quick to respond and steadied her, to Tabitha's relief. He had saved them a trip to the ER and an explanation to her sisters about injuries.

Chapter 26

At the airport a week later, Tabitha relished the hugs. "I missed you two during the holiday," she said to Kym and Rachel.

"We're here now." Kym smiled and looped an arm through Tabitha's while Rachel held on to Aunt Tweet.

"Let's celebrate!" Rachel said.

Later that day, Marcus came to the house for Aunt Tweet's festive birthday mini bash. His brother was with him. Tabitha had a sneaking suspicion Demetrius was there for Rachel and the small party was a cover-up. Thanks to the low humidity, they took the festivities outside. After a while of casual banter, Tabitha cut the cake. The honoree was served first to Aunt Tweet's delight, then Kym suggested a family meeting inside.

"Do you mind entertaining Aunt Tweet?" Tabitha could see the love in Marcus's eyes.

"Babe, you don't have to ask." He reached for her hand and kissed it.

I love you, she mouthed and couldn't stop the blush from spreading as she walked into the house with her sisters.

"Hmm." Rachel teased. "Instead of a family meeting, maybe we should talk about you and Marcus. Things have really heated up since we were here last time."

Tabitha beamed. "Yes, they have."

Kym smiled. "Okay. First things first. Give us an update on Aunt Tweet, then on Mr. Whittington."

"I've had a few meltdowns." She ignored her sisters' shocked expressions. "Ava Elise, my former trainer and now friend, was a caregiver once and suggested I try a nurse's aide to come and watch Aunt Tweet, since her dementia symptoms are advancing. Marcus and I decided, instead of a nurse's aide, an activity might be better—"

"Hold up. You and Marcus? What does he have to do with our aunt's care?" Kym interrupted.

Tabitha didn't like her sister's tone and told her, "He happens to care about me—*us*—and he's my backup." She lifted a brow. "Anyway, he thought it would be a good idea for Aunt Tweet to interact with the children at his day care during story time."

"Go on." Folding her arms, Kym leaned back in the chair and crossed her legs.

"Things were going well until she and Kenny started to tussle over his toy truck. She put his toy in her purse and wouldn't give it back." She didn't want to relive that scene. "We haven't gone back since. Actually," she said, gritting her teeth, "I have been too embarrassed."

Kym grunted. "I can't even imagine that behavior coming from Aunt Tweet."

"Trust me, it wasn't a pretty picture. Next, Marcus and I decided—"

"Don't get me wrong. I like the man. However, all the Knicely sisters need to be involved in decisions involving *our* aunt."

Leaning forward, Tabitha gave them a pointed glare. "Then I suggest you both pack your bags and move back here."

"Me?" Rachel placed a manicured finger on her chest. "What did I say?"

"Nothing." Her mouth twisted in annoyance. "You need to join in on this discussion, especially when Kym and I aren't exactly seeing eye to eye."

"Okay. I agree with big sis on this one. We need to know what's going on. If Marcus is helping, I don't see a problem. I don't know how I'm going to have to tweak my game plan when Aunt Tweet comes home with me after Thanksgiving."

"You mean at the end of October," Tabitha corrected Rachel.

"Are you sure you're not stressed out about the job? It was your idea to change jobs, and surely there has to be another medicine that can help with Aunt Tweet's symptoms," Kym said.

"We've been through this. The ones that would slow down the dementia symptoms have some severe reactions that I'm—no, we—aren't comfortable taking a chance with. My experience with Aunt Tweet is totally different from yours. Rachel's may be different too. What I'm saying is for me, being a caregiver has been stressful. I have moments when I'm fine, then something happens, and I want to hide from reality. Your visits give me the respite I need…to recharge, to enjoy ice cream, a deep hair conditioner, a foot massage…"

Kym waved her hand in the air. "Girl, no problem. We can all go to the spa together."

"No!" Tabitha blurted out. "I need some me moments."

Kym stood and raised her voice. "You say things are going on with Aunt Tweet, but I see the changes in you. We came to be together and celebrate. If she's getting in the way of your budding relationship, say it, and I'll take my dear aunt home with me right now!"

Yes, Tabitha wanted to spend more time with Marcus, but not at the expense of deserting Aunt Tweet, who she loved more than anything. Something within her snapped. Even though she knew in her heart it would be better to hold her peace, she unleashed her pent-up emotions. "You know what? You can leave, but my aunt will stay with me until Rachel takes over."

———

"It's not sounding pretty in there," Demetrius said as they overheard loud voices coming from inside. "Your name has come up at least twice." He raised two fingers.

Marcus squinted through the glass door, then he squeezed his lips together in frustration. "I know, and I don't like it."

Maybe it was a good thing Demetrius had invited himself along; he and Rachel had been talking off and on, and at the moment, he was glad for his brother's presence.

Rubbing his forehead, Marcus debated whether he should intervene. He had seen firsthand how stressful being a caregiver was for Tabitha, but he also saw her love and commitment.

He glanced at Aunt Tweet, wondering if she was clueless about being the object of the sisters' heated discussion. When the shouting started, he and Demetrius scrambled to their feet.

Aunt Tweet was still relaxing with the puppy on her chest, so he left her there and entered the house. He had never seen his little woman so upset. Coming up behind her, he snaked his arm around her waist to drag her away from the shouting match before it turned into a shoving match.

He glanced over his shoulder to check on Aunt Tweet. She hadn't moved. He faced Tabitha. "Hey, babe, hey." He searched her eyes until they focused on him. "What's going on?" As her tears spilled, he wiped them with his thumbs as fast as he could.

"Since you and my sister seem to have it under control, I'm leaving," Kym spat at him before spinning around and hurrying upstairs to pack.

He groaned. It was worse than he thought. When was the last time he and Demetrius had an argument that ended with hurt feelings this bad? They had to have been teenagers. Their dad drilled into his sons to resolve their issues by cooling off, then talking the problem through. Apparently, sister bonds were more easily broken.

With a hand curled into a fist, Rachel marched toward Tabitha, and Marcus nudged her out of harm's way. No punches would be thrown today and land on his woman.

The polished, sophisticated diva was gone. "Move out of the way, Marcus. This discussion doesn't concern you," Rachel threatened.

"The discussion doesn't, but Tabitha does. Will you ladies please calm down?"

Rachel ignored him and raised her voice. "What is wrong with you? Kym is our big sister. We're supposed to be in agreement about Aunt Tweet's care, not fighting. You are so selfish!" A tear fell as she spun around and trailed Kym upstairs.

"Oh boy." Marcus blinked. Selfish? His woman was far from it. His heart broke, knowing the arrows her sisters had aimed had hit their target.

Tabitha turned in the other direction and stormed outside to the patio to join Aunt Tweet.

He wanted to go to her and be her hero, but Demetrius stopped him. "You can't fight this battle. They're going to have to work it out, Bro."

How was he supposed to stand on the sidelines while Tabitha was hurting? Marcus wanted to ask, but he doubted his brother could answer.

Chapter 27

"Mom, I love Tabitha, and I'm worried about her. It's been almost two weeks since she and her sisters have spoken. Plus, she's lost a little weight, despite my efforts to get her to eat more," Marcus confided over the phone when Demetrius was away from his desk. "Even Aunt Tweet seems subdued."

"Poor girl." Sylvia Whittington tsked. "I would think the three of them would be on the same page about something as important as their great-aunt. Anything I can do?"

"From North Carolina? Pray. Hopefully, when you and Dad come next month, their disagreement will be resolved, but I think you'll like her."

"I'm sure it will. Maybe she needs a little motherly love. I have more than enough to give." His mother's cheerfulness came through.

After a couple more minutes, he ended their call with "Love you, Mom."

He wouldn't trade his parents for anything in the world. Marcus prayed that if he and Demetrius ever had to be caregivers, they would be able to work together as a team, like they did in their business. There was a knock on his door, and Latrice peeped inside. "Do you have a few minutes?"

Marcus exhaled. He hoped she didn't have another crisis again so soon. He motioned for her to have a seat in front of his desk.

She did, then swallowed. "Mr. Whittington, why didn't you tell me Victor paid you back his bail money?" she asked softly.

He tapped a pen on his desk. "It wasn't my place." Gauging her reaction, he asked, "Are you okay?"

Latrice sighed and bobbed her head. "I've been praying for

Victor—not so much for us, but for his relationship with our sons. I just don't know if I should trust his intentions with me." She looked to him with expectancy in her eyes.

I'm not a relationship counselor, Marcus thought. He did believe Victor was changing and trying to reach his potential to improve his life, so Marcus grappled for encouraging words. "Latrice, I would say keep praying and giving him the benefit of the doubt."

"I guess you're right." After a slight frown, she thanked him and walked out of his office.

Relationships. Shaking his head, Marcus was about to move on to his next task when he thought about Tabitha. He admired and respected her for wanting to tough it out, but it was time for outside intervention. She was studious and knew more about her aunt's illness than he did, but if he was going to continue to be Tabitha's caregiver, he needed to know as much about Aunt Tweet's illness as possible for himself. He logged on to alz.org.

The site was information overload, so he called the hotline number. As a brief introduction, he said, "My girlfriend is crying out for help from her family, but she's not getting what she needs from them. She needs some alone time," he said, not liking to admit he wasn't enough. "I noticed your website mentions home companions or nurse's aides to assist with light chores and such. Can your agency recommend some places for me to contact?"

"Of course. Plus, we have support groups and events to bring awareness about the disease, such as the Walk to End Alzheimer's in September."

"Right now, we need someone to watch her aunt so she can get that alone time."

"Not a problem," the representative said. "If you give me your email, I'll get a list of some health professionals to you ASAP."

He was impressed by the woman's caring attitude, and before they disconnected, the list came to his inbox. Marcus prayed for guidance and made some calls.

Next, he called Tabitha. "Hey, baby. How's it going?" He hoped the cheerfulness in his voice would bring her some cheer.

"It's going. Thanks for thinking of me."

"All day and every day." He smiled. "Do you trust me?"

"You know I do. More than my sisters right now." The sadness in her voice was apparent.

Marcus hoped her ache would subside with his plan. "The love you have for one another is greater than the circumstances. You have to believe that. Anyway, I spoke with someone at the Alzheimer's help desk about respite care." He paused. "I asked a home health aide to come to your house tomorrow, so we can interview her."

"Umm. I don't know."

He imagined she was going to shoot down his idea before he could explain. "Listen, baby, if I could wash your hair and polish your nails, I would, but I can't. I heard you when you said you need some me time. There's this whole big organization that is ready to help right here in St. Louis. You can't expect help from your sisters far away, even if they came every weekend."

"Does this mean you're pulling away from me?" she asked softly.

Wounded that she would think such a thing, he lowered his voice. "No, girlfriend. It means I'm stepping up even more because I love you."

"I love you too," she whispered, then seemed to regroup. "I'll go along with an interview, but you know my concerns about a stranger."

"Yes. I understand your concerns about someone you don't know in your home alone and leaving Aunt Tweet in their care." Because he anticipated her worry, Marcus planned to surprise her with a wireless security system like the one he had, so when she was out and she had doubts, she could monitor what was going on at home. He'd hold off telling her until they had chosen a candidate.

"Thank you for taking my problem and making it yours."

"When I love someone, it's what I do, and I love you very much."

The loud, juicy kiss Tabitha sent over the phone was deafening and amusing. He laughed the rest of the day, even though he suffered a slight hearing loss for about an hour.

"Finally, you're getting the help you need," Ava Elise said following a morning meeting with the sales reps after Tabitha told her what Marcus had done.

"I said I was willing to interview for the position." Tabitha still wasn't sold on the idea; neither had she discussed that option with her sisters, although she trusted Marcus.

"By the way, I heard your numbers were good last month." Ava Elise grinned. "Doctors are writing prescriptions in your territory." She lifted her hand for a high five. Tabitha obliged, then left for her first physician's office.

The day zoomed by until, finally, it was time to get Aunt Tweet from Bermuda Place. She thought about what her sisters would say about leaving an unsupervised stranger in charge of their aunt's well-being. Almost immediately, she missed their bond. It hurt that they'd hinted she wasn't doing a good job. Maybe they were right. Maybe she wasn't cut out to be a good caregiver. Kym never had any complaints while it was her turn.

Parking the car, Tabitha walked inside, and surprisingly, Aunt Tweet was waiting in the lobby with her purse in her lap, ready to go. That was a first. Usually, her aunt had to be coaxed away from a craft or the snack table. She seemed tired as she stood to greet Tabitha. "Where have you been?" she asked in a scolding tone.

Whoa. After signing Aunt Tweet out and waving at some of the staff, Tabitha explained on the way to the car. "I'm sorry. I was working. Did something happen that you want to tell me?" She silently prayed that her aunt hadn't been subject to any incidents of abuse.

"I want to go with you," Aunt Tweet demanded as Tabitha drove off. Her aunt glanced out the window at their passing surroundings, then looked back at her. "This is a new car, ain't it?"

Tabitha hid a chuckle. Her aunt had cautioned them about using improper grammar when they were growing up. It was odd to hear it spill from her lips. "Yes, this is a company car. I turned the rental in a while back."

She arrived at her house to see Marcus sitting on her steps with a food bag. Yes! All the stress and tension from the day eased away.

Getting to his feet, he grinned, then switched the package to the other arm as he swaggered toward them. He opened her car door. "Hey, girlfriend." He kissed her lips, then walked around and helped Aunt Tweet.

"Why are you so wonderful?" Tabitha asked as he escorted them to the door.

"Because I have a wonderful woman," he answered and pressed a kiss onto her hair. Within minutes, the two had washed their hands as Aunt Tweet attempted to set the table with four plates and three forks.

Not long after they finished dinner, the doorbell rang. Tabitha opened the door, reminding herself not to make any judgment calls until after she could get a reading on the woman's personality.

An older, plump white lady with cherry-red hair smiled and introduced herself as Betty. Marcus came and stood by her side. They both welcomed the woman in. After offering some refreshments, they began the task of interviewing her.

"Miss Betty, what type of background do you have, and how would you handle a combative situation?" Marcus took the lead.

"My job is to provide companionship, activities, bathing, light cleaning, or simply to watch television with the client."

"What about combative behavior?"

She was so proud Marcus had noticed too that Miss Betty hadn't answered the questions.

"I've been a CNA for more than a decade. I'm trained to defuse the situation with a distraction. I allow the client to calm down, then I try to find out the source of the aggravation. Depending on the scenario, it may be best to move the person to a safe environment. If the behavior is a health risk, I am instructed to call 911, then the caregiver."

"As you can imagine," Tabitha began, "I'm struggling to admit that I need your services, and so to be truthful...I have trust issues with a stranger in my house, sometimes unsupervised, since I'm thinking I might need care one or two evenings a week." She shrugged.

"Definitely a Saturday evening," Marcus added with a smirk.

"I understand your concerns. As you are aware, we have to pass a background check, and we are insured and bonded. To be honest, I'm always prayerful that I'm going into a safe environment for myself."

"How about a trial run this Friday for a few hours, so Tabitha can have a hair appointment?" Marcus pulled Tabitha closer, then handed her a gift certificate.

Marcus's gesture caused the potential home-care worker's eyes to twinkle. "Sounds good to me. I never miss my hair appointment."

They all laughed, even Aunt Tweet, who later commented that the woman was wearing a bad wig.

Chapter 28

Friday evening, Tabitha invited Miss Betty to arrive early enough to join them for dinner. While the home companion tidied up afterward, Tabitha indulged in a hot bath—at least fifteen minutes—all the while keeping an eye on the activity in her kitchen area on a monitor. It was courtesy of the home security system Marcus had installed to ease her mind. He had even forfeited a night of hanging out with Demetrius to supervise the first visit between Aunt Tweet and Miss Betty.

After her bath, Tabitha leisurely massaged lotion into her skin, then slipped on a sundress. She sighed as she wiggled her toes before sliding into sandals. Feeling carefree, she bounced down the stairs into the family room. Marcus stood and whistled. She giggled.

She kissed her aunt, thanked Miss Betty, and gave Marcus the tightest hug she could before gazing into his eyes. "Thank you."

He brushed his lips against her forehead. "You're welcome, baby. Enjoy your me time." His eyes sparkled with mischief. "Without me."

Grabbing her bag, she raced out of the house and did a two-step. Inside her car, she screamed, "Thank You, Jesus!"

Crowning Glory Salon II wasn't far from downtown, and she enjoyed the twenty-minute cruise before she exited off I-70 at Tucker Boulevard.

The owner, Constance, greeted her at the door with a smile. "Right on time. My instructions were to give you a deep shampoo." She chuckled. "I think he meant a deep condition, but let's get your facial out of the way first."

While waiting for phase one of the services, Tabitha checked the live home video on her phone.

Nothing seemed out of the ordinary. All three were watching an old black-and-white movie. All of a sudden, Marcus held up a sign behind his back: *Miss you! Why are you watching this? Love you. Take your time, beautiful.*

"No he didn't." Tabitha was amused. How did he know? She kept watching, then realized he was displaying the same message at different intervals. Tabitha loved that silly man. Slipping her phone back in her purse, she thought about her parents. They really would have liked—no, *loved*—Marcus. Aunt Tweet liked him too. Her sisters? She wasn't sure. When Constance instructed her to close her eyes and relax for her facial, Tabitha dozed off.

Tabitha felt rejuvenated when she returned home three hours later. The downtime had done wonders for her psyche. Aunt Tweet was already in bed. Miss Betty was watching television while Marcus dozed on the sofa. Some watchdog he was.

After thanking and saying good night to the home companion, she nudged Marcus's shoe. He sprung up immediately, as if he weren't asleep, and his jaw dropped. His bold, appreciative scrutiny made her feel beautiful. "Wow, girlfriend." Leaping to his feet, he surveyed her as if he had never seen her before, then engulfed her in a tender embrace.

Pulling away, she rubbed her hand against the silky hairs on his jaw while she stared into his eyes. "Thank you so much for suggesting this."

"You're glowing, baby."

She beamed. It was a toss-up which endearment made her blush more: *girlfriend* or *baby*. Feeling playful, she teased him. "Make sure you ask me to marry you." *Really?* Did she just propose to Marcus?

Marcus tugged on Tabitha's hand to see him to the door. He guided her lips to his to kiss her good night, then said softly, "When I do, make sure you say yes."

———

Tabitha was hyped about her and Marcus's official first date. Why had she fought him so hard on it for so long? Was Aunt Tweet really an excuse, or was that the excuse she was using to keep her distance from any type of relationship?

She couldn't remember the last time she had been on a date. Her mind replayed their conversation about it. They were watching Aunt Tweet relax on a bench at the pond. Holding Sweet Pepper, he'd said, "Babe, you've been my girlfriend since the day I realized you couldn't cook."

His declaration made her heart dance. She knew he was referring to the evening she had burned the spaghetti and set off the fire alarm while searching for Aunt Tweet.

That remark had earned him a soft punch in the arm, and he had feigned injury. "Ouch. Seriously, we've been dating since the day you stole that scarf off my front porch."

"Stole?" she challenged him. "I was simply retrieving personal belongings." Their playful banter continued until Tabitha sobered. "It hasn't been very exciting though. I signed up to be a caregiver. You didn't."

Marcus didn't have a clever comeback. What was he thinking? "Nothing happens by chance. I don't care how I met you, Tabitha Faye Knicely." He gathered her hands in his and brought them to his lips. "You showed up on my doorstep. How was I to know you would turn out to be the best gift I've ever opened? Now I can't let you walk away."

Coming out of her reverie, Tabitha concentrated on raiding her closet for the perfect outfit. The intensity of Marcus's sweet words had gotten her through a rough workweek where two doctors she had hoped would be excited about her company's new drug for the treatment of sinusitis weren't convinced enough by the drug's track record to accept samples and monitor patients.

Though clearly unaware of it, Aunt Tweet had, upon her arrival, set the course for Tabitha's unexpected love. Her aunt had given Tabitha so much over the years. Even now, when Aunt Tweet's memory was failing, she had brought Marcus into their lives, who had then become their friend as well as Tabitha's confidant and caregiver aide. Now—she sighed thinking about it—he'd become a special man in her life.

Tabitha yearned to text her sisters about her first date. However, she was certain they wouldn't take too kindly to their aunt's care being left in the hands of someone they didn't know, even though Miss Betty had earned Tabitha's trust.

She refocused and decided on a flirty dress that still had the price tag on it. The lightweight multicolored knit dress with its long fringes at the hem was perfect for a summer evening. Next, she slid her feet into a pair of very high heels that left her toes peeping out. The front was faux leather and the rest was a multicolored fabric that matched her dress.

After her makeup, she tackled her mass of curls. Because of the night's heat, she brushed her hair up into a ball. To top off her look, she chose drop earrings that brushed against her shoulders. Her doorbell rang as she surveyed her appearance.

Pulling herself away from the floor-length mirror, Tabitha grabbed her purse and shawl. Marcus's deep voice echoed from the foyer and sent shivers down her arms. She descended the staircase in a gliding manner, as she and her sisters had done many times as children, pretending to be princesses or beauty pageant winners.

The way his eyes followed her every movement made her silly, childish fairy tale come true. Aunt Tweet and Betty were also staring. Tabitha sucked in her breath as Marcus met her at the landing with a dazed expression.

Without breaking eye contact, he lifted her hand to his lips. Her heart raced. "You're more beautiful every day." Next, he kissed her cheek. "And I am a very blessed man," he whispered, before brushing his lips against hers in the briefest of moments because of their audience. Finally, he twirled her under his arm as if she was his dance partner.

"You look beautiful," Miss Betty said in awe.

"Thank you." She faced her aunt for approval.

"You need a crown like I wore years ago on that stage." Her eyes twinkled.

Tabitha had yet to confirm the story about the beauty pageant. There was nothing mentioned in the newspaper archives or old photos among Aunt Tweet's belongings. Her accolade was a reminder that her aunt was there with her physically but becoming a familiar stranger.

"Thank you," she said, then turned to Miss Betty. "You have my contact number—and Marcus's. Call me…" She was nervous, but not about the first date. Tabitha was having second thoughts. Would Aunt Tweet be okay? Was Miss Betty really, really trustworthy? The doubts continued until Miss Betty seemed to address her unspoken musings.

"Enjoy your night, Miss Knicely. Your aunt and I will be fine."

Tabitha nodded and quietly prayed, *Lord, I'm trusting You to please watch over my aunt.*

Marcus opened the door, and Tabitha almost stumbled at the sight of a black limousine parked at the curb. Her jaw dropped, but no words came out.

He tapped her nose. "For you." Looping his arm through hers, he guided her down the steps and walkway as if they were on a Hollywood red carpet.

Once in the limo, she snuggled against his chest and closed her eyes, in awe of his efforts to make their date memorable. "Thank you," she whispered.

He kissed her hair. "For what?" He nudged her closer as he stretched out his long legs.

"For coming into my life and staying."

He chuckled. "We can thank Aunt Tweet for that."

"Funny, I was thinking the same thing tonight." Angling her body, Tabitha faced him and toyed with his beard.

"I was unjustifiably angry at you; I've seen for myself how she can disappear in a flash." Marcus fingered her chin, then guided her lips to his. His touch, more like a nibble, was tender before he pulled back. "Once you captured my heart, I couldn't walk away." He choked, clearly emotional with his confession.

Tabitha wanted to shed tears of joy, but she wasn't going to ruin her makeup, not even for the man she deeply loved. She was content to rest her head against his chest and listen to his heartbeat until they arrived at their destination.

A few hours later, Tabitha admitted she was having a good time. The *Prince of Broadway* musical was refreshing and rejuvenating. She only wondered about Aunt Tweet once—not counting the time Marcus suggested an update. To ease her curiosity, he urged her to pull up the video, where she saw Aunt Tweet and Miss Betty watching television. During intermission, she called. "Just checking in."

"Everything's fine. As a matter of fact, we were both dozing." Betty chuckled.

"Be careful. That's when my aunt is known to pull her best disappearing acts, when I dozed." Now concerned, she gnawed on her lips as her heart raced.

"No worries, Miss Knicely," Miss Betty said in a professional tone. "I only meant to say that all is well. Your loved one is under good care."

After she ended the call, Marcus lifted a brow. "Everything okay?"

Tabitha patted her heart to calm her heartbeat. "Yes."

"Good." Taking her hand, Marcus tugged her back into the auditorium for the conclusion of the play. About an hour later, they joined others for a standing ovation. With their hands intertwined, they strolled unhurried to their waiting limo, which whisked them off to dinner.

The candlelight, ambiance, and food were surreal. Tabitha couldn't remember feeling so content and happy, like a real-life princess. It had been so long since she'd felt normal. Rachel and Kym would be so happy for her. *I think.* She squeezed her lips together thinking, *Would they?*

"Hey, are you worried about Aunt Tweet?" Concern was etched across his face, and he placed his hand on top of hers.

"A little, but not really." She shrugged and turned away. "Actually, I was thinking about my sisters. We all wondered who would find love first."

"I'm glad it was you…and me." Marcus rubbed her hand with his thumb. "I've been praying for the Knicely sisters to reconcile. I can't imagine a divide like this with my only brother. Even though we can irritate each other big-time, family is family."

"I know." Closing her eyes, Tabitha bobbed her head, feeling worse.

"You may be the middle child, but you can be the leader. I didn't hear everything that was said, but I heard enough to know that it was your frustration talking, and your sisters didn't recognize it."

Although he was right, she didn't want to ruin her evening with bad thoughts. "Can we get back to us?" She smiled, hoping it would distract him. It didn't.

"Most definitely, but when I take you home tonight, there will be no goodbye kiss."

"What?" Tabitha rolled her eyes. That was the highlight of a first date. He had to be kidding. "You give me the most romantic evening, and we won't share a kiss at the end of it?"

"I'm not happy about withholding anything from you, but my relationship with Christ demands we seek spiritual intervention, and the rift with your sisters needs to be mended. My love for you goes beyond physical attraction. I care about you mentally and spiritually as well. I think we should end the night with prayer."

"Why can't we have both?" she asked, then ceased her protests. Isn't this what every woman wanted—a praying man who took his relationship with God seriously?

When their evening ended outside her front door, Marcus stared into her eyes. His were filled with love and shining like stars. Cupping her hands in his, he stepped closer. Tabitha's lids fluttered, thinking he'd changed his mind about their kiss as his lips moved closer to hers.

"Lord." His breath tickled her lips. "Please mend broken hearts. Tabitha needs her sisters, and they need her. Satan, the Lord rebukes you for the division you've caused. God has redeemed Tabitha, and she's taking back the joy you stole from her."

The more Marcus prayed, the more tears seemed to cleanse her soul. "'Let all bitterness, and wrath, and anger, and clamor, and evil speaking, be put away. Be kind one to another, tenderhearted, forgiving one another, even as I have forgiven you,'" Marcus said, quoting Ephesians 4:31–32.

He glanced away. "This isn't easy for me. I wanted to kiss you the first day we met. Your lips were that tempting, and still are." His nostrils flared with frustration. "Get it done, sweetheart, so I can get my goodnight kiss!" With that, he walked off her porch to the limo and didn't look back.

Chapter 29

TABITHA COULDN'T WAIT ANOTHER DAY. TWO WEEKS WAS A LONG time to be angry with her own flesh and blood. *Saying I'm sorry isn't cowardly*, Tabitha coaxed herself, then she admitted she needed their forgiveness as well to move on. She exhaled, situating her laptop between her and Aunt Tweet, then signed in to her Skype account. She connected with Rachel first, who Tabitha suspected Marcus's brother kept updated. Tabitha had been too busy in her own world to ask Rachel to define her relationship with Demetrius.

"Hey, Sis. Hi, Aunt Tweet." Rachel smiled, then waved. "'Bout time you called."

Here we go. Tabitha wanted to remind her that she could have called too, but Rachel wasn't the one who lost control. Tabitha owned, but regretted, snapping like that. After taking a deep breath, she added Kym to the chat.

"Well, hello," her oldest sister greeted, giving no hint of her mood or state of mind.

"Hi." Tabitha's vision blurred. "I'm sorry for being rude and putting you out a few weeks ago."

Kym's laugh eased the tension. "Correction: I packed my bags and left on my own."

Ouch. Ouch. "I'm so sorry," Tabitha repeated as tears spilled from her eyes. Someone else was sniffing, and she couldn't make out who.

"Shh...shh," Aunt Tweet said in a soothing voice and dabbed at Tabitha's tears with a napkin as if Tabitha were a little girl again. The gesture confirmed her aunt was still inside, no matter how faint.

"My outburst wasn't the best way to show my frustration and display my new salvation walk with Christ."

"If you don't stop crying, I'll start," Rachel said with a shaky voice.

Kym sniffed. "No, it wasn't, but I wasn't calling you first." She folded her arms. "As the oldest, you know how stubborn I am, but I love you."

Tabitha rolled her eyes and smirked. "Yes, we know," she and Rachel said in unison.

Clearing her throat, Kym perked up and waved at Aunt Tweet. "How are you doing?" When their aunt nodded, Kym looked at Tabitha. "Judging from the glow on your face, I'll ask: What has your marvelous Marcus done lately? Before you tell me, I'm sure I'll be jealous."

"You will." If she had known Kym would accept her apology this easily, she would have done it sooner.

Yes, forgiveness was a good thing. Closing her eyes, Tabitha exploded with happiness as she shared. "We went on our first date…" She didn't spare one detail.

It felt liberating to end the call on good terms. Immediately, she called Marcus.

"Hey, baby. I was thinking about you. Did you speak with your sisters?"

She nodded as if he could see. "Yes! It was as if nothing had happened, really. We're good. So, when is our next date?" she asked eagerly, anticipating their real first kiss.

"Hmm. Getting antsy, are you?" He laughed. "If it were up to me, it would be tonight, but I doubt if we could get Miss Betty at this late notice." He paused. "I know how hectic your weekdays are. How about Friday night?"

"Thursday," she countered and ended the call, grinning.

⌒

Four days later, Marcus sat at his desk, counting down the hours before he took Tabitha out again. He was fumbling through his mail when a small envelope caught his attention: a formal invitation.

His heart swelled with pride as he read the announcement that Latrice was graduating from St. Louis Community College with her nursing assistant certification. Already? He remembered when she started attending class. "I wouldn't miss the ceremony for anything."

Demetrius strolled into the office, flexing his arm. "Sealed the MOHELA call center deal."

"Yes! That will allow us to add ten people to our payroll." Marcus stood from behind his desk and bumped his brother's fist before wrapping him in a bear hug. They gave each other hearty claps on the back. "The good news keeps coming." He bobbed his head.

"Oh? What else you got?" Demetrius rested his computer bag on his desk before leaning against it. His brother crossed his arms and waited.

"Latrice has completed her CNA certification and is graduating at the end of the month."

His brother's shoulders slumped. "Is that all?" He took his seat behind his desk. "I thought it was business related."

"Changing lives is our business, which is why we started Whittington Janitorial Services, remember?"

"How can I forget?" Demetrius said slowly, then frowned. "But you took on Latrice and Victor's situation as if you were...their caregivers. Isn't Tabitha and her aunt enough?"

Marcus twitched his mouth. The sisters had reconciled. He didn't want to have a falling-out with his dear brother over his girlfriend. "Don't bring my lady into this."

"Come on, Marc." Demetrius didn't back down as he shortened his brother's name, which he very seldom did. "I wonder if you think things through before you try to rescue people. You're essentially inviting yourself into their lives and problems."

Yeah, maybe it was their turn for a blowup. "Family shouldn't be the only people we care about," Marcus snapped.

"True, but you willingly sought a relationship with Tabitha knowing she had no time for you. Then you went and fell in love with her and the auntie. In a few short months, it will be Rachel's turn—"

Ah, now his brother's comments were beginning to make sense. "And you don't see yourself coming to Rachel's rescue."

"Not just her—any woman in that way. Whew." Demetrius shook his head. "I enjoy her humor and sass, but with her aunt in the picture, it's like dating a woman with two or three kids."

Marcus grunted. "I didn't know it was getting that serious with you two."

"Rachel is not a woman who can easily be dismissed with her looks and wits. Yet, I tried my best not to get in deep—you know, with the age difference and all." Demetrius tapped his pen on his desk.

Amused and showing no pity for his brother's dilemma, Marcus turned toward his computer. He burst into laughter. "Good luck, dude. I've learned a Knicely sister is hard to resist."

"Watch me." Demetrius sounded as if he was trying to convince himself. Despite winning the new account, his brother seemed to be in an irritated state most of the day, while Marcus was in a jovial mood. Since dates were a premium as a caregiver, he wanted to make each date with Tabitha count.

Later that evening, Miss Betty opened Tabitha's door and greeted him with a smile. "Hello, Marcus. Don't you look handsome?"

"Why, thank you," he said and strolled toward the kitchen, overlooking the adjacent family room. Aunt Tweet's eyes lit up when she saw him. "Hi, mister."

"How ya doing?" He took the seat next to her, squeezed her hand, and kissed her cheek.

They chatted a few minutes—or rather, he listened while she rambled on about being a teacher. She had such a flair for storytelling. He wished it had worked out differently with the children at his company.

When Tabitha appeared, Marcus met her halfway and wrapped her in a hug. "Hi, gorgeous." He stepped back and admired what she was wearing. "Come on. It's a work night, and I don't want to have you out too late." He winked back at Miss Betty and waved good night to Aunt Tweet, then ushered Tabitha out the door to his car.

Once she was strapped in her seat belt, she faced him. "Where are we going?"

"Dinner" was all he would say until he turned into the parking lot of the Bonefish Grill near the Saint Louis Galleria. Since neither had eaten there before, it was another first for them to experience together.

Tabitha seemed impressed by the understated elegance as she looked around. Her eyes sparkled. Once they were seated, their server pampered them with attention. "What's the occasion?" he asked.

Marcus gave Tabitha a slow appraisal, causing her to shiver, then he faced the server. "Do you see how beautiful she is? A man doesn't need a reason."

Speechless, their server turned red and stuttered, "I-I agree. Would you like to see our drink menu to celebrate?" He recovered with a wide grin.

"We don't drink, so Sprite works for us." Next, Marcus ordered the house signature appetizer, Bang Bang Shrimp, and their meals.

As the young man hurried away, Marcus met Tabitha's stare. "What?"

"You embarrassed him. You could have said there was no occasion."

Leaning across the table, he urged her to meet him halfway. "We're together, so I call that a special event. Plus, you are beautiful." He heard her suck in her breath, and his heart skipped a beat.

In no time, the server brought their appetizer. Marcus took her hands. They were incredibly soft, and that momentarily distracted him. He cleared his mind, then asked for blessings over their meal.

Tabitha whispered "Amen" and glanced up. "Thank you for giving me peace."

"You're welcome. Before we feast, let's make sure the security video is working."

Tabitha couldn't contain her amusement. To ease their curiosity, she retrieved her phone out of her purse and tapped her home security icon. They both released audible sighs when they saw the two women were watching television. After putting the phone away, they sampled the signature dish.

Their Atlantic salmon, jollof rice, and mixed vegetables arrived minutes after they'd devoured the Bang Bang Shrimp. Since both agreed not to discuss work, their conversation was lighthearted and carefree while they enjoyed their meals and each other's company.

"Tonight is a celebration, right?" their server said as he reappeared at their table and insisted they taste a slice of key lime pie.

"Bring it on." Marcus winked at Tabitha.

Minutes later, they had no regrets indulging in the scrumptious dessert. But the night was getting late too fast, so Marcus begrudgingly paid their tab. Taking her hand, they strolled out of the restaurant. "That was nice," she said, patting her stomach.

He wrapped his arm around her waist, and she leaned into him. "We have a quick stop to make before going home."

"O-okay." The detour was to the Barnes & Noble in Ladue Crossing Shopping Center, less than six minutes away.

"We're stopping for a book?" She frowned.

Marcus shrugged. "Just a little browsing," he said and helped her out of his car. He had called ahead to make sure the title he wanted was in stock, so he weaved in and out of sections until his foot touched the multicolored carpet showcasing the children's section. To his delight, they were alone.

"What's going on?"

He chuckled and hoped she would appreciate this date idea he had found online. He spied the perfect seating arrangement in the corner. "Why don't you make yourself comfortable over there?" He pointed.

"We're dressed up, and you want me to sit on a bean bag?" She shot him a bewildered look.

She hesitated until he added, "Please?"

When she complied, he scanned the selection for Rachel Isadora's *The Princess and the Pea*. Taking it from the shelf, he swaggered toward her, then shifted next to her, practically sitting on the floor. "Come closer," he said in a low voice.

Opening the colorful, thirty-two-page picture book written for third graders or younger, Marcus cleared his throat. "Once upon a time..."

Tabitha didn't interrupt, instead looping her arm through his, resting her head on his shoulder, and silently listening until he turned to the last page.

"And the prince and princess lived happily ever after." He closed the book and looked down at her. "You're my princess, and tonight, you remind me of one with your hair brushed up."

"Thank you. That was a beautiful story," she whispered. She rubbed his beard and brushed her lips against his. "I needed that escape from reality. You're so sweet."

He exhaled. "You didn't think it was corny?"

She shook her head. "No, it was beautiful."

He had succeeded in making their brief date memorable. "It might have been a fairy tale, but the reality is I love you." They stood. As he was about to return the book to the shelf, she stopped him. "You're not going to buy it for me?"

"Really?" Marcus smiled, pleased she wanted it.

"Of course." Tabitha held on to the hard copy book until she had to hand it over to the cashier.

Once they were inside his car, she demanded an autograph. "Seriously, you do know I only read the book. I didn't write it." He chuckled.

"But *you* read it to me"—she patted her chest and lifted her chin—"so that makes it special."

"Yes, ma'am." Before he started the engine, he took the book and retrieved a pen from his glove compartment and scribbled *I'm only a prince because I've found my princess*. He dated it and signed *Love, Marcus*.

When he gave it back to her, she clutched the book as if it were worth millions. If it was a sentimental moment for her, it was colossal for him.

Too soon, they arrived in their neighborhood. Standing outside Tabitha's front door, Marcus smiled at her whimsical expression, which made her look as if she was in a daze. Was his childish gimmick the highlight of her night? It wouldn't be for long, as Marcus gently guided her lips to his and kissed her until they both gasped for air.

Chapter 30

"I CAN'T WAIT TO MEET TABITHA!" SYLVIA WHITTINGTON GUSHED from her perch in the back seat of Marcus's car.

Marcus had just picked up his parents from Lambert Airport for their biannual visit to St. Louis. They always reserved a week or so in August; the other week was for another time of the year.

"You're going to have to put that on hold, hon," his father said from the front passenger seat. "First stop, White Castle."

"John Whittington, I can't believe you can still stomach those sour onion burgers," his mother scolded, entertaining Marcus with their light-hearted banter.

His father stood at six three and had a distinguished appearance, with his white hair and mustache. He worked out and was in great shape for his late sixties. Silver hair never looked more elegant on a woman than his mother. She was still stunning at sixty-five, with a dab of red lipstick and no other cosmetics. Their marriage was exemplary, and Marcus wanted to copy it.

Married for thirty-nine years, the couple never ceased acting like boyfriend and girlfriend. While growing up, his father called his mother "sweetheart" so much that Marcus and Demetrius had thought that was her name when they were young children. His parents nurtured them in a warm and loving environment, and that's what Marcus wanted for his own future family.

Exiting off I-170, he drove the opposite direction on Natural Bridge to the closest White Castle. To his mother's dismay, his father asked for the Castle Pack 9, which contained twenty sliders and four orders of fries.

Marcus didn't butt in. His dad would consume at least half before the evening was over, maybe sharing a slider or two with his wife. If her husband hinted of a bellyache, she would dutifully pamper him back to good health. That was love. He chuckled to himself.

Releasing the lazy laugh his father was known for, John turned and faced his wife. "Sweetheart, you should talk. You know you're craving St. Louis fried rice and a St. Paul sandwich."

"Hmph. You got that right." She shrugged and glanced out the window. "Whew, with this St. Louis humidity, right now I'm thinking lemonade or a 7-Eleven Slurpee—something cold. Take me back to the North Carolina beaches." She chuckled.

"I can make a stop for you now, Mom." When she declined, he headed home. "Would you like to see where Tab—"

"Of course!"

Timing was everything. As he cruised down Roland Drive, his heart pounded at the sight of Tabitha stepping out of her car. The white romper against her dark skin was eye-catching. She looked so youthful. He tapped his horn, and she looked up, a slow smile giving way to a big grin that brightened her face.

He parked, leaving the motor running, and jogged to meet her. Tabitha's fragrance mingled with the musk of the scorching heat. She had twisted her hair into a ball on top of her head. The style gave her a sophisticated look, like the princess she was. He finished his assessment, then greeted her with his own smile. "Hey, baby."

"Hi," she said softly, as much in a trance as he was, then she blinked. "I've got to get Aunt Tweet out."

"Got it." Marcus took long strides to the other side of the car and assisted her aunt out, then kissed her cheek. He would have been disappointed if Aunt Tweet hadn't blushed.

"So what are you doing here? I thought your parents were coming to town," Tabitha said, shielding her eyes from the sun.

As if on cue, his father cut the engine, helped his mother out of the car, and they headed toward them. "They're here," he said, chuckling, "but you know I can't go too long without seeing you."

"I didn't want to intrude," Tabitha said softly, lowering her lashes.

"Oh, you aren't, dear." Marcus's petite mother nudged him aside. "We finally get a chance to meet you."

"It's hot," Aunt Tweet said.

Marcus had forgotten that the elderly struggle to breathe in the terrible air quality caused by the heat. Everyone mumbled their apologies. "Get her inside, babe. I'll get my parents settled, and we can come back with dinner."

"If it's not interfering with your plans, then I'll make some fresh lemon-limeade and a fruit salad," Tabitha offered.

Without knowing it, his lady had scored a brownie point with his mother. Sylvia wouldn't be able to resist Tabitha's fresh lemonade with lime and strawberries. Marcus's mouth was watering already. And to think, he teased her about not being a skillful cook. He had been on the receiving end of her and some of her aunt's dishes. Marcus had no complaints. Taking her hand before she escaped, Marcus smacked a kiss on Tabitha's lips, then released her.

"She's pretty, Son," Sylvia announced—he was sure for Tabitha's hearing—as they walked away.

He puffed out his chest in pride as he slid behind the wheel. "Yes she is, and with a caring heart."

"When's the wedding?" his parents teased almost in unison once they'd all strapped on their seat belts.

"Soon." He grinned. He didn't know if he would propose while Aunt Tweet still resided here or after she left to stay with Rachel. If left up to him, a month, tops.

———

A day later, Tabitha worked side by side with Marcus's mother in his kitchen to prepare meat for the men, including Demetrius, to barbecue. Aunt Tweet's task was to arrange cookies on a platter. Twice, Tabitha had looked the other way when her aunt swiped one of the treats and stuffed it in her purse. There wouldn't be a third time because Tabitha was ready to put a stop to it. Evidently, nothing got past Sylvia either, who chuckled softly.

Marcus's mother didn't come across as a woman who purposely enjoyed intimidating her sons' girlfriends. She was warm, friendly, and likeable. Marcus had her eyes, but his other features were a copy of Mr. Whittington's. "Your son is a jewel," Tabitha confided when there was a lull in their conversation. She doubted another man would have pursued her or stuck around, knowing her situation.

"And you're his precious stone." Sylvia's eyes sparkled. "He talks about you and your aunt all the time. From what he's told me, you're doing a great job taking care of her. Trust me, a person can tell when someone is neglected. Your aunt is loved."

"Thank you for saying that," Tabitha choked out. She wasn't expecting high praise. "Marcus has made the difference."

"Since you work through the week, how about doing a little shopping after church tomorrow?"

"I have Aunt Tweet—"

"She is welcome to come," Sylvia said before Tabitha could finish. "We'll visit a few stores, then rest for a cool treat. If she's not up to it, I'm sure Marcus wouldn't mind."

"Mind what?" He walked through the door and squeezed his mother's shoulder, then wrapped his arms around Tabitha's waist, peeping over her shoulder.

"Staying with Aunt Tweet for a few hours while Tabitha and I spend some time together shopping."

"No problem, babe." He sealed his commitment with a brush of his lips against Tabitha's cheek.

The man had no shame in displaying his affections in front of his parents. His father seemed to be amused while his mother appeared pleased by her son's actions.

Within the hour, they were all relaxing on his veranda off the kitchen, which resembled a gazebo attached to the side of his house. A big willow tree gave them shade, and every now and then, a cool breeze would stir its cascading branches to fan them. The conversation was lively, and even Aunt Tweet chuckled a few times as the Whittingtons relived the antics of their sons, to their protests. Demetrius and Marcus blamed each other for their mischievous adventures. When her aunt began to doze, Tabitha called it a night.

Marcus grabbed his keys. "I'll be right back. I'm going to make sure the ladies get home okay."

"Did you forget I drove?" Tabitha asked in a sassy tone.

"Nope." He rocked on his heels. "I'm trailing to make sure you get into the house safely."

Everyone laughed, including Tabitha, who couldn't resist hugging him. "I think it's sweet," she murmured as he kissed the tip of her nose.

On Sunday morning, church was a family affair. Besides the senior Whittingtons, Demetrius tagged along. Once seated in the pews, it didn't take long for Aunt Tweet to hum in unison with the praise singers. A couple of times, she belted out tunes that had been unearthed deep inside of her.

Pastor Nelson had a few remarks before directing the congregation to 1 Corinthians 15:58: "'My beloved brethren, stand firm and let nothing move you from God's calling on your life.' Be encouraged that whatever work you're doing to honor the Lord isn't in vain…"

Every sermon seemed to inspire Tabitha to keep pressing on despite the obstacles she faced at home and work. Once the benediction was given, the Whittingtons commented on how the preacher had given them a reminder not to get weary in doing good things for others. A few hours later, Aunt Tweet declined the outing and stayed behind at Tabitha's house under the watchful eye of Marcus and his father.

During their time together, she had a chance to learn more about Marcus's mother. Tabitha shared tidbits about her upbringing, career achievements, and goals in life. The conversation switched to questions about Aunt Tweet's diagnosis.

"If you feel comfortable with me asking," said Sylvia respectfully.

"Sure." Tabitha gave Sylvia a recap.

"My son told me you and your sisters had a misunderstanding."

Tabitha froze and tried not to squint. "What didn't your son tell you?" She didn't know how she felt about his mother knowing everything about her.

"When you were hurting, he was hurting, and I happened to call him at a time when I sensed he was sad." Sylvia offered a faint smile, then rested one of her hands on Tabitha's shoulder to get her attention. "Trust me, a lot of things I know about my sons are from watching what they do and listening for what they won't tell me." She laughed. "Marcus wasn't forthcoming. I had to pull it out of him, and I'm glad I did, because I've been praying for you ever since he told me what you're doing for your aunt."

Tabitha relaxed. "My sisters and I have reconciled. This has been very stressful for me—all of us—but I'm learning as I go."

Sylvia gave her a tight hug like her mother used to give, then stepped back. "I can't say I know what you're going through."

"Marcus didn't, not at first. I'm so glad he didn't have me arrested."

His mother gasped. "What?" Looping her arm through Tabitha's, Sylvia practically dragged her to a seating area. "He didn't tell me that part." She swung one leg over her other leg's knee and leaned back. "Go. Give me all the details, so I'll know how much of a beatdown he'll get from me."

Judging from Sylvia's expression, if Marcus were a child, he would be getting a spanking when his mother got home. Tabitha laughed. "God has been my peace at times when I didn't even understand how I was holding things together. Marcus has been my sanity, and let me just say, every woman needs a Marcus in her life."

"Since he's my son, I'll say amen to that."

Chapter 31

Tabitha sat in Dr. Phillips's waiting area, hoping that the physician would see the benefits in prescribing Ceclor to his patients.

Although her sales for Porital and Dyabolin had exceeded her quota by 50 percent, she wouldn't see that $30,000 bonus if she didn't reach 100 percent quota with this sinus drug.

In the past, Tabitha thrived on the adrenaline rush of hitting the mark. Ceyle-Norman was no different in their pay structure. This time around, the push was exhausting. If her sales for Ceclor hit 99.99 percent, her bonus would fizzle to $1,300. She'd gotten into this business to make money, not lose it, so it was crunch time.

"Sorry, Tabitha. Dr. Philips will be about another ten minutes," Shirley, the head nurse, said after peeping her head out the door into the waiting room. "Would you like to come back?"

"Oh, no. I'll wait." Even though she had two other doctor visits, she needed Dr. Philips's commitment to prescribe Ceclor to meet her quota. She would camp out at this otolaryngologist's office, if needed.

Ten minutes, huh? She needed a distraction to calm her nerves and to keep from gnawing off her lipstick. Checking the time, she guessed Ava Elise would be on her morning break from the new training class, so she texted her friend, who would understand her anxiety.

Busy?

I have a few minutes. What's going on?

Trying to hit my numbers on Ceclor. I'm at Dr. Philips's office.

Lol. Then that woman is in trouble. You can do it. Ava Elise had faith in Tabitha from day one despite her meltdowns. Take a deep breath and think happy thoughts about your handsome boyfriend.

Immediately, Tabitha smiled. She would have texted Marcus first, but he'd mentioned meeting with a client that morning. I met his mother. Very nice and sweet lady.

Hmm. Does she have mother-in-law potential?

Tabitha laughed. If Marcus and I reach that point. Definitely.

I hope I get to meet your man before the wedding. BIG hint. Got to get back to class. Remember, this is why you were a senior rep at Pfizer. You know how to make it happen!

Before she could type back, Dr. Philips opened the door and waved Tabitha forward. "Sorry to keep you waiting. My phone conference ran over," she said, leading the way to her office. Dr. Philips sat behind her desk and folded her hands. "So, I haven't quite made up my mind about Ceclor. As you know, we see patients with acute and chronic sinusitis after their home treatments have failed them. Our treatment is like a classroom formula: saline nasal irrigation; nasal, oral, or injected cortico-steroids; or aspirin desensitization treatment."

"For your chronic sufferers, that's a complicated treatment regimen," Tabitha said, countering, "which is why Ceclor is designed more as a preventive drug, especially if the condition is associated with allergies."

"Indeed." Dr. Philips nodded. "The patients who have used the samples haven't reported any side effects, but I still would like to see more results from clinical studies."

"I can get you that. Anything else to convince you that Ceclor will help those hard-to-treat patients?" She knew her spreadsheet of pros and cons wasn't enough.

"Yes, discount coupons for Ceclor and whether most insurance companies will cover it."

"Although it's fairly new, United Healthcare, Cigna, and Blue Cross Blue Shield are covering the drug."

"Very well. I'll wait for that additional information before making a decision." Standing, she reached across the desk and shook Tabitha's hand, signaling an end to their meeting. "I do think Ceyle-Norman has a winner, but I want to make sure."

On her way back to her car, Tabitha texted Marcus. Whew. Hard sell.

Is that a yes or no?

A maybe—if I can get information to her ASAP, which will be tonight, because I have two more stops to make.

Bummer. I was hoping for a midweek celebration. Mom had agreed to sit with Aunt Tweet so we could go to dinner. I guess I moved too fast.

Activating her Bluetooth, she called him. "Sorry for the trouble. I'll definitely need a rain check this time."

"It doesn't make sense to let a dinner date go to waste. I want to spend time with you."

She laughed. "Right. What are you going to do, watch me work?"

"How did ya know?" He laughed harder. "I'll pick you up by six thirty, then I'll chauffeur you to a quiet place so you can work or I can help."

There wasn't too much she could say to this man for him to take no for answer. Marcus had no idea how bored he would become. "This won't be a date but punishment."

"Never with you."

If his mother was willing to stay with Aunt Tweet, Marcus wasn't turning down a free caregiver. Since they were within walking distance of his alma mater, the University of Missouri–St. Louis campus, he planned to sign out a study room at the library, where they could bring in carryout. He also brought his headset to watch a movie on his tablet.

But it didn't work out as he had planned once he and Tabitha were settled in the room off the main library. He couldn't bear to watch her tug on her hair, sigh, and grit her teeth. Plus, she hadn't touched the grilled chicken salad he had gotten for them.

"Babe, tell me what I can do."

She exhaled and twisted her lips in frustration. "Not much. I'm searching for clinical trial results from our competitors' drugs for sinusitis."

He pulled up Google and his fingers hovered over the keyboard. "Give me some keywords and I'll do a search. If I find something helpful, it will cut down on your frustration."

Whether it was a challenge or just to amuse him, Tabitha did as he asked. "You can start on clinicaltrials.gov."

"Okay." Searching by diagnosis, his jaw dropped. There were almost three hundred results. Tabitha would have to pull an all-nighter to go through them. Switching into study mode, Marcus concentrated on reading. "Hey, babe, I thought this one might be interesting." He angled his tablet, so she could see. She nodded and typed in the website address.

Marcus felt as if he had been awarded a gold star. With gusto, he dug back into the case studies.

Almost three hours later, Tabitha stifled a yawn, then rubbed her eyes. He coaxed her to stand and stretch.

"We make a good team." Exhausted, Marcus rolled his shoulders. He could only imagine how tired she must be. At least they were five minutes from their homes. "This was exhausting."

Leaning over the table, she saved her work and shut down her computer. "Although I enjoy my job, these last-minute requests aren't fun. I hope it pays off. I used to tuck away my bonuses, so I could travel with my sisters."

Marcus gathered their empty bags and threw them in the trash receptacle. "I would like to think I'll be a better travel companion than your sisters."

She gave him a strange look. No need to show his hand yet, but the next trip she planned would be with him, a ring on her finger and a marriage certificate signed.

Chapter 32

THE FOLLOWING WEEK, MARCUS'S EXCITEMENT AMUSED TABITHA AS he glanced around the massive auditorium filled with balloons and the occasional floral bouquets. They were among thousands of family and friends gathered to witness the graduation ceremony.

The Chaifetz Arena on Saint Louis University's campus had played host to the school's home sports games and sold-out concerts like Beyoncé—even the U.S. Olympics tryouts that gymnast Simone Biles took part in before she became a gold medalist were held on the site.

When Tabitha scanned the program and noted that all four St. Louis community college campuses were participating in the graduation, she braced for a long night.

Marcus had invited her and Aunt Tweet to the Friday evening commencement services the same day he took his parents to the airport for their return flight to North Carolina. Tabitha wasn't sure if she would get home from work in time, but she did and even managed to shower and change out of her suit and into something dressy but casual. Glancing around the auditorium, Tabitha was glad she hadn't dragged her aunt to this event. Lately, Aunt Tweet had seemed more exhausted after her days at Bermuda Place. She was eighty-five years old, so it was a no-brainer that she should rest and have Miss Betty keep watch.

Eyeing Marcus again, Tabitha chuckled to herself. Would he be this antsy at his children's grade school, high school, and college graduations? His exhilaration over the accomplishments of one of his employees was contagious.

"That's her." Marcus pointed to the name Latrice Germaine Allen listed among hundreds of others receiving their nurse assistant certifications.

Her mind drifted to when she, Kym, and Rachel had graduated with honors from Purdue, Temple, and Fisk Universities, respectively. Aunt Tweet had joined their parents in attendance. "You've earned this accomplishment that can never be taken away," their aunt had said to them. "Knowledge."

Once the ceremony started, his eyes sparkled as the class receiving the nurse assistant certificates stood. Marcus's energy was tangible as the dean of the school drew closer to calling his employee's name.

"Latrice Germaine Allen." The young woman's smile was bright as she strolled across the stage.

Jumping to his feet, Marcus released a piercing whistle that seemed to echo throughout the arena. Next, he fumbled with his phone to take pictures until Latrice had exited the stage. Reluctantly, he took his seat when his employee's moment to shine was replaced by the next graduate's. Looking at Tabitha, he exhaled. "This is going on our employee brag board." He pointed to the picture on his phone.

"You okay?" She had never seen him so discombobulated. "You told me a little about her ex-boyfriend and children, but you're reacting to her differently from at the barbecue. Then, it seemed like she irritated you, but I can sense the adoration you have for her. I can see it in your eyes. I'm glad God turned your relationship with her around."

He shrugged. "I like to see people succeed, especially single mothers who are often negatively stereotyped." He paused. "Honestly, I had put a lot of faith in her ex-boyfriend taking the lead."

Slipping her arm through his, she rested her head on his shoulder. "Remember Pastor Nelson's sermon from last week. 'Putting our faith in God will never disappoint us. Imperfect people are known to fail us.'"

Marcus bobbed his head, turned, and met her eyes. "You're right. Thank you for reminding me, my girlfriend."

The ceremony ended sooner than Tabitha had expected. With her hand secured in Marcus's, they weaved through the crowd to find Latrice, who was taking pictures with friends and family. Her face glowed with happiness when she saw Marcus.

"Mr. Whittington, you came!" After a brief hug, she stepped back. "Thank you for believing in me."

"You're welcome." Marcus turned and made the introductions. "This beautiful lady is my girlfriend."

"We met at the company barbecue," Latrice reminded him, and they shared a knowing chuckle.

"Congratulations." Tabitha extended her hand, but the young lady hugged her too.

"Thank you for sharing him with me—us. I'll always remember to pay it forward, to give others second chances," Latrice assured her.

"Does that include me?" A deep voice made everyone turn around. The handsome man was rough around the edges, judging from his sloppy clothes. He clutched an amazing, colorful bouquet.

Two little boys raced his way, shouting, "Daddy! Daddy!"

"That's Victor," Marcus whispered in her ear.

Tabitha had figured as much, seeing the good, bad, ugly, and recycled versions of the man.

"Congratulations, Latrice Germaine Allen. I see now that I was never good enough for you." He handed her the flowers, then heaved both boys into his arms with no effort.

The buzz around them hushed as bystanders seemed eager for her response. Latrice said nothing.

"I'm sorry I've disappointed you and my sons and never been man enough to earn your love and respect." He paused, glanced away, then faced her again. "I'm learning from my mistakes, and one day, I will walk across a stage with some type of accomplishment. You'll see. You might not want me in your life, but I hope to be in my sons' lives."

His heartfelt confession touched Tabitha.

"Then I'll pray that day comes soon because I love you, and if you can accept God's love and salvation, everything will change between us." Latrice stepped closer and wrapped an arm around Victor's neck, then gave him a brief but passionate kiss. "For my heart's sake and our boys', I'll wait from afar. Word to the wise: don't let another man take your place in our lives. Victor, the ball is in your court."

Whoa. High five, girl. Tabitha had to give the woman credit. Latrice loved him but was standing her ground.

"I'll work on me." He bobbed his head as he backed away, then rubbed the top of his sons' heads. "I'll let you celebrate this big day with your family and friends," he choked out, clearly hoping for an invitation.

"Thank you" was all Latrice said.

Victor walked away. His broad shoulders were slumped, seemingly weighed down with a heavy burden. Tabitha turned to Marcus. "What do you think? Please tell me that you believe in a happy ending for them." She was hopeful.

"It's hard to call. Both are determined to do what they think is best. Only God knows."

Moments later, Marcus gave Latrice a card, which probably contained money, and shook hands with her family, introducing Tabitha as his girlfriend, the way he said it always making her blush. Soon, they left the crowd to enjoy a quiet dinner at the Kitchen Sink restaurant.

Once they received their meals, Marcus gave thanks for their food. There was always something comforting about the way he prayed. His voice was deep and strong, but his reverence for the Lord was unmistakably in awe. After they whispered "Amen," she stole one of his fries, dabbed it in his ketchup, and grinned in victory.

"I only let my girlfriend do that." He winked.

"Lucky me—no, I'm blessed." They teased, joked, and whispered their love until Tabitha checked the time. "We'd better head home. My sisters are flying in early in the morning, so we can be together for the long Labor Day weekend."

Wrinkles etched his forehead. "You sure everything's okay? I won't have you upset again." His mouth twitched, possibly indicating that he would be her bodyguard if he felt she needed one.

"Hey." She rubbed his arm and could feel his muscles flex. "We'll be fine. I won't need your private security detail."

Marcus patted his chest. "I'll be on standby to be on the safe side." He signaled to their waiter for the check. "I'm your caregiver, and I care about you more than I have any woman."

His words warmed her heart. "I believe that," she whispered, then repeated it louder.

———

The next morning, Aunt Tweet woke in a combative mood and moved slowly as Tabitha tried to get their day going. She was on the red-scarf binge again and refused to leave the house without it, despite the blistering late-summer heat. Their battle of wills caused Tabitha to be late picking up Rachel and Kym from the airport. Although their aunt's eyes sparkled with recognition, Aunt Tweet called both of Tabitha's sisters "miss." Tabitha could see the pained expressions on their faces.

Back at her house, the atmosphere was so different from before. Kym and Rachel were low-key about going out. Instead, they helped with chores around the house and seemed content with lounging around. That afternoon, while all the sisters were in the kitchen cooking, the doorbell rang.

"Expecting someone?" Kym lifted her brow, teasing, then grinned.

"Girl, please. You know it's Marcus." Rachel bumped Kym's hip. "I wonder if Demetrius is with him," she stated nonchalantly.

"You're crushing on him." Tabitha laughed as she hurried to answer the door. To her delight, Marcus stood larger than life with a smile that made his eyes dance. Unfortunately for Rachel, he was alone.

He stepped inside and graced her with a kiss, then whispered against her lips, "Is everything peaceful?" He stared into her eyes for the truth.

"Peaceful and perfect." Grabbing his hand, she tugged him toward the kitchen. Rachel pouted her disappointment, Kym was cordial, and Aunt Tweet sat patiently at the table, waiting her for an acknowledgment.

He lifted a bag. "Gooey butter cake, ladies." He grinned and kissed Aunt Tweet on the cheek. "Can't go wrong with a St. Louis favorite."

His thoughtfulness was definitely an icebreaker. The rest of the afternoon, they relaxed and watched movies.

Sunday morning, Kym assisted Aunt Tweet with bathing and dressing while Rachel prepared omelets. An hour later, Marcus arrived to chauffeur them to church.

Pastor Nelson was about to preach when Demetrius strolled into the sanctuary. Rachel seemed to perk up. The pastor's message was about empathizing with others by walking in their shoes.

Tabitha and Marcus exchanged knowing smiles before he took her hand and squeezed it.

The next morning, the sisters had their family meeting. "You know, I'm starting to see subtle changes in Aunt Tweet," Kym admitted. "I'm not sure if her current medicine is slowing down the progression of dementia or not."

Rachel looked worried. "I can't help but wonder what state of mind she'll be in when I take her after Thanksgiving."

"Your turn begins the first week in November," Tabitha reminded her. Not that she was trying to get rid of Aunt Tweet, but that was the arrangement. Because of Marcus, she had stopped counting down the weeks and lived moment to moment.

"Ah." Rachel bowed her head before looking up again. "I was hoping you wouldn't mind doing the trade-off the day after Thanksgiving. I mean, we can be together for the holidays."

"We can easily come to Nashville," Tabitha said, recalling Fourth of July, when she had expected her sisters and they'd postponed, opting to celebrate Aunt Tweet's birthday. That had been understandable and reasonable in hindsight.

"I know." Rachel fumbled with her fingers. "I kinda need the extra time." She lowered her voice and swallowed. "I know we were against this, but what about a nursing facility?"

Tabitha's heart dropped but bounced back. Blinking, she waited for her big sister's response.

Shaking her head, Kym exhaled. "We all agreed to this caregivers' pact. Maybe we can revisit this *after* your commitment. Until then, I think we all should spend time with her before it comes to that."

Good advice, Tabitha thought as Rachel gnawed her on lips. The fear of the unknown was plastered on their younger sister's face.

Welcome to my world. Closing her eyes, Tabitha rubbed her temples. She had double circled November 6 on her kitchen calendar, set a reminder in her phone; she and Marcus had planned a dinner-and-movie night. It wasn't to celebrate Aunt Tweet's leaving but Tabitha making her bonus! It had been a nail-biter down to the last day, but the numbers didn't lie. "Okay, we can wait until after Thanksgiving, but you two better remember my flexibility. By the way, Marcus and I are participating in the Walk to End Alzheimer's event in a few weeks."

"Marcus?" Kym lifted a brow, then smiled.

"Yes," Tabitha said smugly. "Aunt Tweet brought us together, and he has been with me every step of the way. No pun intended." She grinned. "Well, maybe just a little." She demonstrated with a slight gap between her finger and thumb.

Rachel hmphed. "I need me a Marcus in my life if I'm going to pull off my six months."

"Sorry. He's one of a kind. Besides, aren't you and Demetrius talking seriously?"

"Demetrius isn't my neighbor. Even if I weren't going to be a caregiver, I don't think we would work anyway. I'm high maintenance..."

Tabitha and Kym succumbed to a fit of giggles. "We know," Tabitha muttered.

Rachel rolled her eyes. "Haters." Getting up from the sofa, she walked toward the kitchen, then sassed over her shoulder. "See if I don't outshine both of you as a caregiver."

"We're all from the Show-Me State," Kym challenged, "so show us."

Chapter 33

WHEN MARCUS HEARD ABOUT THE ALZHEIMER'S ASSOCIATION'S biggest fundraiser, the Walk to End Alzheimer's, he didn't think twice about getting involved. Because of Aunt Tweet, Marcus had experienced firsthand the effects Alzheimer's had on its victims as the dementia symptoms ravished her brain cells.

He was glad to help Tabitha make it a team effort, as she had rallied fellow sales reps to join in. Her sisters flew back to St. Louis to participate in the walk, even though they had the same event in their respective cities. Marcus took it a step further by announcing Whittington Janitorial Services would sponsor their own team on the walk.

Twenty of Marcus's employees pledged to support the Tweety Bird Team. Chess appointed himself to lead the team, but Marcus tapped his former employee instead. Currently a certified nursing assistant at Delmar Gardens nursing facility, where many patients with the disease resided, Latrice was the perfect candidate and immediately said yes when Marcus asked her. Somehow, Victor got wind of the buzz at Whittington Janitorial and called Marcus.

"Is it okay if I donate some money?"

"You don't want to walk in the event?" Marcus asked him.

"Nah. I want to give Latrice space."

"You do realize there's going to be thousands of thousands of people there. Unless you have GPS tracking on her..." Marcus paused. He didn't want to give Victor any ideas that could result in stalking charges.

"Nah, I've disappointed her too many times." Victor was silent, then cleared his throat. "When I come back into her life, and I plan to, I'm comin' a better man. I'm working on it. Anyway, I want to invest that money I got from the lawsuit, so it will last a long time. But it wouldn't be right for me not to give back something for your cause. I got a hundred bucks to give."

"A hundred dollars is a lot of money, and God will bless for your generosity." Before they disconnected, Marcus offered Victor words of encouragement. "Check in with me from time to time and let me know how you're making it. I still believe in you."

"Latrice doesn't." He sounded wounded.

Marcus imparted some encouragement. "You might be surprised how things will turn out. The invitation is open to visit my church."

"Maybe," Victor said and ended the call.

The day of the walk, Kym and Rachel finally got a chance to meet Miss Betty, who stayed with Aunt Tweet during the event. They seemed to genuinely like the home companion.

As members of the Tweety Bird Team were gathering at the starting point, Tabitha was called away by an older couple.

Kym squinted at Marcus. "How come we don't have matching outfits?"

He snickered, knowing exactly what she was hinting at. The back of his and Tabitha's shirts read *Walking for the One I Love*. The meaning was twofold: they were walking for Aunt Tweet and each other. Marcus feigned cluelessness. "You do. Everyone is wearing our company's T-shirts."

"Except you and my sister." Kym folded her arms as Tabitha pulled the couple toward them.

"Marcus," she said, beaming, "this is Ava Elise and her husband, John."

Nodding, Marcus shook their hands. "My father's name is John."

"I've heard so much about you." The woman's eyes twinkled with mischief.

Reaching for Tabitha's hand, Marcus couldn't help but grin like a schoolboy. "Good things, I hope."

"How much time do you have?" Ava Elise rolled her eyes and laughed.

Marcus could never repay the kindness this woman had given his lady before he even knew all the circumstances. He was thankful that her trainer had been behind Tabitha since day one.

Next, Tabitha introduced Kym and Rachel to Ava Elise. While the sisters chatted with the woman, Marcus mentioned his business to John in case he found himself in the need of a cleaning crew for his company. After a few minutes, John and Ava Elise said their goodbyes.

"Rachel, you and I both need a Marcus in our lives," he overheard Kym say. Smirking, he thanked God for their stamp of approval.

Too bad Demetrius had backed out at the last minute. Maybe his big brother would drop that nonchalant exterior, like Marcus had done, and reveal his intentions concerning Rachel—whatever those might be. Marcus doubted Demetrius really knew himself.

When the organizer blew the whistle, Marcus took Tabitha's hand and began their trek. He wasn't going to lose her in the crowd.

It wasn't long before Rachel complained about her aching back, despite reciting her exercise regimen. Clearly, walking was excluded. "What was I thinking?"

"I'm glad I get my exercise walking across campus every day." Kym gave a demonstration of her power-walk stance.

"Sweet Pepper is getting me out walking in the neighborhood," Tabitha announced.

Marcus kept his amusement to himself. Walking the dog? A dog walking its owner burned up a couple hundred calories—tops.

The Knicely sisters lagged behind the others on the team at the end of the two-mile walk. All three moaned for foot massages. The good news was, thanks to corporate sponsors, the Tweety Bird Team raised $4,000.

Hours later, back in their Pasadena Hills neighborhood, Marcus and Tabitha sat in adjacent swings on the playground, holding hands.

They were barely moving, then Tabitha planted her feet on the ground to halt all movement. Facing him, she placed her soft hand on his jaw. She gazed into his eyes, and he saw the evidence of their love. "Thank you for being part of my journey—mentally, physically, and spiritually."

"Thank you for letting me in." When Marcus signed on to be

Tabitha's caregiver, he'd wanted to be her hero. Her thanks always humbled him. He leaned forward and rubbed his lips against hers, then whispered, "You have girlfriend benefits." He grinned.

Laughing, she playfully punched him in the arm, then pushed off the ground to climb higher. Like Marcus had done in the beginning, he chased after her, even if he was in a swing.

——

The last quarter of the year was a busy time for Whittington Janitorial Services, as Marcus and Demetrius started preparing their books in September for the auditors. They had been awarded three more major contracts over the previous year, so they were working long hours, crunching the numbers, assessing costs and profits.

Marcus wasn't happy about breaking dates with Tabitha, but his business paid the bills. The best he had been able to do was call and check up on her and Aunt Tweet, rather than visit as regularly throughout the week.

Tabitha's ringtone interrupted his review of their inventory against sales. "Hey, babe." She was frantic. "Slow down, baby. What's wrong?" Immediately, his senses went on alert.

Crying, she sniffed and said, "Bermuda Place called an ambulance because Aunt Tweet passed out. I'm in Wentzville, but I'm canceling appointments to head to DePaul's Hospital. I'm scared. I don't want her to die." She bawled some more.

"It's okay. Shh." Marcus stood and grabbed his keys. "I'm on my way there."

"What's going on?" Demetrius frowned in concern.

"Aunt Tweet. They called an ambulance. Tabitha is in St. Charles County, so it's going to take her a while to get back up north to the hospital. Since I'm the closest, I'll head over there."

Demetrius held up both hands. "Don't get me wrong, Bro, but that's her emergency, not ours. We're in a crucial time in our business. We both need to be at the top of our game for the audit. Can't you go by the hospital later, *after* your meeting with Energizer?"

"I can, but I'm not. If this were us with Mom or Dad, she would be there for me. Try loving someone and not making them your priority. You can't."

Although Marcus was praying for comfort for Tabitha, he was still going. His hand was on the doorknob when he looked back at the bewildered disappointment etched on his brother's face. "I know you think I've lost my mind over them, but I've surrendered my heart to Tabitha, so I'll keep you updated on what's going on."

"Yeah, do that," Demetrius bit out as Marcus hurried out of the office, bumping into Chess accidentally on his way out.

"Sorry," he mumbled to his employee.

The hospital was close. He heard the sirens behind him on I-270 as he exited on St. Charles Rock Road. He was about to turn into the parking lot when the flashing lights forced him to pull to the side.

Minutes later, when he arrived at the emergency room entrance, Marcus watched as the paramedics lifted a gurney out of an ambulance. Straining his neck, he trotted as close as he could to the vehicle to catch a glimpse of the patient. The woman had silver-gray hair like Aunt's Tweet, but an oxygen mask covered her nose and mouth, making a positive ID sketchy.

He raced inside to the counter, then it dawned on him that he wasn't related to Aunt Tweet, so the hospital personnel weren't likely to give him any information or go wait with her. *Now what?* Pacing the area outside the double doors, he called Tabitha. She answered just as franticly as earlier.

"Babe, it's okay. I got here right behind an ambulance. I think I might have seen her being wheeled in. How far out are you?"

"Just crossing over the Blanchette Bridge."

She had to be driving fifteen-plus miles over the limit to be one exit away so soon. "Slow down."

"Okay." She took a deep breath. "I feel better that you're there. I promise I'll return to sanity and obey the speed limit. Uh-oh. I've got a cop behind me."

Great. Marcus slapped his forehead. The blood drained from his face. "Do you need me to come?"

"No. Stay with Aunt Tweet." She disconnected when he would have preferred she stay on the line.

Police relations throughout St. Louis were still shaky after the Mike Brown shooting in Ferguson years ago. Depending on the officer's mood and mind-set, Tabitha might not necessarily be in safe hands. Now, Marcus had two things to worry about as he took a series of deep breaths, then walked through the double doors. "Lord, in the name of Jesus, please protect my woman from any harm and let the interaction between her and the officer be respectful, and please be with Aunt Tweet. Give her body and mind strength to pull through with thanksgiving. In Jesus's name, amen."

Stepping back inside, he walked to a row of chairs. He flopped down and continued to wait impatiently for Tabitha's arrival, despite his petition for godly intervention. He eyed the paramedics who had exited the ambulance. Did anyone from the facility escort Aunt Tweet here? He hoped she wasn't alone.

He couldn't sit still, so he stood and began to pace the floor until the path led him outside again. He said another prayer, then tried to switch his mind into work mode. Making some business calls would temporarily distract him. "Charles, Marcus Whittington here. I know we're supposed to review our contract in about an hour—"

"I'm glad you called," the man cut in. "I have a bit of an emergency. I'm heading out to get my son. His school called to say he's sick. Can we reschedule for early next week? Sorry to do this to you. I know you're a busy man."

"You are too. I hope your son feels better, and I'll be in touch." Energizer was one of Whittington's biggest clients, employing the majority of their workers at three locations. Charles had recently referred Whittington Janitorial Services to a medium-sized company for business. Marcus was grateful for this turn of events. It seemed the more he strengthened his spiritual walk, the more God gave him favor in situations.

Squinting toward the entrance, he saw Tabitha's sedan speeding his way. He waved her toward him.

"Please tell me you didn't get a ticket." He opened the driver's door and hugged her as soon as she stepped out and collapsed against him. "I'll park the car. You go in and see about Aunt Tweet."

"Okay," she mumbled as if in a daze. "Thankfully, the officer didn't give me a ticket but a warning. Didn't matter. I would have paid it. When he saw my tears, he let me go and told me to slow down."

He nudged her toward the door, then slid behind the wheel of her car. Once Marcus adjusted the seat, he drove away in search of a parking space. When he returned to the waiting room, Tabitha wasn't in sight, so he texted her. Is everything okay?

No response, so he took a seat. About ten minutes later, Tabitha called, whispering, "She's alert. They're running tests to rule out a stroke, a silent heart attack; they're also checking her blood sugar." She paused, clearly frazzled. "Thank you, Marcus, for coming and standing in the gap for me, but you can go. I know you're busy and—"

"I'm not going anywhere." Leaning back to rest his head against the wall, Marcus closed his eyes. Aunt Tweet was alive.

Chapter 34

TABITHA COULDN'T REMEMBER THE LAST TIME SHE WAS SO SCARED. While Aunt Tweet rested, she released silent tears. Her great-aunt could have died while she was locked up for driving almost eighty miles an hour in a company car.

She had to compose herself before calling her sisters. When she did, they became as frantic as she had been.

"I'll fly in tomorrow morning," Kym said in a subdued tone.

"Oh no. Poor Aunt Tweet. I'll hit the road in the morning and be there in the afternoon," Rachel said. "I guess I might as well bring back some of her things with me. I'm so scared I'll have these episodes with her."

"I'll be praying you don't. If we can keep her healthy..." Tabitha paused. Good health didn't mean a long life. Their aunt's life was in God's hands. "Ah, is your mind good enough to drive?"

"Yeah. Nashville is four and a half hours from St. Louis. Less if I speed."

"Please don't," Tabitha said, explaining her ordeal from earlier.

When a doctor opened the curtain before stepping into the examination room, a female resident trailed him. Tabitha paused and tapped speaker on her phone, so her sisters could hear.

"Miss Knicely, you indicated your aunt was a borderline diabetic." Tabitha nodded. "That is no longer the case. Her blood sugar level dropped dangerously low. We're going to give her insulin, but she will need to follow up with her primary care doctor right away."

Tabitha ignored Kym's squeak as she questioned the doctor. "Won't most of those medicines interact with her Alzheimer's medicine?"

The doctor shook his head. "Research shows that many patients who suffer with Alzheimer's have some form of diabetes or disturbed glucose metabolism."

"Our aunt isn't a fan of needles." Rachel voiced what Tabitha already knew. It was going to be a battle giving Aunt Tweet her injections at home.

After thanking the doctor, she let her sisters speak to their aunt, then Tabitha helped her get dressed. "Sorry to be so much trouble," Aunt Tweet said solemnly.

"No trouble." Tabitha's eyes blurred. Her lips trembled as fear lingered. "You scared me." She wrapped her arms around her aunt's shoulders and held her tight. "I love you. I'm glad you're okay. Let's go home."

Out in the waiting room, Tabitha smiled at the sight of Marcus asleep and slumped in a chair. His long legs were stretched out, arms folded, and head resting against the wall. Walking closer, Tabitha admired his features. The lines that wrinkled his forehead were an indication he wasn't at peace either. She loved this man so much.

Leaning over him, she rubbed his jaw. "Hey," she said softly. She watched as his long lashes fluttered. He opened his eyes and strained to focus on her face. Immediately, he straightened up and gave her his attention.

"Is everything…" His voice trailed off when he saw Aunt Tweet. Leaping to his feet, he wrapped his arms around her aunt, then dragged Tabitha into a group hug. "I'm so glad you're okay."

"Me too, mister."

Since the health scare, Tabitha had become clingy, not wanting to let her aunt out of her sight. It was good Rachel had asked to push back Aunt Tweet leaving until the weekend after Thanksgiving. The extra weeks would give Tabitha more time to spend with her.

Everything worked out for the best. Since Marcus was busy with contract negotiations, they agreed to put a date night during the week on hold. The only thing that didn't slow down was the demands of her job.

She had to rely on Miss Betty more as she sequestered herself in her bedroom to work on a project. In addition to reviewing doctors' profiles before setting up visits, she had to find a specialist outside of her territory who had successfully prescribed Porital to his patients. Dr. Rush from Cincinnati was perfect. She exchanged numerous emails with him until he agreed to give a presentation at a fee. After confirming a date, she secured a location and made his travel accommodations.

Weeks later, when the date arrived for the event, Marcus apologized profusely that he couldn't go with her because of a business engagement he had to attend with Demetrius.

"Next time, baby. I promise."

"You don't have to promise," she assured him one morning while she was on the road for a doctor's visit. "Consider us even. I had to turn down accompanying you to a fundraiser."

"We're not going to do tit for tat, girlfriend. Our schedules are crazy for now, but we always have our weekends."

"We do."

That evening, at the last minute, the agency called to advise Tabitha that Betty wouldn't be able to make it. Tabitha's heart dropped. The presentation she had set up couldn't be missed. "Do you have anyone else? I mean, they have to be trustworthy."

"No worries," the man said. "As soon as Betty called in, we started to make calls. I do have another candidate who says she would very much like to fill in for Betty tonight. Her name is Latrice Allen, and she says she met you when she was employed at Whittington Janitorial. Would it be acceptable for the agency to send Latrice to you this evening?"

In desperation mode, Tabitha didn't have any options, so she consented. She thought she'd ask Latrice a few questions when she arrived, hoping that would give her some peace of mind.

Fifteen minutes before she planned to leave, her doorbell rang. After fastening her earrings, she opened the door and greeted the nurse's aide.

"Hi, Miss Tabitha," Latrice Allen said in a professional manner. "Thanks for trusting me to fill in."

Although Tabitha was glad to see a familiar face, she didn't know if the young woman could handle her aunt, and she voiced her concerns.

"I'm trained to expect the unexpected with clients. Every client is special. Knowing how much Mr. Whittington thinks of Miss Brownlee, your aunt is more than special to me."

Tabitha was touched by Latrice's sincerity, but she had a few more questions to make her not second-guess leaving Aunt Tweet in Latrice's care. Satisfied with the young woman's answers, Tabitha gathered her things, then kissed and hugged Aunt Tweet goodbye. Once in her car, she touched the home security video app on her phone to see Latrice pulling a big jigsaw puzzle out of her bag and setting it up on the kitchen table. Aunt Tweet was watching the girl's every move.

"Maybe she will work out." She couldn't wait to tell Marcus who had shown up at her house to care for Aunt Tweet, but he was at a function, and she had to concentrate on hers.

She drove away, praying and trusting the Lord to keep her aunt safe. When Tabitha arrived at her venue, she checked her home security app again. Nothing seemed out of the ordinary as the two women played a card game. Satisfied, she regrouped for her event.

The two-hour function went smoothly. Dr. Rush was an animated, engaging speaker, who, according to an informal survey from some of the other doctors, had won them over. Even Ava Elise complimented Tabitha on organizing a well-thought-out event. The accolades made her miss Marcus's presence even more. She wanted him to witness the fruit of her labor. Immersed in ensuring her guests' comfort, Tabitha only checked on Aunt Tweet one other time but followed up with a phone call. All was going well.

When she returned home, Latrice had washed clothes and was folding them on the kitchen table with Sweet Pepper resting contentedly at her feet.

She stood. "How did the event go?"

"It was a success," Tabitha said in relief and grinned. "How did everything go with my aunt?"

"She's a very smart woman. We talked about a clothing business she owned and that she had fashions from Paris…"

Tabitha didn't try to dispel the woman's shero worship of her aunt.

She had come to the conclusion that eighty-five years was a lifetime of fading memories and experiences. When her aunt told those stories, whether the events had really happened or not, Tabitha accepted them and stopped asking questions.

"When I gave her a bath…"

"My aunt let you bathe her?" Tabitha blinked. A modest woman, Aunt Tweet fussed about Tabitha helping her put on her underwear in the beginning. She protested when Kym and Rachel bathed her too, but Aunt Tweet would be horrified to know a stranger had bathed her.

"Yes, ma'am, but only if I put a lot of bubbles in the water." They both laughed as Latrice gathered her bags and Tabitha walked her to the door.

Chapter 35

MARCUS WAITED UNTIL THE COAST WAS CLEAR, THEN JOINED AUNT Tweet on the sofa. From everyone's vantage point, he was entertaining her while they were busy with the preparation for their Thanksgiving feast. His parents were in attendance as well as Demetrius. Under the watchful eye of his mother, the Knicely sisters attempted to recreate the Whittington family homemade pecan pie recipe.

The ladies seemed to be enjoying each other; his brother and father were already talking smack as the first college football game had gotten underway. Great—everybody was distracted.

Squeezing her hand, Marcus faced Aunt Tweet and smiled. "How ya doing today?"

"Fine, mister," she said, then sipped hot apple cider from her mug.

Mister. He sighed, hoping he could reach a place deep within her soul where Aunt Tweet would comprehend. "I love your niece."

"Me too."

That was a good sign. She was following him. "I want to marry her." When she didn't respond, he pressed on. "I don't know what place you're in today, or if you'll remember me or our conversation, but I'm asking for your permission to marry Tabitha."

Aunt Tweet squinted, then gave him a blank stare. "That's my sister. You need to ask Papa."

Groaning his frustration, Marcus counted to three and tried again. "Since I can't find him, is it okay for me to marry your *sister*? Do you think I will take care of her?"

"I don't see why not." She tilted her head, and he braced for her rambling. "I wanted Rudy to marry me, but that boy didn't want me." A sad expression crossed her face, then she chuckled. "But before long he changed his tune when I took center stage as a model. By that time my puppy love was gone…"

Marcus listened patiently. He hoped that Aunt Tweet would live to see another generation of nieces and nephews.

———

On the surface, it was a traditional holiday celebration with turkey and dressing, desserts and college football. For Tabitha, it would also be the saddest Thanksgiving she would remember for years to come, despite the inspiring message this morning from Pastor Nelson. The service was less than ninety minutes long, and that included Thanksgiving Day testimonies, two selections from the choir, and the sermon.

"1 Thessalonians 5:18 says, 'In everything give thanks.' *Be thankful.* For some of you, it's easy. For others, it may be a struggle not to complain, but it's God's will for us to be thankful despite whatever situations we find ourselves in."

No matter how hard Tabitha tried to be thankful, it was bittersweet. Her six-month bonding time with her great-aunt was coming to an end. During Aunt Tweet's stay, Tabitha had learned so much about herself, relationships, and her aunt. Dismissing the melancholy, she put on a brave face when the men strolled into the kitchen.

They pitched in to help set the table with the turkey and dressing and other dishes. Tabitha situated Aunt Tweet at one end of the table. She and Marcus sat on either side of her. Since everyone was coupled off—Rachel and Demetrius, the elder Whittingtons—except Kym, so she took the other end of the table, which seemed appropriate, as the eldest sister.

"Mr. Whittington, would you ask for blessings over our meal?" Tabitha asked Marcus's father, and they all joined hands.

"Please bless our food for our nourishment and enjoyment, and help us to bless others who might be hungry. In Jesus's name, amen."

Their amens mingled in near unison, then they began to serve themselves after Tabitha fixed a plate for her aunt. The conversation was lively and loud, ranging from travels and childhood memories to careers.

"Aunt Tweet, I sure am going to miss you," Marcus said as he rested his fork on his plate.

"I ain't going nowhere." She chuckled and scooped up another serving of dressing as everybody hushed.

Uh-oh. Tabitha glanced at Marcus, who looked clueless about what he'd said wrong, then she patted her aunt's hand. "You're going to spend some time with Rachel."

"I'm not going to go with that girl!" Aunt Tweet said in a defiant tone and shifted in her chair.

All eyes turned to Rachel. The expression on her face was a cross between horror and hurt. Visibly shaken, Tabitha's baby sister swallowed. Demetrius squeezed her shoulder.

Kym stepped in and defused the situation as best as she could by coaxing Aunt Tweet to talk about the places she had visited and the wonderful souvenirs she'd brought back. It was enough diversion for their aunt to recount her world travels.

Soon, everyone tackled the cleanup and stored leftovers in the refrigerator. Marcus stayed behind after his parents and brother said their goodbyes. Tabitha's sisters were upstairs, preparing their aunt for bed and packing more of her things. Wrapping his arms around her from behind her, he whispered, "Babe, I'm really sorry again about saying something earlier. I wasn't thinking."

Relaxing against his chest, Tabitha shook her head. "There's nothing to be sorry about. It's reality. I don't know where Aunt Tweet's reality is right now. It will be as big a transition for her and Rachel as it was for me."

She turned in his arms, and he brushed his lips against hers. She closed her eyes to enjoy the moment. "I don't know what state of mind Aunt Tweet will be in tomorrow. I'm sure she'll be confused but hopefully not combative."

Tabitha was glad Marcus didn't stay much longer. She was eager to spend as much time in her aunt's presence as possible before her departure. In the beginning, the caregivers' pact had seemed like an easy commitment...until it was her turn. When her aunt arrived, Tabitha had questioned herself daily about whether she was competent to be a caregiver, especially after her initial run-in with Marcus. Months ago, she'd counted down the weeks until she could hand over Aunt Tweet to Rachel. Now, she wanted to rewind time for a couple days more.

Once she was upstairs, she shooed her sisters out of Aunt Tweet's room and looked around. After this weekend, the bedroom would be vacated until her aunt returned in a year. From her research, Tabitha learned that some patients with dementia and Alzheimer's could live up to ten years with the illness. At least next time, Tabitha would have a better handle on being a caregiver.

She tried to keep her tears at bay as her heart broke. She didn't want to cry in front of Aunt Tweet. The last time had been when she apologized to her sisters during a Skype chat. Her aunt had tenderly wiped away her tears as she had when Tabitha was a little girl. The gesture had only made Tabitha want to cry even more.

Scooting back Aunt Tweet's jacquard bedspread, because it was her aunt's pet peeve for anyone to sit on top of it, Tabitha sat on the edge of the bed and mustered a smile.

"I want you to know I love you, and it's been a sincere honor to take care of you. I know I had some rough patches when I became frustrated, but it was still a pleasure to have you here to keep me company. On the days you can remember, I hope there are fond memories of our time together."

Suddenly, Aunt Tweet began to ramble about "mister," which Tabitha understood to mean Marcus. She knew he was going to miss her from the way he held her hand in recent days. There had been a few touching scenes.

"Mister's a good man. A good man…a good man makes a good husband and father and grandfather. You want a man who wants to be with you. Sometimes, I wish I had a man to hold my hand…"

Tabitha held her breath. Aunt Tweet remembered Marcus's gesture? Oh boy, would her aunt have issues being separated from him too? Despite her aunt's smiles and occasional chuckles, it was clear she did have regrets in life when it came to love.

The next morning, true to Aunt Tweet's declaration the day earlier, she refused to get in the car with Rachel. Her sister looked downright overwhelmed.

Tabitha made a snap judgment, surprising Marcus, Rachel, and Aunt Tweet. "I'm going with you." Rachel and Aunt Tweet looked relieved. The passing of the baton was hard. It was a good thing it would be a short trip and a long weekend. She would fly back Sunday night.

"Baby, I can drive you," Marcus offered. "Do you have any idea how crowded the airport will be because of the holiday?"

"I do, but I know you'll be there to pick me up." She kissed his jaw.

The next morning, the sisters tried for the road trip again, this time with very little resistance from their aunt. Marcus was there to say good-bye as if Tabitha were going on a long journey. He had brought flowers for all three of them. She gave him one final kiss and two hugs before she hurried to squeeze in the back seat with Aunt Tweet's belongings.

As Rachel drove away from the house, Tabitha glanced back. Marcus hadn't moved from her sidewalk. At least she had something to look forward to when she returned.

Chapter 36

Tabitha hadn't returned to St. Louis as planned. She'd stayed an extra day in Nashville to make sure her aunt was comfortable and settled. Now, weeks later, Aunt Tweet's absence was tangible.

What was Tabitha supposed to do now with so much free time? For six months, she had scheduled everything around Aunt Tweet, who was now unleashing her combative spirit on Rachel on bad days and confusion on the best days. More than once, Tabitha's baby sister had called in tears.

Tabitha didn't realize her mind had drifted until Marcus cleared his throat.

"Would I spoil the mood if I said I miss her?" he whispered as they both struggled to enjoy the meal they had prepared together.

"Not at all." She loved this man. "I had zoned out on you, wondering how she's doing."

"You still talk to her every day, right?" He wore an expectant look.

"I've been trying to wean both of us. It's every other day. Soon, I'll check on her twice a week, then it will be our weekly Skype chats."

Marcus picked at his creamed corn again. "Why do we sound like empty nesters?"

"I guess, in a sense, we are." Tabitha chuckled. "She's been a part of my life forever and has a flair for making lasting impressions." Although she missed Aunt Tweet, her stress level was down, though not gone. She still worried about her aunt and Rachel. Like Tabitha, her sister really didn't know what she was getting into. And all three of them had experienced different degrees of caregiving.

Reality kicked in for Rachel as soon as Tabitha left for home, and her sister had been frazzled ever since. "One good thing is I'll have time to breathe, regroup, and be ready for next time." At least Kym, Tabitha, and Rachel were in agreement that a trustworthy nurse's aide was a must. With Aunt Tweet's mental state deteriorating, she hoped there would be a next time.

"I guess we should've kept the dog," Marcus said, displaying a boyish pout.

"We?" She pointed her fork at him, laughing. "You mean *me*. I had to walk the dog, feed him, and clean up his poop. The only thing my aunt had to do was pet him. At least Sweet Pepper is with her."

Marcus nodded. "The dog did keep her from wandering off, so it's a good thing."

After they finished their dinner, they cleaned her kitchen and settled in the family room.

It was a chilly December weekend, and both agreed to stay in and let a roaring fire warm them while listening to music. Snuggling under Marcus's arm, Tabitha closed her eyes, content.

Suddenly, shifting in his seat, Marcus startled her. "Let's start over." He angled his body until he faced her. "As if we've just met."

Amused by his excitement, she teased, "You want me to come and stake out your porch? That ain't happening."

His slow grin turned into a deep chuckle. "No. I want to woo, chase, court, and whatever you want to call it to win your heart."

She patted her chest. "You already have it."

His nostrils flared, and his breathing deepened. "Not like a man really wants to. Let's plan something tomorrow."

"It's supposed to snow," she reminded him, which was why he had stockpiled wood on her covered porch.

The forecast didn't seem to deter him. "Like that's going to make me cancel our special occasion."

"What are we celebrating?"

"That you made your bonus and…let's just say I hope the forecasters are 50 percent wrong *again*."

Marcus opened the ring box, scrutinized the diamond, then closed it. Tabitha had no idea he was about to propose. All she suspected was he was rewinding their relationship and dating history. The only wooing he planned to do was to the altar, and tonight was it.

The meteorologists had predicted snow, but none had fallen so far. Snow might shut down cities and businesses, but it wasn't going to keep him from his mission. As any determined man in love, he had concocted a plan B—loading a shovel, a bag of salt, and a portable heater in his truck, just in case.

If only Aunt Tweet were there to see it. Would she remember him asking for Tabitha's hand in marriage? He planned on loving her until Jesus came back for both of them. Until then, he would use his parents' marriage as a model.

Marcus did his scheming while urging Tabitha to redeem his gift certificate he'd given her after Aunt Tweet moved and get the works— hair, skin, and nails. He had gone ring shopping. She wasn't the only one who had gone shopping for something special to wear.

When he had informed his parents that he was going to ask her to marry him, they had been ecstatic. Demetrius was a downer, though, not sharing the same enthusiasm when Marcus phoned him. "Man, have you really had a chance to get to know her outside of caring for her aunt?"

"What Tabitha and I experienced was real life. If love found its way through all that stress and, at times, drama, then I feel God brought us together and will keep us."

"You're a good man." Demetrius laughed. "Good luck."

"Whatever. Please don't mention this to Rachel, because she might say something to Tabitha before I'm ready."

His brother was quiet. Marcus could only assume whatever was going on between him and Rachel had fizzled as soon as Aunt Tweet became a houseguest. That ended all discussion about the Knicely sisters.

Tabitha's ringtone interrupted his musing. He grinned and answered. "Hey, babe."

"Hey. Have you looked out the window?" She didn't hide the worry in her voice.

"As a matter of fact, I did. Nothing is going on," he said in triumph, popping open the ring box again.

"Ah, I think you need to look again," she said as he strolled to look outside his bedroom window and blinked.

"What?" He frowned. When did the sky unleash its fury of snow?

"Yeah. It's coming down heavy. We can do a rain check—or in this case, a snow check." She giggled.

That was not an option. "Babe, I'm not canceling our reservations. Be beautiful, be sweet, and be ready." He chuckled at his own corniness. "I'll see you in an hour." He smacked a kiss in her ear for good measure and disconnected. He couldn't believe the forecasters had nailed it after all. "Time to activate plan B."

He shaved, showered, then donned his tuxedo. Marcus peeped out the window again, and his jaw dropped. The snowfall was unrelenting. He slipped on his boots, grabbed his keys, and left.

Once outside, he scanned his neighborhood's winter wonderland. It was beautiful, but not a deterrent. After starting his car, he cleaned off his windows. He had purchased frozen dinners from Maggiano's. He could pop the entrees into the microwave, or oven, and the pasta would be piping hot and ready to serve along with the other items he had stuffed in a picnic basket. He chuckled—a picnic basket in December was as romantic as he could get under plan B.

Marcus drove the short distance and parked. He stepped out and retrieved the shovel from his trunk. As quietly and fast as he could, he cleared the walkway from the sidewalk to Tabitha's porch. *Done.*

Next, he set up the portable propane heater midway on the path to melt the snow as it fell. *Check.* Finally, he placed portable lanterns in the snow—a winter date idea he'd read on a website. Marcus hiked up the stairs, careful not to slip. He rang the bell, then backtracked to the walkway and waited.

Opening the door, her eyes widened in surprise. The light glowing in the foyer gave the illusion of an angel standing in the doorway.

The moment was surreal as Tabitha gasped and covered her mouth. "Marcus?"

"Put on your coat and come dance with me." He stretched out his hand.

It seemed to take her a few moments to register his request. Once she did, she twirled around and grabbed her coat. *Note to self: Get her a mink on our first wedding anniversary.*

"What is going on?" she asked as snowflakes sprinkled her lashes and he helped her down, step by step, with one hand. His other hand held an umbrella over her head.

Marcus pulled her closer. When she shivered, he guided her to the propane heater until he could feel its warmth against his legs.

Giving her the umbrella, he knelt and fumbled in his pocket until he pulled out the box. "I believe that even in Aunt Tweet's state, she played the matchmaker. Nothing could have kept me from falling in love with you—misunderstandings, bad first impressions, or hardships," he said, staring up into her teary eyes. "You've given me your heart, and I've given you mine. Now this weather won't keep me from asking this question: Will you do me the honor of being my wife for life?"

Wiping away a tear, she choked out, "I once told you if you asked me to marry you, I would say yes. Marcus Whittington, there is no other man I would want as my husband, so yes, I would be honored to be your wife." Taking her shaking hand, Marcus steadied it to slip on the ring.

Leaping up, he balanced himself on the wet walkway before he lifted her off her feet and kissed her. "I love you," he whispered.

"I love you more. I'm still in awe that somehow love found its way into my life at my lowest point."

"Don't question it. Just love me back."

"I do. I will." She squeezed his neck, threatening to close his windpipe.

As the snow began to pile up around them, they still had a clear spot near the heater, so he steadied her, reached into his pocket, and tapped his iTunes to play a rendition of "Thank You" by the late Walter Hawkins.

As she continued to hold the umbrella, he snaked his arms around her and began to sway in a slow dance to the melody. Once the song ended, he hugged her tight. "One chapter of our life has ended. We'll begin the new year with a new chapter as an engaged couple."

Epilogue

TABITHA HAD HOPED FOR MORE TIME TO PLAN HER WEDDING, BUT time wasn't on her side when it came to Aunt Tweet's mental health. Instead of outdoor fall nuptials, she and Marcus had agreed to tie the knot in a candlelight ceremony in early spring.

While waiting in the small, makeshift bridal changing room at her church, Tabitha glanced at her two bridesmaids. Her sisters were elegant and beautiful. Priscilla "Aunt Tweet" Brownlee would be her escort. The moment was somber without her parents' presence. She sniffed so as not to compromise Rachel's makeup artistry with tears. Before the hour was over, she would become Mrs. Marcus Whittington.

"I'm really happy Marcus came into your life. He's a good man," Kym whispered, her eyes glistening with unshed tears. "Mom and Daddy would be proud." Her big sister's hug lingered.

"Thanks," Tabitha whispered.

"Whew." Rachel dabbed at her happy tears, then fanned her face. "I'm trying to hold it together, but I'm glad you found unexpected happiness in the midst of being a caregiver." She hiccupped. Rachel seemed to be in a constant emotional frenzy. Her sister had confessed she felt overwhelmed daily.

When music from the string quartet floated to their room, the sisters readied themselves to leave, but suddenly, Aunt Tweet stated, "You need to pray."

The sisters stared at their matriarch and caught a glimpse of the woman who gave them direction on things in so many ways.

"Right." How had Tabitha forgotten the most important moment before she said "I do"? Taking one another's hands, they moved toward Aunt Tweet to include her in their circle for prayer.

"Father, in the name of Jesus, thank You for this occasion and the man You had for my sister," Kym began, squeezing Tabitha's hand. "Please bless their marriage, my nieces and nephews to come, and... please don't forget about the other two Knicely sisters. We need good men too..."

Once they said "amen" in unison, Tabitha smiled, hugged them one more time, then shooed her sisters out of the room. Turning back to Aunt Tweet, she studied her aunt. Her weight loss was noticeable, but she was still classy in her silk gold suit, stunning hat, and matching gloves. Tabitha kissed her cheek and whispered, "Thank you for everything you've done for me all these years, especially imparting your wisdom. I love you."

"Umm-hmm." Her aunt nodded, then became antsy. "Randolph's waiting."

The mysteries of Miss Priscilla Brownlee would never cease. "Yes," she responded, knowing she had her own handsome and godly Randolph standing at the altar.

Tabitha and Aunt Tweet made their way out of the changing room. When the ushers saw them, they opened the double doors to the chapel. Tabitha took baby steps to keep her aunt steady.

She could feel the tug of Marcus's gaze on her before their eyes connected. When they did, his raw happiness caused her to suck in her breath. With each step, Tabitha's heart pounded. Her life was about to change again, and this time, she looked forward to the new chapter.

Soon, Marcus left his post and met them halfway.

"Thank you, Aunt Tweet," he whispered and kissed her cheek.

Her aunt nodded, then allowed Marcus's mother to guide her to the front pew.

"Ready to become my wife?" He gave Tabitha a tender expression.

"More than ready." In sync, they finished the journey to the altar together.

Pastor Nelson nodded. "Dearly beloved, we are gathered here today in the sight of God and these witnesses..." he began.

"Tabitha Knicely, will you take Marcus Whittington to be your lawfully wedded husband, forsaking all others until death do you part?"

The moment was surreal as Tabitha stared into Marcus's eyes, then blinked when she heard a small voice reciting the vows along with the pastor. It was Aunt Tweet. Even that distraction didn't stop Tabitha from saying "I do" in a strong voice. When it was Marcus's turn, he cupped her hands, resting them against his chest where she could feel the beat of his heart. It seemed as if her own heart felt it and synced with his. Tabitha trembled as the strength of his voice made her weak. She remained in that state until Pastor Nelson said, "Marcus Whittington, you may now salute your bride."

With a smirk that made his nostrils flare, Marcus gathered Tabitha in his arms and delivered a passionate kiss.

"Now that's a whopper!" Aunt Tweet declared loudly.

Author's Note

Many of Aunt Tweet's antics mimic my grandmother Grandma Jessie's, who suffered from advanced symptoms of dementia. The ice cream on the face while the dog went missing was one of Grandma's escapades. As I think back on those days, it makes me chuckle now. Not back then.

Being a caregiver is probably one of the most misunderstood positions. There is joy, sorrow, depression, frustration, pity parties, and more.

If you know someone who is a caregiver, drop them a card, send them flowers, give them a gift card for maid service or a day out… The ways you can bless a caregiver are endless.

For more information about dementia and Alzheimer's, visit alz.org.

Rachel's story is next. Every caregiver's situation is different, and this Knicely sister is about to find that out.

Please take a moment to post a review and purchase a copy of *Lean on Me* for a friend.

Until next time, hug a caregiver and be blessed!

Pat

Reading Group Guide

1. Do you think the sisters' caregivers' pact was realistic? Have you ever shared caregiving with others? How did it go? If you haven't had that experience, would you ever take it on?

2. What did you think about Marcus's interactions with Aunt Tweet?

3. Aunt Tweet is now in the care of Rachel. What do you think is in store for her as the next caregiver? How did Tabitha do as a caregiver?

4. Do you think a single person should place a loved one in a nursing facility when there is no other help? What would you do?

5. How much do you know about dementia and the many diseases that share some of its symptoms?

6. How much do you know about the Alzheimer's Association?

7. Discuss how being a caregiver affects families living in and outside the house.

8. What is your definition of a caregiver? Does it have to be limited to the care of an elderly or physically challenged individual?

9. What did you think about Marcus's relationship with Victor and Latrice? Would you have become involved in their problems?

Read on for a look at book 2 in the
Family Is Forever series
by Pat Simmons

here for you

Coming soon from Sourcebooks Casablanca

Chapter 1

DYING? RACHEL KNICELY REFUSED TO ACCEPT THAT. ONLY THREE weeks ago, her great-aunt Priscilla "Aunt Tweet" Brownlee was the life of the party at the wedding reception. Her eyes had sparkled, her dance moves impressive for an eighty-five-year-old, and her childish giggles made the evening more festive, sometimes stealing the spotlight from the bride and groom. How could she be dying? *Nope, I won't accept that. I need her in my life.*

Closing her eyes, Rachel rubbed her face, trying to make sense of her aunt's rapid decline. The youngest of three daughters, Rachel had made an agreement with her two sisters to share Aunt Tweet's caregiving responsibilities six months at a time, first with the oldest, Kym, in Baltimore, next with Tabitha in St. Louis. Now it was Rachel's "tour of duty" to care for their beloved role model.

Life was suddenly becoming too short. *I'm not ready to lose my auntie yet.* Rachel yawned and stretched on the chaise longue, posted by the bed in the makeshift guest bedroom in the loft of her Nashville condo. She forced one eye open briefly to check on her aunt.

Rachel was drained and wasn't sure how she could be so tired. It was only 2:00 a.m. on a Saturday in a city known for its nightlife. Before Aunt Tweet's stay, Rachel would be out on the town with her best friend, Jacqui Rice, at one of the many "must-attend" events around Music City after a long workweek.

She had tweaked her social calendar until June 1, when Kym would begin the second rotation as Aunt Tweet's caregiver and relocate their aunt to Baltimore again.

Over the past months, she had learned that being a caregiver wasn't a nine-to-five shift. Rachel did what it took to make her aunt comfortable.

Her late nights were now spent watching over her loved one, even more so now as the Alzheimer's-triggered dementia symptoms had her aunt acting out of character.

Rachel had no concept of the term *sundown* until Aunt Tweet began to wake in the middle of the night and wander through her condo trying to get out. Her loving aunt had been downright mean and combative toward Rachel for more than a month. Aunt Tweet's behavior had crushed Rachel to the core.

A trip to St. Louis last month for Tabitha and Marcus's wedding seemed to give her aunt a second wind, then after a few days back in Nashville, her aunt slipped again into another personality.

Aunt Tweet had stopped eating for two days. Two days! Rachel had freaked out and called her sisters, who in turn had a conference call with the doctor—the third one since Aunt Tweet was initially diagnosed more than a year ago. After moving Aunt Tweet from her home in Philly, she had a specialist in Baltimore with Kym, one in St. Louis with Tabitha, and now Dr. Allison Watkins here in Nashville.

"The kind of symptoms you're describing become severe as the patient transitions into the last stages of Alzheimer's," Dr. Watkins had said—too casually in Rachel's opinion as her heart shattered. Was it fair that her designated time with Aunt Tweet was marred with worry that at any time her aunt would slip away?

"Aunt Tweet's doctor in Philly said a patient with dementia can live up to twenty years," Rachel pointed out.

"Yes," the doctor confirmed, "with no other contributing factors, but the average life span is usually four to eight years after diagnosis. Changes in the brain begin before any signs are manifested."

"That's the preclinical period of Alzheimer's," whispered Tabitha, the second oldest and a pharmaceutical rep.

"Yes, also called the mild stage, which allows her to remain active socially. Stages can overlap, so I suspect Miss Brownlee might have moderate to advanced Alzheimer's. It is usually the longest stage and can last for many years."

"Living longer is good news, but not with her condition worsening.

My aunt is the sweetest person on earth." All Rachel wanted was more bonding time with Aunt Tweet, so she could tell her over and over again how much she loved her, admired her, and wouldn't let her down on the expectations Aunt Tweet had set for her three nieces.

"Based on these new symptoms, let me see her in my office to determine if she has progressed to the next stage."

"Which is?" Kym asked, but Rachel wasn't sure she wanted to know.

"The late stage," Dr. Watkins said matter-of-factly. "Unfortunately, the last stage of Alzheimer's is the most severe. Without warning, she can lose the ability to respond to her surroundings or control movements, or she may stop walking, sitting, and eventually swallowing."

When the call ended, Rachel was numb. The conversation had both depressed her and upset her stomach. Dr. Watkins's speculation was one thing, but taking Aunt Tweet into the office to confirm the inevitable was disheartening. Had her aunt stopped eating because she couldn't swallow?

The next day, Aunt Tweet woke with a voracious appetite. Relieved, Rachel cried like a baby. This was proof that Aunt Tweet had not progressed to another stage. She had bounced back. She whispered "Thank you, God" and considered canceling the doctor's appointment.

Kym was the first to veto the idea. "Go, Rach, or I'll fly down there and take her myself," she threatened.

"All right!" Rachel reluctantly agreed.

On second thought, Rachel wondered if all three of them going to the doctor with Aunt Tweet wasn't such a bad idea. Depending on what the doctor had to say, they might need to hold one another's hands.

Unfortunately, one week later, Rachel was on her own as she escorted Aunt Tweet to the appointment. She didn't care what it looked like to others in the waiting room; Rachel held her aunt's hand as if she were a lost little girl, not a twenty-nine-year-old engineer who was at the top of her game.

After the preliminaries, Dr. Watkins gave Rachel the heartbreaking news. "From my assessment and everything you shared on the phone, your aunt has indeed transitioned to the last stage." She was quick to add.

"Don't give up hope yet. It's not over. This stage can last from several weeks to several years. It's not the quantity of time but the memories you have with her that will give you comfort."

Rachel nodded but didn't feel any comfort in her words. It was the memories of Aunt Tweet's laugh, unfiltered conversations about life, and attention to a meticulous appearance that were fading too fast, being replaced by a shell of a woman whose independence had been stolen.

"It's important that you keep a sharp eye on her for signs of pain, since her level of communication may become more limited."

Oftentimes, that meant Rachel sitting at her bedside throughout the night, reminiscing about happy times as a child, unsure if Aunt Tweet remembered or understood, but it was therapy for Rachel.

The influence Aunt Tweet had on the Knicely sisters—especially Rachel's life—was astonishing. Their aunt was all about confidence and character building. Plus, detailed attention to a woman's personal appearance.

Kym inherited Aunt Tweet's wisdom as the oldest sibling. Tabitha's features were almost identical to a younger version of Aunt Tweet as if their parents, Thomas and Rita Knicely, had no say in their daughters' DNA. But as the baby girl, Rachel had a special bond with her great-aunt.

Aunt Tweet seemed to infuse Rachel with her personality: a flair for fashion that included hair, nails, and makeup to be camera ready at all times, a thirst to achieve a high level of intellect with education being the primary goal. Then there were the many lessons on how to act like a lady. And the most important was philanthropy. There was nothing wrong with enjoying the finer things in life, but one had to remember others less fortunate and help them climb to success.

Courtesy of Aunt Tweet, there were many life lessons learned. The only topic her aunt didn't bring up much was living happily ever after with the love of your life.

Wednesday morning, Nicholas Adams was on his way home from work when he received a call from the church office. Overnight, he was a project manager at the Nissan plant in Smyrna about half an hour from downtown Nashville.

By day, afternoon, evening, and night, he worked for his church as a minister. His pastor assigned him and several other ministers to visit church members who were sick, homebound, or hospitalized.

"Hello, Minister Adams," Laura Emerson greeted him when he answered. "I know it's early, but we received a call over the weekend from a Tabitha Whittington with an urgent prayer request. She's a member at one of our sister churches in St. Louis."

"It's okay, Miss Emerson," he reassured the elderly secretary.

"Good, I'll send you the information," she said in a quiet voice. "Miss Whittington would like someone to visit her great-aunt, Priscilla Brownlee, who is staying here in Nashville. I'm sure she'd appreciate your visit—the sooner the better, the note says."

Nicholas nodded to himself. As soon as he said "I'm on it," Nicholas glanced in his rearview mirror. He had planned to get to the barber because a haircut was already a week overdue.

His phone chimed as he took off. At a stoplight, he stifled a yawn as he glanced at the address Sister Emerson had texted him for Miss Priscilla Brownlee. It was in Midtown, minutes from downtown and not far from Vanderbilt University, but a good half hour drive during morning rush hour. It was also a bit early for a house call, so maybe everything would work out. He would make a stop at Hats Off Barbershop in Antioch, which was in the direction of downtown. Hopefully, he could get in and out.

When he arrived, he counted seven heads before him, or maybe his eyes had crossed. Nicholas resolved that he would have to wait longer than he had hoped. Making himself comfortable in an empty folding chair, he mumbled a prayer for Sister Brownlee before he dozed off. A few times, someone nudged him to pull him into a conversation about sports or to give his opinion about a world event from a "preacher's viewpoint."

Two hours later, he walked out a tired man with a fade cut to his wavy hair, a trimmed mustache and five o'clock shadow outlining his jaw. At least he had gone into the restroom to rinse his face with cold water and pop a breath mint. He slipped on his shades after squinting at the sunlight that seemed to have brightened while he'd been inside. Now he felt presentable enough to perform his task.

Once in his car, he confirmed the address again. It was after ten, so surely someone would be awake by now. He tapped the address to activate the navigation app and headed westbound on I-24.

The West End Avenue area was a trendy part of Nashville that attracted graduate students and young professionals drawn to the surrounding downtown nightlife, Lower Broadway, or East Nashville.

Rumor had it that Midtown was so pricey that the rent there was comparable to the mortgage of a custom-built house. Personally, Nicholas enjoyed being a homeowner in a quiet Smyrna neighborhood with a spacious ranch house that was close to his job. To him, that was preferable to living in the midst of a constant bustle of people.

Since the traffic flowed, he arrived in less than half an hour and parked around the corner. He grabbed his Bible from the back seat and headed to the building's grand entrance with a maroon awning and street-level retail shops lining the front windows. He strolled inside. Whoever lived in this place had money with a capital *M*.

The interior resembled a hotel lobby with marble floors and expensive decor. Voices above him made him take notice of a mezzanine overlooking the lobby. *Wow* was the only way to describe the Westchester. A middle-aged gentleman stood from behind a sleek desk in an office with see-through walls and strolled around to greet him.

He asked for Nicholas's ID, which he looked at carefully. "Who are you here to see?"

"Miss Priscilla Brownlee, who is staying with her niece Rachel Knicely in 1402."

"Of course." He returned Nicholas's license and pushed a button to open the elevator doors.

Nicholas nodded his thanks and walked inside, where spotless mirrors, brass trim, and accent lighting surrounded him as the doors closed. He had never visited a residence with this type of security, but it was close to a busy area, so maybe that justified it.

On the ride up to the fourteenth floor, soft music entertained Nicholas until the bell chimed and the doors opened. Should he remove his shoes to walk on the plush carpet? Nah. Overhead, mini chandeliers lit the way to Room 1402, where an artistically carved wood front door would rival the one at his house.

After he pushed the doorbell, Nicholas stepped back and dusted his shoulders from any stray hair he had missed earlier. When he made first-time house calls, he liked to portray an image of a respectable, serious, and clean-cut man. Despite the box some people put a minister in, respect wasn't a given. His attire wasn't dress slacks and a collared shirt; instead, it was his Nissan polo work shirt and jeans.

He was about to ring the bell again when a woman answered. They blinked at each other. It was a toss-up whether Nicholas had awakened her or she didn't care about her appearance. Either way, her beauty wasn't dimmed, even with messy hair, wrinkled clothes, and one large hoop earring, Nicholas had seen worse. He offered a smile.

She looked at him as if she were in a daze. "Yes?"

"I'm Minister Nicholas Adams from the Redeemer Lives Church. I'm here to see Sister Brownlee."

The woman's eyes widened with fear, and she slammed the door in his face.

What? I don't have time for this. Nicholas was sleep deprived and hungry. Maybe his eyes were bloodshot and she thought he was drunk or high on drugs or something. Unfortunately, there were instances where he was met with hostile greetings from families who resented his presence.

Nicholas tried not to take their rudeness personally. This was his calling, and he was going in to see Sister Brownlee. He gritted his teeth and was about to knock again.

He didn't have to when she slowly opened the door with a sheepish expression. "Sorry. I wasn't expecting you."

Clearly. He kept that to himself, then relaxed. He smiled again to ease the tension, and she returned his smile, although hesitantly. "Your sister in St. Louis called our church office."

"Tabitha," she mumbled, then squeezed her lips together. "She hadn't mentioned it."

That somewhat explained her reaction. "Since I'm here, do you mind if I visit with Miss Brownlee?"

"She was alert a few days ago, but she's shut down again. I'm not sure if she'll know you're here. I'm not even sure if she knows I'm here." The look of hurt didn't go unnoticed.

"I'm sure she feels your presence," he tried to console her. "You're Miss Knicely?"

"Yes, I'm Rachel Knicely," she confirmed.

"Nice to meet you. Again, I'm Nicholas Adams." He offered his hand. Hers was noticeably soft.

Before his eyes, Rachel's sluggish demeanor disappeared, replaced with attentiveness as she leaned on the doorjamb, crossing her arms. "First, may I see your ID?" As he reached into his back pocket for his wallet, she added, "I have a photographic memory."

Nicholas contained his amusement at her personality swing from fear to fierceness.

A Yorkie and a cocker spaniel appeared at her side, barking with veiled threats as guard dogs while wagging their tails, undecided if Nicholas was friend or foe.

Back to Rachel. He wasn't offended by her request. Despite the tight security to get to her door, a woman could never be too careful, whether a man was carrying a Bible or not. He had a younger brother, Karl, but if he had any sisters, he would teach them the same precautions.

He handed over his license. She glanced at it, squinted at him again, then handed it back, reciting his license number, height, weight, and eye color to prove she wasn't kidding. Did she say his weight? Seriously, hey, he had lost ten pounds since that was taken. He was lean and all muscle. She didn't need to know that, but he decided to tell her anyway. The woman had some serious mental skills. "Just so you know, I was ten pounds heavier then," he said with good humor.

"And you had a bad haircut," she sassed back and stepped aside for him to enter. He couldn't tell if she was joking about his hair then or now. He refrained from asking.

He sized her up as well, about five foot four or five to his six foot two, messy dark-brown hair, tired brown eyes, curly lashes, and a face that probably could use a morning wash. All in all, she was cute. Very.

He stepped in and noticed the richness of her hardwood floors; they looked as if no one had ever walked across them, only faintly scuffed from her pets. He admired her open space with the dining room/eating area and kitchen on one side.

Nicholas followed her along a hallway that turned a corner as the dogs trailed behind them. They stepped down into a spacious living room with nice decor and floor-to-ceiling windows. The sunlight was streaming through.

They climbed a few steps to a loft overseeing the living room, offering little privacy, except for a trifold room divider. Massive bedroom furniture held court. The dogs had beaten them and had scrambled to a spot at the foot of the bed. "Nice place," Nicholas said, and he meant it.

"Thank you," she replied without looking at him. Her attention was on the woman in the bed. "Aunt Tweet," she called softly. "Nicholas Adams—he's a minister—is here to see you."

Her loved one didn't respond. The slight rise and fall of the cover was proof she was still alive. *Whew.* Nicholas had never witnessed someone taking their last few breaths. He didn't want to see it today.

Chapter 2

HOW EMBARRASSING. RACHEL COULDN'T BELIEVE SHE HAD slammed the door in a man's face—and a minister at that. The doorbell had rescued her from the vortex of a nightmare about a Death Angel trying to get inside her house.

She could thank Jacqui for putting that term in her subconscious. She had mentioned that her family called a priest to administer the last rites to her grandfather, then minutes later, Mr. Rice died.

Still shaken from the dream, Rachel remained leery. She watched Nicholas from the doorway as he perched on the chaise that she had slept on for many nights. Leaning closer, he rested his hand on Aunt Tweet's forehead and softly called her name. "Sister Brownlee, I'm here to pray for you."

Please let his prayer make a difference. The moment was tranquil as she noted his gentle manner. Something she wouldn't expect from a man who had a handsome face with a no-nonsense expression and a body-builder frame. His tenderness was endearing.

Aunt Tweet slowly moved her head but didn't open her eyes. Excitement, hope, and anticipation swirled in Rachel's head at her aunt's response. Next, Nicholas opened his worn leather-bound Bible. The pages seemed to part without a bookmark as if they knew the passage he wanted.

As he began to read from Psalm 23, the softness of his voice deepened to a rich baritone. The sound was like a sweet melody. Rachel closed her eyes, drifting into serenity as she listened.

"'He makes me lie down in green pastures, he leads me beside quiet waters, he refreshes my soul,'" Nicholas read. "'Though I walk through the valley of the shadow of death, I will fear no evil...'"

Death. Wait a minute! Rachel's eyes opened in horror. Her aunt was very much alive, and she was hoping his prayer would keep it that way. Was the minister summoning death for Aunt Tweet? This was too much talk about death—the doctor, her sister, her friend, and now this minister.

The thought ignited a sob from somewhere deep within her, and Rachel couldn't stop the flood. She felt weak in the knees, and she would've collapsed on the floor if it hadn't been for Nicholas's quick movement.

"Are you all right?" he asked in a concerned tone.

She shook her head, unable to answer. He coaxed her to make it to the ottoman. She felt the seat shift as he sat next to her. When she inhaled, a faint scent of his cologne acted as a smelling salt and revitalized her. It was a familiar brand that some of her colleagues and male acquaintances wore.

"Can I get you some water?"

"Yes," she choked out. He didn't know the layout of her kitchen, but she didn't have the energy to go herself as she opened her eyes in a daze and glanced at Aunt Tweet. She was still alive, and Rachel exhaled in relief.

He returned quickly with ice water in a crystal glass. Her best dishes were reserved for entertaining, but he didn't know that and she didn't care as she accepted the glass with trembling hands. Nicholas's hands steadied hers so she could drink. Rachel gulped down the water as if she'd been parched for days. "Thank you."

Instead of returning to Aunt Tweet's bedside, Nicholas took the seat next to her again. "Are you okay?"

"I don't know." She turned and stared into his eyes, noticing the unusual shade of brown. She wouldn't described them as light or dark, maybe sun-kissed, as if sunlight were drawn to them. "I lost it when I heard you say 'death.'"

Nicholas nodded his head, but she doubted he understood the blow, losing the last connection to her father's side of the family. "Death is part of life," he told her, then stood. "If you're all right, do you mind if I pray for both of you before I leave?"

"Sure."

Returning to Aunt Tweet's bedside, he smiled, then reached inside his jacket. He pulled out a bottle no bigger than a sample size portion of perfume or scented oil. Unscrewing the top, he placed a dab of oil on Aunt Tweet's head, then turned to include Rachel. She declined but joined him at the bedside. Closing her eyes, she bowed her head and waited for the prayer.

His short prayer was spoken as softly as the reading that had lulled to sleep Shelby, her cocker spaniel, and Sweet Pepper, Aunt Tweet's Yorkie. He added, "Amen."

"Amen," she repeated, then exhaled.

Nicholas faced her. "If you'd like another ministerial visit, don't hesitate to call the church office."

You mean if my aunt is still alive, Rachel feared. Since that dream, she was having a hard time shaking this death thing.

"If you promise not to slam the door in my face," he added, with mirth dancing in those brown eyes, breaking through her reverie. When he smiled, his dimples made a peek-a-boo through his beard.

So he had a sense of humor. She returned his smile. "You spooked me." Rachel had only seen a woman slam the door in a man's face in the movies. That had been a first for her. She looked away in embarrassment before she tilted her head in a challenge. "You're not going to let me forget that, are you?"

"Consider it forgotten." He gathered his Bible and had her show him out. He offered a slight wave, then walked toward the elevator.

After closing the door, Rachel leaned against it and sighed. Of course death was a part of life, but she didn't want it to happen on her watch. She needed more time with Aunt Tweet—just like her sisters had created recent memories with their great-aunt, Rachel desired that too. She might not get her full six months with her aunt, but if God gave her a couple more weeks...

She sighed. "I'll be so thankful."

Yawning, she pushed off the door and headed toward Aunt Tweet's room. She passed by the hall mirror, then backtracked, screaming at the haunting image staring back at her. Her curls were a matted mess, her face needed attention, and her lounge clothes were wrinkled. She'd taken unkempt to the next level.

If Aunt Tweet were alert, she would have taken Rachel to task about her appearance. "A woman should always get a man's attention, whether she wants to or not. Honey, take the affection as long as your beauty lasts" was Aunt Tweet's mantra. Rachel had pushed all thoughts of men and the dating world aside to focus on caring for her aunt. How Nicholas Adams had broken through her resistance was a mystery.

He was not a man that a woman could easily dismiss, including Rachel. She had appreciated the eye candy for about thirty seconds—no, make that twenty-nine—but he was a minister. She doubted Nicholas gave her a second glance.

Back in the bedroom, Rachel checked on Aunt Tweet. She hadn't stirred. Neither had the two dogs. Her pet had taken to Aunt Tweet the moment she'd arrived, but not to Sweet Pepper. Then oddly, a few weeks ago, the two pets made some sort of dog truce to live in harmony at her side.

Rachel bent and brushed a kiss against her aunt's cheek. For an eighty-five-year-old, Aunt Tweet retained her natural beauty. Flawless dark skin complemented her silver-and-white hair. She was classy, with a larger-than-life personality and the right amount of sass to make a stranger crave being counted among her circle of friends.

"I hope God answers this prayer. I love you, Aunt Tweet," Rachel whispered before descending from the loft. She would shower and prepare a light breakfast in case Aunt Tweet opened her eyes and was famished again before Clara arrived.

Clara Dobbs was a home health aide Rachel employed three days a week to assist with Aunt Tweet's care so Rachel could go to the firm in the afternoons. The other two days, she worked from home to be close to Aunt Tweet.

Since Rachel hadn't set her alarm, the minister's visit was a lifesaver. She pinched her nose. That sounded too much like a pun, but she needed to prepare updates on a project that was almost complete. She couldn't ask for a better boss or company that allowed her work flexibility during her brief tenure as caregiver.

Initially, it wasn't the Knicely sisters' plan to have outside help. They thought the three of them could handle Aunt Tweet's care on their own. Kym sailed through her six months, and Tabitha's six months had been an eye-opener. No medical textbook could have prepared her for the practicum. Rachel expected a less mobile aunt but instead got living a nightmare with whispers of death. None of them were prepared for the dementia symptoms that plagued Aunt Tweet.

When Tabitha had cried out for help, her friend and neighbor Marcus Whittington had answered. The two of them felt a home health aide would relieve some stress. At first, Rachel and Kym had been incensed about Tabitha leaving Aunt Tweet in the care of a stranger, but the woman turned out to be attentive and trustworthy, so Rachel didn't think twice about getting help when she brought Aunt Tweet to Nashville.

Rachel had come to depend on Clara on Mondays, Wednesdays, and Fridays not only to do light housekeeping and patient assistance, but also to guide Rachel as a caregiver. Sometimes that meant Clara had to endure Rachel venting her frustrations. Besides Clara, Jacqui always had a listening ear. And her sisters were only a phone call or flight away.

———

It was after two o'clock when Rachel breezed through the doors of Gersham-Smith, one of the oldest and most successful engineering firms in Nashville. She had worked hard to be respected among her peers and management. She credited Aunt Tweet with inspiring her to study math and science in school before the STEM curriculum—science, technology, engineering, and mathematics—became popular. The subjects were so easy for her, and as a teenager, she was often one of the few black girls in a class.

She also credited Aunt Tweet with the fact that Rachel wasn't intimidated by men in the workplace. She preferred to impress with her brains, wit, and beauty. She didn't believe in leaving the house without being polished from head to toe, not even to walk the dogs. She wanted her appearance to be as exquisite as her intellect. She was fashion-forward and could manage complex projects as though they were building blocks or simple puzzles.

Her boss, Harlan Goode, appeared as she stepped out of the elevator. "Afternoon, Rachel. How's your aunt?"

He was an older man with thinning hair on the crown of his head and a thick mustache. His father started Gresham-Smith, and Harlan expanded the firm to include offices in fourteen states and two overseas. The firm had drawn big-name clients to its roster with cutting-edge designs, including the winning bid to design a deep pump station project for the Metropolitan St. Louis Sewer District.

As a St. Louis native, Rachel took personal pride in handcrafting the design for the sump, dry wells, and other components for a structure that would be 180 feet below ground. It had been an honor to give back to her childhood city in the form of jobs and better living conditions.

Voted yearly one of the top companies to work for, the firm stressed work/life balance, which Rachel had never fully appreciated until she became Aunt Tweet's caregiver. The past four months had been a roller-coaster ride, and it didn't look like the next few months would be any better with Aunt Tweet's deteriorating condition.

"About the same." She mustered a smile. Rachel believed in keeping a professional demeanor among her colleagues and tucked away the meltdowns until she was at home behind closed doors. "My sister had a local minister come to pray with her."

"Good. They say prayer changes things," he said, then continued to his office for the afternoon briefing.

If only she could see a change with her aunt. Although Rachel was hopeful, she was realistic. The body required food and water to thrive, and she would prefer that Aunt Tweet be alert in order to receive both versus having to be fed and hydrated through an IV.

Once in her office, Rachel had to force her mind to focus as she switched to job mode. Her team had been assigned to finding solutions to ease Music City's congestion and reduce travel time for tourists and the ever-growing population. Millennials wanted no part of long commutes. They, including her, were attracted to communities where residents could live, work, and play.

Although Rachel was licensed as a civil engineer, her area of specialty was structural. While the client wanted to preserve some historical aspects in the area, Rachel wasn't convinced their request to build a tunnel for a walkway was sound. She and her team had a brainstorming session to see if the addition that was already underway was going to be able to stay on deadline and within the budget.

After the meeting, Rachel delved into her RISA-3D program to analyze the structures. It was impossible to cram eight-plus work hours into a five-hour shift, but she had to get home to Aunt Tweet so Clara could go home herself. The home health aide was a nursing student and a single mother of an eight-year-old girl. Luckily, Rachel's commute was only seven minutes.

When Rachel slipped behind the steering wheel in her car, a craving hit. Although she practiced healthy eating, a serving of Monell's skillet fried chicken was her guilty pleasure. It wasn't far, but they would close in twenty minutes.

She called Clara. "I know you're off within an hour, but my senses got a tracker on some of Monell's skillet fried—"

"Chicken." Clara smacked her lips and laughed. "Bring me some and all is forgiven."

"Got it, and I'll get some extra in case Aunt Tweet ever gets an appetite again. Any change?"

"No," she said slowly, then added, "But her vitals are stable."

"Okay, thanks." Suddenly, Rachel's appetite dulled, but she practically promised Clara, so she turned north on Second Avenue for the short drive to Bransford Avenue. The reality was her aunt's failing health.

She arrived ten minutes before they closed. While she waited for her order, Rachel's mind drifted to her loved one. "You've got to bounce back, Aunt Tweet," she mumbled. "You've got to."

Returning to her condo, Rachel hoped the chicken's aroma would tease Aunt Tweet's senses, but the only thing that stirred in her aunt's bedroom was Shelby and Sweet Pepper, yet they didn't leave Aunt Tweet's side. Rachel gave Clara her sack from the café and a twenty-dollar tip, something extra as a reminder that the woman's services were appreciated when Rachel returned home late; Aunt Tweet wouldn't have it any other way. Rachel then coaxed the pooches off the bed for a five-minute potty break on the rooftop's pet garden, then she ate alone.

Her aunt had set up a monthly stipend of five thousand dollars for her care. She stipulated that if the time came that she had to reside at a nursing facility, it had to be top tier.

After eating, she checked on Aunt Tweet again before changing into her pajamas. Next, she grabbed her laptop and headed for her balcony. The nighttime view of the downtown skyline was worth the price she paid to live there. The antennas on top of the AT&T building resembled Batman, so she always pretended he was guarding Gotham City.

She loved Nashville, not because it was the state capital or boasted a large African American population, but because of the rich Black history of struggle, determination, and empowerment before and after the Civil War and leading up to and throughout the civil rights movement.

Her mind wandered as she booted up her laptop. There were so many unsung heroes during slavery besides Harriet Tubman. Who would have guessed one of the most famous horse jockeys in the 1800s was an African American man named Isaac Murphy enslaved at the Belle Meade Plantation?

The Harding family was one of the largest enslavers in Tennessee, and they invested heavily in thoroughbred horses. Fast forward to post–Emancipation Proclamation. Education was a priority for freedmen and women, and among Nashville's thirty-two colleges, four were historically Black colleges or universities.

Add other contributions to music and a thriving social scene, and it was a no-brainer why Rachel made the Athens of the South her home after her college graduation. There was never a weekend without an event to attend. And she and Jacqui hit the circuit.

Just like her hometown of St. Louis was more than the Gateway

Arch, Nashville was more than the Grand Ole Opry, even though it was also nicknamed Music City and NashVegas.

Rachel caught herself from further drifting and took a deep breath. Reclining on her balcony was akin to a spa visit. Day or night, it was the perfect place to relax her mind and ease stress from her body. However, she had been zero productive, so she stood, waved good night to Batman, then walked back inside. She padded across her living room floor and up the stairs to the loft-converted bedroom.

She settled in the chaise next to Aunt Tweet's bed and prepared for a long evening of working and watching Aunt Tweet.

Rachel didn't realize she had dozed off until Aunt Tweet's mumbling woke her. Startled, she caught her laptop before it tumbled to the floor. Her aunt's aging brown eyes were watching her.

"Aunt Tweet!" She pushed everything aside, shooed the dogs out of the way, and climbed into the bed next to her. Rachel hugged Aunt Tweet as tightly as she could without crushing her. "You've got to stop scaring me. Hungry? I got you some Monell's. But you're probably thirsty." She scrambled off the bed, more than ready to do her aunt's bidding, then realized she hadn't yet thanked God for answering her prayers.

Shaking her head, Aunt Tweet pointed to the flat screen where Rachel had played countless movies for them to watch together, but her aunt had a fascination with one video. It was a keepsake of her niece's nuptials. The wedding videographer had captured the raw emotion on Tabitha and Marcus's faces that would make a skeptic believe in love.

Rachel had a bargaining chip. She rested her hands on her hips and shook her head. "Only if you drink and eat something—please." After a few rounds of stubbornness on both sides, Aunt Tweet consented in a weak voice to bottled water and toast.

She propped Aunt Tweet up in the bed and fed her. When her aunt became combative about the wedding tape, Rachel conceded she had force-fed Aunt Tweet enough—half of the bottled water and one of two pieces of toast.

If Aunt Tweet stayed awake, Rachel would give her a small snack in a little while. Rachel made herself comfortable, then started the video. Holding Aunt Tweet's hand, they watched in silence as if they had never before seen Marcus dab at one of Tabitha's tears in an emotional moment. Or Marcus's brother, Demetrius, hand him a hankie to wipe the sweat off his forehead. Or Aunt Tweet yelling "That's a whopper" in response to the bride and groom's passionate first kiss.

Somehow, the reruns of Tabitha's wedding sparked a happy place within Aunt Tweet that she had never shared with her nieces. They did know Aunt Tweet was briefly married and then divorced before the Knicely girls were born. Her aunt seemed content without a significant other in her life, but watching the hour and twelve minute video seemed to defy that thought.

A mystery man named Randolph sometimes surfaced on her aunt's lips, and sadness would wash over Aunt Tweet's face. The longing was unmistakable, and Rachel wondered if her aunt had missed out on love, despite men's attraction to Aunt Tweet like flowers to the sun.

Not only did Rachel inherit Aunt Tweet's sass, fashion sense, and other mannerisms, but she also had the physical assets to capture a man's eye. But none had captured her heart—not the way her brother-in-law had wooed Tabitha.

Despite the revolving door of men she allowed into her life—briefly including Demetrius, Marcus's older brother—Rachel never trusted a man to want her beyond her looks, so she had resolved not to expect it.

Aunt Tweet called her by name and pulled Rachel out of her reverie. She smiled. Some days, Aunt Tweet seemed unsure of Rachel's identity, but when she heard her name, her heart warmed.

"Listen to me," her aunt said. Rachel gave Aunt Tweet her full attention. "Make sure you don't let love pass you by, you hear?" She waggled her finger as if Rachel were a little girl again.

"Yes, ma'am." Rachel grinned. The nourishment, although very little, had given her aunt renewed energy.

"A good man isn't always the best looking. He's got to have a good heart too."

"Okay," Rachel agreed, but waking up to an ugly man every morning would be a test in any marriage. Aunt Tweet became more sentimental after each viewing of the wedding video.

"Make sure he holds your hand…prays for you…feeds you…loves you." Her voice drifted off. Oh no, her aunt needed to eat some more, but right before her eyes, Aunt Tweet dozed off, and within seconds, Rachel heard a light snore.

The next morning, Rachel woke and stretched. From her place on the chaise, she glanced at Aunt Tweet, who seemed to be in the same position as yesterday. Had their conversation really taken place? She spied the remote on the bed and knew it hadn't been a dream.

Was there a subliminal message in that wedding tape? If her aunt was hinting that Rachel needed to be next, then Aunt Tweet would be disappointed. Rachel had no prospects, time, or desire to be anybody's wife. She was only twenty-nine. Maybe by thirty-five, she would review her options. Until then, it was business as usual.

About the Author

Pat Simmons is a multipublished author of more than thirty-five Christian titles and is a three-time recipient of the Emma Rodgers Award for Best Inspirational Romance. She has been a featured speaker and workshop presenter at various venues across the country.

As a self-proclaimed genealogy sleuth, Pat is passionate about researching her ancestors and then casting them in starring roles in her novels. She describes the evidence of the gift of the Holy Ghost as an amazing, unforgettable, life-altering experience. It is God who advances the stories she writes.

Pat has a BS in mass communications from Emerson College in Boston, Massachusetts, and oversaw the media publicity for the annual RT Booklovers Conventions for fourteen years.

Pat converted her sofa-strapped, sports-fanatic husband into an amateur travel agent, untrained bodyguard, GPS-guided chauffeur, and administrative assistant who is constantly on probation. They have a son and a daughter.

Read more about Pat and her books by visiting patsimmons.net or on social media.